PRAISE FOR *NEW YORK TIMES* BESTSELLING AUTHOR CATHERINE COULTER

"Her plots are like rich desserts—sinfully delicious and hard to pass up."
—*The Atlanta Journal-Constitution*

"Catherine Coulter romances readers."
—*Colorado Springs Gazette Telegraph*

"Coulter is excellent at portraying the romantic tension between her heroes and heroines, and she manages to write explicitly but beautifully about sex as well as love."
—*Milwaukee Journal Sentinel*

"Delightful . . . witty . . . engaging."
—*Publishers Weekly*

"Coulter's characters quickly come alive and draw the reader into the story. . . . You can hardly wait to get back and see what's going on."
—*The Sunday Oklahoman*

"Charm, wit, and intrigue. . . . Sure to keep readers turning the pages."
—*Naples Daily News*

"Tantalizing."
—*The Knoxville News-Sentinel*

Wild Star

Catherine Coulter

A SIGNET BOOK

SIGNET
Published by New American Library, a division of
Penguin Group (USA) Inc., 375 Hudson Street,
New York, New York 10014, USA
Penguin Group (Canada), 90 Eglinton Avenue East, Suite 700, Toronto,
Ontario M4P 2Y3, Canada (a division of Pearson Penguin Canada Inc.)
Penguin Books Ltd., 80 Strand, London WC2R 0RL, England
Penguin Ireland, 25 St. Stephen's Green, Dublin 2,
Ireland (a division of Penguin Books Ltd.)
Penguin Group (Australia), 250 Camberwell Road, Camberwell, Victoria 3124,
Australia (a division of Pearson Australia Group Pty. Ltd.)
Penguin Books India Pvt. Ltd., 11 Community Centre, Panchsheel Park,
New Delhi - 110 017, India
Penguin Group (NZ), 67 Apollo Drive, Rosedale, North Shore 0632,
New Zealand (a division of Pearson New Zealand Ltd.)
Penguin Books (South Africa) (Pty.) Ltd., 24 Sturdee Avenue,
Rosebank, Johannesburg 2196, South Africa

Penguin Books Ltd., Registered Offices:
80 Strand, London WC2R 0RL, England

Published by Signet, an imprint of New American Library, a division of Penguin
Group (USA) Inc. Previously published in Onyx and Topaz editions.

First Signet Printing, March 1999
First Signet Printing (Updated Edition), March 2002
20 19 18 17 16 15 14 13 12 11 10

PUBLISHER'S NOTE
This is a work of fiction. Names, characters, places, and incidents either are the
product of the author's imagination or are used fictitiously, and any resem-
blance to actual persons, living or dead, business establishments, events, or lo-
cales is entirely coincidental.
    The publisher does not have any control over and does not assume any re-
sponsibility for author or third-party Web sites or their content.

Wild
Star

PROLOGUE

Wakehurst Plantation
Near Natchez, Mississippi, 1844

"Drew just left to visit the Radcliffes, with my encouragement, of course. He took his paints. He'll be gone for hours. I've sent the slaves away. We're alone."

Brent stared at his beautiful stepmother, her soft words dinning in his ears. She was only four years older than his proud eighteen. She was so desirable, her breasts high and full, her waist so narrow he was certain he could span her with his hands, and all that titian hair, loose now, flowing down her back. He watched her tongue glide over her lower lip. She was so unlike the girls he'd loved from the precocious age of fourteen. He'd pictured making love to her, pictured himself thrusting inside her, so deep.

He gulped and took a step back. "My father is your husband," he said. He felt his blood pumping wildly, knew that he was straining against his tight breeches. He hurt.

"Yes," said Laurel. "But he is old, Brent. I am so lonely and he can't love me, not the way you could, not the way I need." She shrugged and the silk peignoir slipped a bit.

Brent forced his eyes away from her breasts, and looked frantically toward the door of her bedroom. He shouldn't have come in here. God, what was he going to do?

"We wouldn't hurt anyone, Brent. Just give each other some pleasure, that's all I ask. You are so young, just as I am. I've wanted you since I came here. You're a beautiful man, Brent, so desirable. I watched you kissing Marissa Radcliffe. Did you know that? I want you to kiss me too."

His body was trembling as he watched her walk toward him, her magnolia scent filling his nostrils.

His hands fisted at his sides. He knew he should walk to the bedroom door, open it, escape her, escape his own frantic lust. Her hand touched his shoulder. He stiffened.

She stood on her tiptoes, looking at his mouth. "I can teach you, Brent, show you how to love a woman. I can give you such pleasure. We won't hurt anyone. No one, I swear it."

She touched her mouth to his, but his arms remained locked against his sides.

"My father," he gasped into her mouth, but her tongue touched his, and he was lost. He'd scarcely ever tried to control his surges of bone-deep lust and found it impossible to do so now. Her breasts flattened against his chest; he felt her belly and her thighs move against him. "My father," he repeated again.

Her small hand found him, began to caress him, and he moaned, knowing that he would spill his seed if she didn't stop. "Laurel," he whispered, "don't. I can't control myself."

"Come," she said. She led him to her bed. Her eyes never left his face as she slipped out of the silk peignoir and gown. She let him look his fill, then began to unfasten his clothes. God, he was beautiful, she thought, lust swirling wildly, deep inside her. So tall and well-formed, so strong. So young. When he was naked, he stood quietly before her, closing his eyes as her hands stroked over him. He gritted his teeth when she caressed him with her fingers and then her incredibly soft mouth, wrenching a moan from deep in his throat. She knew, he realized vaguely, that he would spill his seed if she didn't stop, but still he wanted to yell when she left him. He felt her hands around his back, felt her pull him with her to the bed. He fell on top of her with a wild cry. The shame and the guilt were there, tangling in his mind. "My father," he whispered yet again, the agony of his young body making his voice shake. He pulled away onto his side. But his eyes went to the triangle of dark red hair and he could see her delicate woman's flesh. "No, I cannot," he said, but she straddled him, her hands splayed against his chest.

"Yes, Brent," she said against his mouth. "He will never know. He would not care." Her tongue was in his mouth as he bucked upward against her. His hands tangled in her hair, and he knew nothing else mattered, nothing else existed.

Laurel drew up, and guided him into her. As she drew him deeper, she knew that this time she would not find her pleasure. But it didn't matter. He was so young and vigorous, so splendidly male. There was time enough. All afternoon. All the tomorrows. He would give her all the pleasure she wanted. She felt him stiffen, saw the cords in his neck as he reached his climax. His brilliant blue eyes, deep and mysterious as the stormy sea, narrowed as if in pain. "Yes, Brent," she whispered, and rode him fiercely until he climaxed.

She kissed him, pressed herself on him. To her intense delight, he stayed hard inside her. He was far from sated, far from being exhausted. In the hour that followed, she taught him to pleasure her. The warmth of his mouth, his tongue, made her wild.

"So good," she said, pressing his head closer to her. "Gently, my love, gently."

Brent felt utter power and triumph when her body exploded with the pleasure he gave her. He reared up over her and thrust between her thighs. He pumped into her, lost to everything but the exquisite sensations building in him.

"My God."

It took several moments for his father's voice to penetrate his mind. All sensations ceased as if they'd never existed. He jerked out of her, rolled off the tangled bedcovers, and rose shakily to his feet beside the bed. He stared at his father.

"Jesus, my own son. You filthy little bastard!" His father's face was red with fury. Brent realized his father's eyes had fallen, that he was staring at his sex, wet with himself and Laurel.

"Slut, whore," Avery Hammond screamed at his wife. "God, I'll see you in hell." He rushed out of his wife's bedroom, and Brent could hear his galloping steps down the long corridor.

Laurel grabbed the cover. "He wasn't supposed to come back," she said blankly. "Not until tomorrow."

"He is here," Brent said as he quickly pulled on his scattered clothes.

He was jerking on his boots when his father reappeared in the doorway, a whip in his hand. "I'm going to flay the flesh off your back, you slut."

Brent quickly moved in front of his father. "Father, stop. Please, it wasn't her fault, sir." Brent drew himself up tall and proud. "I seduced her, Father. I forced her. It wasn't her fault. She didn't want me."

Avery Hammond stopped in his tracks, quaking from rage, as his son's words penetrated his mind. His son, his beautiful son, his flesh and blood, his pride. Oh God. Vaguely, as if from a great distance, he heard his wife sobbing. Brent, his son. Wild to a fault, but young. Wild as he himself had been wild when he was his son's age. "You dishonorable bastard." He felt the pounding of blood in his ears. He raised the whip and brought it down, slicing open his son's face.

Brent felt the searing pain, but he didn't move. He felt warm blood trickle down his cheek and off his chin, drip-

4

ping to the carpet at his feet. He found himself wondering if the blood would wash out of his mother's precious Turkish carpet.

"I never want to see your face again," Avery Hammond said as he lowered the whip. His hand was shaking. God, he'd scarred his son. Brent's eyes never wavered from his face, and Avery felt something die deep inside him. Then once again he saw his son's powerful body thrusting between his wife's legs. "You are not worthy to be my heir. I disown you. May you live with this disgrace for the rest of your miserable life. Be gone before dark or I'll kill you."

Brent couldn't bring himself to move.

"Go, damn you."

Brent walked slowly past his father and out of the bedroom. He heard Laurel's sobs, his father's heavy breathing.

He didn't feel the pain in his torn cheek. He felt nothing but emptiness.

ONE

San Diego, California, March 1853

Lunch started well enough. Alice DeWitt ladled out the stew, passing it to Byrony, who in turn served her brother and father. Plump, good-natured Maria had been gone for three months now. They could no longer afford to pay her miserable wage.

There was silence, for which Byrony was thankful. Anything other than silence was usually unpleasant. She glanced at her father, Madison DeWitt, and thought she saw the signs. He was crumbling a soft tortilla between his fingers, and his fleshy jowls were beginning to quiver.

The attack came swiftly.

"Lazy bitch," he roared at his wife. "A man needs his food and you serve me up this garbage?"

He threw a thick earthen bowl filled with tasty beef stew across the dining room to smash against the whitewashed wall. Pieces of beef and vegetables fell on top of the mahogany sideboard. It was her mother's prized piece of furniture.

"Do you think me a pig to give me such swill?"

It wasn't a question, but Alice DeWitt said in her soft, wounded voice, "It's filled with fine beef chunks, Madison. I thought you'd like it."

"Silence. Since when do you pretend to think, you stupid cow?"

Madison DeWitt heaved back his chair and began to pull off his thick leather belt. His heavy face was flushed with rage, the pulse in his throat was pounding above the loosely knotted kerchief. Byrony couldn't stop herself. She slipped out of her chair and moved to the other side of the table to stand beside her mother.

"Leave her alone, Father," she said, her voice shaking even though she was fighting with all her might for calm. "Your temper has nothing to do with the stew, and you know it. You're angry because Don Pedrorena sold his cattle for a better price."

"Sit down and shut your trap," Charlie said, eyeing his father's belt with mild interest. He'd never felt the belt since he was thirteen years old. He leaned back in his chair, folding his arms over his chest. "Don Pedrorena is a damned liar and thief, all the Californios are scum. Someday—"

Byrony turned on her brother. "They are not, and you know it. You're just jealous, both you and Father. If either of you had an ounce of—"

She never finished. Madison DeWitt slashed the belt downward across his daughter's back. She lurched back, gasping at the pain. Alice DeWitt made a soft, keening noise, her hands fluttering helplessly. She made no move to interfere; it would do no good. She felt the pain with her daughter, her sweet daughter whom she'd tried all her life to protect.

"You're as stupid as your mother," Madison growled, and flayed the belt across her shoulders. "Both of you, worthless sluts. God save me from the stupidity of women."

"Not God," Byrony screamed at him, "the Devil."

Byrony felt the cheap cotton of her gown rip as her father struck another blow. She fell to her knees, her arms going up to protect her head and face.

"Father," Charlie said, calmly sipping at his wine, "don't scar her. Didn't you tell me you might get a good price for her? A husband wouldn't appreciate welts or scars, you know."

Madison DeWitt struck another blow before his son's words penetrated his brain. He drew back, breathing hard. "A damned husband wouldn't see her back until it was too late," he said, but he didn't strike her again. "Get up, you little slut," he said. He turned his dark eyes to his cowering wife. "Get me something to eat, woman, and no more slop." He threaded the belt through the loops of his trousers and sat down again, his rage spent, to drink another glass of whiskey with his son.

Byrony slowly inched up and sat back on her heels. She was wounded, in spirit as well as body, and her eyes blurred with hated tears. *Why don't I just keep my mouth shut?* But she knew she couldn't. She had to protect her mother. Her mother, after all, had protected her until just six months ago when Byrony had returned to San Diego at the death of her Aunt Ida in Boston. Aunt Ida, her mother's older sister, who'd always answered the girl's questions with "Your father's a difficult man, my dear. Best you stay here. It's what your mama wants, you know."

Difficult? Dear God, the man was mad, his spurts of violence coming more often now that there was so little money. He'd beaten her three times since she'd returned. Byrony bit down on her lower lip to keep from crying out, both from pain and her helpless anger. It would only bring her father's attention back to her. As silently as she could, she rose and slipped out of the dining room. She heard her father laugh at something Charlie said.

Alice DeWitt entered her daughter's small bedroom nearly an hour later. Without a word, she dipped a soft cloth into warm water and began to sponge the welts.

"I hate him," Byrony said between gritted teeth. "And

Charlie, he's become as much of an animal as your husband."

"Your father has had many disappointments," Alice said. It was a never-ending litany, as if his own failures excused his savage attacks.

"His disappointments are of his own making. Why don't you leave him? Mother, we can go together, leave San Diego. We can go back to Boston. Aunt Ida had so many friends—"

"You shouldn't have interfered," Alice said. "I've told you not to, many times." She must get married, Alice thought. Soon, so she'll be safe.

The wind blew hot and dry across the top of the rise, making the endless sea of chaparral bend and dip. Several buzzards swooped down from the rise to the flatlands below, seeking prey, their flight slow and steady.

Byrony sat in the shade of a lone pine tree, her long legs spread out in front of her, her felt hat pushed back off her forehead. Her mare, Thorny, was tethered some distance away where she could forage at the scraggly bits of wild grass. It was a desolate place, a private place where no one came, except for Byrony. If the day were clear, like today, she could see the ocean in the distance and some of the buildings in San Diego. She shifted her weight and felt a painful pulling across her back. She found herself wondering yet again if all men were like her father and Charlie. Cruel, vicious, unable to accept their own mistakes, their own failures. Unlike her mother, she couldn't excuse her father. He'd lost several head of cattle, all through his own carelessness, leaving them to seek out water from a poisoned well. And those that lived, he'd tried to sell, for little money. And Charlie, carousing in the saloons in San Diego, gambling with the same lack of luck that characterized her father.

She'd thought about escape many times in the past few months. She was nineteen, strong and healthy. She could earn her own way; she knew it. She remembered her brother's words about selling her for a good price. A husband. She shuddered, picturing herself as her mother, bowed in spirit and health, old before her time. The thought froze her with fear. She wouldn't accept violence from a husband like her mother did. She'd kill him first.

I'm beginning to think of violence as a way of life, she thought, as normal. Aunt Ida knew, but she never told me. She remembered her initial loneliness, her childish questions about her brother. "But, Aunt Ida, if Father is so difficult, why isn't Charlie here with us?" And Ida had answered slowly, with finality, "Your brother, my dear, is strong and able to take care of himself. He's safe enough."

She thought of the scores of letters she'd written to her mother during those long years, and her mother's letters to her, filled with love and affection and lies.

She told herself yet again that her mother had protected her. What would her girlhood have been like living with Madison DeWitt?

Thorny nickered suddenly, and she shook off her thoughts. She rose to her feet, shading her hand over her eyes, to see the approaching horse. It was Gabriel de Neve, son of Don Joaquín de Neve, a rich landowner and one of the despised Californios. She smiled at him as he reined in his beautiful bay stallion, Espada, and dismounted gracefully. Gabriel was twenty-one, not much taller than Byrony, his hair and eyes as black as a moonless night. His even teeth glistened white against his tanned face.

Like other rich Californios, Gabriel was dressed flamboyantly, his black pants belted at his waist by a colorful red silk sash, his black vest sewn with gold buttons. His black boots were of the finest leather, and his white shirt embroidered with gold threads.

"Como está?" he asked lazily, grinning at her. He saw a flicker of pain in her fine green eyes, but didn't understand it. It was gone before he could question it.

"I am fine, Gabriel," she said. "I haven't seen you for a week. What have you been doing?"

Gabriel flexed his sore arms. "Working the new horses," he said. "Tough brutes. And you, Byrony, what have you been doing?"

Gabriel's father didn't realize that his son spoke perfect English, a fact that would have enraged him. Nor did his father know that he was seeing a *gringa*, the daughter of a man he considered a fool and a loudmouthed bully. But Gabriel couldn't stay away from her. She was fresh, sweet, and so lovely it made him ache. He was so busy gazing at her, wondering how her flesh would feel beneath his fingers, that he scarce heard her reply.

Actually, Byrony uttered something inane and shrugged. Gabriel had followed her here to her private refuge some months ago, and now he seemed to know when she would ride out here. She didn't really mind, for she liked him. He seemed kind and he loved to jest and laugh. He was a relief from the oppressive atmosphere in her home.

"You are quiet today, *niña*," he said as he looped his stallion's reins over the saddle pommel. He took a step toward her and was appalled when she shrank back. "What is the matter, Byrony? You act as though I were a bull ready to attack you."

It was so apt that she nearly laughed. "Forgive me, Gabriel. I guess I'm just a bit nervous today."

He frowned, wondering as he had many times before what was in her mind. She turned away to gaze out over the desolate landscape, and his eyes were drawn to her breeches. How his mother would screech at the sight of a girl so garbed. Her loose white shirt was momentarily flattened against her breasts by a gust of wind, and he swallowed. After the last time he had seen her, he'd been so filled with a man's physical ache that he'd gone to a whore in San Diego. But it wasn't the same thing.

He'll guess something's wrong if I don't say something normal, Byrony thought. "Tell me about the new horses, Gabriel," she said.

And he did.

The afternoon passed in pleasant conversation. Gabriel spoke of his family, and Byrony found she hungered to hear how pleasant life could be. Had it really been only six months since she'd left Aunt Ida's house, her dear, fussy aunt who'd given her a home and love? And kept her away from men of all ages. She wondered briefly if Aunt Ida, spinster, had believed all men to be like her sister's husband. Not that she'd ever said anything against Madison DeWitt, or any other man for that matter. But she'd never said anything positive either. Byrony brought her wandering attention back to Gabriel who was speaking of his own mother. Doña Carlota, Gabriel's mother, was a laughing, gay woman, plump and loving, who adored playing tricks on Gabriel's father. His brothers were fun-loving and hard workers at the rancho Los Pinos, and his youngest sister, Blanca, was silly, petted, and beautiful.

Gabriel was telling her about the festivities of the past Christmas when Byrony suddenly jumped to her feet. "Oh, my God. It will be dark very soon. My father—I must go, Gabriel."

"I will accompany you home, Byrony," he said as he gave her a foot up.

"No."

She was clammy with fear, and felt sweat begin to trickle down her sides.

"Of course I will," he said calmly, and turned his stallion beside her mare.

She would leave him before they reached the house. Her

brain teemed with lies she would tell if her father saw her. She saw the lights in the distance and dug her heels into Thorny's sides. "Good-bye, Gabriel," she called, turning to wave to him.

"Watch out."

His warning didn't penetrate her mind until the tree branch swiped against her shoulder and hurled her from the saddle. She landed on her back, the breath momentarily knocked out of her. Gabriel jumped from his stallion's back and knelt beside her.

"I'm all right," she gasped. "So stupid."

"Are you certain?" he asked. He put his arms around her as she struggled to her feet.

"Yes, yes," she said, pulling away from him. "I must get home."

"*Querida*, let me help you."

She didn't even hear the endearment. But she saw her brother and father standing in front of the house, smoking cigars. "Please go away," she said to Gabriel, grasping the saddle pommel.

"All right," he said. "I will see you again soon, Byrony."

He wheeled about and galloped away. Byrony drew a deep breath and rode Thorny to the small stable. She dismounted, her body aching and pulling, and began the task of rubbing down her mare. She had nearly finished when she saw her father standing in the narrow doorway of the stable.

"So," he said very slowly, very precisely, "you finally decided to leave your lover, huh, girl?"

She stared at him, not understanding his words.

"The rich little greaser, Gabriel de Neve," he said, and spat into a pile of old straw.

"He is just a friend," she said, her heart speeding up with fear. "Just a friend. I met him three months ago in San Diego."

"And the friendly little greaser rips your shirt, daughter? You like being on your back?"

She looked down at the jagged tear at her shoulder. "I fell," she said. "That's all. A tree branch clipped me and I fell."

"Like hell you did, you filthy little slut. I'll make you sorry you ever—"

"I'm sorry you're my father," she yelled at him. "God, I hate you. You have a filthy mind—"

He lunged at her, but Charlie said from the door, "No, Father. Wait, leave her be and listen to me."

Byrony blinked. Help from her brother? Surely the world had taken a faulty turn. To her surprise, her father, after giving her a look filled with malice, turned to his son.

"Come outside a minute, Father," Charlie said. "It's important, I swear."

"You, girl," he said to Byrony, "get indoors and clean your lover's juices off your body. I'll deal with you later."

Don Joaquín de Neve was informed by Luis, one of his vaqueros, that Señor DeWitt wanted to see him. Don Joaquín frowned, and closed the ledger on his desk. What did that ridiculous man want? It didn't occur to him to deny the man, even though he despised him. He rose from his chair, tall, square-shouldered, and proud. He eyed Madison DeWitt as the man roared into his quiet study like an angry bull.

"Señor DeWitt," he said with exquisite politeness. "What may I do for you?"

As always, the proud, aristocratic Californios put Madison DeWitt off stride. He hated them, but they made him feel somehow insignificant, unimportant, something to be tolerated. "I want to talk to you about your son," he said, drawing up.

"Which son?" Don Joaquín asked.

Foul, angry words stuck in Madison DeWitt's throat. He eyed the splendid rich furnishings of Don Joaquín's study, and felt greed and jealousy flow through him. He managed to moderate his voice. "Your son Gabriel," he said. "The boy has ruined my daughter. Raped her. I want reparation, *señor.* I demand it."

Don Joaquín showed no emotion. "Indeed?" he said, a thin black brow arching in interest.

"Yes, he took her yesterday. I saw him and my daughter, her clothes ripped. He shamed her and her family."

Ah, Gabriel, Don Joaquín thought, saddened, I cannot allow it, my son. He did not bother to tell DeWitt that his son had spoken to him frankly of what had happened the previous evening. He knew that he must protect his family and their proud name. He had no intention of protesting his son's innocence to this miserable creature. It would do no good in any case.

"I demand marriage, *señor.*"

Don Joaquín wondered briefly if all the wretched things he'd heard about this heavy-jowled man were true. Well, there was nothing he could do about the poor girl. He said calmly, "A marriage is out of the question, Señor DeWitt. My son left this morning for a long visit to our relatives in Spain." He paused a moment, realizing that he could possibly spare the wretched girl some of her father's rage. "However, I am willing to give you reparations." He opened a desk drawer, opened the strongbox, and counted out five hundred dollars.

He handed the money to DeWitt. He stiffened as the man counted the bills in front of him.

"It's not enough," Madison DeWitt said. "It's my girl's honor. He ruined her. Who would want to marry her now?"

"It is all you will get, *señor.* Now, you will leave me. I find your presence oppressive."

Madison DeWitt cursed, threatened, but Don Joaquín

stood firm, saying nothing, merely gazing at him with tolerant boredom. When the man finally left, Don Joaquín heaved a deep sigh. It was time, he supposed, that Gabriel did travel to Spain. His grandparents wouldn't live much longer, and there were many cousins for him to meet. Yes, it was time for him to see more of the world.

TWO

Brent Hammond walked out of the dim saloon of the Colorado House into the bright afternoon sunlight. He was smiling with satisfaction. He'd just won two hundred dollars in a poker game with a greenhorn and a cheat. Most of it was from the cheat, and in only four hours. He stretched then turned to look up at Presidio Hill behind him. Up there he imagined one could forget the stench of garbage that lay about in the filthy narrow streets in the flats, and draw a decent breath of clean salt air.

He was eyeing several loose cows wandering about amid the scruffy adobe buildings when he heard the gunshots. He'd whirled about and taken two steps, when a body smashed against him. He rocked back on his heels, keeping his balance, but she went sprawling on the ground at his feet.

Byrony cried out, and let go of her two packages. One of them burst open and flour spewed out, raining down white.

"Oh dear," Byrony said. Her bottom hurt, but she began laughing, she couldn't help it. She struggled up to her knees.

"I'm sorry," Brent said, dropping to his haunches. "Here, let me help you."

She looked up at the man she'd just cannoned into and her breath caught in her throat. He had the most beautiful dark blue eyes she'd ever seen. He was trying to keep from laughing.

"Hello," she said, her eyes never leaving his face. His thick black hair was clean and shone in the sun. She noticed the scar on his cheek, white against his tanned skin, and wondered how he'd gotten it.

"Hello yourself," Brent said. He clasped her upper arms and drew her up.

Byrony was tall, but the man was nearly a head taller. She watched his lips part, and laughter, deep and clear, flowed over her.

"You'd best let me go, or your suit will be white rather than gray."

Brent hadn't realized he was still holding her. He quickly released her arms and stepped back. "I'm sorry I ran into you, ma'am," he said again.

"No, it wasn't your fault," Byrony said, and began shaking out her skirts. "I wasn't paying attention."

"I heard the gunshots," he said.

"Oh, that," she said, her eyes narrowing in ill-disguised contempt. "It was just some of the young men target-shooting, this time. Nothing to worry about."

"I wasn't really worried, just interested. What do you mean 'this time'?"

She shrugged. "Unfortunately, San Diego has something of a reputation for violence. Dueling, gun battles, knife slashings. We've got them all, I'm afraid."

"It shares its reputation then with every other town I've visited."

She raised her eyes to his face again. "I've never seen you in San Diego before."

"No, this is my first visit. Actually, I'll be leaving tomorrow."

"Are you a gambler?" she asked, looking briefly back at the Colorado House.

"Yes, I guess I am."

She continued staring at him, and in an unconscious gesture, her tongue glided over her lower lip.

"Are you enjoying the view?"

She blinked, not understanding, then saw the amusement in his eyes.

"Yes," she said.

Brent wasn't expecting that. A blush, perhaps, a stammered accusation that he wasn't a gentleman. "Well, let me return the favor. You're beautiful even with flour on your nose."

She grinned, but shook her head at his nonsense. She knew well enough what she looked like. Her hair was drawn back in a severe knot at the nape of her neck. Her cotton gown was a dull gray color and about as flattering as a potato sack. But she couldn't seem to look away from him. She realized that he was a very large man, but she didn't fear him. It was odd. "You have very unusual eyes. Forgive me for staring."

He arched a black brown. "I believe they're both still the same color, ma'am, or did the flour get to them?"

"No, it's not that. There's no meanness in them."

He frowned at that. She wasn't being forward, there was no coyness in her manner or voice. Suddenly she stiffened, reached down in a graceful motion, and picked up her packages, quickly folding the flap over the flour bag. "I must go. Forgive me for running into you."

"Wait," he called after her, but she didn't. She picked up her skirts and sped across San Diego Avenue toward the plaza, where an old buckboard wagon was hitched to a railing. "I don't know your name," he said, almost to himself.

She was talking with an older woman, probably her mother, he thought, stepping into the street. He slowed, watching her shake off the remainder of the flour, as she stood by the horses. Miserable-looking beasts.

He stopped at the sight of three young men swaggering in the middle of the street, obviously a bit worse from drink. The middle one was shoving his gun back into its holster.

"Hey, Charlie," one of the young men said, "ain't that your sister over there?"

Brent paused, remembering the condemnation in her voice when she'd said it was just young men target-shooting. Was the anger toward her own brother?

"Yep, Tommy," said Charlie. "You sound like you wanna get to know her better. You ain't got enough money, old fellow. Forget it."

Brent felt a ripple of anger. He looked more closely at Charlie. There was little similarity between brother and sister that he could see. Charlie was swarthy with brown hair, eyes a grayish color, bloodshot from too much drink. He'd met up with his share of young men like Charlie—braggarts, bullies, and sometimes worse.

"She's still a looker," the third young man said.

Charlie hunched his slender shoulders. "Anything in a skirt is a piece of tail to you."

"She sure swishes her tail nice," said Tommy.

Brent didn't hear Charlie's reply to this. Why the hell was he interested anyway? He walked across the dusty street and stopped beside an old man who was sitting in a chair tilted back against the side of the town hall. The old man waved once at the woman, and she nodded briefly. He smelled of spirits, sweat, and cheap tobacco.

"Howdy, young feller," said the old man.

Brent nodded and asked, "Who's the girl over there?"

The old man spit and Brent saw the disgusting brown puddle a foot from the chair. "That there is the DeWitt women. Mother and daughter. Her name's Byrony."

"Byrony," Brent repeated.

"Yep. Her ma was in love with an English feller named Lord Byron, a scribbler of no account at all, Madison told me. Fool name. Madison DeWitt's her pa. One of my best friends, a good man, more's the pity."

Brent continued looking toward the girl, Byrony. He realized that he'd liked her, an unusual occurrence, and that he wanted to talk to her some more. He hadn't really liked a woman in a long time. There was Maggie, of course. And Laurel, when he'd been eighteen. He shook his head at himself. Dear Lord, he hadn't thought of Laurel since he'd gotten a letter from his brother, Drew, over six months ago in Denver.

Drew never mentioned Laurel, but still Brent would remember, usually at odd times, like now. Without conscious thought, he raised his hand and fingered the scar along his left cheek. Nothing more stupid than a lusty young man.

"What's the pity?" he asked finally.

"The girl. Poor Madison's cursed. Told me he'd caught her with her lover, one of the damned Californios. 'Course the boy wouldn't marry her, but his pa gave Madison some money to buy him off. Damned proud greasers. Madison's just hopin' the girl's belly won't swell with a bastard."

But she's so young, Brent thought, probably not even twenty yet. A lover? She hadn't struck him as that type of female. Well, he was probably wrong. Lord knew, he'd been wrong before. She'd probably tried to use her body to get herself married into a wealthy family. An old story. Damnable scheming women. *You taught me well enough, Laurel.* He heard Byrony DeWitt laugh, a sweet sound, and saw her scratching behind the mangy ear of one of the horses.

"It doesn't seem likely to me," Brent said.

"Like I told you, I'm her pa's friend. Tells me everything, he does. The girl's a proud little piece, but still a slut." He spit again, the brown stream landing in the center of the puddle he'd been working on for hours.

"She doesn't look like a slut."

"A silly little slut with a fancy name. That's all she is. Aye, poor Madison. Guess it makes sense, since the girl was raised without her pa in Boston. Now he'll have to find her a husband from other parts. No self-respectin' man would have her now."

Particularly, Brent thought, if you tell everyone you see about her failings. He looked up to see Byrony DeWitt climb into the wagon and take the horse's reins from her mother. For a brief moment she looked directly at him, and she smiled. Then she click-clicked the horses forward, and soon all he could see was the billowing dust from the wagon wheels.

"You stayin' in these parts long, young feller?"

"No, I'm not. San Diego is too quiet for me." And too stagnant, and too dirty. He thought of San Francisco and smiled. Crime, corruption, greed, every negative human behavior imaginable, but dammit, you knew you were alive in that city. A city filled with young men like himself, who wanted to create their own future. Wild, boisterous, invigorating, that was San Francisco. He'd traveled on Edward Bolsom's ship down the coast with half a thought to buying into his friend's shipping line. But it wasn't for him. He knew what he wanted.

"You been up north in the goldfields?"

"Yes."

"Any luck?"

"Enough," Brent said. "Be seeing you." He tipped his hat to the old man and strode back across the street to the Colorado House.

"Who was that man, Byrony?"

Byrony turned her head from the road to look at her

mother. "I ran into him, literally, and spilled the flour all over me. He is very nice, but he's leaving San Diego tomorrow."

Alice DeWitt twisted her hands together, a habit of long standing. "I'm glad your father wasn't in town."

"Why? You think he would have gone after the man and demanded money from him for dishonoring me?" Byrony's voice shook with bitterness and impotent rage.

"Now, dear," Alice said, her voice pleading, "you mustn't be like that. The five hundred dollars was a big help to your father."

"Don Joaquín should have told him to go to hell. Poor Gabriel. God, I wish I were a man." She gave a snort of laughter. "But then I might be like Charlie. You did see him, didn't you? He was with Tommy Larkin and Jimmy Talvo. Worthless scum, all of them. Of course, your husband would be so delighted that Charlie was half-drunk and shooting off his gun."

Alice flinched. Two months after her return to San Diego, Byrony had referred to him only as Alice's husband. "Did much of the flour get spilled?"

"Not more than a dime's worth. Don't worry, Mother. I'll take the blame if he notices." *How can I get away from him? What can I do to escape?*

"I saw the stranger talking to Jeb Donnally."

Byrony gave a mirthless laugh. "So did I. He now believes me the biggest whore in California, if Jeb talked about me at all. Filthy old man."

"Byrony, you mustn't talk like that."

"Why not? What difference does it make? At least it'll save me from *his* marriage plans. I'll bet he didn't count on Jeb bugling all his lies to the world."

But it did make a difference, Alice thought. If Byrony talked like that in front of her father, he would hurt her. She had to get Byrony away; she'd realized that when she couldn't stop her daughter from trying to protect her. But two months before, Madison had found her little stash of money that she'd been hoarding for Byrony. He'd not said a word to her, merely taken the money and gone into San Diego with Charlie. When he'd returned many hours later, he'd still not blasted her with his anger, simply looked at her and said quite calmly, "I know why you did it. But I'll decide what's to be done with the girl, not you. Thank God she doesn't have your looks. I always thought your mother was a looker. The girl has to be worth something."

"She's your daughter, your own flesh and blood." Alice had said, goaded. She had been beautiful, once, many years before.

He raised his hand, then lowered it. "Yes, she is. She's also a hellion, but she'll learn her place. I let you have your way, woman, sending her to your sister. But now she's back and I'll use her as I see fit."

She felt the familiar deadening helplessness sweep through her, but she'd said only, "Byrony isn't a hellion. She's a sweet, kind girl. Why can't you be more loving with her?"

"She escaped her responsibilities for nearly nineteen years. It's time she paid me back."

He was just like his own father, she thought now. And she'd known it, deep down, she'd known it even before she married him. But she'd loved him so much, known that she could change him. "Do you know something, Byrony," she said to her grim-faced daughter, speaking her thoughts aloud, "he did change for a while. He tried, truly tried, but nothing ever went right for him. It made him bitter. That's why we moved to California, so we could begin again, start fresh. If you'd just not talk back to him—"

"And let him hit you? Do you honestly believe that I can just stand there when he's in one of his rages, and watch him strike you? Oh, Mother, let's leave, together. Whatever good you saw in him a long time ago is no longer there. And Charlie's becoming just like him. I can take care of both of us, Mother, I know I can. You've seen that I've gotten some education, and Aunt Ida taught me how to sew and cook. I can find work, support us."

"I can't, Byrony. He needs me."

Byrony heard not only the pathos in her mother's voice but also the underlying strength. She was more trapped than she would have been in a prison cell. "You're right about the five hundred dollars. It will keep him feeling important for a month, hopefully. But then it will be the same again. He'll blame everyone but himself for his failures."

"He needs me," Alice DeWitt said again.

Madison didn't hear about the loss of the flour, and the five hundred dollars was gone within two weeks. He became morose and silent, spending most of his time in San Diego, complaining to Jeb Donnnally about his ill-fortune. Byrony waited for the explosion, but it never came. Instead, one evening Madison DeWitt came into the house, waving a letter in his hand.

"At last," he shouted. "Now, my dear daughter, you'll repay me for all those fancy years you spent in Boston."

Byrony froze.

"What do you mean, Madison?" Alice said.

"I mean," he said with deep satisfaction, "that I've found a husband for your daughter. A rich husband. One of your distant cousins, Alice, Ira Butler."

Byrony didn't move a muscle. Her mind raced to the few conversations she'd had with her Aunt Ida about her family. Ira Butler was a third cousin, from back East. He was old, probably nearing forty.

"The only thing is," Madison said, frowning toward Byrony, "is the girl pregnant? Is she carrying that damned Californio's bastard?"

"Of course not." Alice cried. "She never—"

"Shut up, woman. Our Mr. Butler will be arriving next week from San Francisco. He's going to pay dearly for you, daughter, dearly indeed. He writes of a fine settlement."

"Why does he want to marry me?" Byrony asked, her first words.

"He talks of family ties," Madison said. "He even sent a hundred dollars, for your trousseau, he says. Well, girl, you can have fifty. Do something with yourself, you look like a worn-out—"

"Slut?"

He raised his hand, then thought better of it. "Hold your tongue, girl. I'll brook no insolence from you. Soon you'll be another man's problem."

Alice quickly said, "Come, love, let's go to the kitchen and make dinner. We can talk."

"I won't be here, Ali," Madison called out, his voice obnoxiously jovial. "I'm going into town. At last things are going my way."

"To get stinking drunk," Byrony said under her breath.

"Madison," Alice said, "could you please give me the fifty dollars?"

"Whining bitch," he muttered, but he handed her the money.

Alice heaved a sigh of relief. "It's an answer to all my prayers," she said to her daughter after her husband's heavy footfall had faded in the distance.

"Your prayers, not mine," Byrony said.

"No, listen to me, child. I remember Ira well. He's older than you by some years, but he's a kind man, and handsome, ever so handsome. I remember thinking he looked just like the angels in my Bible, all fair and slender. He won't hurt you, ever. My, my, I wonder at his reasons, but no matter. I haven't heard from him in a good three years. He wrote me from San Francisco back in 'fifty. He was already on his way to becoming rich. A smart man, Ira, and a good man. You'll even have a new sister, Byrony. Her name is Irene, and she's not that much older than you. She's Ira's half-sister, but he's taken care of her since his father and stepmother died some ten years ago."

Byrony listened to her mother run on and on. *A kind man—he'll not hurt you.* Was that all to pray for in a husband? Perhaps, Byrony thought, it was all that she could pray for. But why her? He'd never even seen her. It made no sense to her. But then, nothing had made much sense since her return to the bosom of her family. Oddly enough, before she fell asleep that night, she thought of the man she'd met in San Diego, the gambler. She gave a small half-sigh and drifted into a dreamless sleep.

THREE

Aunt Ida would have said that Ira Baines Butler was a real gentleman, an almost extinct male of the species. Byrony silently agreed as she watched Ira Butler deftly handle each member of the DeWitt family. She remembered Aunt Ida's standards were as rigid as her whalebone corset. For the life of her, she couldn't remember more than a half-dozen males being raised to that exalted station. Ira's light blue eyes swung toward her and he smiled. Despite herself, she felt herself responding and smiling back. No doubt about it, she thought, he was charming, attentive, well-dressed, and said all the right things. Byrony, who was prepared to hate him on sight, had to revise her opinion of him before the end of the first evening of his visit. He treated her father with deferential respect, while her father viewed him with greed, envy, and relief. She saw her mother grow almost pretty again under Cousin Ira's gentle compliments. Charlie's behavior surprised her the most. He had at first been sullen, not at all unexpected, but under Ira's careful handling he soon became like a friendly puppy, eager to win the older man's approval and attention.

And he was rich.

Long after she went to bed that first evening, she could hear the soft rumble of male voices from downstairs. Her father was doubtless squeezing every dollar he could from Ira. Her confusion over the entire situation grew.

The next morning, after breakfast, Ira asked if Byrony would give him a tour of the small ranch. To Byrony's surprise, her father had already hitched up the buckboard, a task he had disdained since she'd come back to San Diego.

"Such a pleasure to finally meet you, Cousin Byrony," Ira said once they were seated in the buckboard. "May I say while we're alone that I am pleased that you have accepted me. Let me assure you that I will do everything in my power to make you happy."

Ira Butler's speech was lightly spiced with a Southern drawl, his voice smooth as honey. Byrony remembered her mother telling her that Cousin Ira Baines Butler was a handsome man, and she hadn't told her daughter a lie. He did look like an angel, Byrony thought, with his silky blond hair, very fair complexion, and pale blue eyes. Oddly, the image of the gambler came into her mind and she thought: And *he* looks like a fallen angel. She said, "Thank you, Mr. Butler."

"Ira, please."

"Ira." She smiled up at him. "I think you misnamed, sir. Gabriel is more appropriate, I think."

A mobile blond brow soared upward.

"You look like an angel. The top angel."

He threw back his head and laughed, showing even white teeth. Why, Byrony wondered, hadn't he married? He certainly appeared to have everything any woman would want.

"I'll bear that in mind, Byrony," he said after a moment. "But I believe that I must prefer being earthbound, unless, of course, you'd consent to share the celestial firmament with me." He wrapped her in his warm smile, and again she found herself returning the smile easily.

She click-clicked poor old Coolie forward. "Have you ever been in San Diego before?"

"Unfortunately not. It's a lovely little town. I venture to say that you will find San Francisco equally as interesting."

"Oh, I have no particular interest in San Diego."

"I forgot. You just came here from Boston, didn't you? A truly fascinating city. No wonder you're not very impressed with San Diego." She nodded, and he continued easily, "You're probably wondering why I proposed marriage to you in such an unusual way." He turned to study her profile.

"Yes," she said, "I did."

"I saw you two years ago in Boston."

She turned her head to face him. "I don't understand."

He looked rueful. "You see, I didn't find out who you were until I was on the point of leaving. But I didn't forget. No indeed. And to discover that we were related—you can imagine my pleasure and relief." He paused a moment, the easy smile never leaving his mouth. "It took me a while to find you."

Was he saying that he'd fallen in love with a girl from just a brief look at her? Byrony couldn't imagine such a thing, but it made her feel somehow very special. After all, he had no reason to lie to her.

"What were you doing in Boston?"

"Business. Boring stuff for such a lovely young lady, I assure you. Such warm, humid weather. I must admit that I couldn't wait to return to San Francisco. It's much cooler. You see, Byrony, San Francisco is like"—he raised his hand—"my thumb here, a peninsula, with the Pacific on the left side, the bay above and down the other side. Our weather is cool all year around. I think—I *hope* you will like it."

"It sounds lovely. I can remember sweat—" She broke off, remembering Aunt Ida's lectures about the subjects a lady never addressed.

He laughed again, patting her arm lightly. "Me too. You

must have drunk gallons of lemonade during the summer months."

"Yes," she said, "I did. Where do you live in San Francisco?"

"On Rincon Hill, it's called. In South Park. Irene and I worked with the architect to make it look a bit like our home in Baltimore. I hope you will feel at home there, Byrony."

"Irene lives with you?" Byrony asked, though she already knew the answer. It seemed a bit odd to her that a sister would continue to live with her brother after he married, but it didn't really matter. It wasn't as if theirs was a love attachment.

"Yes, you will like my sister. My half-sister, actually. I spoke about you to her and she is enthusiastic about meeting you and having a new sister." He was silent a moment. Byrony filled in the silence with points of interest in the landscape.

"You don't mind leaving your family so soon, do you?" he asked after a moment.

"No," Byrony said, "I don't. My mother and her husband realize that you are a very busy man. Do you wish to return to San Francisco after the wedding?"

Married to an absolute stranger. She felt as though she herself were somehow apart from the girl in the buckboard. She shook herself as he said, "Yes, by ship. One of my ships, actually. She's the *Flying Sun* and the accommodations are quite comfortable. It shouldn't take us more than five days to reach San Francisco."

She wanted desperately to ask him how much he was paying her father, but hesitated. It was one of those topics that was doubtless considered a man's business. She prayed it was a goodly amount so her mother's work could be lightened.

Ira looked at her profile, delighted that she was so

lovely. Even if she'd been homely as mud pie, he still would have married her. But her beauty would make every man in San Francisco envious of him. And she was so young, and malleable. Every problem would be solved. He knew all about her father, and had, indeed, despised the man on sight. Miserable bastard. At least the girl had been protected. He had shown himself to her as sensitive to her feelings and very gentle, knowing instinctively it was the way to proceed with her.

He encouraged her to speak of her life in Boston, and did no probing when she glossed over her return to San Diego. He would have liked to tell her that her mother had always been a silly fool, even when she was young, so certain in her belief that she could change the buffoon, Madison DeWitt, but he'd realized quickly enough that she'd appointed herself her mother's protector.

"You will be happy, Byrony, I swear it to you," he said as he helped her down from the buckboard.

"Well, my boy, how are you?" Madison DeWitt clapped Ira on the back, oblivious of the fact that the *boy* was in his late thirties.

"Just fine, sir," Ira said politely. "I was just telling Byrony about my house in San Francisco. Her future home."

Madison's eyes narrowed for a brief instant. It angered him that his slut of a daughter would live in luxury. She didn't deserve it. "Ah, yes," he said. "My little girl will make a fine wife."

He'd been concerned about whom to invite to the wedding. He didn't want Ira Butler to discover Byrony's lustful activities with Gabriel de Neve, at least until after the wedding. He'd made a mistake pouring out his troubles to that old gossip Jeb Donnally. He led Ira into the house for a drink of his prize whiskey, and left Byrony to herself.

Alice found her daughter in the stable an hour later

grooming Thorny, her mare. She said, without preamble, "Do you wish to marry Ira Butler, my dear child?"

Byrony turned slowly, her hand still stroking her mare's glossy neck. "He seems very nice. He is well-looking." She closed her eyes a moment, and said, her voice tinged with bitterness, "And of course he has the most important advantage—he's rich."

"You don't feel he is too much older than you?"

Byrony shrugged. "He is handsome, Mother. He will probably look as he does today in ten years. I think I may come to like him quite a lot." She paused a moment, then asked, "Is he paying your husband enough for me? Will it ease your life?"

"Yes, and he's done it in such a way that I believe he knows my poor Madison's weaknesses. There is a liberal amount of money to be paid into an account with Señor Bandini in San Diego every month."

Byrony sighed her relief. Not one big payment that could be gambled away in a week. "Did you speak private to him about it?"

"No. He just seemed to know. Madison was a bit upset—"

"You mean he ranted and raved at you." Her hands fisted at her sides. "He didn't hurt you, did he?"

"No, not really," Alice said without rancor. "But Ira wouldn't change his mind. I want you to be happy, Byrony, and safe. I had almost ceased to believe in miracles." She hugged her daughter, causing Thorny to neigh softly. "Ira is a good man. He will never harm you."

Byrony blinked, startled by another memory of that man. No, she'd seen it in his eyes. No meanness there. And a blue color that she couldn't begin to describe—dark, so very dark, but not a navy blue. Eyes you could stare into for years and still not know their depths. She had to stop it. It was all romantic drivel.

But it was his face she saw late that night as she lay in her bed, the chirping of the crickets the only sound to break the stillness. Even her mother's husband had fallen into a drunken stupor. She couldn't hear him snoring, thank God. What was the gambler doing? Did he ever think about her, wonder what she was doing, dream about her beautiful eyes?

"You are such a witless fool, Byrony," she said and fluffed up her pillow.

Brent Hammond was sitting very quietly, his face expressionless, as was his wont during a high-stakes poker game. He'd already won three thousand dollars. Five hundred of his dollars lay in the center of the table, along with another fifteen hundred dollars from the three other players. One of the players was James Cora himself, owner of the El Dorado saloon. It was well past midnight, and the game had grown more intense with each passing hour. Brent's concentration remained unbroken. He had to continue winning. He had to, to buy the saloon on the corner of Clay and Montgomery.

"How many, Hammond?"

"Two," Brent said, as he selected the losing cards from his hands. "That'll do it, I think."

James Cora grunted as he dealt the cards. Hammond was good, very good, oblivious of all the distractions Cora always provided. He'd taken only one brief look at Janine's full bosom, then turned away. The other two men he discounted. They were miners out to lose every ounce of gold in their pockets.

Brent gently fanned his cards. A full house, kings over eights. He smiled inwardly, allowing nothing to show on his face. He'd been dealt the three kings, and Cora had given him the two eights. Very nice. Very nice indeed. He studied the other men's faces around the circular table. One very young man was smiling broadly. Young fool. The other, his friend from Nevada City, was looking like he'd lost his best friend. And Cora, no expression on his broad, handsome face. Brent had seen James Cora aboard a riverboat on the Mississippi some five years before. He'd never played against him.

"Your bet, Foggerty," Cora said to the youngest man.

Foggerty licked his lips in evident excitement. "Five hundred," he said, and shoved gold forward to the center of the table.

His partner folded.

Brent paused a moment, then raised five hundred.

James Cora lightly snapped the edges of his cards between his thumb and little finger, with slow deliberation. It was a studied trick that was no longer an affectation. His dark brows nearly met at the center of his forehead. He raised another five hundred dollars.

Within five minutes there was ten thousand dollars sitting in the middle of the table.

"Call," Cora said finally.

Foggerty, a huge grin slitting his mouth, slammed down his cards. "Three aces."

"Sorry," Brent said quietly, "full house, kings over eights."

Cora gave a dramatic pause, and Brent felt his blood turn to ice. He cursed silently, waiting for the ax to fall. Cora looked him full in the face, a twisted smile on his full lips. "I believe, Hammond, that I'm in for some competition." With those words, he tossed his cards in, facedown.

Brent wanted to dance on top of the table; he wanted to shout and laugh and drink a gallon of raw whiskey. Instead, he nodded to each of the men, his eyes resting on Cora's face for a long moment. "Thank you, gentlemen," he said, slowly raking in his winnings. "I hope we play again."

He rose and straightened his coat. James Cora said, "You

play well, Hammond, very well indeed. Give my love to Maggie, won't you?"

Brent started with surprise. How did Cora know of his association with Maggie? Lord, were there no secrets in San Francisco? He said, "Yes, indeed I will. Would you mind keeping my winnings in your safe tonight, Cora?"

"Not at all. Wise of you. I wouldn't bet your staying in a whole hide for more than five minutes if you walked out of here with that much money. The Sydney Ducks have an incredible network, as I'm sure you realize now. Lawless scum."

Brent nodded in agreement, and followed Cora to his back office. The money and gold were placed in a leather pouch and put into the safe. Cora said over his shoulder, "I have men guarding the El Dorado at all times. You needn't worry."

"No, I won't," Brent said. He shook hands with James Cora. "We will play again. I'll try my damnedest to give you that competition, Cora. Give my love to Belle."

"Indeed I will," Cora said. He wasn't at all disconcerted. He and Belle were both famous and infamous. He wouldn't allow his fiery wife ever to get close to Hammond. He was too much a man for Belle's token restraint. She'd have his pants off in five minutes. He saw Brent Hammond on his way, then turned thoughtfully back into his saloon. It was hard to see through all the accumulated smoke. He'd lost two thousand dollars to Hammond, but he wasn't worried. He'd get it back, easily. He wondered at his Good Samaritan streak. It wasn't like him, even if Maggie had practically begged him to give Brent Hammond the stake he needed. A ten-high straight flush. Yes, it had been painful to fold those cards facedown and give Hammond the pot. Not that Hammond's saloon would be any great competition. Lord, there were so many saloons already in San Francisco—over six hundred at last count—one more wouldn't matter. And it wasn't as if Hammond were opening a brand-new saloon. He'd simply be taking over the Broken Mare from that ass Tory Grayson. Why the hell, though, did Maggie care so much? She was hard as nails. Even though Hammond looked like a stud, he didn't think Maggie was after what was in his pants. Well, he thought, accepting a whiskey from his bartender, he'd find out soon enough. He looked up to see Tony Dawson, Dan Brewer, and Delaney Saxton stroll through the swinging doors. They never played for big stakes, but he personally liked the three of them. Good men, and more honest than most successful men were in San Francisco.

Brent Hammond automatically reached for his derringer as he stepped into the cool, foggy night. There weren't too many men about this time of night, just a few drunks and the usual complement of scum lurking in the dark alleys waiting for an unwary victim. He felt nearly light-headed with relief. He whistled all the way to Maggie's house, some three blocks away from Portsmouth Square.

She was waiting for him.

"You did it," she said.

He swept her high into his arms and swung her around, then lowered her and gave her a smacking kiss on her pursed lips. "Yep, Maggie, I did it. Now we can go ahead with our plans."

"This calls for a celebration, Brent. Whiskey?"

"The best you've got, Maggie." He watched her walk in her no-nonsense, nearly military fashion, across her small sitting room, stuffed with so many gewgaws that he wondered how she'd managed to keep them intact with her skirts so full and stiff. He'd met her in a brothel, one of the most elegant in San Francisco. She hadn't serviced him; she was the owner of Maggie's. Strangely enough, he'd forgotten his purpose once they'd begun talking, though he'd believed his need was too great to be diverted by anything or anyone. He told her of that girl in San Diego, Byrony. Silly name, and a girl who appeared to be as grasping as Laurel, and him a randy goat by the time he'd returned to San Francisco. No woman after Laurel had gotten to him like she had, and his admission made him grin at his own stupidity. He wished he hadn't watched Byrony run across that road in San Diego, for at odd moments since, he'd stripped her and seen her long legs wrapped around him. He shook his head and accepted a glass of whiskey.

"Good stuff, Maggie," he said. "To our success."

"To success."

They both threw back their heads and tossed down the whiskey.

"I'm going to name the saloon the Wild Star," Brent said, his voice quiet and pleased. "If that's all right with you."

"The Wild Star and Maggie's. Sounds like a perfect mating. We've lots of work to do before we can open, Brent. How big is your stake now?"

Their plan was quite simple. Tory Grayson's Broken Mare was a huge building, half of which was at the present rented out to merchants for storage. Maggie would take that side and Brent the other. They would be partners, all profits split down the middle. By the time he left Maggie's house, their plans set for an opening in a month, Brent was feeling drunk, blissfully content, and for the first time in nine years, ready to put down roots. He saw not only the immediate profit he would make from the saloon; he saw also the future of this boisterous city with himself a part of it.

The sale was completed the following day in Delaney Saxton's bank office. Maggie grinned at Delaney and offered him her best girl, Celeste, at a discount.

"I don't want Marie taking a knife to me," Saxton said, referring to his French mistress.

Maggie shrugged, imitating Marie's Gallic gesture. "Marie's a sensible girl. You're lucky I didn't take a knife to you, Del, after you stole her away from me."

"Ah, Maggie, you of all people understand the direness of a man's need."

Maggie laughed and gave him a light buffet on his shoulder. "I knew I'd make a fortune in San Francisco."

They parted amicably.

The next three weeks went with startling swiftness as the Wild Star and Maggie's began to take shape. It was only at night that Brent occasionally remembered a pair of warm, laughing eyes. For the life of him he couldn't remember their color, just their directness and their pleasure as they looked at him.

Her image grew fainter as time passed.

It was a shock one morning when Maggie, who had just finished having the main room wallpapered, turned to him and asked, "Who is Byrony?"

Brent could only stare at her.

"Shut your mouth. You look like a silly fish. Don't you know anyone named Byrony?"

"Yes," he said finally, "I suppose that I do—in a way."

"Well, my dear, you knocked the conceit out of Celeste's sails, let me tell you."

"What the hell do you mean, Maggie?" He felt shaken. He didn't like it one bit.

Maggie made a show of shaking out her black silk skirts. "You called out 'Byrony' when you, ah, took your pleasure."

"Shit," Brent said.

"I gather," Maggie said, watching him intently, "that you do know someone named Byrony."

"I knew her for less time than it takes to smoke a cigar."

"Then you, my dear Mr. Hammond, have a problem. Your cigar probably does too. Now what do you think of the wallpaper? You don't think it's too flamboyant, do you?"

FOUR

It was not the first time Byrony had felt nervous on this, her wedding day. But now her nervousness had become terror. It was night now, the evening meal at a close, and they were aboard the *Flying Sun*. She stared hard toward the few receding flickering lights of San Diego. Over and over she asked herself why she had married this man. As always, the reason was obvious enough: she'd had no choice, none at all. Remaining in *his* house, had she refused, would have meant utter misery for both her and her mother.

"I am glad the ocean is calm and the sky clear," Ira said.

"Yes," Byrony said. "The stars look like bright gems. I should like to stay on deck for a while, to admire everything." She didn't look at her new husband; she couldn't. She had no desire to see the cabin belowdeck, no desire to see the bed she would have to share with him.

"I should too," Ira said, and moved to stand beside her. "Like to stay on deck and admire everything, that is. Our fellow passengers aren't as hardy as we are. At least it's quiet and peaceful now." He made no move to touch her.

Her mother's hesitant words of a few hours before flashed through her mind, and her terror grew. "Byrony, love, Ira is a good man. He won't be rough with you. Just close your eyes and lie very still. Let him do as he wishes. It will be over soon enough."

She'd wanted to yell at her mother, "If I don't lie still, will he beat me?" But she'd said nothing. He was her husband, and he owned her. She wasn't stupid; it was the way of the world where women were concerned. Only Aunt Ida hadn't been owned because she'd had enough money to keep her independence, until her death. She hadn't needed a man to support her. Did everything have to revolve around money? Silly question. In her case, Madison DeWitt's lust for money had determined the course of her life.

She remembered her father's words, ugly, obscene words, spoken to her in a low, leering voice before she'd left his home forever.

"If you have any sense at all, girl," he'd said, "you'll pretend to virginity. Cry out a bit when he takes you. I don't want you thrown back to me like a discarded piece of garbage. Praise the saints you're not carrying that greaser's bastard."

She stared at him a long moment, hatred welling up in her. "You are a filthy-minded old man," she said coldly.

He raised his hand, glanced quickly around, and reluctantly lowered it.

"No," she told him, drawing herself up very straight, "you'll never strike me again."

"Watch your mouth, girl," he said, "or—"

"Or you'll what? How about admitting the truth? Announce to the world that you sold me? That since you're incapable of earning an honest dollar, you must have another man support you?"

"You worthless little slut!"

She threw back her head and laughed. "Worthless? Come, what an uncharitable and untrue thing to say."

"You just make sure you keep your new husband happy, girl."

"Or he'll stop sending you money? Now, there's a thought." She struck what she hoped was an insolent pose. His heavy jowls quivered with rage, but Ira was coming toward them and he could say nothing more.

She thought now that she shouldn't have enraged him. He might take it out on her mother. But no, he'd already drunk so much by the time she and Ira had left, he would be snoring now, sodden with whiskey. And he now had money.

"Our wedding was just as I wished it to be—no fuss and no gawking people. Private and simple."

"The parson, Mr. Elks, hates my father. He only conducted the ceremony because of my mother."

"Mr. Elks is a man of discernment. Don't look so surprised, Byrony. I know well your father's reputation, his character. Now you are safe from him."

What about you? Am I safe from you?

"And don't, I pray, Byrony, feel concern for your mother's welfare. That is why I am paying your father on a monthly basis. She too is safe now."

She turned to face him, too startled to speak for a moment. "You are very kind," she said at last.

"It is just that I despise injustice. I need to speak to you, Byrony, then you may judge just how kind I really am."

She jerked at his words. "Yes, Ira?" Was he going to tell her that he wanted their wedding night to begin now? She held herself stiffly.

He remained silent for a few more moments, then said finally, "When I met you, I realized that you were, thankfully, a very kind person yourself. Understanding, I suppose. I know you did not marry me because you loved me, Byrony, just as I know you did not marry me for my wealth. As for myself, I am fond of you, very fond, but I wouldn't have rushed both of us were it not for—"

He broke off, and she saw that his face was very pale and

his hands were clenching and unclenching at his sides. She waited.

He turned to face her and smiled slightly. "You see, Byrony, I must ask you for a very large favor, and I pray that you will give me the answer I must have."

"Yes?" She was more confused than ever.

"I've mentioned my half-sister, Irene, to you. I have practically raised her, our parents dying when she was but fourteen years old. I was all she had in the world. And I still am."

He drew a deep breath and said, "Irene became involved with a man some months ago. I did not discover this liaison until it was too late. You see, the man is married. He lied to Irene, seduced her, and now she is with child."

Byrony stared at him. She heard the anguish in his voice, realized his deep love for his half-sister. "I'm sorry, Ira. Your poor sister."

"You are my wife now, Byrony. I know you are frightened of me as a husband, of my making demands on you. How could it be otherwise? Raised by a maiden aunt who distrusted every man, and a father who is a brutal tyrant. I will not force myself on you, I swear it. But the favor I ask will bind me to you, earn my unending gratitude to the day I die. I ask, Byrony, that Irene's child be yours, that you save my poor sister from a scandal that would destroy not only her but also both of us. I ask that you pretend pregnancy, then, after the child's birth, treat it as your own."

"So," she said quietly, "the only reason for our marriage is to save your sister."

"Yes."

Freedom from a man's demands. Freedom to be myself, to remain untouched. "How could this be done, Ira?"

How very reasonable and logical she sounded. She sensed the relief in him. "I own a home in Sacramento. I would escort you and Irene there as soon as we reach San Francisco. You will remain there for seven or so months, then return home. I fear you will be a bit lonely and confined during that time, but I can see no other alternative. No one must know that it is Irene who carries the child and not you."

"I don't know. It seems outrageous, impossible."

"I also fear for Irene's life," he said. "She is writhing in guilt. I fear she might try to kill herself."

Byrony looked out over the still water. The half-moon cast silver shadows over the gently cresting waves. Again, was there really any choice for her? Why had he waited until after they were married to tell her of this? It was not important, not really, and she had no choice. "You saved me from a wretched existence with my father," she said finally. "I will do this for you and Irene. The money you are sending him each month will protect my mother from his rages. Yes, I owe you a great deal now, Ira." She thrust her hand toward him and he clasped it.

"Thank you," he said.

Brent ruffled Celeste's soft black curls and kissed her lightly on her uptilted nose.

"Perhaps you remember my name now, *mon amour?*"

Before he rolled onto his back and pillowed his head on his arms, he gave her a glittering smile and said, "I know who you are, Celeste."

He felt her fingers glide over his chest, then downward. "Celeste give you everything, yes? Who is this other *grisette* whose name you bleat at me?"

"Do French girls remember everything?" He tensed when her fingers closed over him.

"I think it is not at all polite what you did."

"Forget it. She is nothing to me, a dream, a memory. Nothing."

"Ha! A dream that lives in your mind is not a nothing. But Celeste will make you forget, yes?"

"In an hour, perhaps," he said, his voice dry. "I am only a man, Celeste. Give me a while to garner my strength."

Brent still couldn't believe that he'd shouted her name at the height of his passion. Why? She was only a vague memory, a soft phantom. He hadn't lied. She likely wasn't the *grisette* Celeste painted her, but nonetheless, she would sell herself in any case. To a rich man, a foolish rich man who wanted a beautiful young wife. His jaw seemed to lock until the tension made him wince. He'd pictured an old man's hands stroking her. "Damn all women to hell," he said deep in his throat. Was it his fate in life to be drawn to women like Laurel? At least he'd learned over the past nine years to leave them before they could hurt him. Furious with himself, he turned to Celeste and began to return the deep caresses.

"Ah," she whispered, drawing his mouth to hers. "You are not just a man, Brent. You do such nice things."

"Yes," he said, "I do."

Maggie stood in the center of the opulent room, her gentleman's receiving room she called it. Maggie's was nearly completed, as was the Wild Star. Everything looked grand. She'd had the girls' bedrooms done first, and the gentlemen hadn't minded at all the smell of paint or the hazardous piles of lumber stacked about.

She frowned suddenly, remembering that Lisette was still suffering from violent cramps. She must ask Saint Morris to examine the girl. In fact, her thinking continued, though she was careful to ensure that the men who paid the exorbitant price to spend the night in her establishment were as clean as possible, it wouldn't hurt to have Saint give the girls monthly examinations. She wanted no syphilis in her house.

She walked the length of the sitting room to the large black piano. She lovingly ran her fingers over the smooth finish, then sat down and began to strike a few chords.

Major chords. Only happy sounds. I'm twenty-seven years old, Maggie thought, and I'm going to be very rich and I'll owe it to no one except myself. She smiled at the thought of her stern-faced father, a blacksmith, stepping into her establishment. Self-righteous prig. Horny demanding bastard. Her fingers suddenly settled on a minor chord. Her poor mother, every year of her married life spent pregnant until she'd had the good sense to die, leaving nine children. Maggie had stayed until her father had remarried. She'd then willingly sold her virginity to a rich tobacco planter from Virginia. The money had gotten her as far as Mississippi, where she'd spent seven years of her life as a man's mistress. He'd beaten her only rarely, given her gifts equally as rarely, and hadn't made her pregnant. When she'd read about gold being discovered in California, she'd known that was where she was going, where she belonged. She'd saved nearly every cent Thomas Currson had grudgingly paid her, and she traveled to San Francisco in style. Now I'm a businesswoman, she thought, her fingers moving smoothly to a lighthearted tune. I'll never be a rich man's mistress again.

Maggie looked up to see Brent standing quietly watching her. She nodded and placed her hands in her lap.

"Don't stop, Maggie. You play very well."

She laughed self-consciously and quickly rose from the stool. "I haven't touched a piano in a long time, too long a time. My mother played beautifully, until—well, until she didn't have the energy."

"She was ill, your mother?"

Maggie gave a bitter laugh. "Ill? Yes, I guess you could say that. Now, Brent, what can I do for you? Have you come to admire?"

How closemouthed she was about her past. But it was an unwritten rule of the West. Everyone was entitled to begin again, to bury his past. Just like you, Hammond. "I've never seen such a fancy brothel," he said. "Actually, I wanted to tell you that I've got to go to Sacramento to buy the brass railing for the mahogany bar. Can you believe there's none to be had in San Francisco?" He shook his head in disbelief. "Is there anything else you need?"

"No. When will you leave?"

"Toward the end of the week. It shouldn't take me more than three or so days. Then, Maggie, we'll open, officially."

The pleasure in his voice warmed her. She had never in her life really liked, much less trusted, a man, until she'd met Brent. He was, objectively, a beautiful man, virile as hell, if her girls were to be believed, but she didn't want his body. She wanted his friendship. She wanted to be part of his dream. She'd seen the loneliness in him that first evening she'd met him in her brothel. The emptiness. He'd opened up to her, and she'd known she was the only person he'd really spoken to. That made her special to him. They complemented each other. A madam and a gambler. She giggled. "Yes," she said, "officially. James Cora will gnash his teeth in envy."

"Just so long as Belle doesn't come in and tear the place down."

"Doubtful. James and Belle are experiencing one of their marvelous disagreements at the moment. They're not speaking. Incidentally, I've found you a bartender. He's from New York, more honest than not, and can handle any scum who come in to make trouble."

"Thank God," Brent said. "What's his name? How did you meet him?"

"It was Lucienne who bagged him, actually. His name, if you can believe this, is Percival Smith. He's bigger than you, Brent, and built like a wine cask."

"Send him over and we'll strike a deal." Brent paused, searching Maggie's face. "We'll make a go of it, Maggie, I swear it."

"I know, Brent. I knew we were a winning team five minutes after I met you." She felt a knot form in her throat and quickly said, lightly, "When are we going to have another game of chess?"

"Whenever you want to taste humiliation, you've got it, lady."

They grinned at each other, in perfect accord.

"You never told me, Maggie, who taught you."

Her eyes clouded, but just for a moment. "It was just someone I knew, a long time ago," she said. Thomas Currson had taught her both poker and chess. He'd had his uses.

She shook her head at him and smiled. "You know, I never asked you why you're calling the saloon Wild Star. My name, Maggie's, is pretty straightforward, but Wild Star?"

"I'll tell you if you promise not to laugh at me," he said.

She made a sign of a cross over her breast. "I promise."

"It's kind of silly, I guess, but I was riding out of Denver, at night, and there was this bright star overhead. I just kept riding toward it, thinking that it was like me in a way, always moving, never staying in the same place long, free, if you will, and wild. I decided then if I ever settled in one place, I'd harness that star, but keep the illusion that it was still free, still moving, still wild."

"That's not silly at all," she said after a moment. "You're a romantic, Brent, and that's a good thing for a man to be."

"And a poet, no doubt."

"Perhaps," Maggie said. "Now, I can see you're itching to be off. Will you do me a favor? Could you ask Saint to come over? Lisette isn't feeling too well."

"Sure thing. Nothing serious, I hope?"

"Just woman problems, that's all."

"Mysterious," he said, giving her a wicked look.

"You men are so damned lucky," Maggie said.

"Not always. Celeste just got mysterious on me."

He cocked his hat at her and strode from the stiflingly glorious parlor. Maggie loved yellow. He felt like he'd stepped into a giant daffodil. At least it was better than Belle Cora's garish and tasteless gold-and-red whorehouse.

"It's not at all what I expected," Byrony said to her new half-sister. "It's so barren, but the hills are beautiful and the city is so vibrant."

"Yes, that's true. But we love San Francisco. And there are so many changes. Always changes."

Byrony set down her teacup and looked about the salon. "You've built a lovely house, Ira. Very impressive."

"Thank you, my dear. Do you like your room?"

"I'd be crazy and blind not to! Did you decorate it, Irene?"

"No, Ira did, before he left for San Diego. He wanted everything to be perfect for you."

A silent black woman gently removed the tea service. "Thank you, Eileen," Byrony said.

Eileen nodded, her eyes meeting Byrony's for a brief moment.

Byrony yawned. "Oh dear," she said, "please excuse me. I suppose I'm tired. It certainly isn't the company."

"Why don't you rest until dinner, my dear? I'll escort you to your room."

"I should like that," Byrony said, and rose.

Irene rose also. She gave Byrony a brief hug and said, "Thank you."

Ira left her at her door. "I'll see that you're not disturbed, my dear. Eileen will call you at seven. We dine normally at eight o'clock."

She nodded, and slipped into her new bedroom. She stood for a moment in the center of the room. Her bedroom at Aunt Ida's had been as fussy as her aunt was, crammed with all the bric-a-brac that wouldn't fit into the other rooms. Her bedroom in San Diego had been small, bare, and cold. But not this room. She drew a deep, pleased breath. Large, airy, with huge bow windows facing south to sparsely housed hills. The walls were painted cream and all the furnishings were a pale blue. There were no *things* cluttering any surface. It was her room and it would be she who made it personal. The bed was covered with a pale blue-and-white counterpane.

I'm happy, she thought suddenly. I'm starting a new life. I am in control of it. Well, not really, she quickly amended to herself, her smile fading. She was now, she supposed, officially pregnant. She remembered Irene's soft thank-you. She was relieved. She'd wanted no tears, no apologies, no scenes. How different Irene was from Ira. Ira, fair and slender as an angel, and Irene, small, dusky-complexioned, with deep brown eyes. She seemed somewhat reticent, perhaps shy, but Byrony guessed that the seven months they would spend together would bring about a better understanding of their respective characters.

Byrony stepped to the windows and drew back the heavy cream-colored draperies. She hoped she'd be able to see San Francisco before Ira took them to Sacramento. She'd felt the stirring in her blood when they had arrived, docking at the Clay Street wharf. Life, she thought, that's what San Francisco has, boisterous wild young life. Ira had laughingly told her that he was an old man here, where the average age was well under thirty.

The gambler is here, she thought, and felt a peculiar rush of excitement. But it is too late. I am a married lady. It is too late.

"Fool," she said to herself. "You're behaving like a child, weaving a patched dream from scraps of memory. He's just a man, a man like all the others."

She dropped the draperies over the windows and walked slowly to her bed. She slipped off her shoes and lay on her back, staring up at the cream-painted ceiling. She wanted desperately to recapture that noble image of herself she'd nourished when she'd agreed to Ira's plea, but there was nothing inside her save a growing feeling of despair and disbelief. She would become a mother in the eyes of the world. Irene's child would be called hers. How would they all act? How would she feel then, living this lie? A life of lies.

There was a soft knock on her bedroom door, and Ira's quiet voice calling, "Byrony."

She quickly eased off the bed and straightened her clothes. "Come in."

Ira took in her pale face. "Are you very fatigued, my dear?"

She managed a wan smile. "Perhaps, just a bit."

He closed the door behind him and walked toward her. "Byrony," he said, closing his hands over her shoulders, "you've been thinking, haven't you? Thinking of all the complications, indeed, the consequences of your decision?"

She closed her eyes a moment, wondering how he could have known, but it didn't occur to her to lie. "Yes, I have. It seems impossible to me now, all of it."

Very gently he drew her into his arms. She'd never been held by a man before, and it felt odd, for a man was unyielding, so much stronger than she, and for an instant she felt fear rip through her. He let her go. "Tell me what seems impossible. We will talk of it. I do not want you to be unhappy."

"You're kind, Ira. I suppose I am just homesick."

"Well, perhaps you miss your mother, but nothing else. And you only really knew her for what, Byrony? Six, seven months?"

She nodded.

"You now have a home, my dear, your own home. You are secure, and you are cared for. The child will, I devoutly pray, add to all of our happiness." He paused a moment, then continued quietly, "If, in the future, you wish for a child, you will tell me. You are performing a great deed for my sister and me. I never wish you to have lasting regrets about your decision. Never."

"I hope you are right," she said. Her stomach growled suddenly.

"I'm just as hungry," he said, grinning down at her. "Come now, let's have dinner. Irene isn't feeling too well so she is dining in her room. Tomorrow you and I will visit a very fancy clothier. You will need some new gowns. Friday we will leave for Sacramento. I fancy," he continued thoughtfully as he walked beside her into the dining room, "that you look utterly exquisite in all shades of blue. We will see what Monsieur David can provide."

FIVE

The April afternoon was sunny and cool. The wind blew stiff on the bay, and Byrony clamped her hand on her bonnet while she watched her brand-new trunk carried on board the *Scarlet Queen*. She smiled in delight, thinking of all the new clothes and underthings that were inside, so many things, and all of the finest fabrics. She felt like a spoiled princess. She felt Ira's hand on her arm and turned the brilliant smile to him.

"What's this?" he asked.

"You—well, all the new things you bought me, Ira. I've never had such— Well, anyway, thank you."

"You are most welcome, my dear. Will you wear the sapphire-blue gown to dinner this evening?"

"Yes, certainly. Ira, the boat is so large and beautiful. It must rival the finest riverboats that ply the Mississippi." She looked toward Irene and saw that the woman was looking pale. "Oh dear," she said in a low voice, "I hope the trip won't be too hard on her."

"Why don't I escort both of you to your cabin?"

Byrony nodded, albeit somewhat reluctantly. The bustle of the passengers, the frantic loading and unloading of other vessels, all the smells and sounds of the wharf made her feel so very alive.

"Captain O'Mally," Ira said. "Good day to you, sir. I venture to say we'll enjoy a smooth trip. Allow me to introduce my wife."

"A pleasure, ma'am," Captain O'Mally said. "Miss Butler," he added, bowing slightly to Irene. "You've business in Sacramento, Mr. Butler?"

"Yes indeed. We will see you this evening, Captain."

Byrony followed Ira and Irene along the deck. She peeked quickly into the large dining salon that was enclosed with glass windows. *I am indeed a princess and am aboard my own floating palace.*

Their cabin was small but luxuriously appointed. There was a soft blue carpeting on the floor and two narrow beds along the far wall of the cabin, two chairs, and a dressing table.

"It's lovely. Oh, Irene, come, you must rest. Would you like a cool cloth on your forehead?"

Ira led Irene to the bed and helped her lie down. He sat down beside her and gently stroked her gloved hand. "Yes, Byrony, please," he answered for his sister. "There should be washcloths in the armoire and cool water in the basin."

A silent Eileen appeared at the doorway, looking impassively toward Irene. Without saying a word, she took the damp cloth from Byrony and walked to the narrow bed. "I will see to her, sir," she said, her voice a soft, hoarse drawl.

Ira rose, his brow knit as he looked down at his sister. "You rest, Irene. Perhaps you will feel more the thing by dinner. Byrony, my dear, I will go along to my cabin now."

She walked him to the door and said, "Would it be all right if I explored, Ira?"

"Certainly. You are a married lady now, Byrony. You do just as you please."

She felt a stab of guilt leaving Irene, but her sister-in-law, seeing her excitement, waved her away.

"No need to worry, Miz Butler," Eileen said. "I'll stay with the mistress."

Byrony spent two glorious hours exploring the *Scarlet Queen*. She clung to the rail until the steamboat left the wharf and turned north. She waved to the masses of people on the dock, not caring that she knew none of them. They were never out of sight of land. Desolate land, from what Byrony could tell, and so many islands dotting the bay. She wished she could speak to someone who could tell her where they were going and what she was seeing. Several men looked hungrily at her, but she ignored them. In her short time in San Francisco, every man she'd seen had looked hungrily at her.

"So few ladies, my dear," Ira had said after several men had simply stopped in their tracks and stared at her. "And, of course, you are beautiful."

"But, Ira, I've seen many ladies."

"Not exactly ladies, Byrony. The largest part of the female population are—well, not ladies."

"Whores?"

"Yes," he'd said, looking startled.

She didn't enlighten him. How could she tell him that it was but one of the insults her father had hurled at her head?

Byrony sneaked a look into a small salon that was obviously for men only. There was a thick cloud of smoke, occasional spurts of laughter, and, of course, gambling.

She returned to the cabin to find Irene still abed, Eileen seated in a chair beside her mistress. Eileen placed her finger over her lips.

"She's asleep, poor lady. I'll see that she gets some soup later when she awakens. Come, Miz Byrony, I'll help you dress, but quiet now."

She met Ira outside her cabin, and his soft whistle of admiration made her feel wonderful.

"Lovely, my dear, simply lovely." He looked at the closed cabin door, a question in his eyes.

"Irene is sleeping. Eileen thinks it best."

"Then come along." Ira offered her his elegant black-coated arm.

"We won't be sitting with the captain this evening. There are several business friends of mine who requested a separate table. You will, I believe, enjoy them, my dear."

This proved to be the case. There was a Mr. Lacy, who owned a foundry, a Mr. Dancy, who was an investor from New York, and a Mr. Cornfield, who owned one of the newspapers. She was aware that Ira preened under their attention to her. I do look nice, she thought, straightening her shoulders and sending a smile to the balding Ezra Lacy.

"Gentlemen," she said, "please continue your conversation. I am content to listen and learn."

The dining salon was brilliantly lit; the tables were covered with white linen, the cutlery was silver, the plates fine china. She took a tentative taste of the broiled scallops and found them delicious. She heard a man laugh behind her and turned slightly in her chair toward the captain's table.

She nearly dropped her wineglass. Staring at her, his eyes narrowed and so dark they appeared nearly black, was the gambler. She felt cold and hot at the same time. She shook her head, closed her eyes a moment. It was he, she was certain. She met his gaze again, and smiled. He raised his hand in salute.

Dear God, she thought. She believed her imagination had probably enhanced his male beauty, but it wasn't so. He was wearing black, a pearl-gray vest over his white shirt. His hair glistened as black as his coat beneath the chandelier, and he sported a thick black mustache.

"Are you all right, Mrs. Butler?"

She got hold of herself and said easily, "Of course, Mr.

Lacy. May I ask, sir, who is that gentleman there, at the captain's table?"

"Ah, that is Brent Hammond. He's a new businessman in San Francisco. He's opening a saloon next week, the Wild Star."

"I see," she said. In the same city. Of course she knew he lived in San Francisco. It wasn't fair. Why couldn't he look like a troll? Why did he have to stare at her with those dangerous, beautiful eyes?

She forced her attention back to her table. She heard Mr. Lacy mention something about the "duchess" and her house in conjunction with Hammond. His wife? His mistress? What was this house they were talking about?

Brent continued to stare; he couldn't help himself. It was her, but the difference in her looks astounded him. She was gowned beautifully, quite expensively in fact, and he recognized Monsieur David's handiwork. Her smooth shoulders met the soft white lace of her gown, hinting at the breasts beneath. Her honey-colored hair was piled high on her head and one thick ringlet fell lazily over her shoulder. Her neck was long, slender, exquisite as the rest of her. He glanced at the four men at the table with her, recognizing three of them. After a few moments he turned to Captain O'Mally. "Who is the lady, sir, over there with Ezra Lacy?"

Captain O'Mally turned from Delaney Saxton. "That is the new Mrs. Butler, sir."

Brent, who had been flirting outrageously with Delaney Saxton's bride, Chauncey, felt himself grow cold. Ira's bride. God, the man was nearly old enough to be her father. He stared at the aristocratic, chisel-featured Ira Baines Butler, and felt a surge of sheer hatred for the man. Why the hell should he be so amazed, so disbelieving, after all? He'd known what she was; the filthy old man in San Diego had told him all about her. She'd married a rich man, just as he'd known she would. Another Laurel. His fingers tightened about his wineglass. He wanted to wrap his fingers around her neck. Perfidious bitch. The depth of his anger amazed him. Why the hell should he care what she was? It had nothing to do with him. Nothing at all.

Byrony. Byrony Butler.

Old cold-blooded Ira Butler probably made love to her in the dark.

Brent wanted nothing more now than to finish the damned dinner and get out of the dining salon. Why? To go lick his wounds in private, that was why.

Byrony ate nothing more. She tried to pay attention to the occasional gallant comments laid in her path by the gentlemen. She was aware the instant Brent rose from the captain's table and strode from the dining salon. She watched every step he took. He was larger than she remembered, yet so graceful.

"My dear, are you feeling just the thing?"

"Oh yes, Ira. I guess I'm just a bit tired." Did she sound the least bit guilty?

"Then I shall see you to your cabin."

She bid good-nights to the other men, and gave Ira her hand. There was no sign of Brent Hammond. She felt relieved and, at the same time, disappointed. Ira entered the cabin with her to see Irene. She was still sleeping, Eileen still sitting motionless beside the bed.

"Tomorrow, my dear," he said quietly, and gently kissed her forehead. "Sleep well."

Byrony tried to stay still, but couldn't. She began pacing until she was aware of Eileen's dark eyes burrowing into her back. Suddenly she grabbed her new cloak, sapphire blue to match her gown, and whispered, "I shall go on deck for a while, Eileen."

She needn't worry about seeing him, she thought. He was more than likely gambling. It was, after all, his profession. She made her way along the wide deck, paying no attention to the gentlemen she passed, who all tipped their hats at her. She found a vacant spot, away from the other passengers, and leaned her elbows on the railing, staring at the calm dark waters.

"We'll be passing through the Carquinez Strait soon," she heard a low deep voice from behind her. "We've just come through San Pablo Bay, in case you didn't know."

She whirled about, and her eyes met his throat. Slowly she raised her face until she was looking into his eyes.

"The Carquinez Strait," she repeated.

"Yes, we are now traveling due east, and shortly will be in the Sacramento River."

"There are so many rivers and bays and—so much water."

"Indeed, it would appear so."

"It is a surprise to see you again, Mr. Hammond."

A thick black brow arched upward. "You perhaps remembered that I lived in San Francisco. I should say that I am more surprised to see you. You are a long way from San Diego. I see you quickly discovered my name."

"Yes, yes, I did. I understand you are opening a saloon in San Francisco?"

"Yes, I am," he said, and his eyes glittered. "How lovely you look, ma'am."

She grinned. "A bit different from the first time you saw me, I suspect. I've tried to avoid flour."

"I understand you've married one of San Francisco's wealthiest men."

His tone held barely disguised contempt, and she heard it.

"Ira is rich, so I'm told," she said.

"With your looks and guileless charm, I expected nothing less than a rich man. But so old, Mrs. Butler, nearly old enough to have sired you."

Why was he angry? She searched his face in the dim light. She said nothing.

"What, Mrs. Butler? Doesn't your marriage please you? Have you already discovered that selling your body to a rich man involves less than pleasant duties?"

"I don't understand, Mr. Hammond. Why are you—?"

He cut her off abruptly, slashing his hand through the air in front of her. "There is no need, Mrs. Butler, to pretend anything to me. When I first met you, I thought— Well, no matter. It is not often that a woman is what she appears to be."

"And just what did I appear to you to be, sir?"

"Sweet, untouched, innocent." The words, honest words from the depths of him, were out before he could stop them.

"Until you spoke with Jeb Donnally," she said dully. "I understand now. He's a filthy old sot, a crony of my father, who is equally despicable. You surprise me, Mr. Hammond. I would have thought that a gambler, a professional gambler, would be more discerning about people."

He searched her pale face, wondering at the bitterness in her voice, but he was not to be deterred. "He might be an old fool, but he did tell me that you'd have to search outside San Diego for a rich husband. I gather the Californio's seed didn't take root?"

Without thought, Byrony slapped his face. He grabbed her wrist, feeling the delicate bones grind beneath his fingers.

"You bastard. You know nothing. How dare you believe what you believe, all based on that old man's lying tales?"

He dropped her wrist. "A lady doesn't strike a gentleman, now, does she?"

"You are no gentleman."

"And you are no lady. A word of warning, my dear. You strike me again, or make the attempt, and I shall retaliate in kind."

Byrony said, furious, "Damn you, I had to marry him. Do you understand me? No, don't say any more. It is obvious you'll never understand anything. You are too stupid."

She turned on her heel, but he caught her arm and twisted her around. "So, it is his seed that grows in your lovely body? Well, isn't that interesting. Since you are no lady, and since your dear husband isn't about, why don't we—" He broke off suddenly, bent down and kissed her.

He held her arms tightly against her sides and she couldn't move. His mouth was hard, alien. Just as suddenly, he eased the pressure and she felt his tongue on her lower lip, probing. His hand came up to cup her breast. She burst into motion.

She pulled away, and wiped her hand across her mouth. "You—"

"Bastard?"

She saw red.

"It appears your dear husband hasn't taught you much about pleasing a man yet. You'll learn, my dear. If you are nice to me, perhaps I'll instruct you—"

He yelped in pain, and clutched his groin.

Byrony, shaking from shock and the vicious kick she'd given him, jerked about and ran from him, holding her skirts high.

Brent felt the inevitable wave of nausea and remained crouched over until the worst of the pain passed. He forced himself to take slow, deep breaths. Slowly he straightened, and his eyes went down the deck. She was gone.

"You will pay for that," he said softly.

Byrony ran full tilt to the cabin. She paused a moment, leaning her forehead against the door. Tears burned her eyes, and she rubbed them away. How wrong she'd been about him. *No meanness in his eyes.* What a fool she'd been. He was like all the other men, bullies and worse. She rubbed the back of her hand across her mouth.

Brent remained on deck, thinking of how to get back at her. Unfortunately, each of them ended with him having sex with her. He didn't know how much time passed. When he heard a scream, his entire body stiffened. He jerked about to see a man trying to heave a woman overboard.

For an instant his mind was a complete blank. Then he was running toward them, yelling at the man. He saw him try a final time to heave the woman overboard, saw her long mantle catch between his legs. He pushed her violently into the railing, clouting her back with his fists.

"What's going on here? Hey, stop."

He saw the woman drop to her knees on the smooth deck, gasping for breath.

"Mrs. Saxton? Good God, ma'am. What the hell is going on? Who is that fellow?"

"I'm all right," Chauncey Saxton said, her body shuddering. She raised her white face to his. "He tried to kill me."

Brent cursed. The whole business was insane. Attacked by one woman, saving another. He got hold of himself. "Come, ma'am. He's gone now." Brent picked her up into his arms.

"Del," she said. "Please, my husband——"

A man came rushing up to them. "What the hell?"

"Your wife, Saxton," Brent said. "She's all right, thank God." She began to struggle against him, and he set her on her feet. He watched her run to her husband.

Brent watched Delaney calm his wife. He felt a twinge of perhaps jealousy at their closeness. He met Del Saxton's eyes. "What happened?"

"It appears that someone—a man—tried to throw your wife overboard." Brent lowered his voice, adding, "Perhaps it was an attempted rape." Brent saw the wild anger on Delaney Saxton's face at his words. He heard him say soft, reassuring words to his wife.

"Hammond, did you see his face?"

Brent lit a cheroot, blowing out the smoke before replying. The incident had shocked him and made him wonder what the hell was going on. "He was dressed roughly, a wool cap pulled down over his forehead. When he heard me coming, he ran toward the steerage stairs."

Mrs. Saxton said, "I didn't see him, Del. He was behind me, and I didn't recognize his voice."

"What did he say, love? Do you remember?"

"Something like 'I'm sorry.'"

"A criminal with regrets," Brent said. Why the hell, he wondered, would anyone want to kill Del Saxton's wife? It made no sense, no sense at all. Unless the man was crazy—

"Hammond, would you please ask Captain O'Mally to come to our stateroom?"

Brent nodded, and watched Saxton lift his wife into his arms and walk away with her. He stared thoughtfully after the couple, then tossed his cheroot over the side into the still, dark water. She would have died, he thought, if he hadn't been on deck. If he hadn't been insulting Byrony, the man would have succeeded in murdering Chauncey Saxton. He felt a brief stab of pain at the memory of the words he had thrown at Byrony's head. But they were true. *But what if they aren't? What if she is just what she appears—innocent, sweet?* Damn, he felt as if the world had taken a faulty turn. He didn't want to insult her; she meant nothing to him. It was none of his business in any case.

He went to find the captain, knowing that the chances of tracking down the man who'd tried to kill Chauncey Saxton were next to nil.

Brent helped in the search. He couldn't identify any of the men they questioned. Not surprising, he thought, much later when he finally lay on his bed. Why would anyone want to kill Chauncey Saxton? Why would Byrony marry Ira Butler?

Brent finally slept, but his dreams were of a man trying to push Byrony into the river. He tried to save her; she was screaming his name, but he wasn't in time. He saw her blue mantle spread around her, pulling her under the black water.

He jerked awake, his body covered with sweat. Damn her. He was hard, his body heavy with need. He suddenly remembered her bitter words: *I had to marry him.*

What did she expect, anyway? A child usually resulted from sex. At least Ira had married her. He cursed her again, and turned onto his stomach.

Early the following morning, Brent watched Chauncey and Delaney Saxton leave the *Scarlet Queen*. He didn't blame Delaney at all. Were it he, he wouldn't remain to see if the man tried again. He would protect what was his.

He saw Byrony, flanked by her husband and her sister-in-law. She looked pale. He wanted to smash Ira in his handsome face.

He turned on his heel, refusing to acknowledge her or her damned husband.

SIX

Brent had taken only two steps when Ira's voice rang out behind him. "Mr. Hammond."

He turned slowly, a thick black brow arched upward.

"Won't you join us for a cup of coffee?"

"Yes, do come, Hammond," Ezra Lacy said.

He glanced briefly toward Byrony, but she was staring at her hands, folded in her lap.

"Thank you," he said. "Don't mind if I do."

"You know my sister, Irene. This is my new bride, Byrony. Ladies, this is Brent Hammond, a relatively new business addition to San Francisco."

"Mr. Hammond," Irene said.

Brent nodded. "Miss Butler. Mrs. Butler."

"Sorry business," Ezra Lacy said, shaking his head as he passed a cup of steaming coffee to Brent. "Ira was wondering if he shouldn't take the ladies off, given what happened last night."

"I understand, Mr. Hammond," said Irene, "that you saved Mrs. Saxton's life."

"It was fortunate, ma'am, that I was still on deck at the time," Brent said. He didn't imagine that Del wanted the story bruited about, and said in a dismissive voice, "The

66

fellow is likely long gone by now. An unhappy experience for Mrs. Saxton."

"It is what I thought," Irene said. "The wretch probably wanted to rob her."

Brent blinked at her conclusion, but decided it was for the best. "Undoubtedly you're right, ma'am," he said. He felt Byrony's eyes on him and slowly turned toward her. She looked strained, as if she hadn't slept well, her eyes shadowed. Good, maybe her conscience bothered her enough to keep her awake. He said aloud, his voice tightly controlled, "You're looking a bit peaked, Mrs. Butler. I hope the excitement of last night didn't upset you too much."

Arrogant, mean bastard. "Not at all," she said.

"My wife was tucked safely in her bed at the time," Ira said, patting Byrony's hand.

Brent wanted to strike the man. The thought of him touching her, taking her, made his guts cramp. *I'm losing what's left of my meager mind. All over a woman who was nothing but an insubstantial dream.* He heard Ezra Lacy laugh and say wistfully, "What a bore you new husbands are, Ira. How can I conduct any business with you with your lovely bride about?"

"We accomplished rather a goodly amount last evening, if I recall correctly," Ira said. "But knowing you, Ezra, you want to talk my ear off all the way to Sacramento."

"Well, actually, old man, there are some papers I'd like you to see, if you have the time. Perhaps Mr. Hammond would entertain the ladies for a bit?"

Brent saw Byrony's eyes fly in consternation to his face, but he said easily, "It would be a pleasure, gentlemen. I should be delighted to point out all the sights of interest and make myself generally pleasing." He turned to Irene. "For example, did you know, ma'am, that we're quite close to Hock Farm? Mr. Sutter is in residence, you know, and one of his sons with him. He's much changed, I understand."

"Do you mind, my dear?" Ira asked Byrony. "I shan't be overlong."

What could she say?

"I think I shall return to my room," Irene said. "Enjoy the lovely morning, Byrony. Gentlemen."

Ira helped her to rise and it seemed but a moment later that Byrony was staring at Brent Hammond. She felt as though they were the only two human beings in the world even though other passengers were within three feet of them.

"I think I will also go to my cabin," Byrony said, beginning to rise from her chair.

"What? Afraid? I assure you, Mrs. Butler, that I won't attempt anything so injudicious as kissing you in front of the world or touching your breasts."

She closed her eyes for a moment. "Mr. Hammond," she said finally, "I do not understand why you are being so outrageous and insulting to me. To the best of my knowledge I've never harmed you, never done anything, save spill flour on you."

"It would appear a mystery, wouldn't it?" He lounged back in his chair, crossing his long legs at the ankles. "I believe, however, that we do have some unfinished business."

"What is that, sir?"

"I believe I told you that if you struck me again, I would retaliate in kind. If you recall, you very nearly unmanned me. If your aim had been better, I venture to say I wouldn't have been able to save the fair Mrs. Saxton from her attacker."

"You were the attacker, sir! I was only protecting myself!"

Brent sat forward. She saw the dark brilliance of his blue eyes drawing her toward him. He wanted to touch her, wanted to jerk out all those damned pins, and sift his fingers through her hair. "Were you really, Byrony? It is quite odd, you know." He continued after a moment, "I thought your name so very charming and unusual. Perhaps I even believed for a brief while that you, like your name, would be different from other women. Despite what I knew in my experience to be true. You look quite well surrounded by wealth, so much more sophisticated than the girl I saw in San Diego."

"Mr. Hammond, I cannot address your so-called experience. Whatever disappointments you have known have nothing whatsoever to do with me. Will you please just leave me alone?"

"I have been thinking of retaliation," he continued. "My fingers itch to bare your bottom and thrash you."

"Stop it. I won't listen to any more of this." She jumped to her feet, nearly upsetting the small table.

"Sit down, Mrs. Butler. Surely you don't wish to make a scene. I'm fairly certain that many of the passengers know your husband. What would he say, I wonder?"

There was truth in what he said. She eased back into her chair. He could do nothing to her here, nothing at all. She would simply endure until he tired of baiting her.

"That's better. Tell me, Byrony, does your husband please you in bed? Did it concern him that you came to him a soiled dove? Or did you deceive him and scream at the appropriate time? Perhaps a bit of fake blood?"

Her eyes widened. He wanted to shake her. Guilelessness, the mark of a good actress. Her eyes fell to her lap, and he saw a flush of anger, pain, he didn't know which, color her cheeks.

"Ah, I see your show of ignorance didn't last long."

No, she thought numbly, I know what you're talking about. My dear father told me the same thing. I have to get control of myself. He can't hurt me, not here. Not anywhere. Soon I'll be free of him. That brought an unaccountable pain, and she blinked.

"Mr. Hammond, who is the duchess? And what does she have to do with a house next to your saloon?"

He looked startled, then threw his head back and laughed deeply. "My dear, you have been listening when you shouldn't."

"I thought perhaps that she was your mistress."

He laughed all the harder. "No, she's not my mistress, she's my business partner. Her name is Maggie, and wonder of wonders, she is an honest woman. Diogenes would have been thrilled had he run across her. As for her house it is a brothel. The duchess is a madam, one of San Francisco's finest. Belle Cora and Ah Choy don't touch her in terms of the beauty and skill of her girls."

"A brothel," she repeated numbly.

"Yes, I'm sure you know what that is. A place where men pay to be pleasured. Her house of pleasure connects to my saloon. The two businesses, side by side, complement each other, as I'm sure you can imagine. A man wins, he wants to celebrate. A man loses, he wants to bury his sorrows, and what better place than in a woman's warm body?"

Byrony couldn't believe he was speaking of a brothel and what men did so matter-of-factly. She could think of nothing to put him in his place. He would only laugh if she told him the truth. She'd already told him the truth and he hadn't believed her. All her life, she'd been protected. It was her father had made her feel dirty.

"Perhaps," Brent continued in a lazy drawl when she continued silent, "you will want to visit Maggie. On the sly, of course. A woman who marries an older man for his money rarely stays content for long. A rich husband need only enjoy his purchase; he need have no qualms about not satisfying a lusty little wife. As I said last night, Mrs. Butler, when you tire of the charade, I might consider bedding you. Only, let me be the first. I don't want to be too far down the list of your lovers."

She'd tried not to listen to him, but couldn't help herself. She supposed dispassionately that most men were like him, like her father. Only Ira was different. She rose very slowly and smiled down at him. "Mr. Hammond, are you quite through, now?"

"No, I still have to bare your bottom."

"I believe you are through, sir. My husband is a very kind man, a gentleman. He is, as a matter of fact, the only kind man I've ever known. I told you once that there was no meanness in you. Obviously I was wrong, quite wrong. Good-bye, sir."

She turned on her heel, pausing abruptly when he said, "When is the child due?"

She slowly turned back to face him, her face drained of color. "What do you know of that?"

"I asked," he said, his voice as cold as a winter night. And the truth was on her face. "It seems that you and your sister-in-law are going to be staying for some months in Sacramento. Oh, don't worry, Mrs. Butler, I won't spread it about that the bedding preceded the marriage. But then, were it not for the child, there would have been no marriage, would there?"

She looked straight through him. "No," she said, "you are right about that."

He rose suddenly and towered over her. "So it is true. Damn you, I would have—" He broke off, stunned at the thought that would have so readily formed into words. *I would have married you.*

She saw the rage in his eyes. She didn't understand him or his rage. He had nothing but contempt for her, didn't he?

"I hope you won't lose your lovely figure," he said.

"I won't, Mr. Hammond. But why do you care?"

"I don't, damn you!"

It was he who strode off, quickly, angrily. She stared after him.

"I must go see to Irene," she said aloud. "Yes, I will go see Irene."

*   *   *

Byrony hated Sacramento. It was hot and damp even though it was spring. Ira's house was small, airless, but at least it was close to the river. And the river, thank God, wasn't off limits to her. She sat across from Ira and Irene in the square sitting room, listening to her husband speak.

"Don't forget, Byrony, that you mustn't mingle with the townfolk. I am acquainted with some of them, and it wouldn't do for them to see my wife obviously unpregnant when she is supposed to be."

Byrony shifted slightly in her chair as a trickle of sweat snaked its way between her breasts. She sighed. "All right, Ira."

"I realize this will be a difficult time for both of you, but I can think of no other alternative."

Byrony was tempted to ask him why they couldn't go to Nevada City, for example, where no one would know or care who they were. But she held her peace. She'd given her word and must keep it.

"I have paid your doctor, Irene, to keep his mouth closed. His name is Vincent Chambers. He's a good man, and he will shortly pay you a visit. I know you are a great reader, Byrony, and I'll provide you with as many books as I can find here. Now, if you ladies will excuse me, I must conduct some business before I return to San Francisco."

Byrony let Irene walk her brother to the front door. She knew he was worried about his sister, and since she had nothing really to say to him, it was better this way.

"I made some iced lemonade, Miz Butler. You're looking peaked."

"Thank you, Eileen." She took a deep swallow and leaned her head back against the chair cushion. Brent Hammond's face appeared instantly, as if she'd conjured him. He had about as good an opinion of her as did her father. Why did she care if he believed her a slut? She knew she'd let him believe her pregnant—the crowning blow—but she'd had no choice, after all. She couldn't betray Ira or Irene. She forced herself to rise and walk slowly to the window that looked onto the river. She tried to open it, but it wouldn't budge. She felt drained of energy, drained of hope, and leaned her forehead against the glass, closing her eyes.

Leave me alone, Brent Hammond, she said silently to the man in her mind. Just leave me alone. But part of her wondered what he was doing, wondered how long he would stay in Sacramento. Her hands fisted. Tears mixed with the sweat on her face, but she didn't notice.

SEVEN

Sacramento, 1853

"It's what everyone believes, isn't it, Ira?"

Ira looked at Byrony, knowing that she'd wanted to ask him this for quite a long time. She was quite bright, he'd realized, and wondered why she hadn't brought it out in the open before now. He said very gently, "Yes, Byrony, yes, that's what everyone thinks."

"I'm not surprised, not really. When we return to San Francisco, I with my child in tow, then it will be confirmed. Will anyone even speak to me?"

He truly regretted the isolation he'd enforced on Byrony and his sister. His weekly visit each month had offered some respite, but not much. "Byrony, you will, perhaps, not believe me, but the good people of San Francisco think more of us for removing obvious scandal from in front of their noses. When you return, you will be welcomed gladly, by everyone I know, even the greatest sticklers. It is easier for someone to accept a baby, magically produced before his or her eyes, than watching one grow more quickly than it should. Of course everyone believes we married because you were pregnant, but your absence somehow ennobles you."

"So, we're saving them from themselves," Byrony said.

"If you wish to put it that way, yes. I have been upstairs

to visit Irene, and she assures me that she is feeling fine save for a slight backache. Also, Dr. Chambers agrees that everything appears normal. Is this also your opinion?"

Byrony shrugged. How could Ira appear so cool-looking, his linen so crisp and fresh? She felt like one of Eileen's limp dusting cloths. Even in September, her shift was clinging damply to her back by ten o'clock in the morning.

"Forgive me, Ira," she said, giving him as much of a smile as she could. "Irene is fine. The heat is enervating and she suffers, but she says little. I swear I don't know how people can bear to live here! I can count on the fingers of my left hand how many days have been tolerable."

Ira looked thoughtful. He sipped at his hot tea, making Byrony wince. She'd drunk more iced lemonade and more water during the summer months in Sacramento than ever in her life. Boston in the summer had been hot, certainly, but Aunt Ida's house had been large and airy, and blessedly cool.

"Has Irene spoken to you about—about things?"

If only she had, Byrony thought, it would have served to pass the time more quickly. Irene was like a clam. She shook her head. "No. I do not feel it my place to pry, Ira. If she was ever bitter about that man or the baby, she hasn't let on to me. No, she seems really quite happy about it—content, I suppose you'd say."

"Good," he said, relief in his voice. "All of this has been so hard for her. I've been worried."

What about me? Byrony wanted to ask, but she didn't. She wanted to say that she now understood what it must be like to be jailed, but it wouldn't do.

"The baby is due in about two weeks," Byrony said.

"Yes, I shall return in time. It is important that I be here."

It was odd, Byrony thought, but she hadn't gotten close to Irene over the past months, and she'd tried. But Irene remained somehow aloof, and the baby was Irene's, not hers, and Irene didn't seem to want that to change. If she spoke with any animation at all, it was about the child. Byrony wondered yet again how Irene would act once the child was born. How could she even begin to treat the child as her own? It seemed impossible to her.

"I have a letter for you from your mother, Byrony," Ira said.

Byrony accepted the envelope from her husband. It had been opened, just as the two others had been. The first time, he'd said only, apology in his voice, "It's your father, Byrony. I'm afraid I do not trust him."

"Nor do I," she'd said, wondering what that had to do with anything, but he still opened the letters.

The letter contained little news, not a word, in fact, about her father. Her mother, of course, believed her to be living in San Francisco, happily, with her new husband. She finished the letter and folded it back into its envelope. She would answer it and give it to Ira to post from San Francisco. The deception would be maintained.

Suddenly she felt more lonely than she'd ever felt in her life. Empty. Tears sprang to her eyes and slowly trickled down her cheeks.

"Byrony."

She gulped and swiped her hand across her cheeks. "I'm sorry, Ira, truly I am. It's just that—" She broke off, uncertain of what words would spill out of her mouth.

He rose and crossed over to her. "Poor Byrony," he said, stroking her shoulders. "It's been very hard for you, hasn't it? I shall make it up to you, I promise." He sighed. "You are so very young. You need gaiety and parties."

"People," she said. "I need people." Suddenly she wanted desperately to ask him about Brent Hammond. She had to bite down on her tongue not to. Instead, she said, "Tell me what happened to Mr. and Mrs. Saxton."

He looked relieved, abundantly so. "It's odd, the entire

business. I heard rumors in the early summer that Mrs. Saxton was trailed by a bodyguard. Then there was a fire at one of Saxton's warehouses. They left San Francisco, so I was told, in midsummer and returned some three weeks ago. As far as I know, everything is fine between them. Whatever mystery there was, if there was one, has been cleared up."

She didn't really care, but pretended to listen.

They were both startled at the sound of a piercing scream from above.

"Oh, my God," Ira said, and dashed from the sitting room to the stairs.

She trailed after him. Eileen blocked her at the bedchamber door. "No, Miz Butler. I don't think you should come in. The baby wants to arrive a bit early. Mr. Butler is going soon to fetch the doctor."

"Take care of her, Eileen," Ira said. He looked at Byrony but didn't really see her. "I'll be back as soon as I can."

She stood for a moment in the narrow hallway. As a young girl, she wasn't allowed anywhere near a woman giving birth. She supposed men had made that rule, their belief being that if a woman witnessed the agony of birth, she wouldn't want to go through it herself. Then, she thought, what would happen to the human race?

Byrony sat downstairs, huddled in her favorite chair, a novel on her lap. She heard every scream. It was dreadful. She'd never thought about birthing a child, not really. It went on and on. Dr. Chambers, a small, balding man who appeared to regard his fellow humans as so many insects to be tolerated, remained upstairs. Ira periodically came down. He looked exhausted, and so worried that Byrony's heart went out to him.

"God, how much longer?" he asked, running his hands through his hair. He looked disheveled. She'd never before seen him only in trousers and shirt, his sleeves rolled up. His forearms were very white with light sprinkles of fair hair.

She didn't know what to say. He paced, his eyes going every few moments toward the ceiling. "The baby is a bit early, thank God. She didn't get too big. Why doesn't it come?" There was a piercing scream, and Ira went white. He moaned as if the pain were his, and rushed out of the room. Byrony heard his steps on the stairs.

Byrony's book fell unnoticed to the floor as she rose. She went slowly to the foot of the stairs. She heard two men's voices raised in argument. Then another agonizing cry.

An hour passed, then another. There were no more loud screams. Suddenly she heard a thin wailing sound. The baby. She ran up the stairs, but Eileen blocked her view of Irene at the door.

"No, Miz Butler," she said firmly. "Not yet. The baby's here, a little girl, and the mistress will be fine, I promise you."

It was well past midnight. Byrony, attired in her night-gown and robe, was sitting downstairs, waiting. She looked up to see Ira, his face utterly transformed.

"It's over," he said, rubbing his hands together. "Irene is sleeping now. The child is small but Dr. Chambers believes she will be fine."

"Does the child look like Irene?" She cursed herself the moment the question slipped out.

"It's hard to tell," he said, appearing not to notice. "Actually, she has a lot of almost white hair. Her eyes are blue, but Eileen says that all babies start that way. Jesus, I never want to go through that again."

Irene probably doesn't either, she thought. Byrony had feared that the child would look like Irene's lover, though she hadn't the foggiest notion of what that man looked like. Irene had ignored her one tentative question about him. She saw Ira sag with fatigue into a chair. He was asleep in a moment. It was odd, she thought, watching him. He was her husband, yet she'd never seen him dressed as he was now, never seen him asleep. She didn't know him. A stab of elation went through her. It was over. Soon their exile would end.

Brent looked up from the papers he was reading, and smiled. "Well, Maggie, how was business last night?"

"Much the same. My girls are all exhausted. Lordy, so many horny men." She paused a moment, sighing. "Felice miscarried. Saint tells me she'll be just fine. The little idiot must not have been careful. I will box her ears when she recovers."

Brent knew she was worried, even though she spoke in the most clipped of tones. Oddly enough, this madam cared about her girls, as if, almost, they were her children, which was silly, of course, since several were older than Maggie.

"As for you, Brent, I wish you hadn't removed Celeste."

"I don't like to share my women, Maggie, you know that. Come on, duchess, sit down and relax for a while."

Maggie sighed, and eased onto the plush leather sofa in Brent's office. "Bloody hell, I'm so tired."

"Tired of what? Counting all your money?"

She cocked open an eye at him, until she saw the wicked grin on his face. "You're a bastard, Brent. Talk about counting money. Ah, business is good. We're both lucky as hell."

"That we are. Would you like a drink, Maggie?"

"I suppose a shot of good whiskey wouldn't be amiss," she said. She watched him cross to the small bar behind his mahogany desk. Behind the office were a small sitting room and a large bedroom. "Everything is so homey here. You've done well with the furnishings, Brent."

"Thank you," he said, handing her the whiskey.

"Here's to everything we want," Maggie said by way of a toast. She didn't notice the strange, almost blank look that darkened his eyes. The liquid burned down to her stomach, and she brightened almost immediately.

"Why didn't you want to live with Celeste? Lord knows you've set her up like a queen."

Brent shrugged. "I like having my office and my rooms above the saloon. There's also the possibility," he added, "that one of the girls might lose her way and walk into my bedroom one dark night."

"If that ever happens, you can count on me sending you a hefty bill." She thrust her empty glass toward him. "Give me another, Brent, it makes me expansive."

"Save me from expansive women," he said.

She eyed him thoughtfully for a moment. "What you mean to say is save you from all the women who chase you. You know, Brent, most men would trade about anything to have your luck with women. Have you always had to beat them off with a stick?"

"You exaggerate, Maggie," he said mildly, flinging himself down in his favorite chair, a huge overstuffed affair. "A bit."

"Ha. You haven't had the nauseating pleasure of hearing Celeste go on to the girls about your magnificent self and your prowess as a lover."

"How very boring for you, duchess. Obviously you don't believe her. After all, I haven't ever observed you chasing me. Why, I even forget I own a stick when you come."

There was color in her cheeks, and for a moment she didn't meet his eyes.

He cocked a brow at her. "You're being ridiculous, you know that?"

"Yes," she sighed, "I guess I am. You know something, Brent, you and I are two very aloof people. Loners, I suppose you'd call us. At least that's true of you. You don't need anyone, do you?"

Brent carefully stretched his long legs in front of him and crossed them at his ankles. "I need people," he said.

"But you always keep that distance, as if you consciously

refuse to let anyone close. If there's one thing I do know, Brent," she continued when he remained silent, "it's men."

"Come, Maggie, what's there to know? We're all simple creatures."

"Sex, food, and money."

"In that order? Don't be so shortsighted, my dear. You are forgetting good whiskey and a comfortable bed."

"Oh, Brent, are you never serious? Are you afraid that I'll get closer than you want, so you make silly jests and bait me?"

"Maggie," he said in a very quiet voice, "let it be, all right? What you are, what I am, is no one's business. I know for a fact that you sleep alone. Does that give me the right to demand the reasons from you? I really don't see it as comforting for two people to weep and wail to each other about a past that can't be changed."

"You didn't grow up poor, Brent, so your past couldn't have been so bad. You did tell me a bit about Wakehurst, you know. I suppose I should be ecstatic that you trust me, a woman. Now you've got fire in your eyes. I knew it was a woman who turned you into a loner."

She sounded so pleased with her deduction that Brent curbed his anger. "Aren't women the root of all men's problems?" he asked, drawling his words.

"Well, in my case it was a man—my father, to be exact," she said. "Horny, righteous prig. God, I hated him." She drew herself up, paled a bit at her outburst, and said, "You are a cool one, aren't you, Brent Hammond? Forgive me. Since the last thing you want is for me to weep on your shoulder, I'll stop."

"Don't be an ass, Maggie." He rose and stretched, walking to the window. He said over his shoulder, his voice very cool and calm, "If you wish, I'll beat the shit out of him. Would you like that?"

She laughed. "Oh no— Lord only knows how many

mouths to feed he has now. I wouldn't want the little mites to be orphans." She paused a moment, studying his back. "Have you ever wanted a wife and family, Brent?"

He went rigid, but when he finally answered her, his voice was calm, even humorous. "Can you see me dandling little ones on my knee?" He turned to face her, raising his hand. "No, duchess, don't answer that. If you would know the truth, there was a girl once. Soft, beautiful, sweet. But, of course, it was all a facade, an act. Now, are you quite satisfied?"

"Once, Brent? You mean years ago, or recently?"

"Recently," he said curtly, then shrugged, not fooling her for a minute. "She is what she is, and briefly I was fool enough to think that— Well, enough. We all learn, don't we, Maggie? Incidentally, you're not having any trouble with James Cora, are you?"

Maggie kept her expression impassive. She knew the brief show of bitterness was but the tip of the iceberg. He'd have to be drunker than hell to tell her more. She accepted his change of topic, even as she searched her mind for a likely female candidate. "He's a handsome devil," she said mildly, "I'll grant you that, but I don't want him. A faithless bounder, and Belle knows it. Not that she's a saint herself, of course."

Brent studied his business partner silently for a moment. He admired her, he liked her even when she was being pushy. She was pretty, in an understated sort of way. She did not dress garishly. No one would take her for a whore or a madam. She looked quite prim, actually, with her black hair tucked neatly into a chignon. He wondered idly what her hair would look like out of the severe style. Her high-necked gown was dove gray, so modest in fact that it looked more suited to a schoolmarm.

"Stop staring at me like that, Brent," Maggie said, frowning at him. "I know you don't like what you see, but I don't care."

"Don't be a fool, Maggie. You're a very pretty woman, and that's what I was thinking."

"Well, that's kind of you." She rose to her feet and shook out her skirts. "Next thing I know, you'll be wondering why I don't want a parcel of brats on my knee." She gave a parting shot. "Now, who could this infamous girl be, I wonder?"

"Maggie."

"I'll want a game of high-stakes poker with you tonight, Brent. Don't lose all your money until I've had a chance at you."

Why, he wondered, thrusting his fingers through his hair, had he been such a fool as to mention Byrony? Why the hell hadn't he forgotten her? By now she'd given birth to her child. He felt something stir inside him, and despised himself. He'd made it a point to discover that Ira Butler dutifully traveled nearly every week to Sacramento. And gossip among the upper crust of San Francisco society was, quite honestly, that his bride was pregnant before the ring was on her finger. But she'd left town so as not to embarrass anyone. It was a smart move, and probably Ira's idea, damn the man. He heard some shouting in the street and walked to the window that overlooked Montgomery. Below were two drunken men, miners from the look of them, fighting with great gusto. He grinned. He'd like to join them.

When would she return to San Francisco?

EIGHT

San Francisco, 1853

"Don't touch her."

Byrony straightened like a shot over Michelle's crib at the sound of Irene's furious voice behind her. The baby, who until this point had been looking blurrily up at her, began to cry.

"Now look what you've done. Ah, my poor little sweetheart. Come to Mama, love."

Byrony watched in surprise as Irene leaned over the child and gently lifted her to her shoulder.

"I didn't do anything," Byrony said after the baby quieted. "Indeed, Irene, it was your voice that upset her."

For an instant Byrony froze at the fury she saw in Irene's dark eyes; then it was gone, and she wondered if she'd imagined it. But she hadn't imagined Irene's anger at her attention to the baby.

"Forgive me, Byrony," Irene said, even as she clutched Michelle more closely to her breast. "I was upset about something, and took it out on you. So silly of me, really. Hush, my angel."

"Of course," Byrony said, and left the nursery. She walked to her bedroom and gently closed the door. She looked toward the locked door that adjoined her room to Ira's. My husband, she thought, and laughed, a bitter sound.

They'd been in San Francisco for over two weeks now. Blessed cool weather was Byrony's first thought. She loved the fog, the way it billowed like a fluffy cloud over the bay. Occasionally it blanketed the city, even coming over Rincon Hill. She shook away her thoughts. The weather was stark, cool and clear today, as stark as Irene's vicious words. I've got to speak to Ira. He's got to do something about Irene. And, God, I can no longer remain locked away.

Byrony waited patiently until she heard Ira moving about in his room. Patience. That was something she'd surely learned in the past months. Patience unto boredom. For the first time, she raised her hand to knock on the adjoining door, then lowered it. She'd never been invited into his room, just seen it briefly when he had shown her over his house. A stark, masculine room. She continued to wait until she heard him leave and walk downstairs. She straightened her hair, shook out her skirts, and made her way to his study. Firmly she tapped on the closed door.

"Byrony, my dear, come in." Ira rose to greet her. "How was your day?" She felt his eyes searching her face. What was he thinking, she wondered, when he looked at her?

"I must speak with you, Ira," she said.

"Certainly. Come and sit down."

She did as she was bid, folding her hands in her lap.

"Now, what is the matter, my dear?"

How to begin? How to explain the problem? "Ira," she said, "Irene doesn't want me near the baby."

He withdrew; she sensed it, even though he said kindly, "Surely you are exaggerating, my dear. I agree that Irene is a bit protective of the child, but that is understandable, is it not?"

"Ira," she continued, forcing her voice to remain calm, "Michelle is supposed to be my child. If anyone sees Irene with the baby, with me trailing along like a half-wit nanny, they'll guess that something is very wrong."

He sighed, rubbing his thumb along his jaw in a wide circular motion. She recognized it as a habit he engaged in whenever he was deep in thought. "People aren't stupid," he said finally. "You are, of course, quite right."

"I must at least know the child well enough so she won't start crying when I pick her up. Irene must understand that—"

"Irene must understand what?"

Ira whirled about as if he'd been shot. "Irene. Come in."

"I'm already in," Irene said coldly. "What I would like to know is, what kind of tales is Byrony carrying to you behind my back?"

Byrony gasped. "I'm not carrying tales. For God's sake, Irene, we must work something out."

"Everything would be just fine if you wouldn't meddle."

"That's enough," Ira said. Byrony watched him take his sister in his arms. She knew he was talking to Irene but couldn't make out his words. If only he'll make her see what an idiot she's being. No, not an idiot; a poor woman who's suffered and who must have the child to make her complete again.

Irene's breath caught, and she began to sob.

Oh, damn. Surely Ira didn't have to be so unkind as to make her cry.

Irene seemed to get a hold on herself. Ira patted her back and led her to a chair. "Now," he said, looking away from Irene to Byrony, "we must consider this situation rationally. After all, we want what is best for Michelle. Irene, my dear, you must realize that Byrony is right. You must allow her to become close to the child, else people will wonder. You mustn't appear so possessive. Do you agree?"

Irene hesitated for but a brief moment. "Yes, Ira," she said dully.

And that was that, Byrony thought.

"Good. Now, I've a surprise for both of you. We are going to have a dinner party next Friday night. It's time that Byrony was introduced properly to our friends."

Byrony felt a rush of excitement. "That's wonderful, Ira. Have you made out the guest list yet? Oh dear, we will need additional help. But I'm a good cook and I can assist Eileen—"

"Slow down," Ira laughed, holding up his hands. "One thing at a time. First of all, I have made up the guest list and will go over it with you, Byrony. I've seen to additional servants, and in fact, I've hired a cook. Her name is Naomi; she's a Negro from Alabama. Irene, I want you to be well rested by Friday. Remember it is Byrony, not you, who gave birth. You must get the bloom back in your cheeks."

And that was that, Byrony thought again. The master had spoken. Byrony guessed that Irene was not pleased with her, but what could she do?

Byrony didn't eat much that evening, cutting the chicken breast into neat small pieces, listening with half her attention to Ira's efforts at light conversation. He was a kind man, she thought, looking at him. He tried so hard to keep both the women in his house happy. *His* house. Odd, but she didn't feel a part of this family. She wondered if she ever would.

The next morning, Ira knocked on her door early. Byrony was already up and dressed, and pacing. "Ira," she said in surprise, for she'd expected Eileen.

"Come, my dear, I have a surprise for you."

"What? Another one? I thought you'd already left for your office."

"My business affairs won't float away in the bay," he said, offering her his arm. "Come now, and no, I'm not saying anything more."

Byrony followed her husband outside. "I don't under-stand—" she began, only to blink rapidly in rapturous sur-prise. "Thorny, my mare— Oh, Ira." She hugged him tightly. She whirled away from him in but a moment, and began stroking Thorny's nose. "However did you get Father to part with her?"

"It wasn't difficult," Ira said. "He'd already sold her. I bought her from a man named Joaquín de Neve."

"Gabriel's father. How kind of him. I suppose he felt sorry for me after what— Well, that's long past. Thank you so much. This is the most wonderful surprise I've ever had."

He smiled, thinking it was probably true. Perhaps now there would be peace. Irene didn't like to ride, so the two women would now be separated at least part of the day. He studied her thoughtfully as she continued to talk to the mare. She was thin and far too pale. Hopefully riding would gain her some color, and some weight. He wanted no one at the dinner party to suspect that she wasn't Michelle's mother. He privately thought she'd lost some of her looks after the months in Sacramento. Her lovely hair had lost its sheen and her green eyes their luster. When she turned suddenly to face him, he realized he'd been wrong about her eyes. At least now they were sparkling, full of life.

"I think we should visit Monsieur David again," he said. "You will need some riding habits."

"Oh no. I have my breeches—"

"God forbid," Ira interrupted her, laughing. "We've al-ready scandalized the matrons of society far too much as it is. The sight of you on horseback in pants would boil the pot over."

"You're right, of course," Byrony said on a sigh, "I've never before owned a riding habit."

He felt a stirring of anger at Madison DeWitt, but said

only, "Now you'll have at least three. One must be royal blue."

It was Eileen who accompanied her to Monsieur David's fancy shop on Kearny Street.

"Mr. Butler insists that one riding habit be royal blue," Byrony said, nearly skipping in her pleasure to be out, alone, and free. She'd at first felt a bit odd about Eileen, having lived all her growing-up years in Boston where the few Negroes lived in isolated squalor. But Eileen wasn't a slave anymore. California was a free state. Aunt Ida had hated slavery, and spoken volumes about the subject to whom ever would listen. Byrony had the sneaking idea that it was really the wealthy landowners in the South her aunt hated.

"You will look dandy in royal blue, Miz Butler," Eileen said.

Byrony said, "What a lovely day it is. It's so good to be among people again."

"Lucky for us," Eileen said. "Just you wait until the rains start. I heard tell last year that a mule sank in the mud on Montgomery Street and drowned."

Byrony had insisted they walk to the downtown. It wasn't far and she was bursting with energy. She saw now that Eileen, at least fifty pounds overweight, was wheezing a bit, and slowed her step, feeling guilty. "Oh, look, a saloon!"

"There are more of those places than a body can count," Eileen said, keeping her eyes on the ground ahead of her.

Brent Hammond owned a saloon. Was the Miner's Dream his? No. She shook her head. No, it wasn't fine enough. Only the best for him. She felt Eileen move closer to her, and realized that men were beginning to stop to stare at her.

She wanted to smile at them. She wanted to smile at everybody.

Monsieur David, a dapper little man with snapping black eyes, greeted her personally in his opulent shop. There were other ladies in the outer room, and Byrony recognized one of them. It was Mrs. Saxton.

After she'd picked out the materials she wanted, she walked shyly to the woman. "Ma'am? I don't suppose you remember me. I was aboard the *Scarlet Queen* last spring when there was that—trouble. I'm so glad you're fine now. My name is Byrony. Byrony Butler."

Chauncey Saxton knew all about Mrs. Butler. She hadn't really noticed her at all that long-ago night aboard the *Scarlet Queen*. But she'd had her ears filled the past months. This glowing, diffident girl didn't at all look like a trollop adventuress. But of course, it was only that prig Penelope Stevenson who had said that.

"Yes, now everything is very fine," Chauncey said with a smile. Seeing the curiosity in the young woman's eyes, she added the few words of explanation she and Del had offered everyone else: "The man who tried to do away with me aboard the *Scarlet Queen* is long gone, thank God, as well as the villain who had hired him. It was all a ghastly experience, but my husband and I have survived it. Well, enough of that," she said, patting Byrony's hand. "It's good to see you again. Do call me Chauncey."

"What a lovely name," Byrony said. "So unusual, but perhaps not in England," she added.

"No, it's unusual everywhere," Chauncey said. "As for your name, I fancy your mother was enraptured of Lord Byron?"

"Yes. I've always counted myself lucky, for she could have named me George, after the king."

The two women laughed.

"Madame," Monsieur David said to Byrony. "Excuse me

a moment. I have your measurements, but I think perhaps you are a bit thinner than you were last spring."

"Make them up the same size, monsieur," Byrony said. "I fancy I'll be back to my same figure in no time at all."

She didn't look like she'd had a baby, Chauncey thought, but then again, what did she know about children? "I'm trying, sweetheart, I'm trying." She nearly laughed aloud as she thought of her husband's nightly words.

"Miz Butler, we should be getting home," Eileen said.

The smile left Byrony's face, but just for a moment. "Mrs. Saxton, I mean, Chauncey, we're giving a dinner party next Friday evening. Do you think you and your husband could come?"

How could anyone turn down that sweet request? "We would be delighted, Byrony. My husband is acquainted with your husband, of course, but I know him only as a gentleman who always tips his hat to me."

"Oh, thank you. My husband hasn't gone over the guest list with me yet, but you and your husband must be on it."

This naive bit of information made Chauncey pat Byrony's hand. "If we're not, please write us in."

Chauncey Saxton stood quietly in the middle of Monsieur David's salon, watching the black woman guide Byrony Butler out the door. She was a very sweet girl. She should speak to Agatha about her. And she was close to Chauncey's age. There were so few young ladies in San Francisco, and Chauncey felt a rush of optimism. Anyone would be more pleasant than that snit Penelope Stevenson. Why didn't she marry someone and move somewhere, hopefully out of San Francisco.

"Eileen," Byrony was saying outside the shop, "let's walk around a bit. I've seen so little of the city, and it's such a fine day."

"Very well, Miz Butler," she said, "but not too long."

Byrony watched two Chinese carrying impossibly heavy

loads of lumber on their narrow shoulders across the street. Pigtails, she thought; how very odd. There were so many men, some dressed in the height of fashion and others looking as if they hadn't changed their clothes in months. She drew a deep breath of sheer pleasure. So many different smells, so many different kinds of people.

"Miz Butler," Eileen suddenly hissed in her ear, "keep your eyes down."

Byrony blinked, but before she obeyed, she saw two very beautiful women walking toward them. There were loud compliments from passing men, and whistles, and the women giggled and preened.

She wanted to stare, but she felt Eileen's disapproval. Suddenly she was looking straight at a man's throat; then she bumped into him.

"Pardon me, ma'am. I fear I wasn't watching my progress."

She stiffened as straight as Eileen. His hand dropped from her arm as if he'd been burned. Slowly she raised her head and stared into Brent Hammond's dark blue eyes.

"You?"

"What, no flour today? No, I suppose not. You're far beyond your flour days, aren't you?"

Dear God, he looked so—beautiful. She swallowed, trying to build up the anger he'd made her feel so many months before. But she couldn't. "Hello, Mr. Hammond," she said. It was too soon. She hadn't had the chance to put him into proper perspective.

She's staring at me like a lost lamb, Brent thought. Damn, he'd hoped he wouldn't see her, at least until—

"Miz Butler," Eileen said. "We really must be on our way."

Byrony looked at her with vague eyes. "In just a moment, Eileen. Mr. Hammond is a friend of Mr. Butler's. I haven't seen him since our return. Please, why don't you step into that shop and see if they've any riding hats."

Eileen shot her a puzzled look. "Very well, Miz Butler. Just a few minutes, mind."

"What is she, your keeper?"

"She has been with Ira and Irene for a number of years. She is protective, I suppose."

"You need protection, believe me. If I weren't with you, you'd be besieged by any number of hopeful men."

"I love San Francisco," she said. "All the noise and the activity. I know that I'm truly alive here. And all the men are very nice. They're not forward, not really, just lonely, I think."

"You're looking remarkably fit," Brent said, interrupting her.

"Why ever shouldn't I?"

"Cut line, lady. For a woman who's given birth, quite recently, I expect, you look very fine indeed."

"Oh."

"Although you are a bit skinny, I'd say." She felt his eyes roving over her. "I would have thought that those lovely breasts of yours would be a bit fuller."

"Please, Mr. Hammond, don't—"

"You're right, of course, Mrs. Butler. It's no concern of mine, is it?" Damn her. He'd hoped when he saw her again that he would be able to look through her, with no stirring in his guts. "How long have you been back, ma'am?"

"Two weeks. This is the first time I've been downtown. That odd-looking man over there, who is he?"

Brent turned and smiled at Jeremy Glossop, a newcomer to San Francisco who fancied himself the epitome of a civilized gentleman. "He's from England and a terrible gambler."

"How is your saloon, sir? Where is it?"

"Near Portsmouth Square. The Wild Star."

The sound of his voice made her feel incredibly warm. She didn't want to leave him, not just yet, particularly when he was not insulting her.

"Is business good?"

"Quite. In a town like San Francisco, men have little else to do save gamble, drink, and whore. Of course, we are gaining culture by the day. By January, I hear we'll even have some gaslights installed, to discourage thieves, of course. And realize, please, ma'am, that we have theater groups coming from all over the world to our fair city. Unfortunately, you missed Lola Montez. She's living in the gold country now, I believe, in Grass Valley." Why was he carrying on like this? Because you don't want her to leave, you fool. She was staring up at him with such intensity that he wanted to rip her clothes off on the spot and ravish her. He laughed at himself. A woman who'd given birth as recently as she had couldn't indulge in sex for a while yet.

"How is your child, Miz Butler?" He saw hurt in her eyes, and it angered him.

"Her name is Michelle," Byrony said calmly. "She is quite well, thank you."

"Does she look like you or your husband?"

"She has the look of the Butlers, I understand. Very fair with blue eyes."

The look of the Butlers? Hell, *she* was fair; only her eyes were that soft green color, deep and mysterious. He wanted to ask her if her husband was good to her. Stupid thought. Her gown was expensive. Her doting husband probably gave her everything she asked for. And her husband probably understood well her promiscuous tendencies, else why would he have that huge Negro woman with her? To protect her or to keep her from making assignations with other men?

"Ah," he said, "your protector."

Byrony would very much have liked to dismiss Eileen with a magic wave of her hand. But she couldn't.

She was gazing up at him with that lost, helpless look of hers, and he forced himself to shrug and say, "A pleasure to see you, ma'am. Do give my best to your husband."

"Yes," Byrony said, "I will."

She listened to Eileen describe a bonnet she'd found, but her eyes remained on his tall figure until he was lost from her view.

NINE

Chauncey Saxton looked about the large dining table at all the other guests. Ira Butler had chosen well, she thought. The thirteen guests, for the most part, were kind people and were treating the new Mrs. Butler very well. Byrony looked lovely, gowned in yellow silk, a rich yellow that made her hair look like smooth honey and her eyes a vivid, sparkling green. A very nice girl, Chauncey thought, and understandably nervous. Her gaze turned to Irene Butler, seated now at her brother's right. The little scene they'd been treated to upon entering the dining room still seemed to bother her. She was very quiet, speaking only rarely to anyone except her brother.

A ridiculous mixup, Chauncey thought, feeling compassion for Byrony, who'd tried to smooth it over. How could Irene have so improperly had herself seated at the foot of the table? Surely she was used to her brother's wife by now. It was obvious that Irene hadn't relinquished the mistress's position to her sister-in-law, indeed, had taken for granted that it was her honored place. Poor Ira. It had been he who spoke quietly to his sister and removed her to his end of the table, leaving Byrony pale and smiling nervously.

Chauncey suddenly met the eyes of her nemesis, Penelope Stevenson, across the table, and gave her a sugary

96

smile. A pity that the bouquet of flowers wasn't just a foot to the left; then she wouldn't have to manufacture that false smile. Bunker Stevenson, her wealthy father, was carrying on with a tale of his adventures in Panama. Chauncey's eyes met Agatha Newton's, seated on Byrony's right, and Agatha winked. Bless Agatha. Chauncey had told her about Byrony, and that good woman was regaling her with her own special brand of charm.

"Do try the pork, love, I promise it won't attack you."

"I have and it didn't," she said to her husband.

"You look preoccupied, Chauncey. Is there some man I should begin to worry about?"

"Oh drat, I'd hoped you wouldn't notice. But Bunker is so very—well, how can I put it?"

"Boring? Fatuous?"

"One of these days, Del Saxton, I am going to have the last word."

She kicked him under the table.

"You've made no changes as yet I see, my dear," Agatha Newton was saying to Byrony. "I've always thought that this room and the drawing room needed more of a woman's touch. Of course, Irene doesn't say boo without her brother's approval."

"Yes, that's true," Byrony said, her attention on Brent Hammond, who was flirting outrageously with a very lovely girl whose name Byrony wouldn't soon forget. Penelope the Snob, Byrony had christened her, after the young lady had acknowledged meeting her with only the slightest nod of her head.

Agatha Newton, broad in the beam with a lovely, motherly smile, wished she could reassure the new Mrs. Butler. The girl was naturally nervous. After all, this was her first introduction to the people who counted in San Francisco. Pity that all of them counted, but what could one do? She followed Byrony's gaze to the utterly delicious man next to

Penelope Stevenson. She'd not met him before this evening, but had heard Horace speak of him. "Damned smart young man," her enthusiastic husband had said on more than one occasion. "Old James Cora isn't too pleased with the quick success he'd had with the Wild Star."

What a handsome devil he was, Agatha thought, gently sipping at the very fine French wine from Ira's cellar. She'd stare at him too if she were twenty years younger.

The tender pork tasted like year-old bread to Byrony. She hadn't looked at the guest list, so it was her own fault that she'd suddenly lost her voice when Brent Hammond strolled into the drawing room. I must act natural, she'd told herself over and over. He means nothing to me, nothing. I can't act like a silly twit, mooning over a man who despises me. I am a married lady, and that's the end to it.

Dumb words that meant nothing. Thank God that very nice Tony Dawson was paying a lot of attention to Mrs. Newton. She was a very nice lady, but Byrony couldn't think of anything to say. She heard the kind voice of Saint Morris, San Francisco's finest doctor, according to Ira. She forced herself to turn to him. Like most of the gentlemen, he was young, not even thirty. He didn't look like any doctor she'd ever seen in Boston, pampered and soft-handed. More like a lumberjack.

"I'd like to lay eyes on that baby of yours, Mrs. Butler," Saint Morris said. "Ira hasn't stopped raving about her. Calls her his little angel and all that nonsense new fathers say."

"I take it you're not a father, Dr. Morris."

His dark brown eyes twinkled. "Been too busy, ma'am, to tell you the truth. At least that's what I always tell myself. I meet a nice lady now and again, but I can't seem to bring myself up to scratch. Call me Saint."

"Only if you will call me Byrony. Were you truly christened Saint?"

"That's a long story, Byrony. A long story indeed." He

gave her a big grin, revealing beautiful white teeth. "If I told you my real name, I expect you'd howl with laughter and call me a missionary."

Byrony leaned toward him, enjoying herself. "Is it Horatio?" she whispered. "Or perhaps Milton or Percival?"

One of his big hands covered hers briefly, and he shook his head. "Ah, you should have known my dear mother. What a wit that woman had."

"I see I'm getting nothing out of you, Saint."

"Nope, not a thing. Delicious meal, but you're not eating much, Byrony. If I believed in the efficacy of tonics, I'd prescribe one for you."

"Ah," she said, "so you didn't come West in one of those covered wagons as a medicine man?"

"Not at all, more's the pity. It would have been more pleasant if I had."

"I suppose that's another long, very interesting story you're not about to tell me."

"Delicious wine," he said, giving her a lazy smile.

"Ira tells me you're the best doctor in San Francisco."

"True enough, I expect, but then again, there isn't much competition. At least I do my best not to kill folk if I don't know how to cure them."

Saint watched her look from him to Brent Hammond. Brent was laughing at something Penelope was saying—polite man. Damnation, he thought, so the wind sits in that quarter, does it? Mind your own business, Saint. This Byrony's a good girl and is simply enjoying looking at a handsome man. Look at Agatha staring at him. He'd just about dismissed it from his mind when he saw Brent's eyes meet Byrony's. Saint quickly gave his full attention to his dinner plate. He chewed thoughtfully on the pork, wondering about Brent Hammond. He knew her, it was in his eyes, and he was furious. Saint's mother, bless her soul, had always accused him as a boy of being too fanciful. She was doubtless right. He was always seeing dragons when it was just fluffy clouds. Brent wasn't about to poach on another man's preserves, particularly if those preserves were another man's wife. Still, he thought, life tended to be so bloody complicated. He felt an odd sort of protectiveness toward this young girl. He really couldn't imagine her taking Ira as a lover, but then again, he couldn't really imagine Ira being so foolish as to seduce a young lady. He said, to regain her attention, "Tell me, Byrony, who does the baby take after?"

She looked at him blankly, then seemed to draw herself together. "Michelle has the look of the Butlers, so Ira tells me, so I suppose, sir, that an angel is close enough to the truth. When I first met Ira, that was my thought about him. The angel Gabriel, to be exact."

"Ah, but your particular angel is quite a businessman. If anyone could buy up stock in heaven, it's your husband."

"He is very competent, I understand," Byrony said somewhat diffidently. She had little idea what Ira did. It was simply never discussed.

"Yes, indeed. You need to talk to Del Saxton or Sam Brannan if you want to know the scope of his abilities."

"Sam Brannan frightens the dickens out of me. He's so vocal."

"That he is. He and Ira make a good team. Ira never raises his voice, and Sam rants and raves."

"Ira is a very kind man," Byrony said.

Why? Saint wanted to ask bluntly. Because he married you after he made you pregnant?

She added, "Doesn't Ira bank with Delaney Saxton?"

"That's right. Now, if you want your funny bone to collapse, it's Del you want to talk to. I never can get in the last word with that man. Drives Chauncey crazy, but she gives him a good run for his money. You should hear them—Del with his lazy drawl and Chauncey with her starchy English accent."

There was a brief lull in the conversation and Ira's attention was caught by a sweet rippling laugh from his wife. He turned from Irene and looked down the table. Ah, Saint was amusing her, he thought, grateful. He'd sat Saint next to her on purpose. He knew Saint could get anybody to feel good. All in all, he thought, the dinner was going well. The food Naomi had prepared was delicious, the wine exceptional, most of the guests in good spirits. All except Irene. It simply hadn't occurred to him that Byrony had never taken her rightful place at the table, not until this evening. He wouldn't have noticed this evening had not Agatha Newton blinked in surprise at the seating. Damnation. Irene was hurt. The entire situation was so difficult for her, and he felt helpless much of the time, faced with two vastly different women who both placed demands on him. Having one of his minions go to San Diego to buy Byrony's mare had been an inspiration of which he was justly proud. He knew she was riding all over San Francisco, many times alone, but he had no intention of stopping her. He had given her a small derringer and shown her how to fire it. She hadn't blinked. He doubted she had any concept of what a bullet could do to a body. He winced slightly at loud laughter. Bunker Stevenson was off again.

Brent had determined before coming to the Butlers' house for dinner that he would ignore Byrony. Above looking at her that one long moment, he'd succeeded, giving all his attention to Penelope Stevenson. He was amused by the girl's antics, wondering what Maggie would think of the pretentious but quite lovely little twit. Ah, duchess, what irony there is in polite society. Here he was a gambler who kept a mistress, and was business partners and quite good friends with a madam. He was acceptable, but any *lady* would turn pale and faint were Maggie to be seated at her table, and all these so-called gentlemen would leer and make lewd jokes. He wondered what Byrony would think of Maggie, and nearly dropped his fork. Damn her anyway. And that ridiculous situation with the seating arrangements. She'd looked so helpless.

He wanted to hate Ira Butler.

He realized he'd been silent too long, but could come up with no more nonsense for Penelope's pretty ears. He turned his attention to Chauncey Saxton. "May I say, ma'am, that you've taught your benighted husband quite a bit. I hear that he's making better and bigger business deals every day."

Chauncey laughed, sending her husband a wicked look. "It's all too true, Mr. Hammond. He comes home looking as if he's lost everything, I tell him that he indeed will, then inform him how to proceed so that he won't lose his shirt."

"Aha," Delaney Saxton said. "What tall tale is she telling you now, Brent?"

"We were just speaking about shirts," Brent said, grinning, "and how you're keeping yours intact." He added, "That is an English shirt he's wearing tonight, isn't it, ma'am?"

"Yes, Mr. Hammond, it is indeed. All things English last forever, I tell him."

"Something the English and gamblers have in common, perhaps. We're always around to take care of other people's messes, and we never brag about it."

Chauncey laughed. "And we only fade away in the end, sir?"

"Brent, ma'am. With the look your husband is giving me, I feel as though I'm fading quickly, very quickly, right now."

"Ignore him, Chauncey," her husband told her.

"Why?" she asked, giving him a droll look. "Is he outdoing you as I always am?"

"Women," Delaney said, sitting back in his chair. "I swear that God sent all of you here to earth after he'd already tried famine and pestilence."

"There were also the locusts, don't forget, Del," Brent said.

Byrony had been listening to them, unable to help herself. Why, she wondered, couldn't he act like that with her? Funny and humorous and charming. She chewed slowly on a bite of pork.

"Your attention, everyone," Delaney Saxton called out. "Come on, Tony, get your face out of your plate. A toast: to Byrony Butler, a charming addition to San Francisco."

There was good-natured joking and laughter and everyone dutifully drank to Delaney Saxton's toast. Byrony flushed and murmured thank-yous to everyone within hearing.

Naomi and Eileen served coffee and brandy in the drawing room. Brent Hammond was the first of the guests to take his leave. He lightly touched Byrony's hand and murmured inanities. It was odd, Byrony realized after he'd left, but she felt she was at last breathing normally. She hadn't realized what a strain his presence had been. She turned a bright smile to Penelope Stevenson.

"I don't know why he had to leave so quickly," Penelope said.

"Who?"

"Mr. Hammond. At least he's taking me riding tomorrow."

Byrony felt a dagger of jealousy tear through her. "How very nice," she said.

"Father approves of him, so perhaps I'll marry him."

Just like that? Byrony wanted to box her shapely ears, but instead she smiled. Agatha had mentioned to her that Penelope had also determined to marry Del Saxton before Chauncey had arrived in San Francisco.

Penelope said, "He'll have to give up his mistress and his gambling and all that. Do you know that he is partners with a whore?"

"Not a whore, Miss Stevenson, a madam," Byrony said.

Penelope shrugged an elegant shoulder. "I've seen her. She's old, you know, close to thirty, so you're probably right. No man would want her."

"Ah, my dear, I must interrupt you for a moment." Ira smiled down in understanding at his wife. "Excuse me, Miss Penelope, but Saint wants to see Michelle. Would you like to take him to the nursery, Byrony? No sense in waking the child."

"Did you appreciate my timing, Byrony?" Saint asked her with a smile in his brown eyes.

"You, sir, are the angel," she said. Michelle was deeply asleep, her chubby legs drawn up, her tiny fist in her mouth.

"She looks quite healthy," Saint said quietly. "Who was your doctor in Sacramento?"

"Chambers is his name."

"Don't know him," Saint said. "Are you breastfeeding her?"

"I—that is, yes, of course."

"Sorry, didn't mean to pry or embarrass you. A beautiful baby. She indeed has the look of the Butlers. Does she have your green eyes or Ira's blue?"

"They're blue."

"Ah."

"She's still sleeping, isn't she? You haven't awakened her?"

Both Byrony and Saint turned at the sound of Irene's sharp voice.

"Not at all," Saint said easily. "If a baby could snore, she would. Shall we leave her to her dreams?"

Irene looked undecided, then shrugged. "Certainly. The guests are beginning to leave, Byrony. You must come downstairs. You go ahead, I'll make sure she's well tucked in."

Byrony nodded and walked past her sister-in-law.

"I imagine," Saint said as they walked down the wide staircase, "that it is difficult for a lady who isn't married to readily accept changes. You are lucky, I think, that she cares for the child. It could have gone the other way, I imagine."

Byrony wanted to laugh at his very kind but utterly mistaken observation. "Indeed," she said.

Chauncey Saxton took her hands. "You must visit me soon, Byrony. Are you free for lunch tomorrow?"

Chauncey was surprised to see Byrony look briefly toward her husband before she answered. Ira gave a benevolent nod, and Byrony said, "I would much enjoy that, Chauncey."

"Good. Bring Michelle. I should like to make her acquaintance. Saint stole my opportunity tonight."

Byrony dressed with great care the following morning, then went to the dining room. Ira was already breakfasting.

"I can't believe everything is back to normal," she said, looking about the pristine dining room. "Naomi is a treasure, isn't she?"

"Indeed," Ira said, rising until Byrony seated herself on his right.

"No," she said, seeing his brief frown, "I don't want to sit at the foot of the table. I don't relish shouting to you to be heard. I do hope Irene isn't still upset about what happened."

"Why should I be? After all, aren't you the little wife with all the privileges?"

The woman walked like a cat, Byrony thought, forcing a smile to her lips as she turned to face Irene.

"Please, Irene," Ira said.

"Good morning," Byrony said, her voice neutral. She'd hoped Irene's recent behavior was a passing thing, but she was beginning to wonder. What had happened to the gentle, very quiet woman she'd spent so many months with? "Did you sleep well?"

"No. Michelle was colicky."

"I'm sorry. I didn't even hear her crying."

"Why should you? You aren't her mother."

"Irene," Ira said, his quiet voice holding a touch of warning. "You will please remember the servants."

Irene's shoulders dropped. She took her seat at the foot of the table, shooting Byrony a cold look as she did so. A challenge? Byrony wasn't interested, Irene could sit in Ira's chair for all she cared.

Naomi entered the dining room, carrying a platter of scrambled eggs and bacon and a plate of toast. Ira spoke of the foggy weather until the woman had left the dining room.

"I'm having lunch with Chauncey Saxton," Byrony said, breaking the heavy silence.

"Excellent," Ira said. "A charming woman."

"She wants me to bring Michelle."

"No. That is," Irene continued in a more moderate voice, "the child was sick all night. Surely it wouldn't be wise to drag her around with you."

"Would you like me to ask Saint to stop by and see her, Irene?"

"That isn't necessary, Ira. But she does need her rest."

And that, Byrony thought, is that. She dutifully repeated the baby's problems to Chauncey three hours later. "She's fine now, of course," Byrony said, realizing that Chauncey might think it odd that Byrony had left her sick child. "She is napping." She looked around the drawing room. "You have a lovely home, Chauncey."

"I'll tell Del. I had nothing to do save move in. You just missed Saint, by the way. Do you know he still refuses to tell me how he got that name?"

"You too? He did the same to me last night."

"A lovely dinner," Chauncey said. "Did you enjoy yourself?"

"Everyone was quite nice, really."

"Except Penelope, right?"

"Well, when I met her, she made me feel like some sort of insect. And her mother—I was reminded of a ship under full sail. Oh dear, I shouldn't be saying these things. I'm certain they are both quite pleasant."

"No, they're not. I'll tell you a little secret, Byrony. If I hadn't rescued Del, he might very well have married that girl."

"Ira did tell me that you arrived here from England just last winter, and you and Mr. Saxton were married two months later."

To Byrony's surprise, Chauncey dropped her eyes a moment. "I am very lucky," she said. "Now, instead of having lunch here, Del invited us out with him. There's a new restaurant that opened on Clay Street, Samuel's Chop House. If you like, afterward we can do a bit of shopping."

Byrony readily agreed. Lucas, a pirate of a man if Byrony ever imagined one, drove the two women to Montgomery Street. "We will meet you here at four o'clock, Luc. All right?"

"Certainly, ma'am," Lucas said.

Chauncey said behind her gloved hand, "I think there's a real romance brewing between Lucas and my maid, Mary. Luc looks so ferocious, but he's gentle as the proverbial lamb. I fear he will let Mary ride roughshod over him without a whimper."

Byrony was grinning as they walked into the Saxton and Brewer bank. They were the only females in this den of males, but it was obvious to Byrony that Mrs. Saxton's appearance wasn't a surprise. Hats were politely tipped, gentle greetings made. Chauncey introduced Byrony to several of the gentlemen, one of them, Dan Brewer, Del Saxton's partner.

"You have a lovely bank, sir," Byrony said, having never before in her life even entered a bank.

"I agree, Mrs. Butler," he said, winking at Chauncey.

"We'll see you later, Dan. Now, it's time I rescued Del from his labors."

Chauncey knocked on a closed door, then opened it and walked in, Byrony on her heels.

"Oh dear, I didn't realize you had someone with you."

Byrony stopped dead in her tracks. It wasn't fair, dammit.

"Not at all, Chauncey. Do come in. Ah, Byrony, welcome. Brent and I were just finishing a bit of very profitable business."

Byrony heard Chauncey's light, charming voice, but she didn't hear her words. She didn't realize she was backing up until Brent Hammond said, "How pleasant to see you again, Mrs. Butler. Were you going somewhere?"

"Yes, she is," Del said. "The ladies have graciously consented to have lunch with me. Won't you join us, Brent?" When Brent paused, Del added, "Surely you don't have a high-stakes poker game going on at noon?"

Brent forced his eyes away from Byrony and said, "If I did, Del, I'd leave you in a flash. Most of my customers are too impatient for poker, you know. Let them spin a roulette wheel or take their chances at vingt-et-un and they're happy. So I'll be happy to join you. Thank you."

I'm cursed, Byrony thought.

"Mrs. Butler?"

His voice was light, mocking, at least to her sensitive ears. She looked at his offered arm as if it were a snake to bite her.

"I thought," she said, her eyes lowered as she slipped her hand onto his forearm, "that you were taking Penelope Stevenson riding."

"Indeed I am, ma'am," he said, arching a black brow at her. "Surely you don't expect me to spend all afternoon with you?"

Go to hell, Byrony wanted to say. Instead she said, "Why

not, sir? Perhaps you'll learn how to conduct yourself in the company of ladies."

Brent threw back his head and laughed deeply. "Instead of what, ma'am?"

"What's all this?" Del asked.

"Mrs. Butler just informed me that she could beat me at poker. Five-card stud."

"Most ladies have many more talents than you gentlemen care to admit to," Chauncey said. "I'll wager she can beat you, Brent—yes, indeed I do."

"Oh yes," Brent said under his breath to Byrony, "I would wager that you have many talents. I'm simply wondering when I'll be the lucky recipient."

"When hell freezes over."

"Such language from such a perfect little lady."

TEN

Byrony leaned over Michelle's crib, making nonsense sounds that made the baby kick her legs and wave her arms in excitement. Byrony laughed and picked her up, hugging her. "You still don't care who pays attention to you, do you? Well, I understand that in a couple more months you're going to become very choosy."

"She has a cold. Put her down."

Byrony didn't turn at Irene's voice, but she felt herself going stiff with dread. "A cold? She seems just fine to me."

"What would you know about a child?" Irene took Michelle from her, held her tightly against her breasts, and walked to the other end of the nursery.

"I imagine that I could learn a little something, if you'd but let me."

For many moments Irene merely looked at her, saying nothing. Then, very softly, bitterly, she said, "Don't you already have everything? Why must you have what is mine?"

"I have nothing," Byrony said without thinking, then realized she meant it.

"You little fool. You have all the pretty clothes you want, you have nothing to worry your empty head about. You have the Butler name."

"So do you."

"Hardly the same thing. God, I wish Ira had never married you."

So do I, Byrony thought. "Ira married me for you, Irene," she said, surprised at how very calm and detached she sounded. "I am trying to fulfill my end of the bargain, but you are making it difficult. Why can't we be friends?"

"I am going to take Michelle out for a while," Irene said.

"What?" Byrony asked, a bit of irony lacing her voice, "I thought she was so very ill with a cold."

"You little slut, what do you know about anything?"

The viciousness of her attack left Byrony breathless, but just for a moment. Cleansing anger shot through her. "Slut, Irene? I wasn't the one who got pregnant. I wasn't the one who was stupid enough to have relations with a married man."

She regretted the words the moment they were out of her mouth. She said quickly, "I'm sorry. I didn't mean that. Surely we can live in the same house without so much discord."

Irene said not another word. Byrony left the nursery and went to her room. I am twenty years old, she thought, and I was right about something—I don't have anything, except a mockery of a marriage and the reputation of having become pregnant before I married. I live a lie and I hate it. She felt further alienated that evening when she followed the sound of Ira's voice and found him and Irene in the nursery playing with Michelle. She crept away before they'd noticed her presence.

The house was quiet now, the quarter-moon outside her window nearly obscured by dark clouds. She tried to imagine her life in this house in five years, but couldn't. She couldn't imagine her life continuing in this vein for another month. She was a well-treated boarder, nothing more. Eileen was kind to her, she supposed, in her matter-of-fact way, but it was to Irene she went for her orders. As did Naomi.

She walked to her bedroom window and leaned her face against the glass. Her thoughts went to Brent Hammond. He wouldn't stay out of her mind and she'd given up trying to keep him out. She hadn't seen him for two weeks, not since that lunch with Del and Chauncey Saxton. Surprisingly, he'd stopped baiting her after his initial remarks. In fact, the lunch had been enjoyable. She hadn't wanted it to end even though she knew he was being pleasant only because he had to be in front of Delaney and Chauncey. It had seemed the most natural thing in the world to agree with Chauncey that she wanted to see Brent's saloon.

They'd only peeked inside, of course. Ladies didn't venture into such male lairs. She found that she was just as interested in the other half of the large building. The brothel. Did she expect to hear seductive laughter? See scantily clad women?

Because he'd been so nice and proper during lunch, very much the gentleman in fact, Byrony was held speechless when Brent whispered in her ear, "Shall I ask Maggie if she'd allow a very proper little lady to use one of the very nice bedrooms upstairs? I could meet you there, of course. Should you like that? The mystery of it? Just imagine, my dear, what I should do to you."

"I will not listen to you, Mr. Hammond."

"Ah, yes," he said, keeping his voice so soft she could barely hear him. "I would much enjoy having you. You can't begin to imagine the things I'd do to you."

"Stop it," she said, wanting to strike him, but knowing she couldn't, not with Del and Chauncey standing so close.

"Stop? Why, I haven't even begun. I'll bet you taste very sweet, Byrony, between your lovely legs. Do you have lovely legs? It's so difficult to tell with all the damned clothes you women wear. Perhaps I could write to some of your former lovers—talking to Ira wouldn't be too very prudent—and ask them what you like. Or were they fumbling young boys?"

Byrony whirled about and said in a high, thin voice, "Chauncey, I must get home. Michelle—she must be hungry."

"Ah, I'd forgotten about your breasts," he said. "Perhaps soon you'll share your warm milk. I would like to taste you, you know."

Even after two weeks, she remembered every one of his hateful words. Irene had called her a slut, and obviously Brent believed her to be one. Suddenly she started laughing, softly, then more loudly. It was all too ridiculous. She should tell Brent Hammond that he was the only man who had ever kissed her. What would he say to that? She laughed so hard she hugged her aching sides. She wasn't certain when the laughter turned to sobs.

"Well, since my two very best friends are here, I will tell you my news."

Byrony and Agatha looked at Chauncey. She looked ready to pop, she was so excited.

"Don't keep us in suspense!" Agatha said.

"Very well, I'm going to have a baby."

Agatha hugged Chauncey and patted her back. "I am so happy for you, my dear, so happy indeed."

"Yes," Byrony said. "Is Del pleased?"

"Oh yes," Chauncey said. "He acted like a wild Indian, shouting and whooping about last night. Mary and Lin and Lucas came rushing in wondering what was going on. At that point, Del was waltzing me around the room. Among the five of us, we drank two bottles of champagne."

"What wonderful news, my dear. Have you seen Saint?"

"He visited me yesterday and confirmed what I'd hoped. You should have seen Mary hanging over him, telling him what she thought and giving him instructions. He just laughed at her and told her to get herself married to Lucas so he'd have another baby to deliver in the future."

"He said everything was just fine?" Byrony asked.

"Saint assured me I was as healthy as any horse he'd ever seen. With this twinkle in his eyes, he told me to continue everything I was doing until he told me to stop."

"I'll wager Del was happy to hear that," Agatha said.

Chauncey flushed a bit, then laughed. "What my dear husband said, Agatha—his exact words were, 'Ah, at last there will be fruits to my labors.'"

"Has he been working too hard, Chauncey?" Byrony asked.

Both women stared at her, then broke into gales of laughter.

Chauncey saw that Byrony didn't realize what they were laughing about, and quickly said, "You must bring Michelle to visit. It's time I got used to babies, and she is so sweet. I'd hoped you would bring her today."

"She has a cold. Irene didn't think it would be a good idea to take her outside."

"Has Saint seen her?" Agatha said.

"No. I didn't think it was necessary."

How very curious, Chauncey thought, after the two women had left. Byrony had truly not understood their jest. Indeed, so many things about Byrony simply didn't fit together. She said as much to her husband that evening over dinner.

"And she simply didn't understand, Del. It's true, I suppose, that our jesting was just a bit improper, but we are all married women, for heaven's sake."

Delaney laid down his fork and raised his eyes to her face.

"And her child, Del. She's never brought her here to our house. In fact, the only times I've ever seen Michelle are with Irene hovering about. It's all rather odd."

"Perhaps you're reading too much into this, love."

"Maybe."

"Did I tell you that Ira's becoming a total bore? He's always been reticent, I guess you'd say, except when he talks about his child. Do you think I'll become like him?"

He raised his hand quickly when he saw the twinkle in her eyes. "All right, I guess I'm already a total bore about my wife, so my friends will believe me much more interesting after the baby comes."

"I should be so lucky."

Later that night, when Chauncey was settled in for the night, her cheek pressed against her husband's shoulder, she murmured, half-asleep, "I am worried about Byrony, Del. There's something wrong, I'm certain of it. Sometimes I think if I invited her, she'd move in with us."

"A very pretty girl. I shouldn't mind."

Brent hadn't been at all gentle in his lovemaking with Celeste. But then, she liked him to be fierce and demanding. She'd already curled up against his side and was fast asleep. He lay on his back, his head pillowed on his arms, and stared up at the dark ceiling, reviewing the day's events in his mind. He thought about Delaney Saxton's proposition to buy into his shipping business. The Orient, he thought. I'd like to go there.

"You've got to do something smart with all the money you're raking in," Del had said over lunch. "All you're doing is piling it up in my bank."

"You're right, of course." Brent fell silent a moment, his thoughts going to his father's plantation, Wakehurst. It would have been his, had he not been such a bloody fool. He unconsciously rubbed his fingertip over the scar on his cheek. So many years had passed, yet he still remembered those terrible few minutes so vividly. He had betrayed his father. But you were only eighteen, a stupid boy, he'd tell himself, but the guilt was still there. Damn, but he missed his father. All because he'd been a randy boy, all because Laurel had wanted him—

"If you don't take me up on it, Brent," Del had said, "I think I'll talk to Maggie. Now, there's a lady with ambition."

"I think every man who gambles in my saloon pays her girls a visit. They lose fifty dollars to me, then pay her a hundred."

"That's one thing I've always admired about San Francisco," Del said, swirling the beer about in his glass. "Men are men and don't apologize for it. It isn't at all that way back where I grew up."

"It had to be worse in the South," Brent said. "Everyone wanted to be wicked, and indeed everyone was, but so discreetly, and with such hypocrisy."

"You're originally from Natchez? Don't look surprised, Brent. I asked Maggie. She told me you are a planter's son."

"Yes, I am. Or was. My father disinherited me."

Del raised a brow, but asked no more questions. He said after a moment, "That's another thing I like about the West and San Francisco in particular. A man's—or a woman's—past is nobody's business. You are, out here, what you make of yourself. I sometimes believe my own father would have booted me out if it hadn't been for my older brother, Alex. He was always the great peacemaker."

"Is your brother in the shipping business?"

"He builds ships, in New York. And like me, he's married to an Englishwoman. Therein lies a tale, but unfortunately, I don't see him and Giana, his wife, often enough to weasel it out of them."

"Speaking of tails—" Brent broke off and grinned.

"I've got the spelling, go ahead."

"I understand you very nearly tied the matrimonial knot with Penelope Stevenson."

Delaney rolled his eyes. "I'll tell you, Brent, that girl

needs to be thrashed, probably about three times a day. Even before Chauncey arrived, I'd decided I would rather slit my wrists than marry her. Why? You've got ideas in that direction?"

Brent shrugged. "The lady's persistent. If I didn't know better, I'd think it was my body she was after, and not my noble heart. The dowry's tempting, you must admit."

"I suppose so, if a man was willing to give up his peace for dollars."

"And power. Hell, Del, you could keep her pregnant and out of your hair easily enough."

"I wouldn't wager fifty cents on that. I'd think carefully, Brent, before I shifted toward Penelope."

Brent grinned and tossed down the rest of his beer. "I'm just spouting nonsense. Don't listen to me. I have no intention of marrying—any woman."

"You'll change your mind, once you meet the right lady. Incidentally, you can congratulate me. Chauncey's pregnant."

To Delaney's surprise, Brent became utterly still. What the devil was wrong? Then Brent seemed to get hold of himself, and smiled. "I'm happy for you. Is Chauncey feeling well?"

"She has so much energy, it's terrifying. Saint assures me she'll slow down a bit. I'll tell you something, though," Del added, "I won't say anything to Chauncey, but I'm terrified. I was in New York in fifty-one when my sister-in-law went into labor. I've never felt so utterly helpless in my life. Hell, I'd be willing to pay Saint any fee he asked. Thank God, he's here in San Francisco."

What if Byrony becomes pregnant again? Was she in danger with her first child?

"Yes," Brent said, his voice clipped. He couldn't bear the thought of Ira even touching her hand, much less possessing her. Get used to it, you fool. That, or leave San Francisco.

"Well, it's time for me to get back to the grindstone," Delaney said. "Think about my proposition, Brent. But don't take too much time, all right?"

"Tell you what, Del. I think I'm going to go riding this afternoon myself—no Penelope—it'll clear my head. I'll get back to you tomorrow."

Brent stabled his horse, an Arabian stallion, whose unlikely and unaristocratic name was Curtis, at Jem Bradley's stable on Kearny. The afternoon was clear, fortunately. The rainy season was nearly upon them, and then, he knew, Curtis wouldn't get too many workouts. He rode beside the plank road to the Mission Dolores, then headed Curtis toward the ocean. This part of the peninsula was barren, nothing but whirling sand and high, shifting dunes. The constant wind off the ocean whipped the sand inland, covering trails and paths within twenty-four hours. He remembered stories of the miners newly arrived in San Francisco. They'd pitch their tents and go to bed, only to awake the next morning sanded in.

Sea gulls squawked overhead, the only noise of life around him. It was desolate land, savage land, yet comforting, and he loved it. He urged his horse over the last rise, holding his reins tightly so he wouldn't slip in the sand, and the Pacific came into view. God, it was beautiful. He'd been raised inland, and had never before seen the ocean until just two years ago. The tide was coming in, and the stiff ocean breeze was whipping up the sand on the beach. He looked north, to the raised, jagged cliffs. It was then he saw the other rider.

It was a woman seated on a mare some hundred yards up the coast. She was sitting very still. For a moment he frowned, for he wanted to be alone. Then, after what seemed to be hours, the woman turned and click-clicked her mare toward him. Brent froze.

What an unlucky bastard you are, he thought, laughing at

himself. It was as if he'd conjured her up. She was never far from his conscious thoughts, and he wondered briefly what she'd do when she saw him. Then he didn't care. He nurtured the seed of contempt, realizing vaguely it was his only and last defense against her.

He urged George forward, keeping him but a couple of feet beyond the encroaching tide. At least the wet sand was firm and his stallion wouldn't stumble.

"Good day, Mrs. Butler," he called to her, and doffed his black felt hat.

"What are you doing here?"

She sounded frightened and it surprised him. Was she afraid he would pull her off her mare's back and ravish her on the sand?

"I'm riding, as you can see. Does your husband know that you're out alone? This isn't exactly a civilized city yet, ma'am."

She was wearing a royal-blue velvet riding habit and a rakish little blue hat on her head. Her hands were gloved in the finest leather. She looked so beautiful, and so wary, that he had difficulty breathing.

"You don't look particularly civilized, Mr. Hammond. But I am always careful, I assure you. You look more like a desperado than a fancy gambler." It was true, she thought, staring at him. He was wearing black trousers, a full-sleeved white shirt, and a black leather vest. The black hat and black riding boots completed the picture. He looked like the devil, and so compelling that she wanted to ride toward him, and run away at the same time.

"And untrustworthy?"

She ignored him and forced herself to urge her mare away from him. His hand shot out suddenly and grabbed the reins. "I thought you were probably afraid of me."

"I'm not afraid of you."

"Excellent. Let's walk along the beach for a while."

Damn you for an idiot. Why didn't you just let her ride away?

He quickly dismounted and walked toward her. She stared down at him, her eyes wide and wary on his face. "I'm not certain—" she began, and licked her lips.

His hands clasped her waist and easily lifted her off her mare's back. He didn't release her, but gently and slowly slid her down his body until her feet touched the sand. Blood drummed loudly in his ears. His body reacted instantly, and he didn't deny himself. He pulled her against his chest and kissed her. The plume in her riding hat brushed his cheek.

Byrony struggled, pushing her fists against his chest. His arms only tightened around her back. "No, please, Brent, no."

Her words brought his head up. "God, you're so bloody beautiful. Why you, dammit?"

"I don't know." She slipped away from him, turning her back to him. She wasn't frightened of him. She wanted him. It was the oddest feeling, one that she had never before experienced. Was this desire? She stared blindly at the crashing waves.

His lust calmed, and he said brutally, "You want me and Lord knows I want to bed you. Just once, and I imagine you would be out of my mind for all time."

He saw her stiffen but she didn't turn to face him.

"One more man wouldn't make any difference. I won't leave you unsatisfied, I promise you that. And I won't get you pregnant."

Slowly Byrony turned to face him. Her heart was beating wildly, and no matter how many deep breaths she'd taken, it wouldn't calm. She wondered vaguely if he could hear it.

"I don't understand," she said, staring him full in the face. "Why do you want me? You don't know me, not at all. You hate me, I'd say."

He pulled off his hat and ran his fingers through his hair.

"It's strange," she continued after a moment of silence. "I really thought you different from other men when I met you in San Diego. But I guess that was foolish of me, wasn't it? Mr. Hammond, the truth of the matter is that—"

"Is what?" His voice was harsh.

She cocked her head to one side, and she looked so innocent, so sweet with that damned little feather arching over her cheek, that he wanted for a brief instant to beg her forgiveness.

"If I did what you wished, would you stop hating me?"

He stared at her, no words coming to mind.

"Please, I'm only trying to understand. I cannot think why you feel it necessary to insult me every time we meet. I really don't understand why you would want me to—that is, what you want is so intimate. Why would a man want intimacy with a woman he despises?"

"I don't despise you."

"You've a strange way of showing liking then, Mr. Hammond."

"Brent."

She sighed. "Very well, Brent."

"I don't dislike you," he said, trying to get a grip on himself, but failing. "Dammit, I despise what you've done. You talk about not understanding. Well, I don't understand why women sell themselves, and why they lie and cheat. Why they feel they must play games and tease men. Does it give you a sense of power to know that men desire you?"

"I have no power at all," she said. "As for what I've done, I had no choice. It was out of my hands."

"Ah, yes. Once his seed was planted in your belly, it certainly was."

Slowly she said, "Mr. Hammond—Brent—please, no more. As you once said to me, I've made my bed and now must lie in it. I sincerely doubt that happiness has anything to do with real life, but I would like peace. Won't you please just leave me alone?"

"Nothing would give me greater pleasure." He raked his fingers through his hair, his frustration mounting. "You're like a wretched sickness, and I doubt I can be cured until I've had you in every sense a man can possess a woman."

"So," she said slowly, "if I give myself to you, you will leave me alone?"

He wanted to fling her onto the sand and rip off her clothes. He wanted to shake her and tell her to stop acting like a wanton. He wanted—

"Brent?"

"Go to hell, Byrony," he said, rigid with fury, both at himself and at her.

"I'm already there," she said, and turned to walk across the sand to her mare.

ELEVEN

"It's beautiful, Ira. Thank you."

Byrony lifted the thick chignon at the nape of her neck to allow her husband to fasten the exquisite pearl-and-diamond necklace about her throat.

He kissed her gently on the forehead and said, "Merry Christmas, Byrony. You look lovely indeed."

Byrony wanted to laugh when Ira presented Irene with a very similar necklace, one of sapphires and diamonds. Poor man. He tried so hard to keep his half-sister content. Yet with me here, it's impossible, she wanted to tell him. She'd made Ira a shirt, her careful stitches small and exquisite, just as Aunt Ida had taught her. Irene had bought her brother a beautiful Spanish leather saddle. Her own gift, in comparison, was meager indeed, but she had no money.

Eileen and Naomi served them steaming mugs of buttered rum, and received, in turn, their presents. Byrony sat back to watch Irene playing with Michelle while she unwrapped the baby's many gifts. The baby gurgled happily and waved pieces of the gay wrapping paper in her hands. Irene is an excellent mother, Byrony thought. How would I feel if I had to pretend to others that my child weren't my own?

Ira laughed at the baby's antics.

"She looks more and more like Irene every day," he said, "except for that mop of blond hair."

Yes, Byrony thought. The shape of the baby's face was Irene's, and the dark brown eyes.

Irene opened Byrony's present to Michelle, a tiny hand-sewn ribboned petticoat.

"She is much too young, of course," Irene said, and tossed the small garment aside.

So much for the goodwill at Christmastime, Byrony thought.

There were only the three of them for Christmas dinner. It was a delicious meal—a stuffed goose, fresh green beans, potatoes, and Naomi's rendition of a Christmas pudding. Irene sat next to Ira, the baby on her lap.

Here I am alone in splendid solitude, Byrony thought, gazing down the long expanse of dining table. She supposed, honestly, that this Christmas was more pleasant than the previous one. Her father had gotten drunk and her brother had gone off with some of his worthless friends to gamble. And her mother, of course, had said nothing.

Ira had also given her a book for Christmas, a collection of Lord Byron's poetry. "Your namesake, my dear," he said.

She spent the remainder of the day curled on the small settee in front of the fire.

Brent and Saint shared Christmas dinner with the Saxtons.

"Your bulk, Chauncey, is charming," Brent said, smiling at his hostess.

"Come now, I'm not that ungainly yet."

As for Saint, he studied Chauncey for a long moment and said, "Go upstairs at once and loosen those stays of yours."

Chauncey threw up her hands.

"Just do as you're told, sweetheart, and you'll get no orders from me," said Del.

"What marvelous male ambiguity," his wife said.

Brent said, "I fear, Chauncey, that it's too late to change any of us blighted specimens. What do you think, Saint?"

"I think," said Saint slowly, "that this is the happiest household in San Francisco."

"What is this? You dismiss the Butler household?"

Saint gave him a long, thoughtful look, and Brent found himself squirming. Why the hell hadn't he just kept his mouth shut?

Del, who'd just turned to them, added his two cents. "Yeah, Saint, and don't forget the Stevensons."

"All right," Saint said agreeably. "Give me a drink, Del, and I'll be mellow as a duck by the time Horace and Agatha arrive. They are coming after dinner, aren't they?"

"Well after dinner," Del said, laughing. "Don't worry, you can give your greed full rein." He added as he handed Saint his whiskey, neat, "What I've got to do is marry the both of you off."

Saint choked on his whiskey.

Brent gave Delaney a raised eyebrow.

"I'll have you know, Saxton," Brent said, "that after Saint and I gorge ourselves here, we're going back to the saloon, there to have a real Christmas party with Maggie and all the girls."

"Oh, Lord, don't have me guess what you two unworthies are getting for Christmas."

Brent merely smiled. *Celeste already gave me my Christmas present*, he thought, *two of them as a matter of fact, both this morning.* He still felt pleasantly relaxed. *I give her presents and she gives me her body. A fair exchange.*

"It wouldn't be the same thing with a wife," he said, then realized he'd spoken aloud.

"What wouldn't?" Saint asked.

"The entire system of barter," Brent said easily. "If a man has money, he can buy his pleasure and not have to worry about it nagging at him."

"Cynical bastard," Delaney said to the blazing fire in the fireplace.

"He's got a bit of a point," Saint said, rubbing his ear. "Not everyone's as lucky as you, Del."

"Just look at that poor fool Butler. Lord knows he didn't have to marry her," Brent said.

Delaney leaned his shoulder against the mantel. "Ira is a lot of things, but he isn't dishonorable. Byrony, despite your obvious dislike of her, Brent, is a lady. Whatever happened between them, well, Ira did the right thing. Women have so little power."

Brent snorted. "They have what men want and are quite willing to pay for."

"Who has what you men want?" Chauncey asked as she walked into the room.

"We were just talking generalities, love," Del said.

"I just bet you were. Now that I'm in the room, your conversation will degenerate into proper nothings, fit, I'm sure you will tell me, for a lady's delicate ears. Come, tell me what wickedness you were talking about."

"We were talking about the fact that women have no power," Brent said. "At least Del subscribes to that notion."

Chauncey, to his surprise, stiffened a moment, then said, "It's true, you know, very true indeed. A woman can't go out and find a position, for example. Who would hire her? And if someone did—a man, of course—he wouldn't have the slightest respect for her, and she would probably be open to whatever advances he chose to make. It isn't fair, it really isn't."

"Coming from one of the richest ladies in San Francisco," Saint said, "your words surprise me."

"No, Brent," Del said, "it wasn't a case of barter. Chauncey had more money than I. I keep telling her that's why I married her."

"I wasn't always rich," Chauncey said. "Believe me, I understand powerlessness firsthand. It is not pleasant."

"But if a woman is beautiful, she is immensely powerful," Brent said. "She has but to pick her quarry and he will probably fall all over his feet giving her whatever she wishes."

"I called him a cynical bastard already, love," Del said.

"I would say rather that he was hurt quite badly by a woman," Chauncey said.

"How about a whiskey," Brent said.

Chauncey was feeling sated and lazy after one of Lin's marvelous Mexican-Chinese dinners, tamales with ginger.

"I don't think this wretched rain is ever going to end," she said to Byrony. "I do thank you for spending the evening with me."

Byrony nodded, listening to the steady downpour outside. She'd begun to feel dizzy and nauseous earlier in the evening, but had said nothing. She finally admitted to herself that she was sick.

"I hope Del comes home before midnight. But the gentlemen and their political meetings. Ira is at the Pacific Club this evening too, isn't he, Byrony?"

"Yes. He was delighted that you invited me to spend the evening here with you. He doesn't like me to be lonely." Her throat was scratchy, and she felt very hot. Her head was beginning to pound.

Why should you be lonely? Chauncey wanted to ask. You've a baby and there's Irene to keep you company.

"Here it is almost the end of February," she said instead, "and May seems an indecent decade away. Did you feel as lazy and contented as I do? And as impatient?"

"What?"

"When you were pregnant."

"Oh, well, yes, I suppose I did. It all seems a long time ago, actually."

How odd, Chauncey thought, looking at Byrony from beneath her lashes. Here I am feeling so protective toward her, and she is far more experienced than I. "All Saint will tell me is that it hurts. Did you have a very bad time of it?"

Byrony cleared her throat and said carefully, "I suppose it wasn't very pleasant."

"Byrony, are you all right? You're looking very pale."

Byrony forced a weak smile. "Do you know, I think I'm coming down with something. I haven't felt quite the thing all day, and now, well, I think my head's going to burst."

Chauncey was at Byrony's side in a moment. She laid her palm over Byrony's forehead. "You've a fever. Shall we send Lucas for Saint?"

"Oh no, Chauncey. I think I'll just go home and tuck myself into bed."

"This dreadful rain. It's a wonder that all of us aren't sneezing and sniveling about. You just sit still, Byrony, and I'll tell Lucas to bring the carriage around to the front."

Byrony didn't feel like doing anything else. In fact, she wanted to curl up into a ball and sleep for a year. She felt so hot, and the high collar of her gown was choking her. She pulled at it, then shuddered when a sudden chill raced through her. She could count on her fingers the number of times in her life she'd been ill, even with a cold. She hated the weakness, the feeling of helplessness.

"Come on, love. I'll help you to the front door. Here, let me bundle you up."

Byrony stood docile and quiet while Chauncey tied her scarf about her neck and helped her into her long cloak. "I'll check up on you tomorrow, Byrony. If you're not better, I'll see to it that Ira fetches Saint. Ah, Lucas. Hold the umbrella high for Mrs. Butler."

It was so cold. Her bones felt like they were shivering.

Byrony huddled in the closed carriage, her eyes closed. She couldn't see out the windows in any case because of the driving rain and the thick fog. Ira's house was but a half-mile from the Saxtons'. When the carriage came to a stop, she drew on her reserves and allowed Lucas to help her to the front door. The house was dark.

"Thank you, Lucas. You needn't see me in. I'll be all right."

But he waited, his eyes narrowed in concern, until Byrony had unlocked the front door and disappeared inside.

Where were Eileen and Naomi?

Byrony knew the house well and made her way up the stairs in the darkness. She supposed that Irene and the baby were both asleep. Good, she could be miserable in peace. Her hand was on the doorknob of her bedroom when she chanced to see a gleam of light from beneath Ira's bedroom door. How odd, she thought, staring at the light. Could Ira be home already? He'd told her he would be quite late and not to come back early from her visit to Chauncey Saxton.

Perhaps she should ask Ira to fetch Saint. She walked toward his closed door. She raised her hand to knock, then paused, frowning. There were noises coming from within. Strange noises. Was that a moan? Could Ira be ill? She gripped the doorknob and turned it. The door opened easily, silently, and Byrony peeked into the room.

There was one lamp lit, casting dim shadows.

There was another moan, from the bed.

She started to call out his name. Nothing came out of her mouth. It wasn't a man moaning, it was a woman. She stood frozen, shock and surprise holding her silent.

"Ira, please, please."

"Yes, my love. God, yes."

Irene's voice. Ira's voice. Lovers' voices.

Bile rose in her throat and she stuffed her fist into her

mouth. She saw Ira's white body rise, saw Irene's parted legs.

She heard Irene gasp for breath when Ira covered her.

They were lovers. No. Irene was his half-sister! No, it couldn't be. *No.*

Their bodies were entwined. They were one.

Michelle had the look of the Butlers. No, she looked like Ira.

Byrony clutched her arms around her stomach as the truth burst into her mind. Dear God, no wonder Ira didn't want her as a real wife. He already had a wife and a child.

Slowly she backed through the doorway. She gently pulled the door closed.

Michelle was their child. He'd married her to save his half-sister, to keep her and their child in his home. She was only for appearances. For show.

She was going to be sick. She ran back down the stairs and jerked open the front door. She fell to her knees in the thick mud and vomited.

She shuddered with dry heaves. Finally she quieted. Her body felt battered, her mind blessedly numb, but just for a moment. I can't go back, I can't go back.

She staggered to her feet, clutched her cloak about her, and started running. She saw the lights coming from downtown and kept running toward them. Across Market Street. She stumbled into deep pockets of mud, pulled herself up, and kept going, doggedly. She felt the rain soak through her cloak, to her skin.

I can't go back there. I can't.

Her mind focused on the lights. The new gaslights, installed just last month. Hazy lights with the fog shrouding them. She stumbled past saloons, past men who didn't realize she was a female until she was well beyond them. She heard men calling to her but didn't slow. She had to keep going. Keep going.

Some part of her mind knew exactly where she was going. To the Wild Star. To Portsmouth Square. To Brent Hammond. She wondered, briefly, why she didn't go to Chauncey. Chauncey was her friend, she would take her in. But her feet didn't slow. She saw Brent in her mind's eye, and knew deep down that despite everything, he would take care of her. He would protect her. And she wanted his protection, no one else's. God, she just wanted to see him, have him hold her, have him make the awful nightmare go away.

Her breath was jerky, she had a painful stitch in her side. Her head pounded in time with her heart. Her teeth chattered until her jaws ached.

She heard her shoes clattering on the wooden sidewalk on the east side of Kearny, a soggy, hollow sound. She wasn't aware of time passing. She was conscious only of putting one foot in front of the other. Conscious only of escaping.

The Wild Star was brightly lit. Men gambled and whored in all kinds of weather. Suddenly she heard a man's gruff voice, felt herself pulled to a stop by a strong arm about her shoulders.

"Jesus, Chad, lookee what I got. A little bird. A very wet little bird."

"Let me go," Byrony screamed, but the words were only a hoarse whisper. She didn't have her derringer.

"I should say you've got yerself a prize, Neddie. What are ye doin' out of bed, honey? You need yerself a warm man for the night?"

They were drunk and they were going to hurt her. "Please, let me go."

She jerked away from the one man, but the other caught her and pulled her against him. She felt his hot, whiskey breath against her mouth.

She screamed, a thin, wailing sound that was muted by the pounding rain.

"What the devil is going on?"

"Help me. Please, help me."

Brent stared at the bedraggled woman in the grip of the two drunks Nero had just assisted bodily from the saloon.

"We just found us a little whore out for a stroll," Chad said, tugging Byrony against him.

"She doesn't look particularly willing to me," Brent said, watching the struggling woman with growing anger. "Let her go. Now." Damnation. All he'd wanted to do was go to Celeste, and now this. He felt the rain trickling down the back of his neck, and strode forward.

"Lookee, Hammond, it ain't none of yer business."

Byrony found the strength to jab her elbow into Chad's stomach. He yowled, and raised a meaty fist to strike her.

"You damned bastard." Brent was on him in an instant, his fist connecting with Chad's wet jaw. Jesus, he was thinking, was it one of Maggie's girls? Chad dropped back, and Byrony stumbled toward Brent. He caught her against his side. She was trembling violently.

"That's enough, gentlemen," he said.

"There's two of us, Neddie. High-and-mighty Hammond ain't got no say out here!"

A shining derringer appeared as if by magic. "I suggest that you two leave, now. No," Brent continued, his voice soft, almost amused, "don't try it. I'll blow your brains out."

Byrony vaguely heard the argument, heard the two men cursing vilely. Then they were gone.

"What the hell are you doing out here?" Brent asked, easing his derringer back into its small holster. "Didn't Maggie teach you anything?" She felt herself being shaken. The hood to her mantle fell back.

Brent saw a sodden, tangled mass of hair, and impatiently shoved it back. He sucked in his breath, then cursed. "You. Jesus, Byrony, what the hell—"

He broke off abruptly. She was looking up at him with utterly blank eyes.

"What's the matter with you? Where's Ira?"

In bed with his half-sister. She wanted to laugh, but the sound that emerged was a wet cough.

"Dammit, what are you doing out in this miserable weather?" He pulled her in under the wooden overhang and clapped his hand over her forehead. Fever. She was burning up with fever. He felt panic and fear. God, no, she mustn't be ill. "Damn you, where is your precious husband? Come on, I'll get you home!"

"No!" She jerked away from him so quickly, he didn't have time to react.

"Byrony—" he yelled after her in fury.

He saw her stumble off the sidewalk, weave in the thick mud, and sprawl forward onto her side.

TWELVE

He cursed as much from fear as from anger. He walked after her, picking her up, nearly tripping into the mud with her.

He managed to stumble back to the sidewalk. What the hell was he supposed to do now? There was really no question, and he tightened his grip on her as he strode to the back of the Wild Star. "Don't you dare be ill, you little twit."

He managed to unlock the back entrance, and strode up the stairs to his rooms. Black-haired, sloe-eyed Felice saw him and he said, "Get me Maggie at once."

Why was she unconscious? Had that bastard hurt her?

"What's going on, Brent?" Maggie took in the wet, filthy bundle in his arms.

"It's Byrony," he said. "I don't know what's wrong. She has a fever. She's unconscious."

Byrony, Maggie thought. So it wasn't some woman he'd known a long time ago. She became brisk. "She's filthy and we'll have to bathe her. I'll have Caesar fetch Saint. Since Felice has already seen you, and the girl can be trusted to keep her mouth shut, I'll have her help us. Don't move, Brent."

Byrony stirred in his arms and muttered something about

a baby. He tightened his grip, whispering to her, "What about a baby? Your baby? Byrony?"

Her head fell back against his arm. So long, he thought, so long since he'd even seen her. Now she was ill. He realized after a moment that he was praying. He looked at Maggie like she was the angel of mercy when she came quickly back into the room.

"All right, Brent. Take her into your bedroom. Felice is heating water. No matter if she's ill. She'll be even sicker if we don't get her out of those sodden clothes. Caesar's off to get Saint. Pray that he's home. But then again, nobody but an idiot would be out in weather like this."

Brent carried her into his bedroom, a place he'd fantasized about having her. At his mercy. Having her want him and admit to it. Having her sprawled on his bed, her arms raised to him.

"Just put her here on the hearth. Get out your tub, Brent." Maggie looked up at him, realizing he hadn't moved. He was staring down at the girl, his face pale.

"Brent."

Gently he eased her onto the cold floor in front of the fireplace. "She's ill," he said.

"I know. I'll get her undressed, and you do the same for yourself. You're as wet as she is"

He nodded, thankful that someone knew what to do. He didn't leave his bedroom, merely stepped back and methodically began to strip off his wet clothes, dropping them on the floor at his feet.

He heard a gasp from the door, and turned to see Felice holding a bucket of hot water in each hand. He didn't realize that he was quite naked.

"In the tub," Maggie said. "Help me, Felice, and don't gawk at Mr. Hammond. Lord knows, he's just a man, and you've seen enough of them."

Brent shrugged into a dressing gown. He stood helplessly as Maggie and Felice lifted Byrony into the tub.

"I hate to wash her hair, but we've got to," Maggie was saying to Felice. "Quick, hand me the soap. I don't want her in here any longer than necessary."

"Why is she unconscious?" Brent asked.

"I don't know. Don't worry. Saint will be here soon."

He'd wanted to see her body ever since the first time he'd met her, so long ago, it seemed. But he didn't look. His eyes remained on her shadowed face. She was so damned pale. "I'll kill that bastard," he said.

"You're not going to do violence to anybody, Brent. Get me another one of your dressing gowns. The burgundy velvet one."

Felice wrapped Byrony's wet hair in a thick towel while Maggie quickly dried her. Brent handed her the dressing gown.

"All right. Put her into bed, Brent."

She's thin, he thought as he lifted her into his arms.

They covered her with three thick blankets.

Felice removed the towel from her hair and began to untangle the strands, smoothing them away from her head onto the pillow.

"That's fine, Felice. Thank you. Please see to it that Dr. Morris comes straight up when he arrives. And, Felice, not a word, all right?"

"But who is she, Maggie? What's she doing here?"

"None of your business, Felice. Be on your way now."

"Why is she unconscious?" Brent asked again when they were alone.

"For God's sake, I don't know. I do know she has a fever. It's probably the influenza. Now, Brent, this is your Byrony. Who is she?"

My Byrony. The Byrony whose name he'd yelled when

he'd taken his pleasure with another woman. "Byrony Butler," he said.

"Ira Butler's wife?"

"Yes. Dammit, she's nothing to me, Maggie. I haven't laid eyes on her in a long time. I have no idea why she was alone and—"

"Obviously she was coming to you."

"No," he said. "She wanted me to leave her alone. She wanted peace. She told me to go to hell." *No, you were the one to say that.*

"Then where was she going?"

"I don't know. All right, something obviously has happened to her—"

"Something awful, I should say, and she was coming to you because she had no place else to go." Maggie fell silent a moment, then laid her palm on Byrony's forehead. "She's so young," she said. "Are you going to send someone for her husband?"

"Hell no. That is, when I told her outside that I was taking her home, she yelled at me that she didn't want to go. I don't know what I'm going to do."

"Well, let's see what Saint has to say," she said as he came through the door.

"This better be good, Brent. Dragging a man out on a night like this— Hey, what's this? Byrony."

Saint's eyes flew to Brent's face, but Brent only shrugged.

"Maggie thinks it's influenza. But she won't wake up, Saint."

Saint had at least half a dozen questions, but he said nothing as he shrugged out of his coat and hat and tossed them and his umbrella into the corner. He sat down beside Byrony and gently pressed his palm to her cheeks.

"I'm going to leave now, Brent," Maggie said. "We don't want any talk, obviously. Call me if you need me."

"Maggie, thank you."

"You want to tell me what's going on here, Brent?" Saint asked, not looking up.

Brent talked and Saint grunted.

"So your guess is as good as mine," Brent said. He watched Saint pull open the dressing gown and lean his cheek against Byrony's breast. "Lungs are clear," he said. Saint was on the point of closing the dressing gown, when he suddenly stopped. He stared at her white breasts with their small pink nipples. He shook his head, bemused.

"What's the matter?" Brent asked, moving closer to the bed.

"Leave me alone for a while, Brent. I don't think my patient would appreciate you being here while I examine her."

"To hell with what she thinks," Brent said, but he did walk to the fireplace.

Saint pulled open the dressing gown and studied her. She was on the verge of thinness. He asked, "When did Byrony have her baby?"

"I don't know. About six or seven months ago, I guess. Why?"

"Just wondering," Saint said. If Byrony had ever carried a baby, he was president of the United States.

"Pour me a shot of brandy, Brent. I want to bring her out of this." What was holding her from consciousness? Shock?

Saint forced the rim of the glass between her lips and tilted it. She choked, and Saint quickly lifted her.

"Take it easy, Byrony. Here, drink a bit more. It'll warm you up."

Byrony heard a man's voice, and forced her eyes to open. He was a blur. A stranger. He was touching her, he was going to hurt her. "No." She tried to get away from him.

"Move, Saint." Brent captured her flailing arms and brought her close to his chest. "Hush, Byrony. It's all right. I promise you. It's Brent. You're all right."

"Brent." Her eyes cleared and she stared up into his dark eyes. "I'm sick," she said.

"I know. Saint's here. He'll make you feel better in no time at all."

He started to ease her down, but she threw her arms about his neck and held on tight. "No, please—don't go."

"All right, I promise I won't go. I want you to lie down now. Just relax. That's it. Close your eyes. Good girl."

Saint said not a word. He measured out a few drops of laudanum in a glass of water. "Make her drink this," he said.

He listened to Brent, his voice soft as he spoke to Byrony. He watched him gently stroke her hand as she drifted into drugged sleep.

"I'd say, old son, that you've a problem the size of a house."

Brent forced his eyes from Byrony's face. "I've got to find out why she ran away," he said. "Will she be all right, Saint?"

"Yes. She's a strong girl. I gather you're going to keep her with you tonight?"

"Do I have a choice?"

"Nope. None at all that I can see, unless you want to get Ira. He is her husband, you know, and she's his responsibility."

Brent rose and stretched out his hand to Saint. "I'll see you tomorrow," he said.

"Keep her warm, and if and when she wakes up, give her lots of water."

Saint pulled his leather hat low on his brow, drew a deep breath, and thoughtfully walked down the back stairs and into the rain. So, it was Irene's baby. However did that damned woman manage to get herself pregnant? Why did Byrony consent to go along with the charade? God, what a bloody mess.

* * *

She mumbled in her sleep, meaningless sounds that made no sense to Brent. He sat in a chair beside the bed, his fingers steepled together, tapping softly, his eyes never leaving her face. She'd evoked emotions in him since the first time he'd ever seen her. Strong emotions that made him uncomfortable, made him want to strike out—at her. He saw perspiration beading on her forehead. He rose, dampened a cloth, and gently wiped her face.

Always they'd fought. Rather, he amended to himself, he'd always insulted her. He studied her features, the delicate straight nose, the stubborn chin, the high cheekbones. Her lashes were dark, and fanned like tangled black shadows against her pale cheeks. Her brows were slightly arched, darker than her hair. He slowly reached out his hand and wrapped a hank of hair around his fingers.

He told himself yet again that she'd sold herself to Ira Butler, borne his child. She'd made her bed, damn her, let her wallow in it. She had nothing to do with him.

Why was she coming to him? She hated him. He knew she was very good friends with Chauncey. Why had she run like a madwoman in the rain all the way downtown? God, it was so dangerous, it made his blood run cold to think of it. What if he hadn't been on his way to visit Celeste? What if those men—

He jumped when the clock struck twelve strokes. Midnight. He'd been sitting silently watching her for two hours. Slowly he rose, locked the door, and turned off the lamps. He shrugged out of his dressing gown and slipped under the blankets beside her.

He resolutely stayed away from her, forcing himself to close his eyes.

He awoke in the middle of the night, alert, and aware of a warm body nestled against his chest. How many times he'd wanted her in bed with him, arching against him.

Lightly he touched his palm to her forehead. She was

cool to the touch. No more fever. His fingers clenched. He wanted to reach out and feel her. His sex was hard, his muscles rigid with tension.

She muttered something in her sleep and twisted away from him.

He flipped onto his back and stared up into the darkness. A first time for everything, he thought. You should take her and be damned. But he didn't move.

Byrony blinked at the bright sunlight that was warming her face. Slowly she opened her eyes. It wasn't raining. Memory suddenly flooded her.

"It's all right. How do you feel, Byrony?"

"Brent?" Her voice sounded low and gravelly, totally unlike her.

"Yes."

"But what— Oh, I remember now. Where am I?" She tried to pull herself up.

"You're with me, in my rooms above the Wild Star. Do you remember coming here last night?"

She closed her eyes, trying to rid herself of the vivid memory of Ira and Irene. "I remember running. I guess I was coming to you. I don't know."

"Here," he said. "Drink this. It's barley water, a donation from Maggie."

Dutifully she drank, then lay back against the pillow.

"You're being nice to me," she said, and stared at him.

"Yes, a miracle of circumstance. I want you to tell me what happened to you."

Why I went home early, not feeling well, you understand, and just chanced to see my husband making love to his half-sister.

Laughter welled up in her throat, not healthy laughter, but hysterical laughter. For an instant he saw the horror in her eyes.

"Byrony."

The laughter was hot and fast. Then she choked. He held her, clapped her on the back.

She breathed in deeply, trying to get hold of herself.

"Did you have a fight with your husband? Is that why you ran away? Did he hurt you?"

How angry he sounded. "No," she said. "There was no fight." She felt the headache worsening. I'm still sick, she thought, but I can't stay here.

"Then why?"

Why wouldn't he leave her alone? She could just imagine herself telling him exactly what had happened. He wouldn't believe her, of course. He'd never believed anything she'd said to him. But that wasn't the point, not really. She couldn't, wouldn't say anything until she decided what she would do. It was her problem, hers alone, no one else's.

"I have to leave now."

"Like hell you will."

"I must go home before I'm missed."

Brent, furious with himself and with her, jumped up from the bed. "Did your dear husband push you too far? Demand too much? Sully your little lady's ears?"

His anger was, oddly enough, a relief. At least his anger was something she was used to, something she understood. She couldn't handle his brief bout of gentleness.

"Yes," she said coldly. "He wanted to take me on the dining-room table and I resisted."

He turned away from her, and she watched, fascinated, as his hands fisted and unfisted at his sides. He was wearing a dressing gown. There was dark stubble on his jaws. He hadn't shaved. It must still be early. Early enough. Her mind had already begun working through possible lies she could tell Ira.

She realized suddenly that all she was wearing was one of his dressing gowns. It was warm and so very soft. It carried his scent. Slowly she eased her legs over the side of the bed. She felt weak, but the dizziness was gone. Her throat hurt still, as did her head.

"Where are my clothes?"

"Ruined. Maggie will lend you something."

"The duchess."

"You insult her and I'll thrash you silly."

She gave him a tired smile. "Please, Brent, I must leave, very soon. Could you please ask her for something? I promise to return anything she gives me."

She looked so bloody defeated and alone. He left the bedroom without another word. It was Maggie who brought her clothes a few moments later. She didn't ask any questions.

"Thank you," Byrony said. "I appreciate your kindness."

The dove-gray wool gown was too short, but Byrony didn't care. Brent came into the room just as she pulled a shawl over her shoulders.

"Nero will take you home," he said. "The carriage is hired, so your husband won't recognize it. I suppose you have several believable lies to tell him?"

"I hope so."

"After this, do try to keep to your bargain. I don't relish being dragged into your sordid little adventures."

"No, it was unfair of me. I'm sorry."

"Stop acting like a whipped dog."

Byrony smiled for the first time. "Don't you mean 'bitch'?"

She turned to Maggie, whose eyes were narrowed on Brent's face. "Thank you again."

She wanted to laugh when, twenty minutes later, she crept silently into the house. No one was about. There was no one to see her. She went to her room, carefully removed Maggie's clothes, and folded them away. She pulled a warm nightgown over her head and crawled into her bed.

She wondered if Ira and Irene were sleeping together on the other side of the adjoining door.

I've got to do something, she thought yet again.

The answer was so simple, really.

She pulled the covers to her chin and slept.

THIRTEEN

Byrony paused in the doorway of Ira's study, then forced herself to pull the door quietly closed behind her and walk forward. She studied him a moment, seated behind his oak desk, before he saw she was there. He was reading a newspaper, totally absorbed. There was a quietness about him, a serenity that used to soothe her, calm her, just being in his presence. No more. Did she somehow imagine that he would look different? Now that she knew? But he didn't, of course. His fair skin, pale blond hair, only two shades darker than his daughter's, the beautifully sculptured aristocratic bones. An angel indeed, she thought. His hands had always drawn her admiration—long, narrow, the fingernails perfectly shaped. Gentle hands, hands that caressed his half-sister's body. Oh, God.

"The idiots can't really mean to do that," Ira said to the newsprint. He sensed her presence then, and slowly began to fold the paper before he looked up. "How are you feeling, my dear?" he asked, rising from his chair. "You're still looking just a bit pale. I was worried about you, you know."

"I'm fine now, Ira. Thank you." How very normal we both sound. She drew a deep breath and said, "I must speak with you, Ira."

"Of course, my dear." He was tired today, having dealt with labor disputes at the foundry the past two days. The last thing he wanted or needed was another damned household fight. "Here, sit down."

"No, I don't want to, really." How many times during the past three days she'd gone over and over in her mind exactly what she'd say to him. He touched her hand, and she jerked away.

He frowned, but said nothing.

"Ira," she said very calmly, "I know."

He remained silent, his expression telling her nothing. He knew exactly what she meant, understood her perfectly, but he said, nonetheless, "What do you know, Byrony?"

"I know about you and Irene and Michelle."

"I see." It was over, and he felt an odd surge of relief, then a coursing of fear. They'd been so careful. Had Eileen said something? No, of course she wouldn't. "May I ask how you know?"

"I saw you. Both of you, in your bed."

There was distaste in her voice, and he suddenly hated her, wanted to strike her for despising something she could never understand. But of course he couldn't hit her, he'd never struck a woman. His father had taught him very early that women were to be cherished, to be protected. Long-buried memories raced through his mind. His father and Irene's mother were dead, killed in that unexpected winter storm. They were alone in the house, and his grief had over-whelmed him. Then Irene, only fourteen but so wise, had come to him. Held him. He'd not had many women in his twenty-eight years, and never a virgin. She'd given herself to him completely, suffering her virgin's pain in silence, loving him. Forever, she'd whispered.

How odd, Byrony thought, looking at him closely. He still looks like an angel; even my new knowledge of him doesn't change that. But she wasn't blind to the pain in his eyes.

"May I ask what you intend to do?" he asked her, his voice polite, almost uninterested.

"I will do nothing. I will say nothing, if you will release me from this farce of a marriage and—"

His brief moment of relief was dashed, and his expression tightened into anger and distrust. "What is this 'and'? For a blackmailer, there must be more."

"You must continue to give my parents the same sum of money you are now sending them each month. It isn't that I care about my father, but without the money, I imagine he would quickly turn on my mother. I don't want her hurt."

"That is all you want?" he asked as he turned away from her. Don't trust her, he told himself.

"Yes, that is all."

"What do you mean 'release'?"

"I've thought about all the problems. I'm willing to leave San Francisco, willing to let it be believed that I deserted my husband and my child. Your secret will remain safe with me."

He turned again to face her and she saw that he was thinking frantically. She could see it in his eyes.

"I'm not a blackmailer, Ira, but I would ask, though, that you give me, say, one hundred dollars. I don't have any money, as you well know. I doubt I could get very far from San Francisco even if I sold all the clothes you've bought me. And I don't think it wise for me to sell the necklace you gave me at Christmas. Someone might recognize it, perhaps wonder, and ask questions."

"You have considered this carefully, I see."

"Yes, I have. I've had nothing else to do for the past three days, save think. I do not wish you ill, Ira. It's true that I do not understand your feelings for Irene, nor hers for you. But it is not for me to be your judge. There's just one more thing, Ira. I fully intend to keep in touch with my mother. If I learn that you've stopped sending them money, I will ruin you."

"I will think about it," he said finally.

Byrony left the study without another word. She closed the door behind her and sagged against it. She was trembling with relief. What had she expected him to do? Scream at her, try to justify his relations with his half-sister? Ira, the consummate gentleman. God, it was over. She left the house and rode her mare to the ocean. It wasn't raining, but there was a high wind, and she felt grains of sand whipped against her face, stinging her eyes.

It didn't surprise her at all to see him there, astride his big Arabian stallion, still and alone.

"Hello, Brent," she said, wishing the sight of him didn't bring her such pain. His thick hair was tousled by the stiff ocean breeze, and his eyes roamed over her.

He said nothing for several moments, merely studied her face. "You are all right?"

"Yes, I'm fine. Just a bit of a cough left, but nothing more." She climbed off Thorny's back and walked to the edge of the water. Her booted foot crunched on a shell, and she leaned down to pick it up. She examined the pink striations with great concentration, fully aware that he was standing behind her.

She turned slowly. "I hoped you would be here. I wanted to thank you for taking care of me."

"You gave me no choice. I couldn't very well leave you in the mud."

"No," she said, smiling, "I don't suppose you could."

"You still aren't going to tell me what happened, are you?"

"No. I can't."

Brent turned away from her, striking his riding crop

against his thigh. He'd ridden out here for the past two days, like a damned fool. But he hadn't been able to help himself. "Did you manage a believable lie for your dear husband?"

"I had several prepared, but no one saw me come in. No one even knew I'd been gone."

"Don't forget them. I'll wager you'll have need of them in the future."

She said, surprised, "Why should I?"

He wanted to shake her. "When you take another lover, Mrs. Butler."

She drew back her hand and slapped him hard.

Her head snapped when he slapped her back. She gasped, more in surprise at his action than in pain, though her cheek stung.

"Damn you," he said, and jerked her into his arms. He kissed her fiercely, not a lover's kiss, but a furious man's punishment. She felt his hands in her hair, felt his lips gentle as they touched her jaw, her cheeks, her nose. He was devouring her. He was marking her.

Byrony stopped struggling. She felt his teeth nibbling on her lower lip, felt his tongue try to probe between her lips. "Open your mouth," he said.

She did. He didn't thrust his tongue into her mouth, or savage her, but slowly, and very gently, he entered her mouth, then withdrew, giving her time to get accustomed to him. Brent felt the exact moment she responded to him, and something deep within him stirred. She gave a small cry of surprise, then willingly pressed herself against him, rising on her toes to fit herself better against him.

I've gone mad, he thought. Utterly mad. He stopped kissing her, looking down at her parted lips, moist from him. She was trembling. She wanted him. At last. She opened her eyes, and he saw they were filled with disappointment that he'd stopped. Dreamy eyes.

"I want you, Byrony," he said, pressing his mouth against her temple. "Not here. Tonight. Come to me tonight."

The marvelous new sensations that had been crashing through her body abruptly stopped. She shook her head, trying to clear her mind.

"Say yes to me. I'll give you pleasure, more pleasure than that old man you're married to ever gave you. More than your other lovers."

Tears stung her eyes. So many lies, so many deceptions. Very softly she said, "I've never had a lover."

She saw the flash of disbelief in his dark eyes. So blue they were like midnight without a moon to lighten them. Eyes that mirrored his thoughts, at least in this moment.

"I've never had a lover," she repeated.

His hands tightened on her shoulders. "I don't want your lies. I don't care if you've had a dozen other men. They don't matter. All that matters is that I have you." Suddenly he laughed deeply. She watched the muscles contract in his throat. "Shit, I wouldn't care if you had the damned pox."

"Stop it, Brent," she said very calmly, very precisely.

She was stiff now, unyielding. He'd let her desire fade. Her eyes were clear, her expression unreadable.

"Let me go," she said.

He dropped his hands. "Are you frigid, Mrs. Butler? Is your passion all an act? Or is your coldness an act? Do you like to tease men, make them crazy with lust before you let them take you?"

She raised her hand, but he grabbed her wrist in an iron grasp. "Be glad I stopped you, Byrony. I'm very close to taking you right here. The way I'm feeling right now, I seriously doubt you would enjoy it."

Suddenly he jerked her hand downward and pressed her fingers against his sex. "Does that please you, Byrony, to feel how much I want you? Does it make you feel powerful?"

She was silent with shock. She felt him straining against her hand. A man. It felt hard, alive, dangerous, and terrifying. And so hot. She felt the heat of him through his clothes. Her fingers clutched inward, closing around him, and his moan shocked her.

He was panting, his whole body shaking with need. When she jerked her hand away, he managed to focus on her pale face, on her wide, uncomprehending eyes.

Another act, damn her. "Your hand is nice, Mrs. Butler, as I'm certain you've been told before. I would prefer your mouth, of course. Are you skilled with your mouth and that pink tongue of yours?"

"I don't know," she said. She had a sudden vivid image of her on her knees in front of him, taking that part of him into her mouth. How could she possibly do that? He'd felt so hard, so large, against her hand.

"It's a quite acceptable way, as you know, to pleasure a man and avoid pregnancy. Perhaps you are not so skilled. I would be delighted to instruct you. Tonight, Byrony. I want you to come to me tonight. With all the lies you've prepared for your husband, it shouldn't be so difficult."

His words flowed over her. Why, she wondered, did she continually think about him, want to see him, be with him, when he did nothing but insult her? All he wanted from her was her body. He wanted nothing else. For an unwanted instant her body reminded her of the startling sensations he'd made her feel. Why not go to him before she left?

"I can't," she said, not in response to his words, but in answer to herself.

"I'm not a whore, Mr. Hammond."

He grinned at her. "No, of course you're not. Whores, my dear girl, are really quite honest."

"I'm leaving San Francisco."

Brent froze, undefined thoughts, feelings, and pain racing through him at her stark words.

"I suppose I wanted to see you one last time before I left. Why, I don't know. Perhaps I just wanted to thank you again for helping me that night." She shrugged. "Well, now it doesn't matter."

"Why did you come to me that night? Why?"

She said quite honestly, "Because for some inexplicable reason a part of me trusts you completely. I'm really quite a fool, I suppose. But you did help me, and I thank you for it. Now, good-bye, Mr. Hammond."

"Why?" he yelled after her. "Why did you want to see me again? Not just to thank me, I know." She paused a moment, but didn't turn back.

He stood on the beach, the soothing sounds of the lapping waves in his ears, watching her climb onto her mare's back. She never looked back.

"Where is she?"

"Eileen said she was eating dinner in her room. We needn't worry about her. What are we going to do, Ira?"

"Have we a choice? She is willing to leave. I will divorce her quietly. Then we will be free, Irene. And our child."

"Will we?"

He was arrested by the odd note of bitterness in her voice. "Of course. I believe Byrony."

"Then you are a fool, Ira. Does she plan to return to her father's house in San Diego?"

"She didn't say, but I'm certain she won't. She hates him, and Madison DeWitt, well, he's an animal."

"Just what do you think will happen when she runs through the money you'll give her? Become a shopgirl? Make bonnets, for God's sake?"

"She isn't a bad girl, Irene," he said patiently. "I know,

love, that you've had problems, the two of you, but I've never seen her behave viciously or maliciously."

"There will be talk, awful talk. You speak of a quiet divorce. It won't be possible, Ira. We'll be dragged through scandal."

"You know as well as I that the woman is the one blamed. And Byrony will be seen as deserting not only me but also her child."

"People will wonder why she left, and of course, she won't be here to blame. I don't like it, and unlike you, I don't trust her. She will always be there, and we will always wonder and worry."

Ira sighed deeply, and thrust his hands into his trouser pockets.

"We must protect Michelle."

Ah, his baby. He would do anything to ensure that she was safe. Anything. "What are you saying, Irene?" he asked finally, meeting her eyes.

The jealousy she felt toward Byrony threatened to choke her. She couldn't simply blurt out what she wanted to do to the little bitch. She was a threat. She would be a threat forever. She'd seen Ira softening over the months toward her. She'd been terrified that he would treat her as his wife indeed.

"She mustn't leave," Irene said.

"She will leave, Irene. She won't stay here, not after—"

"I realize that." She rose from her chair and walked into his arms. She rubbed her cheek against his shoulder, feeling the tension in his body begin slowly to ease. He hugged her to him, and she felt his desperation, his fear, his love.

"I think she should die."

He shoved her away, his face pale with shock. "I am not a murderer," he said.

"And when she spends the money, do you really believe

she won't return? Won't continue to threaten us? Ira, for God's sake, think of Michelle."

"I am not a murderer," he repeated.

She knew him well, knew he wouldn't change his mind. She wondered vaguely if she could cause Byrony's death. He was gazing at her with something akin to horror in his eyes. She felt herself go pale, and quickly said, "No, no, of course neither of us could do it." She threw herself against him and sobbed softly. "I'm so afraid, Ira. So very afraid."

"I know, my darling, I know."

I love him, she thought, but he is sometimes weak. I must protect what is ours. I must protect my child. "Ira," she said, gulping down her sobs, "I think I know what we must do."

That night, Brent lost nearly a thousand dollars to James Cora. He tried drawing to an inside straight, but couldn't manage to bluff his way with the damned three of diamonds he'd been dealt. He drank steadily, and occasionally cursed vilely, for no particular reason that James Cora could see.

"My dear fellow," Cora said, leaning back in his chair as Brent scraped up only about a hundred dollars from the center of the table. "Surely you could have won a bit more if you'd been paying the least attention. Three kings. Lord, I only had a pair of jacks. Colin over there was ready to go the limit with his queens and eights."

"I'm a fool," Brent said in the very precise voice of a man who'd drunk too much and was trying to act sober.

Cora laughed, lit one of his thick cigars. "Woman trouble, I'll wager. No, don't try to deny it. I've far too much experience, you know. Lord, what Belle hasn't taught me."

"She's a bitch and a liar."

"Ah. I trust you're not referring to Belle? No, of course not. Do I have the pleasure of knowing this paragon?"

Brent got a belated hold on himself. "No, you don't."

"You lie as poorly as you're playing tonight, old fellow. Look, one woman's as good as the next. I'll continue taking your money, but you really aren't much sport. Go see your Celeste. When you plunge that sex of yours into her, just shut your eyes. You'll see anything you want. Elephants, birds, anything."

Brent grunted, and drank the rest of his whiskey.

"Keep swilling that rot, and you'll barely be able to stiffen your tongue."

Brent laughed, he couldn't help himself. "You've a big mouth, Cora."

"So Belle tells me," he agreed, grinning.

"I don't need your advice. Lord knows, I've had my share of women and their shenanigans."

"All right," James Cora said agreeably. "Here come two big spenders. They'll not take you for more than ten dollars. Hey, Del, Dan. Come on over, boys. I've got a piss-ass gambler on my hands who's lost everything but his boots."

Del Saxton cocked a brow at Brent. "You look like shit," he said.

"Thank you, Saxton." He cast a blurry eye toward Del's partner, Dan Brewer. "Sit down, don't just stand there looking like an ass."

"Same to you, Hammond."

"Maggie told me I'd find you here," Del said, sitting next to Brent. "She's a bit worried about you."

"Damned women. Tell her to mind her own business."

"My, you've got a foul mouth tonight," Dan said.

Brent wanted a fight, but not with Del. Lord, he was making a fool of himself. And it was all her fault. "I'm sorry, Del," he said, drawing a tired breath. "Excuse my damned mouth. Shit, I don't know what I'm even doing here."

"Losing lots of money," Del said. "By the looks of it. Look, Brent, you want to talk about it?"

Brent got unsteadily to his feet. "Nope. You might be my partner in that shipping business of yours, Saxton, but you're not a priest. Now, gentlemen, if you'll excuse me, I think I'll go find less demanding company."

"What happened to him?" Dan asked as he watched Brent walk very slowly and very carefully between the tables to the front door of the El Dorado.

"Your guess is as good as mine," Delaney Saxton said. "Since we're here, you want to lose your roll of dimes?"

FOURTEEN

"Celeste, just keep your hands to yourself. I'm not going anywhere, none of me."

She gave a soft, amused laugh. Brent was sprawled in a large overstuffed chair, his legs stretched out in front of him. She unfastened the rest of the buttons on his trousers and gently closed her fingers over him again. "Such a little problem," she said, stroking him.

"Thanks a helluva lot for the compliment."

"My little *amour* doesn't realize what pleasure is in store for him."

"Your little *amour* is in the throes of a drunk. Why don't you pour me another drink and keep your compliments to yourself?"

"I am a woman, Brent, not a miracle worker," Celeste said. "Another drink and he would be as the dead. Now, hush."

Brent sighed and closed his eyes.

"Ah, not so very little now," Celeste said a short time later with satisfaction, raising her face to his. "Come, let me undress you."

"I don't want to move. I don't want to think. I don't want to have sex."

"So stubborn. What happened, Brent? No one is gambling anymore?"

"Yeah, me. I lost a thousand dollars to Cora."

"Very bad shape," Celeste said, shaking her head. She regarded her handiwork and frowned. It took her a good ten minutes to get him stripped and into her bed. He cursed her, cursed the world, and fell, finally, sprawled spread-eagled.

"Now," Celeste said, easing over him, "I'll see to it that you stop your vile curses and moan just a little."

Instead of moaning as he should, Brent muttered, "I'm a fool, a randy goat, with no sense at all. She's nothing to me and soon she'll be out of my life and my mind. Stubborn, foolish, so beautiful—"

He moaned finally when she eased him deep within her. He raised his hands to clasp her hips, and Celeste, looking down at his restless face, asked softly, even as she moved over him, "So stubborn? You mean she won't let you bed her? Your Byrony?"

Brent arched up, his fingers digging into her hips. "No," he cried. "Christ, you women have memories like traps. Stop raping me, Celeste."

She slowed, her movements torture. "Hush, *mon cher.* You enjoy and forget that other woman."

He did, for at least five minutes. He fell into a drunken stupor, but Celeste pulled him against her breasts, stroking his hair. His snores filled the silence of the room. My mighty man has fallen hard, she thought, and he probably won't ever admit it to himself. She didn't love him, but she was fond of him, and accounted him an excellent and quite generous lover. He'd sworn up and down, many times, that he would never marry, never let a woman get her clutches into him. "You poor fool," she murmured, stroking her hands over his back. What had she meant when he said that she would be out of his life soon? Was she leaving? Was this the reason for his drinking?

"We will make all the necessary arrangements for you this week, Byrony," Ira said.

The three of them were sitting at the breakfast table, tense and silent until Ira had spoken.

"You will abide by my wishes, Ira?"

"Yes, certainly."

"You've given him—us—little choice," Irene said.

Byrony took a bite of scrambled egg before she said, her voice filled with irony, "Can you imagine my remaining here, Irene? If you were I, wouldn't you want to leave, demand to leave?"

"You have a very easy life," Irene said. "You have the Butler name, all the clothes you want, social position—" She broke off at the incredulous rage she saw on Byrony's face. "Well, I can't imagine you being content as a shopgirl."

"At least there won't be any more lies, will there?"

"One gets used to lies," Irene said.

Not an hour after breakfast, Byrony felt a wave of nausea. She clutched at her stomach at a sharp cramp, but it passed. The remains of the influenza, she thought, drawing a deep breath.

She accompanied Ira and Irene to church, as was their habit. After the service, she spoke to Chauncey and Del, agreeing to have lunch with Chauncey on Tuesday, exchanged pleasantries with Agatha and Horace Newton, and watched uncomfortably when Saint nodded politely to her, then studied her closely. She intended to spend the afternoon riding Thorny, but she felt so weary after lunch that she went to bed instead.

"Are you certain you've recovered from your influenza?"

Ira asked her at breakfast the next morning, concern in his voice.

"Perhaps not entirely," Byrony said. "I feel a bit tired."

"Should I call on Saint? See if he can come by?"

"Oh no, it's not necessary. I think I'll just rest a little." She toyed with her jam-covered toast. "I would like to leave by Friday, Ira," she said.

"Yes, you shall," he said.

"He's mean as a rattlesnake," Maggie said to Saint. "Say hello to him and he looks at you like you're calling his honor into question."

Saint grunted, then resumed his train of conversation before Maggie had interrupted him. "I don't know what to do about Felice, except dose her on a little laudanum every month like I've been doing. She's always had bad cramps, she tells me. She's concerned that her profession might be making it worse."

"Silly girl," Maggie said. "How about a cup of coffee?"

He nodded. "Black, Maggie, please."

When she was seated across from him, each of them with a cup of coffee, she continued her own train of thought. "I know it has something to do with Byrony Butler. Celeste, who has the warmest heart and the loosest mouth, told me that Brent was mumbling about 'her leaving.'"

Saint's head jerked up, just as Maggie had suspected it would. "That's ridiculous," he said, and immediately closed his mouth. God, ethics were tough. Where did one draw the line? Maybe it would be best if Byrony left. The poor girl deserved something out of life, something besides pretending to be the mother of another woman's child. But Ira seemed so solicitous of her, at least he had at church yesterday. Jesus, they appeared the perfect couple.

"Would you talk to him, Saint?"

He heard the concern in Maggie's voice, felt the same

concern himself. He sighed deeply. "It's none of my business, Maggie. None at all."

"You're his friend, aren't you?"

"Yep, and as his friend, I won't pry."

"Just wait until he turns on you. Then you'll want to do something, I wager."

"What will you wager, Maggie?" Brent said from the doorway.

Maggie jumped. "Can't you knock, Brent? Why, Saint and I might have been doing something very private."

Saint choked on his coffee. He looked up as Brent crossed the room. He looked different, drawn, weary. He'd lost weight.

"I wouldn't see anything I haven't already seen a hundred times," Brent said, sprawling uninvited into one of Maggie's velvet chairs. "From the guilty look on your face, Maggie, my wager would be that you've been gossiping. Of course, all women are just born that way, aren't they?"

"Don't be so nasty, Brent," Maggie said.

He cocked a dark brow at her. "Me, nasty?"

"The nastiest bastard I've seen in a long time."

"Let's have some peace, you two," Saint said, raising his hand.

"How do you spell that?" Brent said.

Saint frowned. Maggie was quite right. Brent was behaving outrageously. He said "I ran into Ira Butler this morning." He hadn't, but he wanted to see Brent's reaction.

It was swift in coming. Brent stiffened in his chair, his eyes narrowed, and he said through his teeth, "What the hell was that bastard doing?"

"Search me," Saint said, and rose. "Thanks for the coffee, Maggie. Felice should wake up feeling just fine. I'll see myself out. Brent, I've some free advice for you—medical advice, of course. Stop drinking."

"Go to hell."

"A saint in hell? Impossible."

Chauncey faced Eileen at the front door of the Butler house.

"I would like to see Mrs. Butler," she said again, wondering why in the world the woman was blocking her way.

"Mrs. Butler is ill, Mrs. Saxton. The doctor won't let her see anyone."

"Ill? What is wrong with her?"

Eileen shrugged. "You'll have to ask the doctor, Mrs. Saxton. All I know is that she keeps to her bed."

"Is Mr. Butler here?"

"No, ma'am. I must go now, Mrs. Saxton." And with that, Eileen closed the door in Chauncey's face.

"Of all the bloody nerve," Chauncey said as she returned to her carriage. "Let's go home, Lucas. Mrs. Butler appears to be ill, and no one can see her."

Lucas frowned over Chauncey's head as he gently assisted her into the carriage. "Still the influenza, ma'am?"

"I don't know. I don't understand it at all. She was supposed to have lunch with me today. She must be very ill indeed not to send me a note."

"Well, you mustn't worry, Miss Chauncey," Lucas said. "Mr. Del wouldn't like it."

"I know. He thinks this is the very first baby to be born."

But Chauncey didn't forget about Byrony and mentioned it to Del that evening. When she finished, she asked, "What should we do?"

"Do?" he asked. "If she's ill, I would imagine that Saint is seeing to her, Chauncey. Why are you so worried?"

Chauncey fretted with the fringe on her shawl—an item Del insisted she wear in the evenings to protect her from the nonexistent drafts in the house. "The Butlers' servant, Eileen. She acted funny."

"Tell you what, sweetheart. I'll ask Saint what the trouble is. Tomorrow. All right?"

"Yes, thank you. I saw Lucas kissing Mary," she added, a twinkle in her eyes.

"Oh Lord, now this is a story that I want to hear. Is it time for me to haul Lucas off to a corner and demand his intentions? Shall I prime my shotgun?"

"You're being silly."

"You're probably right. Mary can handle him quite well without our interference. She is one tough woman."

"He's up in his office, Dr. Morris," Nero said. "I don't think I'd bother him if it ain't real important."

"Thanks for the warning, Nero. It's important, or I wouldn't risk my ears."

"He beat the hell out of a drunk last night," Nero added. "I had to haul him off the guy."

"Good," Saint said. "He ought to be too tired to go after my hide."

He knocked on the closed door and heard a very reluctant "Come in. What do you want?"

Saint firmly closed the door and walked into Brent's small office. He took his time seating himself.

"Well?"

"My, we're irritable, aren't we?"

"Saint, if you're here at Maggie's behest—"

"Oh no, not at all. I just wanted to hear what you know about Byrony Butler leaving San Francisco." Aha, he thought, that got his attention.

"All I know is that she's leaving. All right? Leave me the hell alone." Brent closed his eyes. He felt so tired, so miserable, he couldn't stand himself.

Saint relaxed further into his chair, crossing his long legs at the ankles. "It's odd," he said after a moment.

"What's odd?" Brent said, straightening, his eyes intent on Saint's face.

"She isn't gone."

"So," Brent said, exhaling a deep breath. "She even lied to me about that. I should have known it was all an act, all—"

"She's ill."

Brent went pale. He jumped up from his chair and strode across the room to stand in front of Saint. "What do you mean?"

"I mean that I ran into Del this morning. He told me that Chauncey went to the Butlers' house but their servant wouldn't let her in. Told Chauncey that Mrs. Butler was in bed and the doctor wouldn't let her see anyone."

"You're her bloody doctor! What's wrong with her, Saint?" Suddenly Brent drew back as if he'd been punched in the stomach. "She's pregnant again, isn't she? That is what's wrong."

"I doubt it," Saint said. "Ira hasn't called me. I don't know who's seeing to her."

Brent mentally counted the number of days it had been since he'd last seen her. Four, no, five days. She'd told him she was well again, she just had a slight cough. "You've got to go see her," he said.

Saint had already decided to drop by the Butler home. He supposed that he had to test the waters for himself. "I think I will," he said, rising.

"You will tell me what's wrong, won't you?"

"Yes," Saint said. "I'll tell you."

"Are you out of your bloody mind?" Saint couldn't believe what he'd just heard.

"I said, Saint, that my wife has her own doctor. She's being well taken care of."

"Marcus Farnsworth is a damned charlatan. He's a quack.

He knows as much about medicine as my horse. No, less. At least my horse doesn't kill people."

Ira rose from his chair. "I agreed to see you, Saint, because I thought you wanted something. I didn't agree to have you attack me or my judgment."

"Ira," Saint said, "I want to see Byrony."

"No. Marcus thinks she has brain fever. He believes that it's some sort of female hysteria."

"Bosh."

Ira strove for patience. It would be stupid to lash out at Saint. Very stupid. "Listen, Saint, Marcus knows what he's doing. I'm sorry you don't approve of him, but I do. He's helping her, I know it."

"I want to see her," Saint repeated.

He won't budge, Ira thought, studying a man he respected, liked, and, now, feared a little. He threw up his hands in exasperation. "Very well. If you wish it, come by this afternoon about two o'clock. All right?"

At two o'clock precisely, Saint was ushered upstairs to Byrony's room. Marcus Farnsworth wasn't there, which was probably just as well, Saint thought. He'd like to take a strip off that fool. Female hysteria, indeed.

Byrony was asleep. A drugged sleep.

Saint sat beside her on the bed and gently felt for her pulse, then leaned down to listen to her heart. Pulse a bit thready, heart sounded all right. Her color wasn't good. She was pale, fragile-looking.

"What'd he give her?" he asked Ira.

"Laudanum, I believe. I'd hoped she wouldn't be asleep. I wanted you to speak with her, of course. But evidently, this morning, she had a bad time. Out of her head, almost violent."

Dear God, Saint thought, frowning down at her, what the hell should he do? He brushed his fingers through his hair, his eyes never leaving Byrony's face. Dammit, it was none of his business if Irene and not Byrony were Michelle's mother.

"Tell me, Ira, what does Farnsworth think will happen?"

"He's hopeful," Ira said. "But he says this type of illness is difficult. He's asked me if he can call in a doctor from Sacramento, a man who's dealt with this kind of problem."

I'm seeing things that don't exist, Saint told himself as he rose from Byrony's bed. He was on the point of leaving when there was a soft moan from the bed. He turned on his heel and swiftly strode back to the bed.

"Byrony?"

She felt a great weight resting on her mind and on her body. It was so hard to keep her eyes open. She wanted only to sleep. But she'd heard Saint's voice. "Saint," she whispered. "I'm so thirsty."

"Of course you are, my dear," he said, and quickly filled a glass of water from the pitcher on the bed table. "Here. Slowly, now."

It took so much energy to swallow the water. "What are you doing here, Saint?"

"I was worried about you." He gently closed his fingers around her limp hand. "How do you feel?"

"Weak. So very weak."

"It's the laudanum, I expect. You'll be well in no time. Then—" He broke off. She was unconscious again. He rose, his jaw set, his mind made up. "Thank you, Ira," he said. "I think she'll be just fine soon. Yes, just fine."

"It is my hope also, of course," Ira said. He was sweating.

FIFTEEN

Byrony awoke to the sound of voices—indistinct, low, and upset. Her mind felt fuzzy, heavy, without focus. She tried to concentrate on those voices. It was Ira and Irene.

Ira's voice, worried. "Saint is suspicious, I swear it."

Irene's voice, contemptuous, dismissive. "What can he do, for God's sake? Nothing, I tell you, nothing at all."

"No more, Irene. I mean it. Whatever you're putting in her food, it must stop. I'm going to let her go. Do you hear me?"

"No, Ira, no— Please, you must listen to me."

The voices moved away.

Stop putting what in my food? Her mind cleared, and she realized suddenly that Irene was poisoning her. But that was crazy, wasn't it? Why would she? *Because they're afraid you will tell the truth about them. That you'll blackmail them forever.*

"But I promised Ira I wouldn't," she whispered. Her throat was parched; her voice sounded scratchy to her own ears.

She was fully alert now, and, thankfully, alone. She remembered Saint sitting next to her, speaking to her. What had she said?

What am I going to do?

You're going to leave, that's what you're going to do. I have to get my strength back, she thought. And I don't dare eat or drink anything. She pushed herself upright and swung her legs over the side of the bed. Slowly she rose, only to fall back, her legs too weak to hold her weight.

Byrony covered her face with her hands. She didn't cry, she was too afraid. She'd never felt so alone in her life. Why couldn't Aunt Ida bustle through the door? Tell her the Misses Perkins were here to visit. Tell her— There was no one.

You have to rely on yourself once you leave. You must begin now.

She looked toward the windows. It was late afternoon. Anytime now, Irene or Eileen would bring her something to eat. She had to pretend. Tonight, she had to be strong enough to leave tonight. She thought of the beautiful necklace Ira had given her for Christmas. She couldn't wait to sell it. I'm going to rest now, she thought. Tonight, late, I'll sneak out the window. I'll ride Thorny south, toward San Jose. I'll be all right.

She was asleep when Irene quietly opened her door and peered in. She frowned a moment, then shrugged and carried the tray of food back downstairs.

It was near to midnight. San Francisco was fogged in. It was eerily gray, the air so thick and heavy that it was difficult to make out anything beyond several yards away.

Brent rode his stallion across Market Street and cut over to South Park, to the Butler house. The fog was lighter here. He reined in just a bit down the road. It was dark, thank God, not a single light. He'd found out from Saint which room was hers. She wasn't sleeping with her husband.

He wondered briefly if Saint had any idea what his words would result in. Probably; the man was damned perceptive.

"So," Saint had said, his eyes nearly closed, "I suppose

I'll just go see her again tomorrow. Hopefully she won't be too drugged."

Brent could still remember his rage.

"Of course, it's really none of your affair, Brent. But you said you wanted to know." Saint rose, stretched as if he hadn't a care in the world, and added, "I think I'll try my hand at some rouge et noir downstairs."

Then Brent had asked him where Byrony's room was.

And Saint had told him.

"So she has her own separate room, does she? Not still sleeping with her husband?"

Saint had merely smiled at him. "Who knows?" was all he said.

Brent hadn't really questioned his own decision. He made it, and that was that.

What would she say when she saw him? Would she refuse to come with him?

He shook his head, and quietly dismounted. He tethered his stallion to one of the few pine trees and walked toward the back of the house. He stopped in his tracks, a wide smile on his face, and tossed aside the rope he'd brought. A skinny pine tree was nearly touching the side of the house, rising to the second story.

Byrony had packed a valise. She was shaking from weakness. I've got to get dressed now, she thought, I've got to. But she simply had no more strength. She sat down on her bed, looking blankly at the lone flickering candle. It would gutter out soon, she thought blankly, and there aren't any more. How can I dress myself in the dark?

She jumped at the noise. Her heart pounding, she stared toward the window. She watched it pushed open. She watched a man swing his leg over the ledge.

Brent.

His eyes met hers in that moment, and he grinned.

Byrony could only stare blankly at him, not really believing that he was here.

"Good evening, madam," he said, and swept her a bow.

"Brent," she whispered. In the next instant she stumbled off the bed and into his arms. "Are you really here? I'm not imagining you?" Her hands were clutching at his arms, his shoulders.

"I'm here."

"I didn't know what to do. I knew I had to escape, but I didn't have the strength to dress myself. The candle is nearly gone."

He held her tightly against him, not speaking for several moments. She was trembling. He felt her sag against him, and lifted her into his arms.

"You don't have to do anything now," he said as he set her on the edge of her bed. He lightly cupped her chin in his hand and raised her head. "Will you come with me?"

She looked at him as if he had asked an incomprehensible question. "I thought I was alone," she said. "Have you really come to take me away from this house?"

"Yes," he said. "I see that you managed to pack."

She was clutching at his sleeve. "Please, can we go now? Sometimes, sometimes they look in on me."

He studied her pale face for a moment. Her eyes were feverishly bright. Her long hair was pulled back and tied with a simple ribbon at the nape of her neck. He lightly touched his fingertips to her cheek. "Sit still."

She watched him toss her valise out the window. "Now, Byrony, this might be a little tricky. I'm not certain just how strong that damned tree is. Shall we give it a try?"

She nodded, and tried to rise.

"No, no." He fetched her heavy wool cloak from the armoire and wrapped it around her. "Just hang on." He lifted her over his shoulder, his arm across the back of her thighs.

Byrony closed her eyes. If this was a dream, she didn't

want to wake up. Not yet. She breathed in the scent of him, felt the strength of him.

A branch cracked. Brent cursed softly, momentarily losing his footing. But Byrony made no sound. She lay over his shoulder as if it were the safest place in the world to be. "Good girl," he whispered. "We're almost there."

He reached the ground and lowered her to her feet. "You've lost weight," he said.

She was leaning against him, his arms supporting her. "So have you."

"How do you know? You haven't looked at me."

"Your face is thinner. Have you been ill too?"

He wanted to laugh, but didn't. Maybe later. "Come, we've got to get away from here, and now." He picked up her valise.

He lifted her over his shoulder once again. She trusts me, he thought as he walked as quietly as he could toward his stallion. It was a surprising realization, given the way he'd always treated her. No, she'd trusted him before, when she'd come to him that rainy night. He managed somehow to climb on his stallion's back, holding both her and the valise.

He wanted to know why the hell her husband would want to hurt her. If indeed he had been trying to hurt her. Probably, his thinking continued, because she was going to leave him. The jealous, possessive sort. Maybe Ira was furious because she was taking their child with her. But she'd said nothing about the child, expressed no concern, nothing. He frowned, thinking that the puzzle pieces simply didn't fit cleanly together. He didn't understand her or this bizarre situation. And now he was in the middle of it. Irrevocably.

Brent pulled his horse to a halt in the alley behind the saloon. To his complete surprise, Saint came out of the shadows.

"Good evening, Brent," he said. "I was expecting you a

bit sooner, but I guess rescues take a goodly amount of time these days."

"You sneaky bastard," Brent said as he carefully dismounted, Byrony in his arms. "You knew, didn't you? You knew what I was going to do."

"Sometimes you're about as transparent as a windowpane. Take her upstairs and put her to bed. I'll take a look at her while you take your horse back to the stables. I trust no one saw you."

"No."

Brent handed Saint the valise, then shifted Byrony into his arms. She leaned her face against his shoulder.

Once she was lying on Brent's bed, Saint said over his shoulder, "Get out for a while, Brent. Let me examine my patient."

"Saint? Did I dream it or did you come to see me?"

"I saw you, Byrony," he said, smiling down at her. "You'll be well in no time, my child."

She gave him a weak smile. "Child? Why, you can't be more than seven years older. Child indeed."

"All right. Now tell me your symptoms and when they started."

She looked hesitant for a moment, then said, drawing a deep breath, "I told Ira I wanted to leave him. He agreed. Then that night, after dinner, I didn't feel particularly well. But last Sunday, I was fine again. Remember I saw you in church?"

"I remember. Did you have an upset stomach, nausea?"

"Yes. Then I started feeling so weak. I didn't know until after you'd left, I guess, what Ira and Irene were doing. I overheard them arguing." She closed her eyes a moment, blocking out the horror. "I think they were poisoning me."

"Yes, I agree," he said quite calmly. "Doubtless it has to do with the fact—well, never mind that now. Did you eat any dinner? or drink anything?"

"No, nothing."

"How about something now? I promise to taste it first."

"I'm not too hungry," she said.

"In a little while, then. Hold still now." He gently slipped his hand under her nightgown to her belly. "Does that hurt?"

"No."

"How about here?"

She shook her head.

"Good." He straightened her nightgown and rose. "Ah, here's your rescuer. She'll be all right, Brent, I promise."

"Why does she look so pale?"

"She's been in bed for five days, hasn't eaten today, has some kind of poison in her system. I think that about covers it."

"I'm going to kill that bastard."

"No. Please, Brent, don't tell him where I am. Please."

For a man who appeared by word and attitude at least to despise this particular woman, Brent, in Saint's eyes, looked stricken. He watched his friend sit beside her and take her hand between his large ones. "No, I won't. You must rest now, Byrony. Get your strength back. We'll decide once you're well again what we're going to do."

"All right." Byrony paused a moment. "I'm not alone anymore," she whispered, more to herself than to Brent.

"No," Brent said, "you're not."

She raised her hand and tentatively touched her fingertips to his jaw. "You need to eat something, Brent. Are you certain you haven't been ill?"

Brent heard a chuckle from Saint and said, "No, not at all. I'll tell you what, Byrony. I'll get us both some hot soup, something nourishing. All right?"

"Yes, all right," she said. "I don't think I would have managed to ride to San Jose tonight."

Saint stayed to make certain the chicken soup, Maggie's

own private recipe, didn't make her sick. He looked rather pleased with himself when he left an hour later.

"Thank you," Byrony said.

"I'll call on you tomorrow, Byrony. You sleep now."

"She'll be asleep in ten minutes," Brent answered for her. In fact, she was asleep when Brent returned to the bedroom after seeing Saint on his way. He stood over the bed a moment, staring down at her still face. What the hell have I done? He laughed softly at himself.

"I don't bloody believe it. That bastard."

"It would appear that he's anxious to have her back, that and to cover his tracks," Saint said.

Maggie looked toward the closed bedroom door "Where did you hear it, Saint?"

"From Del Saxton. He told me that Ira was frantic, telling everyone that his poor wife is suffering from female delusions—crazy, in other words. He's offered a huge sum of money for information about her. The poor child, he says, must be confined for her own protection. Hints of violence to herself, and all that. Pretty smart of old Ira, I'd say."

"The bastard," Brent said again.

"I just don't understand any of this," Maggie said.

Saint merely shrugged.

"Well, Brent," Maggie said, turning to him, "it looks like you've set yourself firmly in the middle of this mess. What are you going to do?"

"I haven't the foggiest notion. Any ideas?"

"First, obviously," Saint said, "Byrony has to get well again. I don't suppose you want to send her on her way until then, right, Brent?"

"I'm not a monster." Actually, he had no intention of letting her leave, ever.

"Of course you're not," Maggie said, shooting a surprised

glance toward Saint. "You rescued her. That was very noble of you, Brent."

Saint rose. "Well, I've got other patients. I hope we can keep Byrony's whereabouts a well-kept secret."

"Can you imagine Ira ever thinking that his wife was in bed in a saloon, next to a brothel?"

"Good point, Maggie. Brent, keep feeding her whenever she wakes up. And Brent, no arguments, all right? You know," he said from the doorway, "I think Del might be a help to us in this situation. What do you think, Brent?"

"I agree, but let's give it a few days before we speak to him."

Byrony slept twelve hours. Deeply and dreamlessly. When she awoke, she stretched under the covers, queried her body, and received a painless response.

"Good. You're finally back to the land of the living."

She opened her eyes and smiled at Brent. "I feel marvelous, I think," she said. "Is that food you've got? I'm starving."

She pulled herself to a sitting position. "Brent," she said, her voice tight with embarrassment, "could you leave, please?"

"Leave?" he said, frowning down at her. "Whatever for?" Then he understood and grinned. "I'm pleased that you're functioning again. I'll be in the other room. Call me if you need anything."

She discovered she was still a bit weak, but she managed to relieve herself without accident. She stared at herself for a moment in the small mirror above Brent's dresser.

"You look just fine. Come back to bed now."

She ate everything he gave her—the warm crusty bread piled with butter, the chicken soup, the thick cocoa.

She sighed, and leaned back against her pillows. "If I die now, it will be with a smile on my face," she said.

"No dying. I forbid it."

"It would ruin all the nice things you've done for me, wouldn't it?"

"Very true," he said.

"Why?"

"Why what?"

"Why did you rescue me? I didn't think you—well, you've never given me any reason to believe that—I don't understand you, Brent."

"Ah, Saint forced me into it. Convinced me that I should start paving my own private Christian road to heaven. What could I do but agree?"

"Oh."

He leaned down and wound a lock of hair around his finger. He heard her breathing quicken and felt a jolt of lust so powerful he pulled back abruptly, yanking her hair. She yelped. "I'm sorry," he said, and turned away from her. His desire for her was evident, and he didn't want her to believe that he'd saved her just so he could have her in his bed. Why *had* he saved her? Brent shook his head, and said over his shoulder, "Anytime you would like to talk about all this mess, I'm willing to listen. In fact, Byrony, I demand to know just what I've gotten myself into."

He turned then, but her eyes were lowered, staring at her clasped hands in her lap. "You've gotten yourself into nothing," she said finally. "I will leave just as I had originally planned. You will not be involved."

"Damn you, I am involved. Don't you prattle at me as if I'm some stranger off the street who just happened to pull you out of the window of your house."

"I'm sorry."

"And don't give me that ridiculous whipped-dog routine. Just tell me the truth, Byrony. That's all I ask. That night I dragged you in out of the rain—what were you doing? What had happened to you?"

"It doesn't concern you, Brent. Please. I'm very tired. I plan to leave tomorrow."

He stared at her, feeling utterly infuriated and utterly helpless. "I fully intend to beat you when you're well," he said, then turned on his heel and walked from the room.

SIXTEEN

Maggie brought her dinner that evening. She arched a brow at Byrony, saying, "Whatever did you say to Brent? He's in a snit again."

"He wants to know things," Byrony said. Her chin went up at Maggie's chuckle. "They're really none of his business."

"Well, I won't ask any questions. Would you like to get out of that bed to eat your dinner? I imagine you're feeling quite bored by now."

"That would be wonderful," Byrony said, and slipped out of bed. "Saint said as far as he could tell I was just fine now."

"Here, put on Brent's dressing gown. It's just a bit chilly in here. After dinner, would you like a bath?"

"Indeed I would." Byrony pulled Brent's dressing gown around her. It was as if part of him were next to her. His scent was in the velvet, and for a moment she inhaled deeply, closing her eyes.

Maggie watched her closely, a small smile tilting up the corners of her mouth. This *affliction,* as Brent acidly referred to Byrony Butler, appeared to be shared. Her smile disappeared. The girl was going to be badly hurt. Whatever women were in Brent's past, they'd made him wary and untrusting. But he had saved her, twice. He must feel something for her.

"What do you mean, he's in a snit again?" Byrony asked as she chewed on a bit of roast chicken.

"Did I say that? Oh dear, I should learn to keep my mouth closed."

Byrony gazed at her expectantly.

"Oh well, after you left here the first time, he was like the proverbial bear with a thorn in his paw. You appear to have the ability to disturb him excessively."

"Yes, but it isn't my fault, truly, Maggie. He thinks I'm an awful person. No, it's true, he really believes that. He's done nothing but insult me since I saw him again."

"Again?"

"I saw him first in San Diego. We didn't exactly meet, but we did speak for a little while. I thought he was a very nice man." She sighed. "So much has happened since then."

Brent paused in the sitting room just beyond the open bedroom door. He shouldn't be eavesdropping, but he was. He straightened, walked into the bedroom. "Ladies," he said. "Maggie, you have some customers. I'll stay with Mrs. Butler for a while."

Maggie rose and shook out her deep wine velvet skirts. "Never keep a customer waiting," she said, rolling her eyes. "Byrony, I'll send Caesar over with some hot water for your bath. Brent, try to maintain a veneer of civility, all right?"

"Thank you, Maggie," Byrony called after her. "She's a very nice person," she continued to Brent. "She's been so kind to me."

"But surely you disapprove of her business?" He had to keep his distance from her, so he moved quickly to lean his shoulder against the mantelpiece.

She continued eating her dinner. "I suppose," she said at last, "that men are very different from women. Actually, I'd never really thought about things like that before."

"How odd. I would have sworn that it was one of your major concerns."

"You *are* in a snit," Byrony said. She shrugged, and waved her fork at him. "Actually, I feel more comfortable when you act sarcastic. When you're nice, I don't know what to do or say."

He cursed.

"I thought only my father knew those kinds of words. And my brother, of course."

He frowned at her, thrust his hands into his trouser pockets. "I'll see that your bathwater arrives. Do you need any help?" His question was innocuous to begin with, until his mind gave him a vivid picture of her naked in his bathtub with him looking on.

"No, I'll be all right."

"Good. I'm relieved that you're looking so fit."

"Yes. I should be well enough to leave tomorrow."

"I doubt I'll be that lucky. Do I next rescue you in San Jose?"

Her chin went up. "I have only one favor to ask of you, Mr. Hammond. I have no money—"

"What very poor planning on your part. I would have thought that you'd saved quite a bit by now. Married nearly a year, right? Ira wasn't such a besotted fool, then?"

"—but I do have a very valuable necklace that I will have to sell."

"So you did manage to get something out of him?"

"Yes, a Christmas present. I would appreciate it if you would sell the necklace for me."

"Perhaps I can sell it back to your husband. Better yet, perhaps I should have a talk with your husband. Ask him why he came to detest his bride in such a short time. At least that's the way it seems. He wants you back only to have you shut up away from the world."

She stared at him. "What do you mean?"

"Saint told me that your precious husband is spreading the tale that you're suffering from delusions, female hysteria, that sort of thing. Says you're a danger to yourself and should be confined for your own good."

She was silent for many moments, her eyes on the roasted chicken on her plate. "Irene," she said. "It must be Irene's doing."

"Is he right?"

"What do you think?"

"I think you are the most maddening female it has ever been my misfortune to meet. I'll see you later, much later."

He walked from the bedroom without a backward glance. She heard the door to the sitting room slam.

Brent stood by Nero, his assistant, a huge black man who'd lost his right ear at the hands of his owner in Georgia. He trusted Nero as much as Maggie trusted his brother, Caesar. Both men had managed to escape and make their way to California the year before.

Business was good. But then, it always was. There was one fight, and the two combatants were quickly and efficiently hauled outside by Nero. Brent roamed about the huge room. He didn't want to gamble, nor did he want to drink. He wanted to go upstairs and make love to Byrony. There, he'd finally admitted it to himself, brought it into the open. What difference could it make, anyway? He had saved her. Didn't she owe him?

He shook his head. He was being a crude bastard. He felt himself stiffen suddenly. Through the front swinging doors walked Ira Butler with Stephan Bannion, a lawyer and business associate. Brent's eyes glittered. He walked to the table where the two men had just sat down.

"Good evening, gentlemen," he said. "Welcome to the Wild Star. Your first time here, Butler. Have you come to try your luck?"

Bannion answered, "Old Ira needed some cheering up. How 'bout some of your whiskey, Hammond?"

Brent signaled the bartender, then turned back to the two men. He studied Ira Butler. He did look depressed as hell. Brent's eyes fell to Ira's pale, narrow hands, an aristocrat's hands, he thought, and saw those long fingers stroking over Byrony's body. "What's the problem, Butler?" he asked. "Oh, I forgot. It's your poor wife, isn't it?"

Ira felt furious and utterly helpless. He wished he hadn't allowed Stephan to drag him here. He'd gone over and over it in his mind. She obviously had escaped out her bedroom window. But where had she gone? She hadn't taken her mare. Someone had to have helped her. But who? Why? He'd sent one of his men to Saint's house, but she hadn't been there. Was Saint hiding her somewhere? Had some of the city scum caught her and killed her? His head ached. He became aware that Hammond was talking about Byrony, and blinked. "My wife? Oh yes, my wife."

"The poor demented girl," Stephan Bannion said, shaking his head. "We've looked everywhere. Still no sign, no word of her."

"I'll find her," Ira said. "I've got to find her."

"Such a pity," Brent said. "Her illness came upon her so suddenly, didn't it? Here is your whiskey, gentlemen." He walked away, knowing that if he'd stayed, he would probably have baited Ira to the limit, perhaps made him suspect something. He also wanted to kill Butler with his bare hands.

He went upstairs, unable to stay in the saloon. He locked the door to his office and walked through his sitting room into the bedroom. Byrony was looking healthy and scrubbed from her bath. She was wearing his dressing gown over her nightgown and was sitting up in his bed, reading one of his books.

"How very comfortable you look," he said furiously. "I see you've helped yourself to everything you wanted."

Slowly Byrony closed the book, a collection of Molière's plays. "I'm sorry," she said. "I'm being very careful—"

"Just shut up," he said. "Your husband is downstairs looking the worse for wear, drowning his worries in whiskey, and swearing that he'll find you."

She turned utterly white.

"Don't worry. I didn't announce that you were upstairs in my bed."

"Did he say anything?"

"Not really. Bannion did all the talking. You're a poor demented girl, and Ira is obviously suffering tremendously with worry."

Byrony swallowed. He was downstairs. God, what was she to do? Brent was angry again, probably because he was in the middle of this damnable mess. "I'm sorry."

"If you say that word one more time, I'll strangle you."

"All right," she shouted at him, finally enraged. "What do you want me to say? What do you want from me?"

"It's really very simple. I want you to tell me the truth."

She fidgeted a moment with the bedspread, fighting the need to tell him everything. "I can't," she said finally, raising her eyes to his. "It doesn't concern you, Brent. I refuse to involve you any further in this—"

"This what?" he yelled. "I'm involved up to my neck." Suddenly he paused, his eyes darkening. "You know, Byrony," he said, watching her carefully, "you haven't mentioned your child once. You plan to desert her?"

He saw the flash of—what was it, horror?—in her eyes before her lashes came down. He pushed. "I see that you haven't spared a thought for your child. You don't care that she'll be raised by that fool husband of yours? Don't you care, damn you?"

"No, it's not like that."

"Not like what? You're as miserable a mother as you were a wife?"

"Please, Brent, don't—"

"Don't what? Lady, you're a miserable human being from all I can see."

She wailed, a high, thin sound, her hands slamming against her ears to keep out his words. She was shaking, the horror and pain so dreadful that she felt she would die with it. Sobs broke from her throat. She stared at him, unaware that tears were streaming down her face.

Brent cursed, sat down beside her, and drew her into his arms. "Stop it. Stop your bloody crying." But she couldn't.

His face twisted with his own pain as he tried to calm her. He buried his face against her neck as he stroked his hands down her back, pressing her face into his shoulder. He felt her breasts heaving against his chest, felt her delicate bones beneath his probing fingers. God, he wanted her. Now. "Byrony," he whispered, kissing her temple. "Hush, love. Hush."

She shuddered, even as she raised her face. His mouth closed over hers. He tasted her tears, felt her start of surprise. But she didn't withdraw from him. He felt the moment she wanted him, but it wasn't right, and he knew it. But he couldn't stop himself. His kisses deepened, his tongue probed to enter her mouth. When she parted her lips, he thought he would explode from the sheer pleasure of it. She tasted so warm, so sweet, so yielding.

She was his now, all his. His hands swept over her. He couldn't get enough of her fast enough.

She arched against his hands, pain, desire, astonishment, all mingling together as the urgent feelings whipped through her. His hands were on her breasts. How could that make her feel so wild?

"Please," she whispered.

Brent tried to slow himself. He'd wanted her for so long.

He wanted her pressed against him, naked flesh against naked flesh. He wanted to stroke her, kiss and taste every inch of her. Fill her with himself. He tried to pull her arms from around his back. "My clothes. I have to get off my clothes."

She didn't want to let him go. He was her anchor. He was safety, he was the source of her passion. Her fingers fumbled wildly with the buttons on his vest.

Brent managed to strip himself, despite her help. He had to rise to pull off his trousers and boots. He looked down at her and thought he would drown at the passion in her eyes. When he was naked, he yanked back the covers, slipped into bed beside her, and pulled her against him. "Oh, damn," he said, and jerked off the dressing gown. Her nightgown presented many small buttons and he ripped the gown off her.

What am I doing? The question came to her sharply, but she dismissed it, not caring. She cared only about this moment, having this man who'd haunted her since that long-ago day in San Diego. She didn't care that he would continue to despise her. She pressed her hands against his chest. He felt warm, his flesh so smooth.

She felt his rigid sex against her closed legs. He'll come inside me, she thought. He'll fill me with himself. Her body rippled with anticipation, and she whispered his name.

He couldn't get her close enough. When she said his name, helplessly, eagerly, he thought he couldn't wait. He pulled his mouth away and drew several deep breaths. But it was no good. He'd wanted her for so long. His hand stroked over her breasts and downward to her flat belly. She felt him cup her, his fingers searching, then finding. She cried out, arching upward.

She was warm, wet. She wanted him. He was shaking, he couldn't wait. "Byrony—" He said her name as if in pain. He spread her legs, and moved over her. He should wait—

give her pleasure— But he looked down into her face, saw that her eyes were glazed, saw her reach for him.

He raised her hips in his hands and slid himself slowly into her. He felt her pain before he was aware of the cause. He realized only that she was very small and that her body was fighting him. She cried out, struggled against him. He pressed forward with difficulty. Then he felt her maidenhead.

He went utterly still, his body frozen over her, his mind fighting against what he realized to be true. He stared down at her.

She cried out his name.

"No," he whispered. "Oh God, no." He tore through and seated himself to his hilt. He felt pain convulsing through her body, felt her shuddering beneath him. He reared back, beyond all reason, and let himself go. For many moments he was insensate. She didn't move.

Reality, with its enormous complications, reared its head.

"Byrony," he said, propping himself up on his elbows to relieve her of his weight.

She opened her eyes and stared up at him. Her lashes were matted with tears. Her eyes were clear, her expression unreadable.

He could think of nothing to say. He'd taken a virgin, a girl who was vulnerable, and he'd hurt her, badly.

"You can't be," he said slowly, as if the words themselves would cancel out the truth.

"I didn't know it would hurt so much," she said. "I thought it would be very nice."

"It is, just not the first time. I didn't know, Byrony."

"No, how could you?" She spoke so calmly, but her mind was reeling with what had just happened between them. She waited for his guilt to turn to anger.

"Why didn't you stop me? Why didn't you tell me you'd never been with a man before?"

"I didn't want to stop you, and I did tell you. You simply didn't believe me."

"You told me you'd never had a lover, Byrony, you had a husband and a baby." No sooner were the words out of his mouth than he realized many things. Saint, when he had examined her, had known she hadn't birthed a child. Obviously the child was Irene's. Obviously her husband had married her to protect his sister. Brent tried to pull out of her, but she clasped her hands around his back.

"No, please don't leave me."

Her words made him instantly hard, and it shocked him, this instant and intense reaction to her. "I must," he said. "If I stay inside you I'll hurt you again. No."

He came out of her. "Are you all right?" He pulled her against him, his fingers massaging her shoulders and her scalp.

"Yes."

"There's much we have to talk about," he said, wondering where to begin, what to say.

He felt her head nod slowly against his shoulder, then felt her body go slack against him. She was asleep.

Brent pulled the covers over them, and leaned over to douse the lamp beside the bed. He wanted to laugh, and it took all his will to keep still.

"You randy fool," he said to himself and the silent room. "You just took a virgin." Life was made up of the unexpected, and certainly he'd had his share of surprises, but this floored him. He remembered everything he'd said to her, all the very graphic sexual images. He realized that he knew nothing about her, nothing at all. And all she knew of him was what he had shown her.

He wasn't a good man.

What was he going to do?

Tomorrow she would tell him the truth, all of it. And if she refused? He'd make love to her until she was crazy.

Would she withdraw from him? Remember the pain and be afraid of him? He drew her closer. "Byrony," he whispered against her temple, "I'm sorry."

She mumbled something in her sleep and pressed closer, her hand fisting against his chest.

SEVENTEEN

Byrony awoke suddenly, disoriented, and aware of soreness between her legs. She frowned a moment, not remembering. She felt the warmth of him, felt his hand touching her hip. Brent moved closer to her, and she slowly turned her head to look at him.

His dark hair was tousled, his cheeks covered with dark stubble. There was a slight smile on his lips in his sleep.

I'm a woman now, she thought, and swallowed, easing slowly away from him. She felt sore and sticky. She jerked up, lowering the covers. There was blood on her thighs and on the sheet beneath her. My blood, she thought. She remembered the pain when he'd entered her. She wondered if blood signified her passage into womanhood. No one had ever told her about that. She remembered at the age of fourteen she'd begun her monthly flow. Aunt Ida had merely nodded when Byrony had told her, fear thick in her young voice, and told her, her eyes not quite meeting Byrony's, it was something she would have to bear for many years.

"What the hell happened to your back?"

She'd pulled her hair over her shoulder and unconsciously begun to weave her fingers through it to get out the tangles.

"Byrony, answer me."

She felt his fingers lightly touching her and shivered. She grabbed the covers and pulled them to her chin, but of course her back was bare to his eyes. Slowly she turned her head to look at him. "What do you mean?"

"There are scars on your back, faded, but there. Who the hell beat you?"

She'd expected his anger, indeed, was ready for it. But his anger was directed against another this time. "It was a long time ago," she said.

"Who, Byrony? That husband of yours?"

"No, Ira never touched me."

He laughed roughly, falling off into a near-moan. "God, I know that well enough—firsthand."

"It's raining," she said, staring toward the windows.

"Who, Byrony?—And yes, I see it's raining."

"My—my mother's husband."

"Your stepfather?"

"Father."

"Why?"

"I couldn't let him beat my mother," she said calmly. "Not in front of me, at any rate."

It was that acceptance in her voice that shook him profoundly.

"He'd hurt her so many times before, you see. That was why she sent me to live with her sister in Boston. To protect me. I'd only been back in San Diego for six months when I first met you."

He lay back, pillowing his head on his arms. She was still sitting up, her long hair rippling over her shoulder, the covers to her chin, her back naked. She looked so beautiful, so innocent, so accepting, that he wanted to yell.

His hands clenched, but he kept them where they were. If he touched her, he'd make love to her again. He was hard. He raised his knees slightly under the cover so she wouldn't see. She wasn't ready for that. He had no intention of hurting her again.

"I remember when I met you in San Diego," he said finally. "I spoke to that old man, my thought at the time merely to learn your name. I told you about him and what he'd said."

"Yes, I remember."

"It was all a lie."

"Of course. I told you it was."

"Why would a girl's father lie about her, Byrony?"

She made a slashing movement with her hand, and now there were bitterness and anger in her voice. "He is an animal. He called me a slut, and much worse. I had only one friend, a young Californio, named Gabriel. My father accused me of sleeping with him and carrying his bastard. He went to see Gabriel's father and extorted money from him." She paused a moment, then continued, her voice very sad and soft. "Poor Gabriel was shipped off to Spain. He was a nice boy, a friend, someone I cared about."

She shifted, then bowed her head.

"What, Byrony?"

"I have no one to ask. There's blood on me, and I was frightened. Is that natural?"

He swallowed, a shaft of pain in his belly. "Yes, it's natural. It won't happen again. Come here, Byrony." He saw the wary look in her eyes, and added quickly, "I won't make love to you again. I just want to hold you."

Still wary, she watched him as she slipped onto her back to lie beside him. He brought his arms down, and very slowly, not wanting to frighten her, drew her against his side.

She didn't know what to do with her hand, and gingerly laid it on his chest. She felt him stroking her hair, and eased, resting her cheek on his shoulder.

He said after a moment, "Then Ira Butler came to San

Diego? No, Byrony, it's time for the truth, all of it. I won't let you be hurt again, I swear it. Please trust me."

He could practically feel her thinking, arguing with herself, weighing his words now against his past actions toward her. "Yes, Ira came then," she said finally, her decision made. "He wanted to marry me. He is a distant cousin of my mother's, and very rich. I agreed to it because he signed a document stating he would pay my father so much money a month. I did it for my mother. My father, I learned quickly, isn't so violent if there is enough money for him to spend." She sighed and fell silent for a moment. Brent said nothing, merely waited. "There was nothing for me in San Diego. I begged my mother to escape with me, far away from my father, but she refused. So I accepted Ira. I remember telling you once that I'd had no choice, and I suppose it's true. At least I thought it would be, had to be, a calmer life. He was very kind to me. It was on the trip to San Francisco that he told me the real reason he'd married me. Irene was pregnant, he told me, the father of her child a married man. He'd married me to save Irene from a dreadful scandal. Her child was to be mine. I felt so very sorry for Irene and proud of Ira for being so caring of his sister. I agreed, of course."

"So that's why Butler kept the both of you in Sacramento," Brent said.

"Yes. Michelle was born and we returned to San Francisco. There began to be problems, of course. Irene didn't want me near her child. The situation was becoming dreadful. Ira tried to keep peace, but it wasn't always possible. The servants' loyalty was to Irene, not me. I was nothing more, really, than a boarder."

"That night you were ill, and I saved you from those two drunks—had you had a fight with Irene?"

To his surprise, she began to shake. He eased her onto her back, balanced on his elbow, and stared down at her. "Tell me what happened. Byrony, tell me."

"I don't know what to do."

"Tell me, Byrony."

It was as if the dam had burst, and she said, "Michelle is Ira's daughter."

He didn't understand her, not at first, and she continued, speaking quickly. "I was visiting Chauncey one evening, but I wasn't feeling well—the influenza. Lucas drove me home. There was no one about, and I can remember being surprised that none of the servants were there. I heard noises coming from Ira's bedroom. I remember thinking that perhaps Ira had the influenza too. I was worried about him. The noises— Oh God, he was in bed with Irene."

Incest, he thought, stunned, a subject never spoken of. He closed his eyes a moment, seeing in his mind's eye what she must have seen, feeling what she must have felt. "You ran from the house and came to me."

"Yes," she said. "I came to you."

"You came to me knowingly, because you trusted me."

She was nearly undone by the gentleness in his voice. She'd heard it so seldom since she'd known him. Tears stung her eyes. "Yes."

"You confronted Ira after that, didn't you?"

"Yes, I told him I knew the truth and I wanted to leave. My only demand was that he continue paying the money every month to my father. Otherwise I told him I would ruin him. I could think of no other way to protect my mother. I thought it was little enough to ask of him; considering what he'd done."

"Obviously," Brent said, "he didn't believe you'd keep your end of the bargain."

"It was Irene, I think, not Ira. That was when I became ill."

"Saint saved you."

"No, you did."

They both fell silent.

Suddenly Byrony giggled. It was so unexpected that Brent jumped. "Here I am, in bed with you. I don't have any clothes on and I can feel you."

Unconsciously he lowered his body a bit until her breasts were pressing against his chest. That elusive pain gnawed at his guts again. He closed his eyes, wishing he could also close his mind, but he couldn't. "I won't let him near you," he said. "Never again."

Her low laughter turned into a sob. "I don't know what to do now. Please, Brent, you must sell the necklace for me. I swear I'll leave. You've helped me so much—"

"Shut up. I'm getting up now," he said in a very calm voice. "If I stay here with you, I'll take you again." He pulled away from her and rolled out of bed.

He knew she was staring at him, and he was as hard as the floor beneath his feet. "Close your eyes."

For some odd reason, he was embarrassed. He'd never before had a hint of modesty with a woman, but now— "Oh, hell," he said, and grabbed for his dressing gown.

"I never thought that a man—well, you have a very nice back."

He smiled, but refused to face her. "And you, my dear, have the most beautiful breasts I've ever seen." He heard her suck in her breath, and turned to face her. "You're not going anywhere, do you understand me, Byrony? You're staying right there until I can figure out what we're going to do."

"But I must leave San Francisco."

"Maybe," he said. "Stay put."

He left her thirty minutes later, having said only, "I'll be back soon. It's not that I don't trust you, but Nero is downstairs. Continue reading my books."

He could only shake his head at his own stupidity. There was a driving rain and he felt water drip down his neck. It was a ten-minute walk to Saint's house on Clay Street. His housekeeper, Lydia Mullins, ushered him into the small sitting room.

Saint came into the room, wearing an old dark blue dressing gown. He merely stood in the doorway, a thick brow cocked at Brent. "Well?"

"I need your help," Brent said simply.

"Not until I've had some coffee," Saint said. "I was up half the night bringing a child into the world. The child died, dammit."

"I'm sorry," Brent said.

"Not anybody's fault."

Brent found that the strong black coffee calmed him.

"All right," Saint said, seating himself comfortably across from Brent, "tell me all of it."

"You knew Byrony hadn't birthed that baby," Brent said.

"Yes."

"Why didn't you tell me?"

"It wasn't any of your business. I am a doctor, you know, ethics and all that. Now that you've got that out of your system, tell me what's happened."

"I made love to Byrony and discovered that she was a virgin. She isn't now, needless to say."

"Ah."

"The child is Irene's."

"I imagined as much."

"The father is Ira. I don't think you imagined that."

Saint sucked in his breath. "Good God," he said softly. "So that's why—"

"Yes, that's why. It took me long enough to get the entire story out of Byrony, but there it is. She wanted to leave him, swore she wouldn't say a word, but of course neither Ira nor Irene believed her. Now the question is: what to do?"

Saint uncrossed his legs, stretched them out in front of him, and crossed his ankles. "An interesting problem," he said.

Brent drew a deep breath. "She still insists that she wants to leave."

"That doesn't seem like such a good idea to me," Saint said, his lashes nearly closing, making him look sleepy.

"No, it doesn't. Indeed, it's out of the question. The girl has no more idea of how to survive than a puppy."

"And she has no money, does she? Of course, it's conceivable that she is pregnant—now." Saint grinned at his choice of words.

Brent stared at him blankly. He hadn't thought. "Shit," he said.

"There is that," Saint agreed. "And she's legally married. Quite a problem, I'd say."

"The marriage wasn't consummated. It can be annulled."

"Hmmm," Saint said. "I think, my boy, that we'd best go see Del Saxton. Among the three of us brilliant specimens, we ought to come up with a reasonable solution."

Del, when presented with the facts, turned to Saint.

"The fact of the matter is, Del, that the marriage needs to be annulled. Byrony needs to be freed."

"Why?" Del asked.

"So Brent can marry her, of course," Saint said.

Brent leapt up from his chair across from Del's desk. "Marry her. Jesus, Saint, I never—"

"Oh, I take it then that she, the deceitful, cunning woman, seduced you, Brent?"

"No. I don't want to get married." Even as he shouted the words, he knew it wasn't true. He'd wanted her for so long, and it wasn't just lust. She stirred emotions and feelings in him that scared him to death.

"Too late. It appears to me that you understand procreation well enough. You want your child born a bastard?"

"Who said she'd get pregnant? It was just once, Saint."

"Calm down, Brent," Del said. "Saint, stop poking him. The man's a wreck already. Now, listen, both of you. I have

196

a friend, a very powerful friend, in Sacramento. The marriage can be annulled there. There's going to be a scandal, of course, no way around it. What bothers me is that Byrony will be the one to suffer the gossip—a wife deserting her husband and child. Unless—"

"Unless," Brent said, "we force Ira to admit that the child is Irene's." He turned to Saint. "I see no reason for the incest to come out, if Butler agrees to the annulment. Do you think anyone would draw that conclusion?"

"Unlikely. Weren't you shocked, disbelieving at first?" Saint asked.

"So," Del said, leaning back in his chair, "there will be a scandal all right, but the two of them won't get what they really deserve."

"Of course," Saint said, "Byrony could simply leave San Francisco, and the scandal wouldn't touch her. She wouldn't be here."

"No."

"Well, Brent, you don't want to marry her, you just said so. Of course, even if she isn't pregnant now, how could she ever marry? Women are funny about that, you know. They're raised to believe they should be virgins when they marry. I suppose she could say she's a widow—"

Brent writhed in guilt. But it was more than feeling like a rutting bastard for taking her virginity. Oh no, he'd fine and fairly caught himself. He rose from his chair. "She's not leaving," he said, his decision made.

"Good," Saint said. "I suggest, gentlemen, that we waste no more time. Let's track down Ira Butler."

EIGHTEEN

Eileen reluctantly ushered the three men into the Butler drawing room. Both Ira and Irene were present, and it was her face that drew Brent's attention. She's scared silly, he thought. And they both know. Oh yes, they know why we're here.

"Gentlemen," Ira said in a thin, calm voice. "May I ask why you have honored my sister and me with your visit?"

Del Saxton moved forward. "Do you want your sister to remain, Ira?"

It was Irene who walked forward, her hand on her brother's shoulder. "I will stay, Mr. Saxton."

"Very well then," Del said.

"We are here about Byrony," Brent said.

"So," Irene said, "the little slut came running to you. What filth did she tell you?"

"It's no use, Irene," Ira said. He sounded incredibly weary.

"What do you mean?" Irene said. "For God's sake, Ira, get a hold of yourself. These *gentlemen* know nothing."

Brent saw clearly what Byrony's life had been like. But he also saw the fear, the desperation in Irene Butler's face.

"We happen to know everything, finally," Brent said. "If

you hadn't tried to poison her, Butler, if you had but trusted her, she would never have said a word. Never."

"She ran to you, her lover," Irene said. "I know her sort—a tramp, just like her silly mother. I knew she would betray me, I—"

"That's enough," Brent said. He looked from Irene to Ira, then said, "It is time to end this farce. If you do nothing foolish, I doubt anyone will ever think that Michelle is a product of your union. But don't doubt it, you will do exactly as we say, or you won't survive."

"What is it you want?" Ira asked. He turned away as he spoke, and walked to the front windows. He appeared almost disinterested.

Del said, "The marriage will be annulled, immediately. None of us feel it precisely fair that Byrony be considered a fallen woman—a wife who's deserted her husband and child—thus you will bear the brunt of whatever scandal there is. You will admit that the child is Irene's, that the child is the result of her relations with another man, a man who was tragically killed, if you wish. I'm certain that if you put your heads together, you'll come up with a very affecting tale to justify what you did. As Brent said, I can't imagine that anyone would draw the conclusion that Michelle is the result of incest. If you do it properly, I imagine that San Francisco society will forgive your charade in a very short time."

Saint spoke for the first time. "Ira, I've known you for several years. What you've done—I don't refer to you and Irene, that's none of my business—but what you did to Byrony, well, that's tough to swallow. You hurt her badly, and I don't refer simply to your use of poison and your tale of her being insane. I have to admit that for the first time in my life I want to strangle another human being. You'll do as you're told, Ira."

"Yes," Ira said, his back still to them, "I will do as you

ask." He turned then, slowly. "I would like to know one thing," he said, his eyes on Brent. "I had no idea that Byrony even knew you, Hammond. Is Irene right? Has she been your mistress?"

For a long moment Brent simply stared at him. Then he threw back his head and laughed deeply. "My God, man, did you know your—wife—so little? If you weren't so pathetic, I'd knock your teeth down your throat."

"Please don't do that, Brent," Saint said. "Ira's got healthy straight teeth."

"She was, wasn't she, damn you, Brent Hammond." Irene shouted. "God, that's where she belongs. Running off with a gambler whose partner is a whore!"

Brent's expression became quite cruel, but his voice was an amused drawl. "You amaze me, Miss Butler, you truly do. You appear so determined to paint Byrony a slut—I would suggest that you look to yourself instead. As for Maggie, she is honorable and loyal and you aren't fit to be in the same room with her. For your information, Butler," he added, "your wife was trying to escape you that night. I was fortunate enough to be on hand to help her."

Ira felt ill. Indeed, he looked so white, Saint moved to him. "No," Ira said quietly. "Living a lie—well, one isn't always rational. So many things to regret— We will do as you wish. Don't send Byrony back to her parents. Her father is cruel. He would abuse her endlessly."

Del said, slanting a look toward Brent, "Who knows? Perhaps it would be best for her to return home. After all, what does she have here?"

Brent said very clearly, "As soon as the annulment is granted, I'm going to marry her."

Byrony sat in Brent's favorite chair, her legs tucked beneath her, a book lying unread on her lap. Nero had come to check on her once, to make certain, she supposed, that she wasn't preparing to bolt. Maggie had shared lunch with her. But now she was alone again.

When have I ever really not been alone? she wondered. And now, soon, she would be alone again. She shook her head to clear her mind of the endless stream of questions that had no answers.

She heard the door to the outer office close, heard Brent's footsteps coming toward the bedroom. It was odd, she thought, that she knew it was he, recognized the sound of his step. She met his eyes as he stepped into the bedroom. For a long moment they simply stared at each other, not saying anything.

Brent was looking at her with new eyes. He never denied that he'd been attracted to her from the first moment he'd seen her in San Diego, and no longer did he deny that he had endless lust for her. He'd admitted he felt fond of her, protective of her. The other, deeper, swirling feelings, he kept at bay. Yes, his fondness for her would be enough. It would not exceed that.

"How do you feel?" he asked, not coming into the room.

"I'm fine, really."

"Good. Maggie told me that you ate a healthy amount for lunch."

"Yes."

He walked to her. "What is this? Don't shrink away from me. I of all men won't hurt you, God knows."

Her eyes dropped, and she fiddled with the leather binding on the novel in her lap. "I know you won't," she said. "It's just that everything is such a—mess. I don't know what to do."

"You don't have to worry about anything now. The mess is in the process of being cleared up."

"What do you mean?"

"Saint, Del, and I met with your husband and sister-in-law. Del is leaving today for Sacramento to have your marriage annulled. As for Ira and Irene, they will admit that the child is Irene's, the father I suppose will become some sort of military hero who was killed before he and Irene could be married. You will not be blamed."

She could only stare at him. "But it isn't necessary, really, Brent. I have no intention of remarrying, I assure you. I'm leaving San Francisco. There's no reason for them to—"

"Be quiet, woman." He frowned down at her, turned, and walked to the fireplace, leaning his shoulders against the mantelpiece.

"Brent," she said very calmly, "you know that I am leaving San Francisco. Why have you forced Ira to do this?"

"You're not leaving," he said shortly, almost angrily. "You, Byrony, have no more sense than a hummingbird. Just how do you think you'd survive anyway? The precious proceeds from that bloody necklace wouldn't last long, you know."

She raised her chin, a gesture he now recognized as digging in her heels. "I will do just fine, thank you. I do not intend to be anyone's *affliction* in the future."

Here he was making her angry. He hadn't intended to. Where had she heard that "affliction" business? "Byrony, I want you to marry me."

The novel fell to the floor with a sharp thump. She jumped from the chair, her fists at her sides, and stared at him in utter disbelief.

Some reaction, he thought, taking in her flushed face, to his very first proposal of marriage. "Yes," he repeated, "I want you to marry me just as soon as your marriage to Ira is annulled."

"Why?"

"Well, that's short and to the point, isn't it? I venture to say that there are many very valid reasons."

What had he expected anyway? For her to fall to her knees in thanksgiving to him?

"I don't think it would be a good idea," she said finally. "You don't like me, not really."

That made him laugh. "Not like you? I can scarcely keep my hands off you."

"That's not the same thing, is it?"

He saw the pain in her eyes, the need for reassurance. Dear God, she thought so little of herself. "Do you care for me, Byrony?"

That damned gentle tone of voice. He used it to such devastating effect. "Yes," she said. "I'm probably the biggest fool alive."

He had no intention of reminding her that she could possibly be pregnant with his child. He could just imagine how she would react to that.

He shoved his shoulders away from the mantelpiece and walked to her. He clasped her shoulders. "Byrony," he said in that same gentle voice, "I care for you too, you know. I want you to be my wife. I will try to be a good husband to you."

He meant what he said. He wasn't certain he could manage to keep that promise, but he intended to try. When she raised her eyes to his face, he saw that she believed him. "You are so lovely," he said, and leaned down to kiss her. He felt her stiffen. "Don't be frightened of me," he said quietly against her pursed lips. "I won't hurt you, I swear it."

She thought with a sense of wonder that he was telling her the truth. He had no reason to lie to her. She wanted to tell him that she more than cared for him. She wasn't exactly certain when it had come about, but she loved him. She pulled back slightly so she could look up at him. "Will you continue to insult me?"

Brent cupped her face in his hands, his thumbs lightly caressing her jaw, and gave her a crooked smile. "What will you do if I continue in that bad habit?"

"I don't know," she said honestly. "I have so little

experience with men. You are so unpredictable, but you would never hurt me, would you—like my father?"

He felt pain in his gut, and for a moment he couldn't speak. He pulled her tightly against him, but this time he felt no lust for her. "No one will ever harm you again."

"You truly wish to marry me?"

"Yes, I truly do. Will you?"

She smiled, a dazzling smile that quickly made his lust return with startling force. "Yes," she said. "Since you beg so gallantly—"

"Byrony."

"Byrony what?"

"If ever I want to insult you, I'll take you to bed instead."

"Perhaps that wouldn't be too bad."

His eyes went to his bed. He pictured her naked, felt her flesh beneath his hands. He swallowed convulsively, but held himself in control. It wouldn't be right, or fair to her. He said, "I hope Del Saxton returns quickly from Sacramento."

A week later, they were married at Delaney Saxton's house. Byrony was wearing one of Monsieur David's creations, a white satin gown that was sewn over with at least five pounds of lace. I'm married, really married, she thought, staring about the Saxton drawing room. The Newtons were there, Saint Morris, Tony Dawson, Dan Brewer, Maggie, and of course Chauncey and Del. She knew she should be ecstatic, but each time she'd left Brent's apartment, she'd seen people staring at her, seen the speculation in their eyes. She'd said nothing to Brent. She'd seen him rarely, as a matter of fact.

"Well, wife, what do you think?"

She jumped, spilling some of her champagne. He looked so handsome, she thought. His suit was pearl gray, as was his vest, his shirt white as new snow.

"It's fine," she said. "Everyone has been so kind."

"What did you expect—a stone-throwing party at sundown?"

"My ring, it's beautiful."

"I'm glad you approve," he said, his voice equally as formal as hers. "It belonged to Chauncey and I bought it from her."

"Chauncey? Not Del?"

"Some women do have money, you know," he said, not meaning anything by his words.

And I have nothing, she thought as she watched him turn to speak to Dan Brewer, Del's banking partner.

"What's this, Mrs. Hammond? Grim thoughts already?" Maggie grinned at her, patting her arm.

"Oh, Maggie! I didn't know—that is, I was just thinking that I don't have any money. I was wondering what it would be like to be rich, to have real control over your life."

"Few women ever have that feeling, my dear. Not unless husbands die and leave them money, or they endeavor to go into business for themselves. But that, Byrony, I wouldn't recommend."

Maggie flinched when Byrony raised lost eyes to hers and whispered, "Then I am to sit doing nothing and accept this husband's bounty as I did the last?"

"Oh, Byrony, don't. Everything will work out all right, you'll see. May I ask you a question?"

Byrony nodded, her eyes on her new husband. He was laughing, a beautiful, rich sound. She watched his hands slash through the air as he made a point. Hands that had touched her. It seemed a long time ago, that night when he'd made love to her.

"Do you love Brent?"

"Yes," she said so softly that Maggie had to lean close to her to hear the small word. What woman wouldn't fall in love with that clever, handsome bastard? Maggie wondered.

"Well, may I join the conversation?"

"Lin's buffet is lovely, Chauncey," Byrony said.

Chauncey patted her rounded stomach. "Junior here is an obvious glutton. I thought he'd be asleep by now, but he's still jumping about. Saint told me to drink a glass of champagne to calm him down for a while."

So much for light conversation, Chauncey thought. She thought she'd been just a bit amusing. Byrony looked lost and frightened.

"Thank you for the diamond, Chauncey. Brent said you sold it to him."

"It is lovely, isn't it? The best of the lot, I thought."

At that point Delaney called out for everyone's attention to propose a toast. Byrony downed two more glasses of champagne in rapid succession.

"Am I going to have a drunk bride?"

"No, of course not."

"Good, it's time for us to leave." He turned immediately to Maggie. "You'll come back with us. I don't trust you with that lecher Dan Brewer."

"I?" Dan said. "I'm a staid banker."

"Ha," Maggie said, grinning at him. Dan flushed.

Byrony survived the constant flow of compliments and congratulations. In the carriage, she leaned her head on Brent's shoulder and closed her eyes against the wave of dizziness.

She listened to Brent and Maggie talk about this and that with the ease of old friends. A madam and a gambler. Surely this is odd, was her last thought before she drifted into sleep.

"Good grief," Brent said when the carriage pulled in front of the Wild Star. "I've got an unconscious bride on my hands."

"Just carry her upstairs, Brent," Maggie said. "The poor girl's had a very trying day."

"Perhaps," Brent said, arching his black brow at her, "but I hadn't intended for her night to be at all trying."

"Knowing your appetites, I wouldn't bet on it."

He lifted Byrony in his arms and carried her up the back stairs to his rooms. He started to shake her, when Maggie whispered, "No, why don't you just let her sleep for a while?"

Byrony awoke with a start. The room was dark. She was lying on the bed, covered with a blanket, still dressed in her wedding gown. "Oh dear," she said. Slowly she swung her feet to the floor and rose. Where was Brent? The bedroom door was closed. Why had he left her? Why had he let her sleep? She padded to the door and slowly turned the knob. Her hand paused at the sound of Brent's voice.

"Dammit, Maggie, don't preach to me about my duty."

What was he angry about? What duty?

"I simply asked if you'd spoken to Celeste. I know, my friend, that you spent several evenings with her before your marriage. I suppose you considered that the height of nobility, leaving Byrony alone until the ceremony."

Who was Celeste? Why had Brent spent evenings with her?

"Celeste has the biggest mouth," Brent said in disgust. "Can't women ever keep anything to themselves? And no, Maggie, I haven't spoken to Celeste. For God's sake, why should I?"

"A man newly married doesn't need a mistress, Brent. Surely you don't intend to be unfaithful to Byrony, or should I say, continue in your randy ways?"

"Byrony is my wife. I will treat her as my wife. I married her, didn't I? I really didn't have a choice in the matter. Come, I intend to take very good care of her. Now, Maggie, if you're quite through I think it's time I woke up my bride."

Byrony didn't move. She couldn't. Serves you right for

eavesdropping, she thought. She heard their voices move away. Maggie was leaving. Brent would come to her very soon.

My husband.

At least he was spending this night with her and not with his mistress.

Brent was shaking his head as he doused the lamps in the sitting room and locked the door to his apartments. Maggie should mind her own business. Of course he was going to speak to Celeste. The last thing he needed now was a mistress. He opened the bedroom door quietly and entered. He was smiling now as he looked toward his bed. He whispered her name, but there was no answer. He lit the lamp beside the door; he didn't want her to awaken too abruptly. As he straightened, he saw his wife standing in the middle of the bedroom.

In the next instant, the porcelain basin from the commode flew at his head.

NINETEEN

"You bastard."

He ducked the porcelain basin in the nick of time. It crashed against the wall behind him, shattering at his feet.

"Byrony. What the hell—"

The small lamp from the table beside the bed struck him on the shoulder and bounced off, breaking into two big pieces.

"Byrony, stop it. No, not my brass candlestick."

He managed to catch the candlestick at its base. In the next moment he was struck full in the chest by his leather-bound copy of *The Works of Aristophanes*.

He heard her panting, saw her raise his volume of Voltaire to hurl at him. "That's enough, dammit." He dashed toward her, ducking Voltaire. He dropped the candlestick and lunged at her. He grabbed her arms, forcing them to her sides.

"I hate you. You miserable, lying—"

He shook her until her head snapped back. "Stop it. What the devil is the matter with you?"

He was too strong for her, but still she struggled. Brent said nothing more, merely waited for her to exhaust herself. "Now," he said finally, his voice more puzzled than angry, "you will tell me why you suddenly hate me."

"Let—me—go."

"No. If you don't give a good damn about my belongings, I do." He shook her again as he stared down at her face. Tears were in her eyes, eyes wide and dark and filled with anger and something else. He gentled his voice just a bit. "What is wrong? Why am I a miserable, lying—" He stopped dead in his tracks. Damnation, she'd overheard his foolish discussion with Maggie; he knew it. "You are my wife," he said, holding her so tightly that she thought her ribs would crack. "You are my wife," he repeated again.

"Why?"

The one small word was anguished, her anger gone, buried in a haze of misery. He closed his eyes a moment, trying to remember all the stupid things he'd said.

"It was all a mistake," he began. "I didn't mean—Maggie was preaching and I—"

"Why did you marry me? Why did you lie to me and tell me that you cared for me? You had a choice, Brent, what you said to Maggie wasn't true. You had a choice."

"That isn't what I meant. You heard us talking."

"Yes. Wasn't it ill-bred of me to have woken up and eavesdropped? I suppose one deserves to hear the truth about things when one does that."

Such a short time ago he'd promised her he'd never hurt her. He'd meant, of course, that he would never hurt her as her father had—but somehow, this seemed just as bad, maybe worse.

"Let me go," she said again. "I promise I will leave *your* belongings alone."

A muscle in his jaw jumped. "I didn't mean that, precisely. They're your things too now. Even my *Aristophanes.*"

"And what about Celeste? Just what is hers?" Good God, could she be jealous? He supposed that wives should be angry to overhear their husbands talking about their mistresses. And she wasn't really a wife yet. She was a bride. It was her wedding night and she'd heard him talk about his mistress.

"Celeste," he said very precisely, "is absolutely none of your concern. She has nothing to do with you. Nothing. Now, if I let you go, will you stop acting like a wild thing?"

"Yes," she said.

Brent released her. She stepped back from him, rubbing her arms. He wondered if he'd bruised her, and frowned.

"Good," he said. "You will now remember that you are a lady and my wife."

The numbness evaporated. She looked at him, her lips thin. "And what of you, Brent? Are you not a gentleman and my husband?" She didn't wait for him to reply, her fury too powerful. "Why is it you used to accuse me of all sorts of awful things? Why is it that I, a woman, am to be called a slut, a harlot, a—and you, a man, can bed as many women as you like, and still hurl your vile insults at me? Why?"

He'd never before thought of a man's physical desires in that light before. Hell, he'd never before been married. "Women," he began, trying to sort through a logical explanation, "are different. They don't seem to want—that is, they are more—"

She achieved a creditable sneer. "Ah, so if I am different, then why did you think me like you—a harlot and a—"

"That isn't what I meant, exactly." He raked his fingers through his hair. "Look, Byrony, I was wrong about you, completely wrong. When I was young, there was a woman who, well, taught me things that weren't exactly correct."

"You're telling me that you were seduced? But women don't like that sort of thing, Brent. Or did you pay even then, as a young man?"

"No," he said, and she heard the ripple of remembered pain in his voice, saw the bitterness in his eyes. "She was my stepmother."

Byrony refused to feel sorry for him. "So you paint all women with the same brush, is that it, Brent?"

"I suppose that I have," he said slowly. "It was wrong of me. Particularly when it came to you. It's just that I was drawn to you from the very first, Byrony. I won't lie to you. Maybe I wanted to believe that old man's lies in San Diego. It kept the world sane for me. It kept me intact and whole. When I saw you again, so beautiful, so sweet, I thought— Well, never mind what I thought because it didn't last long. You had married Butler, a rich man, and were pregnant. And I laughed at myself for believing you were different."

"And you hurt me."

"Yes, and I was wrong." She was still looking at him with incredulity, and something else. Anger, more than likely. She was probably remembering his words to Maggie. He didn't owe her any explanation, none at all. He was a man and her husband. He could do precisely as he pleased. With discretion now, of course.

"Enough of this foolishness. I want to make love to my bride."

She stared at him, disbelieving. "Go to Celeste. Go to your mistress."

He turned away from her and began to pull off his clothes. When he'd stripped to his breeches, he said over his shoulder, "Would you like me to assist you out of your *wedding* gown?"

"No. I am sleeping in the sitting room."

He whipped around at that. "The devil you are." He unfastened the buttons on his trousers.

"Stop that."

"No." He stepped out of his trousers and methodically folded them and laid them over the back of a chair with his other clothes.

He straightened, his hands on his hips. "Look well, Byrony.

I hope you like your husband's body, because I am the only man you will ever see naked."

"No," she said. "Maybe not."

He drew on his patience. "Byrony, you are my wife and I fully intend to make love to you. We can do this one of two ways. You can fight me or you can enjoy me. Which is it to be?"

Her head fell and her shoulders slumped.

He said nothing, merely walked behind her and began to unfasten the myriad small satin-covered buttons down her back. He wanted to kiss the nape of her neck. The smooth flesh with the tiny wispy curls. He didn't want to hurt her. He wanted to make her forget his ill-chosen words, he wanted—

"There," he said, pulling the gown downward. "Would you like me to help you with the rest?"

"No," she said. "Please, Brent, just leave me alone."

He shook his head, and said aloud, "No. But I will have a bit of brandy while you finish."

He forced himself to walk away from her.

Byrony wondered if all women were born under an unlucky star, then thought of Chauncey Saxton, and sighed. Delaney Saxton was handsome, clever, and terribly kind. And she, fool that she was, cared for this man, a man who looked upon her as a possession, as a thing to do with just as he pleased.

"I don't intend to drink brandy all night," she heard him say from behind her. "You have five minutes, Byrony."

She jerked off her chemise, petticoats, and underthings. She was reaching for her nightgown when she felt his hand on her bare arm.

"No," he said. "I want you now."

Something inside her snapped at his tone of utter and absolute command. He turned her to face him. She brought up her fist and smashed it with all her strength into his stomach.

Brent sucked in his breath, grunting more in surprise than in pain. When he felt her fingernails rake his shoulder, he grabbed her about the waist and flung her onto the bed on her back. He landed on top of her, jerking her arms above her head and holding her wrists together with one hand.

"Enough," he said, staring down at her. He saw the wild fury in her eyes, and grinned. "So, I'm to ride a wild mare on my wedding night?"

Byrony tried to squirm away from him, and quickly realized that her movements only excited him all the more.

"I hate you."

He was still grinning. "I will make you forget those words. And no, I'm not going to rape you. Now, I suggest that since you are quite ignorant, you simply lie still and let me teach you." He dipped his head down and kissed her lightly on the mouth. "And you will enjoy it, Byrony, oh, you surely will."

She felt the length of him swollen against her belly, felt his chest against her breasts. "No," she said, "I won't."

That startled him, and for a moment he merely stared down at her. "So that's the way it is to be. We will see, Byrony. We will see."

He released her wrists, but she did nothing, merely lay there looking up at the ceiling. He rolled off her and balanced himself on his elbow beside her. He took his time to study her. "You will fill out," he said, hoping to get a rise from her. He touched her breast, gently stroking. He cupped her, felt her heartbeat. It quickened under his palm, and he smiled. She had such beautiful breasts—he'd told her that already. He continued to stroke her as he looked downward. She was a bit on the thin side, it was true. Lord, he'd be thin too if he'd lived the way she had the past weeks. Her skin was soft, and very smooth. He kneaded her belly and felt her muscles tighten beneath his fingers. Lightly he brushed his fingertips over her dark blond curls. He heard her indrawn breath, felt her stiffen.

"You have nice legs," he said, thinking that an understatement. They were long and very white and shapely. Quickly he cupped her breast again and felt her heartbeat soar to a gallop.

"Please," Byrony said. "No."

"Yes, sweetheart. Now, I want you to open your legs."

"No," she said again.

He wedged his hand between her thighs and parted them slightly.

Byrony closed her eyes tightly. She knew he was looking at her, studying her. His fingers stroked the insides of her thighs, drawing ever nearer. He bent her legs and parted them. She didn't fight him. She felt strangely languid, but no longer apart from him. No, she was beside him, feeling him touch her.

He moved quickly between her legs, pressing up against her.

Byrony jerked upward.

"No, I won't let you! I—"

He pressed his full weight on her and kissed her. His body was already moving against her rhythmically, and she was frightened, remembering the pain from before. She felt his urgency and began to fight him in earnest.

"Byrony," he said into her mouth, "stop it. Love, lie still."

"No." She turned her face from side to side to avoid his mouth. "You promised you wouldn't hurt me. You're a liar, like all men, you're—"

He rolled off her and drew her against him. "Hush," he said, stroking his fingers through her hair. "I won't hurt you. I'm not a liar." He shook his head at himself. Lord, he'd lost control. The last thing he wanted was for her to fear his lovemaking. He held her gently. He kissed her hair and did nothing else. When she quieted, he eased her away so he could see her face.

"Let's go to sleep," he said. "All right?"

She blinked, not understanding him. He rose and doused the lamps, then returned to the bed and eased them both under the covers. "Come here, Byrony. I want to hold you. That's all."

She came to him, knowing he would force her to if she didn't obey him. She lay stiffly against his side, her cheek on his chest, her thoughts desolate and bitter. To Brent's surprise, he heard her breathing quickly even into sleep.

He cursed, then smiled into the darkness.

It was still and calm and very dark when he awoke, a smile still on his lips. She was lying relaxed and yielding against him, her palm open on his chest. Very slowly he eased her onto her back. She mumbled something in her sleep, but didn't awaken. He lightly stroked down her belly, found her. She was soft and warm. He stroked her slowly, felt her woman's dampness and felt as if he would shout with the pleasure of it. He eased his finger inside her. He closed his eyes a moment, almost feeling himself coming into her.

Slowly, he thought, very slowly. He began caressing her again and heard her moan softly. Oh yes, Byrony, let me invade your dreams.

He had invaded her dream. She was standing atop a hill, a barren hill with a wide green valley beneath her. Strange, intense feelings were welling up inside her, making her squirm, making her breathless, making her want to move closer to the edge of the hill. Her hips moved, and in her dream she was looking down into that green valley, crying, not knowing what to do.

Brent deepened the pressure and her hand came up to touch his shoulder. She hovered between dream and reality, wanting to keep the softness and ambiguity of sleep, yet her body sought consciousness, sought the unbelievable pleasure. Suddenly her eyes flew open, and she felt her body convulse. She cried out, not understanding what was happening to her, only feeling and wanting more.

Brent could see her face now in the dim light of dawn. He saw her look of utter bewilderment as she reached her climax. "That's it," he said, coaxing her to feel more and more. Before her pleasure subsided, he eased between her legs and came into her. He felt her muscles tighten about him, drawing him deeper.

Byrony came abruptly awake. She stared up at him, felt him deep inside her. She cried out, the feelings still streaking through her, and wrapped her arms about his back. She wondered if she would die from the pleasure of it.

Brent felt her passion swirl around him, felt her giving, her need. He drove his full length and let himself go. He fell on her, straining, panting.

He closed his eyes, felt the deep-seated sensation of belonging, a need so long buried inside him that he'd forgotten its existence. I've come home, he thought, somewhat dazed by his insight.

"Byrony," he said, her name sounding wonderful to his ears.

He kissed her face, eased his tongue into her mouth, felt her arms still tight around his back. "Byrony," he said again, and fell asleep, sated, his head on the pillow beside her.

Byrony was stunned. She didn't move. He was heavy on top of her, yet she didn't want to shove him away. He was still inside her, and she marveled at the feel of him. You have been properly loved, she thought, and closed her eyes. She'd never imagined that such feelings existed. Feelings so strong, so powerful, that nothing else was important. She felt the relaxed muscles in his smooth back. Slowly she ran her hands down his back, then upward again. So different from her, she thought, so very different. He moved slightly and she felt a sharp jolt of pleasure. She blinked into the gray morning light, trying to quash it. But it wouldn't stop. She wanted him. Again, yet for the first time.

Her body seemed to know what to do. She moved beneath him, arching upward, and she felt him grow inside her.

Brent responded quickly, for he'd wanted her so long, so powerfully. He reared up over her, nearly withdrawing, then thrust deeply, his fingers going between them to find her. He heard her sob, her face pressed against his neck. She nearly bucked him off her.

When he felt her stiffen and convulse in her climax, he kissed her deeply, thrusting his tongue into her mouth as his sex was thrusting inside her belly. Then he was beyond her, yet at one with her in his own pleasure.

"Ah, Byrony," he said, and drew her tightly against him.

TWENTY

Byrony's nose twitched away from the rough hair on his chest. Very slowly she raised her head and looked down at his sleeping face. His dark hair was messed, a thick lock falling over his forehead, his jaws covered with black stubble. He looked exquisite. She even admired his ears.

She realized that her leg was over his groin, one of his arms under her, even in his sleep holding her firmly, his fingers splayed on her hip.

My husband, she thought. He is my husband. She held herself very still, remembering the previous night—no, morning. He'd known she would be more cooperative if he waited until she slept. And she had. She was still stunned at her wild response to him. She'd had no idea, no inkling from Aunt Ida or her mother that such feelings existed. Byrony grinned, thinking of the look on Aunt Ida's pleasantly thin face were she to say, "Yes, Aunt, and then I yelled and squirmed about and never wanted him to stop. Oh yes, Aunt, to have a man deep inside you, filling you, moving over you, kissing you—" She let herself marvel at it for a few moments before she set herself to thinking clearly again. She needed to get away from him now, physically, but was afraid to move. He would wake up and probably make love to her again. Make love. What a curious thing to say, but that is what he called their wild coupling. She felt sticky between her thighs. His seed. Inside of her. Never before in her life had she felt her womanness as she did now, now that she knew what it was men wanted of women, and, she added silently, still marveling, what women wanted of men. She lifted her leg, easing away from him. He muttered something unintelligible and tightened his arm about her back.

"Byrony," he said suddenly, opening his eyes. He looked up into her face and smiled. "Good morning, wife. Come closer, you're warm and soft, very soft."

He brought her tight against his side again.

"Did you sleep well?" His question was filled with satisfaction. She felt the warmth of his breath against her temple.

"Yes," she said.

He turned to face her and held her against him. She felt his sex swelling against her leg and drew in her breath. "Surely—" she began.

"Surely what?" He nibbled at her ear. She heard rich amusement in his voice. He knew he'd won, but she thought suddenly, hadn't she won also? But what of last night? she wanted to ask him. Had anything changed?

"I don't know."

"Make you speechless, do I?" His grin was irresistible, and her mouth curved in response. She felt his hand glide over her stomach and cup her.

"Oh. Brent, surely you—"

"So warm," he said.

"And sticky. From you."

She was amazed when he closed his eyes a moment as his fingers probed, searched and found her. "Yes," he said softly, "from me." She felt him tremble and for a brief instant knew a moment of power over this man. Then she was on her back and he was easing into her. She gasped at the feel of him, and he stopped cold. "Am I hurting you, Byrony? Are you too sore for me?"

She looked into his eyes, seeing the sudden worry for her, and was lost. "No." She arched up to take more of him.

But he was frowning, and for one of the few times in his adult life, concern for another took precedence over his own lust. Very slowly he began to ease out of her, but she locked her arms about his back, holding him to her.

"All right," he said, looking down into her face, "but we'll go easy, Byrony. You are unused to a man." He dipped his face down and kissed her. "I am relieved that you enjoy me."

She blinked, the wild urgency building slowly deep within her. "But you knew that I would. Doesn't everyone?"

He wanted to laugh, but didn't. "No," he said, "not everyone. We are quite good together."

He was pressing down on her even as he moved more deeply. She groaned softly, arching upward. "Brent, please."

He watched her face saw her eyes darken with pleasure, and increased his pace. When he slipped his hand between their straining bodies to find her, she cried out, and was gone in a maelstrom of nearly painful pleasure. He held himself in firm control until the spasms lessened, then drew her onto her side and took his own release.

"Now you're *very* sticky," he said against her throat.

"Yes," she said, and he grinned at the pleased sound of her voice.

There was a knock coming from the outer office door. He lightly flicked his finger over her nose and pulled away from her. "Stay warm, I'll be right back. It's probably our breakfast."

She watched him walk naked from the bed and pull on a dressing gown. "Don't move, Byrony," he said over his shoulder. Why had he said that? Was he afraid that she would leap from the bed and try to escape him?

He paused a moment in the doorway and almost unwillingly turned to look toward the bed. Her dark blond hair was tangled around her face. She looked so lovely that he wanted nothing more than to fling himself on her again. Rutting bastard.

When he returned to the bedroom, a tray on his arms, she was sitting up in bed, pulling her dressing gown around her.

He frowned in disappointment, but just for a moment. He would have preferred to see her naked, but of course she was unused to a man, even her husband, seeing her unclothed.

"I've a kitchen downstairs," he said easily. "When I don't feel like eating out, Caesar brings me food up here. Would you like some coffee?"

She nodded.

"Don't tense up on me, all right? Here."

She took the steaming cup of coffee and sipped it. It tasted better than any coffee she'd had in her life.

The bed dipped as Brent sat down beside her.

"And croissants, from Pierre's bakery."

"Thank you."

"You can't be embarrassed now," he said, his voice warm. "After all, you've taken my poor body—what is it?—three times in less than—how many hours?" He bit into a flaky croissant. "You know, Byrony, we haven't discussed where to go on our honeymoon."

"Not Sacramento," she said.

"No, certainly not." He was silent a moment, watching her. "It would be wise, I think, if we did go somewhere, however. There will be talk, and unfortunately, even if Irene and Ira keep their respective mouths tightly closed, I think it likely that some people might not treat you as they should."

"I know."

"It occurred to me also, that being a married man now, I should probably build us a house. Living above a saloon and next to a brothel can't be considered exactly respectable."

"I like it here," she said. "Really, Brent, I don't want you to have to do anything you don't wish to. And Maggie is a good friend."

Her eyes were serious upon his face. "I don't want you hurt anymore," he said, his voice rough.

"That is kind of you," she said, but her thoughts were of Celeste, his mistress. Wasn't that considered hurt from his man's perspective?

"Thank you."

"May I ask you a question?"

He arched a black brow.

"I guess I'm rather ignorant," she began.

"But very receptive."

"Does a man want to make love all the time?"

"Not more than every hour or so." She looked horrified, and he had to laugh.

Then she looked down, her expression all demure, and said, "Has it been an hour yet?"

He'd never seen her flirt before and he was enchanted. "Very nearly," he said. He wondered briefly if he would ever have his fill of her. It was a heady thought, having a wife. It was also a commitment and a responsibility he'd never before considered, and that was scary as hell. He leaned toward her, delighting in the fact that she wanted him too, and took the tray from her lap.

"Now, sweetheart," he said, "my hour is up and you can have your way with me again." He cupped her face between his hands and began kissing her. He quickly forgot about their honeymoon, building a house, and an unknown future filled with responsibility. He'd also wanted to speak to her about their fiasco argument of the previous night, but not now. No, not now.

"You are looking quite splendid, Byrony," Chauncey Saxton said, smiling at her friend. "I see that marriage agrees with you."

"Brent is—" Byrony paused a moment. "He is, oh, I don't know. Thank you for shopping with me, Chauncey."

"My pleasure. I thank the elements it isn't raining. Come, love, let's have a cup of tea, and let me rest a moment." She patted her growing belly. "This little brute is jumping about, and Saint told me tea—only mint tea, mind you—would calm him down."

Byrony quickly agreed. They entered the small pastry shop called Mortimer's on Market Street and the smiling, very rotund Timothy Mortimer led them to a small table. "Ladies," he said.

After they'd ordered, Chauncey sat back in her chair and drew a contented sigh. "Oh course, Saint has no idea how to calm down this wild child of mine, but his suggestion of mint tea—with lemon, of course—I find delightful. You must give me your advice, Byrony, if you would be so kind. Del and I will be married a year next week and I haven't the foggiest notion of what to give him."

But Byrony was silent.

Chauncey looked up and saw Mrs. Stevenson and Penelope in the doorway to the shop. "Ignore them," she said. "Besides, we don't know which of us they disapprove of more. Dear Penelope has always been a mild thorn in my side. It's all too silly, you know." She nodded toward the two women.

"Ah, our tea. Thank you, Timothy."

"Certainly, Mrs. Saxton. Tell Del that the new oven is working better than I ever dreamed it would."

At Byrony's questioning look, Chauncey said, "Del loaned him some money for the famous oven."

"At least he spent it on an oven and not in Brent's saloon."

Chauncey laughed and toasted Byrony with her cup of tea.

"How is the new *bride?*"

Byrony slowly set her teacup into its saucer and raised her eyes to Penelope's face. "Hello, Miss Stevenson."

"The new bride looks marvelously happy," said Chauncey, "doesn't she, Penelope?"

Penelope considered this a moment. "Do you always look marvelously happy when you marry, Mrs. Butl—Mrs. Hammond? At least for a short time?"

Byrony locked her eyes on the blue-and-white-checked tablecloth.

"I saw your child the other day. What is the poor little thing's name? Michelle?"

"Poor Penelope," Chauncey said, shaking her head. "It must be so difficult to ignore facts and wallow in fiction."

"I should say that most of the ladies in San Francisco think it appalling that a woman would leave her child and husband to marry her lover. Don't expect to be greeted fondly, Mrs. Hammond."

Brent had warned her, of course. Still, chilling looks were easier to take than this direct attack. I can't allow Chauncey to continue protecting me, she thought, and raised her eyes to Penelope's face. "I think, Miss Stevenson," she said slowly, very precisely, "that you shouldn't have any lemon with your tea. Your lips are pursed so tightly now, you just might find yourself permanently wrinkled."

"Indeed, Penelope," Chauncey said, "take yourself off and regale your mother with all your nasty little tales. Better yet, find yourself a husband, then you'll be kept too busy to spread gossip about other people."

"She's so very pretty," Byrony said as she watched Penelope flounce away from their table. "She seems to have everything a girl could want. Why is she so very nasty?"

"Saint thinks she needs to be beaten every morning. Clear her of evil humors, he says."

"Oh no, not that."

Chauncey frowned. "It was just a jest, my dear. Now, we

must plan a small dinner party. I'm not bragging, mind you, but I fancy I have just as much social power as Mrs. Stevenson and her little group. And of course Agatha Newton could sway a battleship. Indeed, I'll never forget—"

Byrony listened to Chauncey ramble on, not really attending, her thoughts on her very bizarre situation. She still didn't know what to do about her mother. The money would continue to be sent to her father, of course. Ira had promised. She supposed she must write and tell her at least some of the truth. Dear Mother, she thought, I have a new husband, but I never really had a husband before, much less a child. No, you aren't a grandmother, not really. . . .

"Everything will work out."

Byrony tried to manage a smile. "Yes, of course." She shrugged. "I think I should have left San Francisco. Brent really didn't want to marry me, as I'm certain you realize. Perhaps I should simply—"

"Stop it, Byrony. You're being a simpleton. Brent Hammond does nothing he doesn't choose to do, believe me. He wanted to marry you."

"He has a mistress."

That drew Chauncey to a halt, but she said, "So did Delaney. Her name is Marie."

That gave Byrony pause. "I don't think I'll ever understand how things work. Men are expected to dally about, but if a woman does it, she's a miserable, dishonest—"

"Yes, all of those things. It doesn't make any sense, does it? How do you know about this mistress of Brent's?"

"I heard him talking to Maggie—on our wedding night. When I rather heatedly asked him about it, he told me she had nothing to do with me. In short, it's none of my business."

Chauncey frowned. She liked Brent Hammond, found him charming, and he had saved her life. But he didn't seem to be dealing well with his new wife. What on earth was the matter with him? Byrony was a lovely girl whose disposition seemed as sweet as her face. She knew that many wives simply ignored such behavior, but Byrony wouldn't. "It is your business," she said. "He is your husband."

"And I am his wife, as he so kindly informed me. It's like I'm some sort of possession. I don't like it."

Chauncey leaned over and patted Byrony's hand. "Do you love him, Byrony?"

Byrony went utterly still.

"Forgive me, it's really none of my business."

"No, it's just that I haven't thought of love." *Liar. To be loved, to belong, is something you've wanted all your life.* "All I know is I wanted to kill him when—Well, I'm rather a fool, aren't I? Oh, damn, Chauncey, I suppose I do love him. But it doesn't make a whit of sense."

"Good," said Chauncey. "He will come around, you'll see." And he would, she was certain of it. Del had told her that Brent was something of a womanizer and a loner. "But," Del had said, grinning at her, "I think for the first time in his life, Brent has been fairly caught." Chauncey chose to believe Del. "Shell we visit Monsieur David now?"

Chauncey said as they left the pastry shop, "I shall have to tell Saint that his prescription of mint tea and lemon worked well."

It was a foggy, damp night. Byrony shivered and moved closer to the fire. Brent was downstairs in the saloon. Maggie had visited her earlier in the evening, and given her an enthusiastic response to her two new gowns.

Where was Brent? It was past midnight. I've been married three days, she thought, and smiled. Married for the second time for three days. She closed the volume of Voltaire and stared into the leaping flames. "The best of all possible worlds," she said softly. Byrony sighed. She had to write to her mother. She was a coward.

She started up at the sound of the office door opening and closing.

"Not in bed yet?"

She turned to face her husband, and drank in the sight of him. His coat and trousers were black as his hair, his shirt a startling white. "No," she said.

She rose and walked quickly to him. "I'm glad you're here," she said, and flung her arms around his back.

"Me too," he said, his hands caressing her through her dressing gown. He breathed in her special scent, feeling himself drawn to her. It was a scary feeling, and he didn't like it. Suddenly his hands were gripping her arms and he was gently pushing her away. "I'm sorry, Byrony, but I must leave again, just for a little while. I've got to go to the El Dorado and see James Cora."

She wondered wildly if he made love to her if he would still have the strength or desire to visit his mistress. She didn't believe for a second that he was going to see James Cora. "Can I come with you?"

Brent laughed. "Hardly, sweetheart." He tucked an errant tendril of hair behind her ear.

She warmed at his endearment, foolishly, of course. He meant nothing by it. Damn him, he probably called Celeste his sweetheart.

"Your hair is so soft," he said, winding a long strand around his fingers.

"I washed it this afternoon," she said.

He gathered a handful of hair and brought it to his nose, and breathed in deeply. "What is the scent?"

"Gardenia."

He drew back, his eyes going cold. Laurel had used gardenia. Had drenched her bathwater with the scent, had lavishly sprayed it all over her body.

"It isn't my favorite," he said. "I should prefer another scent, perhaps jasmine or rose. I shall buy it for you."

She winced as though he'd struck her.

But Brent didn't notice. He'd quickly closed Laurel from his mind and was trying to figure out a way to stay with Byrony. "Oh, damn," he said. He quickly leaned down to kiss her. "I'll be back as quickly as I can."

She finally went to bed and lay awake for two hours. He hadn't come in by the time she fell asleep.

Actually, Brent finished his business with Cora, a joint purchase of poker tables from Baltimore, but was detained by Maggie. He looked impatient, but she merely motioned him into her parlor.

"You've got to get her out of here," Maggie said without preamble. "The damned talk will continue if you keep your wife here."

"Byrony said she liked it here," Brent said.

"Don't be a stupid ass," Maggie said. "Do you know that two of my girls, Felice and Nora, visited her this afternoon? No, I didn't think you did. I shudder to think of what they talked about. Nora is a half-wit and Felice can talk of nothing but men and their preferences. Is that what you want for your wife?"

"Shit," said Brent.

"Exactly. Now, I'll miss her, don't get me wrong, Brent, I'll miss you too for that matter. But it just isn't right. Another thing. Byrony asked me to go out with her tomorrow. Can't you just hear the talk now? Mrs. Hammond in the company of a madam? I told her no, of course, and she was hurt. She really doesn't understand, Brent."

"Give me a brandy, Maggie."

"Idiot man," Maggie said under her breath. When she'd handed him a snifter of brandy, she asked, "What do you intend? Keeping her here until she's pregnant with your child?"

He choked on the brandy. Pregnant. "I'm not ready to be a father, for God's sake!"

Maggie grimaced at his outraged tone. "Oh," she said sarcastically, "she is still a virgin then? You haven't laid a hand or any other part of your man's anatomy on her? You've given her instructions on how not to conceive?"

"No, I've loved her until we're both exhausted."

"Such an intelligent man." She gentled her voice, very slightly, at the stunned expression on his face. "Look, Brent, you've been with a very different breed of woman until now. Celeste, Felice, Nora, they all know the rules. They made the rules, for God's sake, and they're all growing quite prosperous off the horny men in this city. What does Byrony have?"

"She has a husband," he said.

"Such a lucky girl. Just what do you expect her to do with herself? Knit perhaps,while you're gambling downstairs? She's a bloody prisoner, Brent. For God's sake, get her out of here."

Brent tossed down the rest of his brandy, snapped the snifter on a side table, and rose.

"Let me tell you another thing, Brent," Maggie said. "Saint also thinks—"

"Damnation. Is everyone minding my business for me? Hell, is Delaney going to track me down tomorrow with his advice?" He held up his hand when Maggie's mouth opened.

"All right, I'll think about it." He raised his eyes to the ceiling. "Lord, life was so bloody simple."

"It still could be if you weren't such a stubborn fool," said Maggie to his departing back.

TWENTY-ONE

Brent stared wistfully down at her sleeping face, then slowly, resolutely, pulled away. She stirred, said his name, and he stilled. He felt her warm hand glide downward and sucked in his breath. "No," he said, grabbing her hand.

Byrony blinked away the sleep, but the dreamy, soft feelings still held her. "I missed you," she said, stretching against him.

"I've got to go," he said, twisting away from her.

"Oh no, not yet. It's still so early, and don't you always want—" She broke off. She'd wanted to tell him that she enjoyed their early mornings together, enjoyed how, since that first morning, he'd always awakened her with his lovemaking. What was wrong?

He's probably exhausted from spending all those hours last night with his mistress.

She was coldly awake now. "I didn't hear you come in last night," she said. "Were you very late?"

"Late enough," he said, his body warring with his mind. Maggie's words had haunted him a good hour before he'd finally fallen asleep. Pregnant. Marriage was too new to him to consider creating a son or daughter. It was damned terrifying, as a matter of fact. What if she were already pregnant? He'd dismissed it because he'd wanted to. After all, hadn't he made love to her only that one time? Of course he'd ignored Saint. But there was no excuse, no logic at all for what he'd done since they'd been married. It took Maggie's sarcasm to penetrate his brain. It shook him, and he quickly pulled away from Byrony and rose. The room was chilly and he shivered as he pulled on his dressing gown.

"Brent?"

He didn't turn until his dressing gown was firmly belted at his waist. "Yes?"

"I don't understand."

No, you probably don't, he wanted to tell her. You're used to me falling all over you in the mornings, aren't you? But he wouldn't again, not until he'd found out how to prevent conception.

"Nothing to understand," he said easily. "I've got a lot to do today and want an early start." He didn't mean to look at her again, at least not until he had a firm grip on himself, but he gazed briefly over his shoulder as he headed for the washbasin and his razor. He would have had to be a blind man not to see the pain and confusion on her face. He cursed softly.

"Byrony," he began, his voice desperate to his own ears, "please, sweetheart, I— Would you like to take a ride with me to the ocean today? If the fog clears, it will be beautiful, and we could stop at Russ Gardens, perhaps visit the racetrack—"

"You are probably too busy. Maybe Maggie could—"

"No. That is I won't be too busy. I want to go. All right?"

"If that is what you wish."

"I believe I've told you before that I don't particularly care for your whipped-puppy routine," he said, frowning at her lowered head. He watched the bedcovers slip a bit and considered the odds on making love to her only one more time.

Her chin went up. "Very well. When do you wish to leave?"

He thought quickly. Celeste usually slept very late, that is, if she'd spent the night with him. He hadn't seen her since he'd married Byrony. He supposed he could ask Maggie about contraception, but he shied away from that. He didn't think he could stand the patronizing smirk she'd doubtless give him. *You, Brent Hammond*, he could just hear her, *you who have rutted your way West don't know how to prevent conception?* And she'd preach, he didn't doubt it for a moment, about his responsibilities, about his selfishness—

"How about after lunch?"

She nodded. She'd seen the myriad shifting expressions on his face. So, she thought, feeling numb, he no longer wanted her, he wanted his mistress.

Byrony watched him go through his now familiar morning routine. "I'll have Caesar bring up your breakfast," he said, bending down to kiss her cheek. "Why don't you go back to sleep?"

She made a noise that he chose to think an affirmative.

"Byrony," he said, "how do you feel?"

She looked at him, startled.

He tugged on a lock of hair behind his left ear, and cleared his throat. "That is, ah—When was your last monthly flow?"

She stared at him as though he'd asked her when she'd last traveled to the moon.

"When, Byrony?"

"Just before we were married," she said, not meeting his gaze.

Brent closed his eyes a moment. He wished he hadn't asked. "Go back to sleep," he said again, and left.

She fluffed up her pillow and leaned back. What was she to do? *Leave San Francisco now.* But something deep within her rebelled. That was the coward's way. And Brent had told her that he disliked her so-called whipped-puppy routine. Very well. He'd soon see just how submissive she really was. She threw back the covers and bounded out of bed. As she bathed, she thought he would at least have breakfast before he visited his mistress. She splashed more of the gardenia scent into her tub. Why, she wondered blankly, had he asked her about her monthly flow? She would never understand him.

Forty-five minutes later Byrony stood in the shadow of the saloon, waiting for Brent to come out. The air was heavy with fog, and she drew her cloak more closely about her. Had she been wrong? Of course you're not wrong, you silly fool. But she continued to dither and argue with herself. Then she heard his voice. She swallowed, watching him walk out of the saloon and down the street.

She followed him, weaving her way through the increasing numbers of tradesmen, wagon drivers, vendors, and workmen.

He walked quickly, turning onto Clay Street. She watched him walk up the steps to a narrow wooden house on the corner of Clay and Kearny.

She waited a few minutes, then crept up the steps. To her surprise, the front door was unlatched. She opened it quietly and looked inside. She walked into a small vestibule. Stairs leading upward were directly in front of her; there was a sitting room to the right, a dining room to the left. She heard a woman's voice floating down to her, heard Brent's voice.

"Damn you, Brent Hammond," she said and stalked up the stairs.

She paused outside a bedroom door that was partially open, and listened.

"You come here at the break of dawn for what?"

"Celeste, look, I'm sorry to bother you but it is important. And it's a long way from dawn, for God's sake."

"Do you want me to stay in bed?"

How seductive his mistress's voice sounded. Byrony's hands fisted at her sides.

Here I am eavesdropping again. But she couldn't bring herself to move.

"Don't you want to join me, Brent? It's been such a long time."

Long time, ha. Since last night.

"Look, Celeste, I need your advice on a very important matter."

She heard him cross the bedroom. He was going to get in bed with her. Byrony felt pure rage flow through her. She flung the door wide and stomped in. She pulled up short. Brent was standing next to the fireplace, his shoulders resting against the mantel, fully dressed. But it was his mistress who drew Byrony's eyes. Celeste was reclining in the large bed, a frothy pale yellow negligee tossed over her shoulders. One very shapely leg was bent at the knee and quite bare. Byrony could see the swirl of dark curls at the top of her thighs. She was beautiful, and Byrony wanted to tear her glossy black hair out. Why couldn't she look like a crow in the morning? Her hair tied up in rags? her face covered with white cream?

"Byrony. What the hell?"

Brent stared at his wife, standing rigid as a statue in the doorway, her eyes on Celeste.

"My, my, what have we here? Isn't it your little wife, Brent?"

"Shut up, Celeste. Byrony, what are you doing here?"

Byrony raised blank eyes to her husband's face. "I followed you," she said. "I wanted to be certain you were coming to her. You were, of course."

"I want you to go home, Byrony, now." He felt an utter fool. He wanted to throttle her, wanted to kick himself. "I will be back soon. We will talk."

"Soon, Brent? I beg you won't hurry on my account. I'm

afraid I didn't give you enough time to make yourself comfortable." She turned away, saying over her shoulder, "Excuse me for interrupting you."

He was across the room in an instant. He grabbed her shoulders and twisted her about to face him. He shook her until her head snapped on her neck. "No more," he said. "I was not here to make—dally, dammit."

"'Make love.' That is the strangest way of saying it. Let me go, Brent, now."

"No." He shook her again. "I'm telling you the truth, Byrony." Why the hell was he explaining anything? She'd followed him, not trusted him. "We're going home now, together."

"But, Brent," came Celeste's amused voice, "what was it you wanted of me?"

"Later. Come along, Byrony."

Byrony gasped at him. "Later? I don't believe you. Why, I wouldn't go to Sacramento with you."

"You will do as I tell you." He shook her again. "I will have no more scenes." He pulled her from Celeste's bedroom, his mistress's laughter sounding in his ears. "I don't believe this," he said to himself as he dragged her out of the house. He felt her straining away from him. "Behave or I swear I'll thrash you."

Byrony was too furious to react to his threat. "You just try it, Brent Hammond. I'll carve you up, I'll shoot you."

"Just shut up. And here I thought I'd married a lady."

She whirled about and slammed her fist into his belly.

He grunted in surprise.

"I'm no lady," she yelled at him. "I'm your wife."

Brent was marginally aware that people had paused to stare at them. He tightened his jaw and his hold on her arm. By the time they'd reached the saloon's back entrance, Byrony was silent and white. What have you done, you idiot? She'd embarrassed him, that's what she'd done. Infuriated him. Made him look like a fool. The list went on in her head until Brent opened their apartment door and shoved her inside. She stood quietly, rubbing her arms.

"I won't beat you," he said as he very calmly closed the door, "for the simple reason that I promised you I would never hurt you. But you deserve it, Byrony. Now, I want you to tell me just what you were doing there."

It seemed to Brent that she hadn't heard him, and he said more sharply, "I told you that Celeste was none of your affair. She has nothing to do with you."

"I'll be gone by tomorrow," she said, not looking at him. "I want nothing from you, Brent. I have the necklace Ira gave me. I intend to sell it. It will give me a start somewhere else."

He ground his teeth. "You're not going anywhere."

She cocked her head at him, clearly puzzled. "You don't want me. You only married me because—well, I'm not really certain why you did. Guilt, perhaps, because you seduced me—not the harlot you believed me to be, but a virgin? Or was it pity for a homeless waif?"

"I married you because I care for you, you little idiot." He saw she didn't believe him. Even to his own ears, his words sounded like gibberish from a confused man. It was pity, guilt, but not all, for God's sake. There was more, so much more. It seemed like he'd wanted her forever.

"But you also *care* for Celeste."

"It's not the same thing." He ran his hand through his hair, quite aware that he was digging himself in deeper and deeper. How dare she question him like this.

"And when you don't care for Celeste any longer, there will be another woman, won't there?"

"No. Byrony, listen to me. I didn't go there to make—to sleep with her."

"Oh? To have breakfast, then? To have a chat about your

day's activities? To ask her whether or not she wanted to go riding with you, tomorrow perhaps, when you'd be free?"

"No, I went there to ask her how to prevent conception."

Byrony drew up short. "Prevent conception," she repeated. "I don't understand."

"Because I don't want you to get pregnant. Christ. It's too soon, Byrony, much too soon. You're too young, and I— well, I—"

"You what, Brent?" She went pale as the truth dawned on her. "If I became pregnant, you'd be truly tied to me, wouldn't you? Your freedom would be well gone."

"It's not like that," he said. "We need time to learn about each other, time to—"

"Time to see whether you get bored with me? And when you do, you hope I will still have the infamous necklace to sell so I will be gone from your life?"

"No, dammit."

"I'm just another mistress to you, aren't I, Brent? A mistress who dares not even look at another man because she belongs legally to you. I thought— Well, it's no longer important." Byrony whirled around, unable to face him further. She felt tears sting her eyes, and viciously wiped them away. She heard him coming toward her, and quickly moved to the other side of the bed. "Stay away from me, Brent."

He was angry, tense with it, rigid with it. How dare she follow him, then accuse him of such things? He said, "It doesn't really matter what you want. As you said, you belong to me legally. You will do as I tell you. Since you have such a vivid imagination and poisonous tongue, I think I will really give you something to rant about."

She looked at him, then saw the purpose, the determination in his eyes. "What do you mean?"

"Take off your clothes. As you almost said this morning, my dear, I much enjoy waking up to lovemaking. And you know it, don't you? Perhaps you even enjoy me as much as I enjoy you?"

"No," she said. "I don't want you."

He shrugged. "It doesn't really matter. I've heard it's unusual for a wife to enjoy sex. Usually, I understand, a wife forces herself to bear it. Husbands are animals, the saying goes, thus wives are relieved if they take their dark lust elsewhere. But I am a faithful husband, Byrony, despite what you choose to believe. Now, take off your clothes."

She searched his face for a brief moment. There was something else in his eyes now. It was desire. She ran to the door. The door slammed hard just as she opened it. He was behind her, his hand flat on the door, above her head. She heard his breathing, felt the heat from him.

She wanted to beg him not to humiliate her like this. But no, she wouldn't be a weak, whipped puppy. Very slowly she turned to face him. She forced a cold smile. "Very well," she said. "Shall I lie naked on the bed for you or shall I put on a negligee and pose with my knee provocatively bent, like Celeste?"

She'd surprised him; she could see it in his eyes. He was utterly taken aback. Damn him, he'd wanted her to plead, to cry. Well, she wouldn't, ever again.

"Yes," he said finally. "I want you naked, on your back. I will part your legs when I wish to."

I haven't the experience to fence with him, she thought. But she wouldn't give up, not now. She shrugged with elaborate indifference. "All right. Odd, isn't it, Brent? I feel particularly fertile now. Do you think I'll become pregnant?"

His eyes narrowed, but it was the only sign that she'd shaken him again. He laughed. "My dear," he said, stroking her hair, "you need to be taught so many things. No, don't try to pull away from me. Just listen. I suppose you do know that it is my seed that creates a child. But it isn't necessary that I spill my seed inside you. It is more pleasurable for me of course, but I shall survive. I'm an impatient man, sweetheart. Come now and do as I bid you."

He wanted to laugh at her expression, but he didn't. "You're an intelligent girl, Byrony, and perhaps, just perhaps, you can best me in the future. The distant future."

"I hate you."

"No, no you don't. You're just being a poor loser." His fingers were on the buttons on the back of her gown.

Please, she wanted to say, please don't do this to me. But she remained mute. She felt the buttons part swiftly, and the thought that he'd had so much practice undressing women made her forget her indifference.

"No." She jerked away from him. "No, I won't let you do this, Brent."

He paused a moment, stroking his long fingers over his jaw. Then he turned from her and locked the bedroom door. He could hear her frantic breathing. "I will master you, my dear," he said very calmly, turning back to face her. "I will master you in all things. And no, Byrony, I won't rape you, although I venture to believe that such violence on my part would please you in some twisted way, reaffirm that I'm a bastard like your father and that miserable brother of yours."

"You are. All of you men are. No, stay away from me, Brent."

But he didn't. He held her very firmly and stripped off her clothes. She was wearing only her chemise and stockings when she went limp against him, worn out from her struggles.

"I'll scream," she said.

"If you do, I'll gag you." Once he had her on the bed he stripped off the rest of her clothes. "Now," he said, stepping back, "please don't move, Byrony. Go ahead and cover yourself if it makes you feel better."

Byrony pulled the blanket over her and stared up at the

ceiling. She heard him undressing, but she didn't look at him.

Brent eased down beside her. She ignored him. So that was the game she was going to play now. She didn't realize that a woman who'd known pleasure would have a difficult time being lifeless and without feeling. He slipped his hand beneath the blanket and found her breast. She tried to pull away from him. He tossed off the blanket and covered her, holding her still beneath him. Balancing himself on his elbows, he studied her face.

"I am your husband," he said, "the man you willingly consented to marry. I am the man who took your virginity and taught you pleasure. Feel me, Byrony." He was hard against her closed legs.

"No," she said, turning her face away. "No, I won't."

"You're such a child," he said, and began to kiss her. "Be a woman for me, Byrony."

She tried to lock out any feeling; she tried to concentrate on his lies, on his mistress. She felt him moving down her body, felt his mouth close over her nipple. She lurched up, unable to help herself. He was nibbling and licking at her, caressing the underside of her breast, his hands kneading her waist, her belly.

"No," she whispered, to herself, not to him, but his hands, his magic fingers and clever tongue were roving over her. She felt the growing intensity, felt herself becoming warm and open. "No."

She felt him open her legs, felt his warm breath against her belly. "You are so white and soft," he said, and she knew he was looking at her, studying her, and it seduced her, she couldn't help it. "And that soft curling hair, such pleasure for a man." But he didn't touch her there, only lightly caressed her with his fingers. He kissed the insides of her thighs, speaking to her between his kisses, telling her how lovely she was, how delightfully responsive. But he didn't kiss her where her need had become so overwhelming, so shattering, that she began sobbing deep in her throat.

Brent had planned, in the beginning perhaps, to punish her, to bring her to the point of her release, then leave her. But he couldn't. God, he wanted her, and he wanted her pleasure.

He waited until she was heaving upward against him. Then he closed his mouth over her. Dear God, the intense pleasure at the sweet taste of her, her openness, the incredible softness of her. He held her hips, feeling the spasms of pleasure course through her. He heard her moaning. He eased the pressure, then quickly reared over her and came into her. She cried out, shuddering, her thighs closing about his flanks.

You mustn't, he told himself, even as his thoughts became blurred, but he didn't want to stop himself. He didn't think he could withdraw from her. He gritted his teeth, and with a cry of fury at himself, pulled out her, his seed flowing onto her belly.

Byrony was still shuddering from the waves of pleasure, the small shocks of intense feeling.

"You left me," she said, her voice sad, defeated.

"Yes," he said. He pulled himself away from her, his body weak and clumsy. He wanted to jerk her into his arms and kiss her and caress her until she slept against him. He drew a deep breath to steady himself, and her scent, Laurel's gardenia scent, filled his nostrils. He rose and stood beside the bed, staring down at her.

"You've learned a valuable lesson, Byrony. Never again will you try to deny me. You will only lose." But she'd won, he thought. She'd drawn him into her, made him want to lose himself in her. He stiffened, his eyes narrowing. He said in a lazy drawl, "No rape, was there?"

She raised weary, disillusioned eyes to his face. "No, there was no rape." She slowly pulled the blanket over herself and turned away from him onto her side. She felt hollow, empty, discarded. She felt the stickiness of him on her stomach. She curled up, bringing her legs to her chest, and buried her head in her arms.

He had to get away from her, he had to regain his control. He dressed quickly, not looking at her again, but when he reached the bedroom door, he couldn't help himself. He stared back. She hadn't moved, nor was she crying.

He cursed very softly, and firmly closed the bedroom door behind him.

TWENTY-TWO

"Byrony, what's going on here? What are you doing in bed?"

It was evening, Byrony realized vaguely. The bedroom was dark. The light from the sitting room, silhouetted Maggie in its gleam.

"Come, what's wrong? Do you feel ill?"

Yes, she felt ill, but she didn't need Saint. She forced herself to unbend, and pulled herself up onto the pillow. She pulled the blanked to her chin. "No," she said, "I'm not ill. Just tired, that's all."

Maggie, eyes narrowed, came into the bedroom. She lit the lamps, then came over to stand beside the bed. "Are you pregnant?"

Byrony laughed. "Pregnant? Me? I'm too young to be pregnant."

"Stop it, Byrony." What, Maggie thought, was going on? "Where's Brent?"

"Brent? Brent who?" She started giggling again, her voice hoarse and raw. She stopped abruptly on a hiccup. "Have you asked Celeste?"

"Where is your dressing gown? Ah, here it is. Put it on. You don't need to catch a cold. And comb your hair. I'll have Caesar bring you up some dinner."

When Maggie returned to the bedroom, Byrony still lay in bed, the dressing gown tossed across the blanket, her hair tangled around her face. What had that damned fool Brent done now?

"Even if you are pregnant," Maggie said, "it's too soon for you to be showing any signs. So why are you lying here in the dark?"

"I told you. I was tired."

"You must have had a sublime argument with Brent."

"Oh no. He just wanted to prove to me who was master, as he put it. It's been proved. He is. There's no doubt about it."

Maggie heard Caesar's knock on the outer office door. "You're going to eat something," she said.

When she returned, Byrony had put on the dressing gown. Maggie placed the tray on her lap. There were thick slices of roast beef drowned in brown gravy, mashed potatoes, and fresh peas. "I'm not hungry," she said.

"I don't give a damn. Eat."

Maggie pulled Brent's favorite chair next to the bed and sat down, her fingers a tapping steeple. She said nothing, merely watched Brent's wife take a few bites. She said, "I saw Mrs. Saxton this afternoon and she asked about you. I, of course, had no idea that you were burrowed in your bed like a mole. She's a nice lady. Keep eating. As for Mr. Saxton, I believe he's downstairs in the saloon, probably here at his wife's request to see that you're all right. Take another bite of beef. That's it."

"Where is Brent?"

"I don't know. I haven't seen him."

"Go to Clay Street. That's where Celeste lives."

"Your husband, Byrony, hasn't visited Celeste since before your marriage."

"He was with her this morning," she said. "I followed him."

"Oh, no," Maggie said. Several possible scenarios flitted through her mind, each more lurid than the last.

"He wasn't doing anything, Maggie, or perhaps I was just a little early. He forced me back here."

"And?"

Byrony said not a word.

Maggie sighed. It really wasn't any of her business. It was probable that Brent had been utterly furious, that he'd acted the domineering male and ripped up at his young wife. And then? Maggie suddenly became aware of the smells in the room. Dinner smells, the faint scent of gardenia, and sex. So, the idiot had forced her, punished her, then slammed out.

"Maggie?"

"Yes, love."

"I'm not much of a person, am I?"

"What in heaven's name do you mean?"

"I'm not a good person, or a strong person." Maggie watched her stare down at the tray. She hated the look of misery on Byrony's face.

"That's bosh, and you know it, Byrony."

"I'm sorry, Maggie. I'm boring you. And I'm acting like a whining child. I've always loathed people who carried on about their problems, burdening other people with them. I've always believed that one should act. Lord knows I managed to act, not at all wisely perhaps, with Ira. Now here I am a shivering—" Byrony leaned back against the headboard and closed her eyes. "Thank you for the dinner, Maggie. You've been very kind to me."

"You are not a whining person, Byrony. Felice is a whiner. I think perhaps you would act if you knew what action to take."

Byrony laughed. "There's a good deal of truth in that, I suspect."

"I would say, though, that you're very confused and unhappy with the present situation. Brent is occasionally the most stubborn, bullheaded man I've ever met. but he's also kind and loyal. He's so used to being alone, Byrony, to never *giving* himself completely to another. He's twenty-seven; and he's been alone for nine years. That's a lot of years to depend only on yourself. I'm not defending him. But you need to understand him. I've seen him the angel and I've seen him the devil. I guess most of us have both in us. Now, would you like to tell me about it? I'm accounted a good listener."

She said, her voice calm, almost singsong, "I wish I'd never seen him in San Diego, never felt about him the way I did when I first saw him. But that's all in the past now. I'm married to a man who doesn't love me, who is afraid I'll become pregnant so he'll be tied to me." She turned to face Maggie, her face white, her eyes swollen. "I only want someone to care about me. Is that so much to ask, Maggie? I don't want to live my life without feeling some happiness, some sense of being important to another person. Oh drat, this is ridiculous. I swore I wouldn't shed another tear, and just look at me. A weak woman crying her bloody head off because she's too immature to take charge of her life. Just look at you, Maggie. You're strong, independent, sure of yourself. I want to be like you."

Now, that is a revelation, Maggie thought, both touched and amused. "All right," she said. "You want to know what I would do?"

"Yes, please."

"I would buy myself a whip, and when words failed, I would take it to his tough hide. Sometimes, I've found, it's difficult to get a man's attention."

Byrony stared at her. "You wouldn't just pack up and leave?"

"If I hated the man I would, and without a backward glance. However, if I thought I could salvage him, if I *wanted* to salvage him, I'd keep pounding some sense into his thick skull."

It sounded so logical, Byrony thought, so straightforward, and—yes, easy. But Brent wasn't around. She laughed, nodding.

Maggie felt as though a great weight had been lifted from her shoulders. There was strength in her, strength, fire, and determination. Damn Brent anyway. Why did he have to be such a blind idiot? "Now," Maggie said briskly, "I have some work to do. Shall I ask Caesar to have some bathwater sent up to you?"

"Yes, please." Byrony threw back the blanket and nearly bounded from the bed. She hugged the other woman tightly. "Thank you, Maggie."

"You just get that whip, my dear. It there are any wagers to be made, my money's on you."

Byrony giggled, this time a pure, happy sound.

"Heavens, this room is a mess. I must straighten it up."

Maggie left her rushing about, filled with purpose. It wasn't until much later that Maggie learned that Brent was gambling with James Cora at the El Dorado, drunk as a loon, and itching for a fight, which he got. He was delivered to Maggie's doorstep, bloodied, still drunk, a stupid grin on his battered face.

"We didn't want to take him to his new wife, ma'am," said Limpin' Willie. "Didn't wanna scare the sh—the hell out of her."

So what am I? Maggie wanted to ask sarcastically, his mother?

"Bring him in, boys."

She stood over Brent, hands on her hips, her lips pursed. A woman cries and a man gets drunk, she thought. Well, just maybe it was a good sign. He hadn't gone to Celeste.

Brent was singing, a very graphic ditty about a gambler

and a saloon girl. She poured black coffee down him between choruses.

"Now, do you want Saint? You're a bloody mess, Brent."

He cocked a brow at her, and winced as he grinned. "You should see the other fellows."

"Yeah, I'll just bet you won that one."

"Sure did," Brent said. He felt like hell and he wanted another whiskey. Suddenly he felt so tired he couldn't hold his head up. He fell asleep on Maggie's sofa, snores filling the room.

"Idiot," she muttered as she covered him with a blanket. She sent for Saint.

"You finally beat the hell out of him, Maggie?" were Saint's first words upon his arrival some forty-five minutes later.

"It appears I'll have to line up for that," she said. "Sorry it's so late, Saint, but his face looks like chopped meat."

"Where's Byrony?"

"Asleep, I hope. The boys brought him here. They wanted to spare his wife."

Saint began to sponge the blood off Brent's face. "Not as bad as it looks," he said. "His handsome face is still intact. No need for stitches. Wouldn't want anything to interfere with that romantic scar of his."

"Stop it, Byrony," Brent protested, trying to push Saint away. "That hurts."

Saint grinned at the sound of Brent's slurred voice, and shoved his hand back to his side. "I want you to know, my friend, that you interrupted a very pleasurable interlude. It's bloody inconsiderate of you."

"Byrony," Brent muttered. "Don't do that, love. Come here and let me kiss you. Lord, you're so beautiful—so beautiful."

"Now he remembers he has a wife," Maggie said in some disgust.

"Now, Maggie, he's just a man," Saint said. "A very confused man. He'll realize soon enough, I imagine, that what he's finally got is more than what most men ever have."

"Whatever he is, he's going to feel like hell tomorrow."

He did, but Byrony, with new eyes and delighted with the fact that he hadn't slept with his mistress, merely said to him, "Here is some cocoa, Brent. Saint said the sugar would make you feel better."

He drank the cocoa.

"Saint also said a big breakfast would help. Lots of eggs—"

Brent groaned. "Please, Byrony, let me die in peace."

She placed a fresh damp cloth over his forehead, gently smoothing back his hair as she did so. "All right. You rest. I'll be here if you need me."

He fell asleep again and Byrony stood over him, staring down at the rough black stubble on his jaws, the steady rise and fall of his bare chest. When Maggie and Saint had half-carried him into the bedroom some hours before, Byrony thought he'd been hurt.

"No, no, love," Maggie said, "he's just stinking drunk. Maybe you won't need that bullwhip for a while."

"Let him sleep, then mother him when he wakes up," Saint said. "As for you," he continued, his eyes searching her face, "you get some rest as well. And, Byrony, don't you worry too much, you hear?"

Byrony heard Maggie say to Saint as they left, "And you, I suppose, Dr. Morris, are back to continue your pleasurable interlude?"

"Unfortunately not. Poor Jane, she was so sad when Limpin' Willie came for me."

"Get yourself a wife, Saint, that's my advice to you."

Saint said something Byrony couldn't hear. Maggie's

bright laugh came back, clear and filled with fun. "Then," she said, "let's rouse Felice. The girl's in love with you."

Byrony quickly closed the bedroom door. She had no intention of ever eavesdropping again in her life. She looked back at her sleeping husband, shook her head, and settled down with Lord Byron's *The Corsair*.

Thank God I'm young and strong and have a thick head, Brent thought. He felt no aftereffects of all the whiskey he'd drunk, but he was sore, damnably so. He flexed his fingers, looked at his raw knuckles.

"Saint said there's nothing broken," Byrony said. "Did you give a good account of yourself?"

Brent wasn't certain how he'd expected Byrony to act—he hadn't even thought about it—but this smiling girl somehow didn't fit the image a man had of a wife who'd been deserted for drink and a bloody fight for most of the night. "Yes," he said, "I did."

"How many were there?"

"Four, maybe five. Then everyone got into it. I owe Cora a good three hundred dollars for damages. I'd be broke if most of the fight hadn't happened in the street."

She said nothing about the money, merely pointed to the tub in the corner of the bedroom. "I've had bathwater brought up for you. In about an hour, Smiley from the stables is bringing over a landau. I'm taking you for that ride to the ocean. Saint said it would be great medicine for you. The fresh air and all."

Brent nodded and flung back the bedcovers. He was naked and Byrony found herself staring at the ugly bruise over his ribs. "Are you truly all right?"

He gave her a cocky grin. "Nobody kneed me, it that's what you're worried about."

Back to normal, Byrony thought. She said, "I think I'll go out for a while. I won't be long."

"Where are you going?"

She smiled at him. "I'm going to buy a bullwhip," she said, and left him standing in the middle of the bedroom, a look of incomprehension on his face.

The afternoon was cloudy, the fog thick and heavy as they neared the ocean. Brent said, "I won't be able to see you in a moment. What are you going to do with that whip anyway?"

He'd been eyeing it, surprised that she'd actually bought it.

"For peace of mind," Byrony said, her voice serene. "How do you feel?"

"Just a bit sore, that's all. What peace of mind?"

"Mr. Hobbs told me it was quite efficacious, but never to use it on geldings. Just stallions."

"I see," said Brent, who was beginning to. "I thought any kind of violence repelled you?"

"It does." She shrugged. "One must adapt, however."

"The fog is too thick," Brent said and turned the horse around. "Let's get out of here." The breeze was stiff, whipping up whorls of gritty sand.

"As you wish," Byrony said easily.

"Byrony," he said, gazing at her profile, "I don't think I like your tone."

"I suggest you wait until you have the horse doing what you want before you go after the mare."

She was laughing at him. He didn't like it, not one bit. He said in his most affected drawl, "I intend to mount the mare, sweetheart. No bridle, of course, that's not necessary, but perhaps a few nips on the back of her neck."

She gave a bright laugh that made him grit his teeth. "And you want the mare to try to buck you off? Or perhaps if the mare decides to let you ride her, you'll decide to punish her by dismounting?"

He was so hard that he hurt. "No," he said, his eyes between the horses's ears, "No more dismounting. After I nip her neck, I fully intend to ride her until she's trembling and sweating."

"I wish you luck," Byrony said lightly, "with your mare."

"I don't need luck, just opportunity."

"Oh, incidentally, could you please just leave me at the Saxtons' house? I promised Chauncey I'd come by."

"No chance. Didn't you know that the stallion always herds his mares, keeps them under his watchful eye?"

"Is that so? Well, perhaps the stallion had best come to the realization that there is the occasional mare who refuses to share him. Maybe you know of such a stallion, Brent?"

That did it, he thought. "If the mare were more of a mare," he said brutally, "perhaps she could keep the stallion content."

"Or," Byrony said, manifestly amused, "if the stallion were more of a stallion, he could be content in his own pasture. I venture to say that there are some mares who are just as possessive as their stallions. Have you ever heard of a mare nipping her stallion's neck?"

"All right," he roared, scaring the horse, "that does it. Enough of this ridiculous imagery. If you ever raise that whip to me, Byrony, I will make you very sorry."

"How, if you don't mind my asking?" she said with great seriousness. "We mares like specificity, you know."

He ground his teeth. "I don't know," he said finally, "but you can be certain I will come up with something."

"Until you do, then I shall keep to my present course."

"Which is?"

"Keeping my stallion to myself," she said, "using whatever means are necessary."

"We stallions also appreciate specificity."

"Do you now?" she said, and very lightly trailed her fingers up his thigh. She felt his muscles tense, heard his sharp intake of breath.

"Perhaps," she said, "this stallion will shortly be too exhausted to leave his pasture."

"I will do just as I please, Byrony."

"So shall I, Brent. So shall I."

"You'd best remove your hand, else I'll take you right here."

She laughed, and with great concentration straightened her bonnet. He gave her a black look as she began to hum, as if she hadn't a care in the whole damned world.

Brent fully intended to make love to her until she was utterly exhausted when they returned, but it was not to be.

Caesar met him outside. "It looks important, Brent," he said.

Brent took the wrinkled envelope and stared down at it. "Oh no," he said.

"What is it, Brent?" Byrony asked.

"A letter, and not from my brother, Drew. It's from my father's lawyer in Natchez." His hand was trembling; he couldn't seem to control it. He ripped open the envelope and pulled out the neatly scripted two pages.

Byrony watched his hands clench, watched the myriad expressions on his expressive face. She heard him curse very explicitly and very quietly.

He turned to walk away from her, but she grabbed his arm. "What is it, Brent?"

"My father's dead, and of all the insane things, he's made me his heir."

TWENTY-THREE

"Why shouldn't you be your father's heir?"

Byrony followed her husband into the sitting room and firmly closed the door behind her. He looked utterly abstracted. She repeated her question.

"Heir? I shouldn't be, even though I'm the eldest. He kicked me off the plantation and out of his life nine years ago."

"Would you like a brandy, Brent?"

"Yes."

She handed him a liberal dose and turned away to remove her pelisse and bonnet. She said over her shoulder, "Why did he do that?"

"Because he caught me in bed fucking his wife."

Byrony felt as though someone had slammed a fist into her stomach. She turned incredulous eyes to his face. "What?"

"I was eighteen, Laurel was only twenty-two. She wanted me and had me, for what it was worth in those days. My father came in, quite unexpectedly, of course." Unconsciously he rubbed the scar along his cheek.

So it had been his father who had punished him, she thought. Nine years, Maggie had told her, nine years completely on his own.

"But you were only eighteen. What about your stepmother? Did your father kick her out?"

Brent laughed, waving the letter at her. "That's the irony of it, sweetheart. I was gallant at eighteen, so gallant that I took the blame for that fiasco. Perhaps I shouldn't have. It would have spared my father later. Evidently he, poor besotted fool, finally realized that she'd only married him for money and position. He's given me the plantation, Wakehurst, and also left me Laurel's trustee. In other words, I will control all the money. I do wonder just how she feels about this."

"What about your brother, Drew?"

"Father left him quite a bit of money in his own right, in addition to what our mother left him upon her death. Drew's twenty-six now, and an artist. He lives in a bachelor apartment near the main house and has for over two years. When I was removed from my home nine years ago, Drew was readying to leave for Paris, to study art there. Actually, the only contact I've had over the years with my former home has been an occasional letter from my brother. Lord only knows what he thinks about all this." Brent stopped abruptly, downed the remainder of his brandy, and eased into his chair. "Byrony, I've got to go back. The lawyers can't do anything without me."

"Then we will go," she said, her voice brisk.

"We?"

"Of course. Unless you don't want to go back."

"It appears I have no choice in the matter. It's my intention, however, to sell the plantation." But it sounded to Byrony as if he were hesitant.

"It was your home for eighteen years, Brent."

He sighed, running his fingers through his hair. "I know. I'd be lying if I said I hadn't missed it over the years. It's a beautiful, graceful old place, Byrony, just south of Natchez, quite near the Mississippi, and just north of the Louisiana border. My grandfather built it before the turn of the century. There's quite a bit of Spanish influence, of course."

"Please tell me more about it."

"The slaves. When I left nine years ago, there were more than five hundred Negroes at Wakehurst."

"Doing what, for heaven's sake? It sounds like a small army."

"The majority are field hands, backbreaking work in the cotton fields from dawn to dusk, and there are artisans—blacksmiths, coopers, bricklayers, carpenters—and of course, house slaves, well over two dozen waiting on the white folk. Mammy Bath, old and wrinkled as a prune, was like a second mother to me. At Wakehurst, their existence was better than at most other plantations. That is to say, they got two meals a day, had a hospital of sorts, and for infractions could only receive twelve lashes from the overseer, or the head driver, a slave also, but a more intelligent one. Had I stayed, I probably wouldn't have given it a great deal of thought. It's simply a way of life, you see, and an economic necessity. But now—I don't know if I could stomach seeing it again." He laughed. "Now I'm the *massa*, and you, my dear, would be the *missis*."

"Free them," Byrony said without hesitation.

"To do what? They're ignorant, appallingly so, thanks to the white man. Oh, hell, maybe you're right. As for dear Laurel—"

"If nothing else, dear Laurel had excellent taste in men. But I don't think it quite fair for her to seduce an eighteen-year-old boy." *And, as a result, make you so distrustful of women. Make you so distrustful of me.* Byrony couldn't wait to meet Laurel. She wanted to take the bullwhip to her.

"Lord, you're probably right, but I was a horny little goat. I had my first taste of sex when I was fourteen, and was the scourge of the county by the time I was seventeen. Hell, I even bedded a couple of young Negro girls. Every man did it, you see, every white man, that is. The ladies called me the *enfant terrible*, and giggled behind their gloves. My father was quite proud of me, I think, until that day. Now you know my rather reprehensible past, Byrony, at least how it all got started."

She grinned at him. "On the way to Natchez, you can tell me the really reprehensible parts, as in what you've done during the past nine years. Have the ladies called you *homme terrible*?"

"I imagine that some of them did. But no matter now. Are you certain you wish to go back with me, Byrony?"

"You did promise me a honeymoon, you know."

"What about the whip?"

"My constant companion," she said. "I'm sorry about your father, Brent."

"So am I. I don't know why he didn't write to me himself before he died. I would have come back."

"I suspect it probably had something to do with pride."

He twisted around to look at her. "You're pretty smart, you know that?"

"I bought a whip, didn't I?"

The next evening, the Hammonds, dressed formally, arrived at the Saxtons' home for dinner. Horace and Agatha Newton were there, as well as Saint Morris and Tony Dawson.

"How lovely you look, Byrony," said Chauncey, giving her a brief hug. "Del is delighted you came. He told me he's forgotten how a normal woman is supposed to look. I think he wants to add me to his shipping line."

"You look noble, Chauncey," Brent said, "a clipper, perhaps, under a sail of blue silk."

"Tony's my dinner partner?" Saint said to Del as they strolled into the dining room.

"Sorry, old man. Bear up. Tony here can be quite amusing when the muse strikes him."

"Chauncey isn't due for another month. I wonder you invited me at all."

"She's so big, I'd forgotten," Del said. "Excuse me, Saint, but you can't compete with this vision." Del turned to Byrony, who was seated at his right. "The gold silk becomes you, my dear. As for this village idiot," he continued at Brent, "I'm delighted he isn't dead. I heard about your fight."

"Just a mild difference of opinion," Brent said easily. "Actually, it wouldn't have mattered if that other fellow ever had the same opinion. In fact, I don't even remember any opinions being exchanged."

"Nothing like a good fight to reaffirm your manhood," Byrony said to Chauncey and Agatha.

Agatha sent a fond look toward her husband. "The days aren't too far past when Horace got drunk to the gills and raised a little hell."

"Poor Saint," said Byrony. "I don't know how you manage to keep your male image intact. You're too large for anyone to want to fight you."

"The good missionaries used to tell me that God always balanced the scales. A huge fellow like myself is gentle as a lamb. It's only the scrawny little ones, like Brent, who are constantly trying to prove themselves."

"Missionaries?" Brent said, quirking a dark brow. "Where the devil did you find that sort?"

"On a little island called Maui. It's part of the Hawaiian Islands in the Pacific. I was a doctor on a whaler. When I first traveled to the main town on Maui, Lahaina, I decided to stay for a while. It's a constant battle between the missionaries and the sailors."

"I say, Saint," Tony said, "I didn't know about that. A

great story for the *Alta*, I think. What do you say? All the gory details?"

"Later, my boy, later. There are ladies present."

Byrony turned to say something to Chauncey, but she seemed lost in thought.

It was Agatha who drew Chauncey's attention. "My dear, what is to be the name of this prince or princess?"

"How about Beauregard Saxton?" Tony said.

"Or Percival?" said Brent. "After the fellow who was supposed to be my bartender but didn't show up. We mustn't forget he'll be half English."

"Actually," Chauncey said, "we can't agree on a name. Del is digging in his heels and simply won't be reasonable."

Saint said, "What is this? What name do you want, Del?"

Delaney shook his head, and calmly continued eating his baked chicken.

"This is ginger, isn't it?" Brent asked. At Delaney's nodding grin, he added, "Amazing. Never a predictable moment in this house." He said to his wife, "I think I'm beginning to like it when things aren't just as one expects them to be."

"They will continue not to be what you expect, too," Byrony said.

"She wants to keep me happy," Brent said.

"So that's what she meant," Agatha said.

Later, as the guests were all seated in the Saxton sitting room, Chauncey suddenly jumped and dropped her cup of coffee. "Oh dear," she said, looking toward her husband.

Saint smiled and rose from his chair. "I'm glad you waited until after dinner, my dear."

"The baby's coming?"

Agatha laughed at Del's stunned expression. Saint was bending over Chauncey, his large hand splayed over her belly. When he felt her tense with a contraction, he gently patted her shoulder. "How long have you felt the pains, Chauncey?"

"Since this morning. Nothing impressive, until now."

"Chauncey," Del shouted at his wife, "why didn't you tell me? Jesus, you stubborn—"

"Now, Del, if I'd told you, you would have been in an absolute panic all day." Another contraction seared through her and she gulped. "I think you can panic now."

"No need," said Saint calmly. "Why don't you come upstairs with me now, my dear. My, my, a month early. The little beggar is eager to see the world."

"Wait. That is, shouldn't I do something?"

"My dear Del, you've done quite enough," Saint said. "After all, you did invite me to dinner. Agatha, why don't you come with us. You can help Chauncey into her nightgown. Del, have a drink. The rest of you hold his hand and keep him amused, all right?"

Byrony jumped to her feet. "I'll help you," she said.

"No, my dear. You stay downstairs."

"But—"

"Byrony," Brent said sharply, "sit down."

Delaney helped Chauncey to her feet, and held her when she doubled over. "Don't worry, love. I'll be with you."

"Lord, that's all I need," Saint said, "a husband who won't obey me."

Tony, Byrony, Brent, and Horace were left in the sitting room to stare at each other. Brent felt Byrony's hand close over his sleeve. "Shouldn't I go up and be with her? I am a woman, after all."

"You haven't had a child," he said.

"What would you know about it?"

To her utter surprise, Brent paled a bit. "Unfortunately, I didn't know much of anything. If I had, perhaps Joyce Morgan might still be alive. As it was, I buried her and the child."

"I say, Brent, what are you talking about?" Horace Newton asked, leaning forward in his chair.

"It was a long time ago," Brent said. "In the wilds of Colorado. I was riding to Denver and overtook this wagon. A very young woman was driving, and in great pain. She was alone and in labor." Brent stopped, aware that he'd begun to sweat. He forced himself to shrug. "That's all. I tried, she tried, but nothing was good enough."

"Where was her husband?" Byrony asked, her throat dry.

"He was in Denver, selling cattle. When I found him, he'd gotten into a fight and been killed. It was probably just as well. The way I was feeling, I might have killed him myself. He'd left her close to her time, you see, with no one to help her."

The fury he'd felt, the utter hopelessness that had paralyzed him for weeks thereafter, returned in full measure. He wasn't aware that his face mirrored that nearly forgotten pain. He bounded to his feet and began to pace. "Chauncey will be all right," he said, looking upward for a moment.

"Of course she will," said Horace.

Brent paused a moment, and wiped the sweat from his brow. It occurred to him that this was the real reason he didn't want Byrony to be pregnant. She could die. He'd buried the memory just as he'd buried the young woman and her baby, so deep that he'd hoped never to remember it again. He shot a look at Byrony, but her head was bowed, her eyes on her folded hands.

Tony began to talk, to everyone's relief, of David Broderick. "He just gets more and more powerful. To say that California is the land of opportunity is an understatement. Here was Broderick, a New York saloon keeper and a Tammany henchman, and now he's a United States senator."

"Careful, Tony," Horace Newton said. "He's so powerful, I think he has spies everywhere. I just hope Del doesn't get it into his head to go against him."

"Del isn't stupid," Tony said. "Our dear mayor, Garrison, keeps Del informed of what is doable and what isn't."

There was a scream.

Everyone froze.

"That's it, love, yell," Del was saying to his panting wife. "As loud as you want."

Chauncey was clutching his fingers so tightly they were turning white. "It hurts so much," she whispered.

"I know," he said, but he didn't, of course. He met Saint's eyes.

"Move aside a minute, Del. I want to talk to your wife."

At first Chauncey wouldn't let him go. When she did, he backed up only two steps. Saint sat down beside her. "You're doing quite well, Chauncey," he said calmly. "Quite well indeed. The baby's not at all large, since he's a bit early. In fact, I think you'll have your son or daughter by midnight. Incidentally, that was a fine dinner. I noticed you didn't eat much. Just as well."

"Midnight?" Delaney nearly shouted. "That's three hours away."

"This is also your first child," Saint continued, lightly stroking Chauncey's hand. "Not a long time at all, actually. Now, practice breathing as I taught you to. That's it, pant, and don't fight the pain." Saint stood and moved away to wash his hands again in the basin of hot water Lin had brought up. "Now," he said, moving to the foot of the bed, "let's see where the little fellow is now."

Chauncey felt his fingers slip inside her just as a strong contraction made her feel as if she were being torn apart. "Pant, Chauncey."

Close to an hour later, Agatha came into the sitting room. "I'm here to reassure everyone," she said, eyeing the faces staring at her. "Chauncey's just fine. Delaney's even alive, but barely. A round of whiskey for everyone, Horace. Byrony, come with me a moment. I'd meant to speak to you this evening. Now's as good a time as any."

Byrony followed Agatha from the sitting room to the entrance hall. "Is she really all right?"

"Yes, my dear. I promise. Saint is telling her jokes right now. She's smiling, but poor Delaney is looking ready for execution. Now, I just wanted to tell you that I'm relieved you and Brent are leaving San Francisco for a while. The end of the week?" At Byrony's mute nod, she continued. "It's Irene, of course. She didn't institute the gossip, but on the other hand, she didn't actively try to stop it. She doesn't play the martyr well, let me tell you, but Sally Stevenson and that snit daughter of hers don't care. You may be certain that while you're gone, Chauncey and I will do our best to obliterate all the nastiness and innuendo. I think that when you return, everything will have blown over. Who knows? Maybe some intelligent person might even strangle Penelope."

"Thank you, Agatha."

The older woman smiled gently and patted Byrony's hand. "Everything will work out, my dear, you'll see. Now, I'm going to go back upstairs. I've never thought it reasonable that a woman in labor should be surrounded by men. Lord, what do they know?"

Chauncey felt Saint's fingers kneading her belly. "Come here, Del. Feel your child."

Delaney tentatively placed his palm over his wife's stomach. He felt the contraction, and winced. "Can't you ease the pain, Saint?"

Saint shook his head. "Not yet, we don't want the contractions to slow or stop. We want the baby born as soon as possible. I'll give her chloroform when it's time."

Chauncey screamed, a high, thin wail that made Delaney shudder. "Oh, shit," he said frantically.

"I think we're there," Saint said. "The baby's coming now, Chauncey. Keep pushing. That's it. Del, help me, and don't faint. No time now to give her anything."

Delaney saw the blond mop of hair. Saint quickly moved aside, and watched with a pleased smile as the baby girl slipped out into her father's waiting hands.

"Oh, my God."

"A real beauty, isn't she?" He kept talking as he quickly clipped the umbilical cord. "Now, Del, give her to Agatha and Lin. Listen to those lungs. She's not too small at all."

Delaney Saxton felt as though he'd just run a mile. He stood very still, watching Saint speak to Chauncey as he pressed her belly to remove the afterbirth, watching Agatha and Lin wash his little girl and wrap her in a soft blanket.

The clock downstairs chimed twelve strokes.

"Are you never wrong, Saint?" Chauncey asked.

"Never about babies. Now, say something to your poor wretch of a husband. He looks ready to collapse."

But Chauncey said, "I forgot to ask you where you got your nickname. Now you'll probably never tell me."

It was Saint who brought Alexandra Aurora Saxton downstairs to the assembled group.

"I am so relieved," Byrony said to her husband sometime later as she climbed into bed beside him. "Such a beautiful child. She looks like the female counterpart of Del."

"Chauncey's labor was blessedly short," Brent said, as if in surprise. "Of course she had a doctor and her husband with her."

He turned beside her and took her into his arms. "What is this thing? A nightgown on my bride?"

"It's cold."

"I can guarantee you'll be sweating soon enough."

"So, the stallion is ready to mount his mare?"

The hand stroking the nape of her neck stilled. I won't fill her with my seed, Brent thought. I can't. He released her abruptly and turned onto his back, his arms pillowing his head.

"What is this?" Byrony asked, balancing herself on her

elbow above her husband. "You wish the mare to mount the stallion?"

"I'm tired," Brent said, not looking at her. "Let's go to sleep. There's a lot to be done tomorrow if we want to leave for New Orleans on Friday."

She moved closer and he felt her breasts against his chest. He gritted his teeth. "No, Byrony."

Byrony realized what was on his mind. He was afraid she would become pregnant. He was afraid she might die, and he would hold himself responsible. She was utterly relieved to learn that his wish for her not to become pregnant was because of his terrible experience and not because he didn't want to stay with her. At least that's what she thought were his motives. "Very well," she said. She slowly, gently spread her fingers over his chest, tangling them in the soft tufts of black hair. "You feel so warm." He was very still beneath her hand. Her fingers drifted downward.

"No, Byrony." He sounded like a drowning man even to his own ears.

"Why, Brent? If you are worried that I'll become pregnant, I will accept that. But why shouldn't I give you pleasure?"

Her fingers closed over him at that moment, and he trembled with the shock of it. She felt him swell in her hand. "Felice told me that men liked this," she said, her warm breath on his belly. He felt her hair streaking over his chest, down over his groin, and then he felt her mouth close over him. He nearly leapt off the bed.

He thought he'd die.

"I love how you feel and how you taste."

His fingers were in her hair, and he knew it was nearly over for him. Her inexperience and her obvious interest in what she was doing to him were an exhilarating combination. "Byrony." He moaned again. "Oh God."

He gritted his teeth, forcing himself to control. "Stop it,

Byrony, now." His chest was heaving as he pulled her off him and onto her back. He felt her legs close about his hips, felt her tremble as his fingers found her. "You'd make a saint forget himself." He went deep into her. His control was nearly gone and when he would have pulled out of her, she closed her thighs tightly about his flanks and arched upward.

"I'm giving you nothing," he panted. "Byrony, you're my wife."

There was a wealth of possessiveness in his voice, and to her surprise, Byrony felt her body respond. She was enjoying her power over him until that moment. She wrapped her arms around his back. When his tongue was inside her mouth just as his sex was in her body, she cried out, unable to help herself. He took her soft, keening wails into his mouth, and forgot his fear, forgot everything but her, his wife, her pleasure, and his.

She raised her face and kissed him. She nestled close, and said sleepily, "There's so much to be done tomorrow if we're to leave on Friday."

"I can't believe it," he said more to himself than to her as he fitted her against the length of his body. "Seduced by a very proper little lady."

TWENTY-FOUR

Laurel Hammond breathed in the sweet scent of magnolia blossoms as she walked from her small music room at the back of the house into the garden. A glorious day, she thought, neither too warm nor too humid. She walked slowly through the garden toward the gardenia bushes. She would pick the blossoms for Mammy Bath, bossy old crone, to make her more perfume. The meager supply Drew had dutifully bought her from Paris was gone. The thought of Drew brought a frown. He was a grown man, damn him, yet he was so slippery—no, elusive. If she dared question him, he called her "Stepmama." She hated that.

As she plucked the gardenias and laid them in her small wicker basket, her thoughts went inevitably to Brent. No word, nothing. It had been well over six months since his father's death. She had to assume that he'd been notified by the lawyers, for after all, Drew knew he was in San Francisco. Why hadn't he written? She'd wondered so many times what kind of a man he'd become. What did he think of her? Did he hate her? After nine long years? Of course he couldn't. It had been he who had seduced her, after all. It hadn't been her fault, not really. She'd just been so lonely, so unhappy with her husband, cold, domineering Avery.

The will, that wretched document. Laurel shivered under

the shade of a huge moss-strewn oak tree, and walked into the bright sun. Drew, insolent bastard, had dared to laugh when that pompous, bewhiskered old fool Mr. Jenkins had read it aloud to them in the library two days after the funeral. She'd been too surprised to say anything, too surprised and too frightened. She dropped a gardenia onto the green grass. The fear was still there.

"You must be more careful, Laurel."

She watched Drew lean gracefully down to pick up the blossom. He looked like an aesthete and a well-bred Southern gentleman who had never lifted his hands in work—slender, pale-skinned, his light brown hair swept back from a broad, clear forehead. None of the look of his brother, she thought, with his thoughtful brown eyes. But of course, she really didn't remember all that well what Brent did look like, except for his midnight-blue eyes, penetrating eyes, so compelling and intense, even when he was only eighteen. Drew straightened and handed her the blossom with a flourish.

"Thank you," she said. "Why aren't you painting?"

"The beautiful day drew me out. That"—he paused a moment, his brow furrowing—"and a premonition."

Laurel arched a perfectly plucked auburn brow. "You and that witch Sinda are more alike than I imagined."

"Oh no," Drew said easily. "I don't wring chickens' necks and dance about a fire preaching the end of the world."

"That was something, wasn't it?" Laurel shook her head, smiling at the memory. "I'll never forget that incident. The slaves refusing to work because the day of reckoning was shortly to arrive. More fear for God's wrath than Mr. Simmons's whip."

"Father and Mr. Simmons handled the situation very nicely, as I recall. Poor Sinda. When the earth didn't end, she was severely flogged."

"So what is this premonition of yours?"

"I'm not really sure," Drew said slowly. "Something will happen today, something out of the ordinary." He shrugged and looked a bit rueful. "Don't mind me. It's probable that my mind has heated up before the weather has. Perhaps my paints have finally reduced my brain to shadowy mysticism."

"You need to leave the plantation more often than you do, Drew. There are so many very pretty young ladies hereabouts, just waiting for an offer from Mr. Drew Hammond of Wakehurst. Why, Melinda Forrester was telling me just the other day how she so much admired your paintings—"

Drew held up a slender white hand. "Spare me, Laurel. Melinda Forrester is—well, suffice it to say that I have no interest in the girl." He got a dreamy, faraway look in his deep brown eyes. "I miss Paris," he said simply. "Oh, all this is beautiful, but it's not mine."

"No, it's all Brent's now, isn't it?"

Drew's eyes focused on his beautiful stepmother's face. "Why so bitter, Laurel? I don't know why Brent left Wakehurst so long ago, but he is father's heir. Of course the plantation must belong to him. The question is, what will he do about it?"

"And I was your father's wife. How dare he make Brent *my* trustee? Why didn't he leave me money in my own right, like he did you?"

Drew merely cocked an eyebrow at her. He'd been home for two years now, and wasn't by any means blind. He'd discovered she was having an affair with another planter, the blustery Mr. John Lattimer. If he'd known, surely his father must have. The fact that his father hadn't left her her own money seemed to be proof. Of course, to be fair about it, Laurel was young and beautiful and his father had been old and infirm.

He reached up and pulled down a piece of Spanish moss dangling from a low branch of an elm tree.

"Perhaps," he said slowly, "you should consider remarrying—after your period of mourning is over, of course. I understand that Mr. Elias Standford is infatuated."

Laurel shrugged. "He's old and a bore. And his children hate me. No, thank you."

"I seem to recall that Brent and I weren't any too happy when father turned up with you on his arm. But that was a long time ago, wasn't it? Why don't you visit New Orleans for a while? Good hunting there, I understand."

"Drew, don't be nasty. Lizzie?"

Laurel's near-yell brought a small Negro girl running toward them.

"Yes, missis?" the girl panted, her eyes on her dirty bare feet.

"Take this basket of gardenia blossoms to Mammy Bath."

"Yes, missis."

"Tell her to make my perfume."

"Yes, missis."

"So, Drew, have you bedded her yet?"

"For god's sake, Laurel, she can't be over thirteen years old." He stared after the girl, knowing she'd heard Laurel's words.

"I've already noticed the head driver, Josh, eyeing her closely."

"How odd it is, to be sure," Drew said in a sardonic voice. "If you had your way, Lizzie would have a baby within a year and be a grandmother by the time she was thirty. How would you like to be a grandmother, Laurel? After all, you are well past thirty, are you not?"

Laurel shuddered, but her voice was hard. "Spare me your European sensibilities, if you please, Drew, and I am not *well* past thirty."

"I have been home for two years now, and you haven't celebrated a single birthday."

"Drew, why don't *you* go visit New Orleans?"

"All right, Laurel, I'll cease and desist. It's going to get hot soon. I don't know how you ladies can bear all those heavy clothes."

"To be quite honest, it is very uncomfortable. But what is one to do? I can't very well stroll about in breeches and an open linen shirt as you do."

He laughed. "A sight to boggle the mind."

They were drinking lemonade under the shade of a huge cedar when Mammy Bath, wheezing and yelling all at the same time, came dashing into the garden. "Missis. It's the massa. He's home, my little boy is home."

Laurel grew very still. "Your premonition, Drew."

"It would appear that I do possess powers of which I was unaware. Well, my dear, it's been nine years, hasn't it? My wandering, wild brother, home at last."

"I suppose it's time for me to face my trustee," Laurel said. What is he like? she wondered yet again. Will he still find me beautiful? Of course he would. There would be no problem, she would see to it. And if there were—

Byrony allowed Brent to assist her from the open carriage. "Wakehurst," he said.

"It's beautiful, and just as you described it. But the trees and flowers, Brent. I couldn't have imagined anything so old or so glorious. Those are azaleas, are they not? And magnolia trees? And gardenias? Everything is so green, so lush."

Brent smiled at her excitement. "Yes, yes, and yes, and I agree," he said. "Now, are you ready to meet the inhabitants?"

The first inhabitant was Mammy Bath. She flew down the deep steps of the mansion and into Brent's arms. "My baby. Lordy, my baby is home. Oh, you handsome boy. And so big." Her gnarled black hands explored every inch of his face, her smile huge and unwavering, her teeth as white and healthy as Brent remembered as a child.

"Mammy, come now, you'll make this lovely lady jealous. I want you to meet my wife, Byrony Hammond."

"Mercy, mercy, you've got yerself a missis! Look at that little alabaster face. Where did you find this sweet baby?"

Byrony was too taken aback to move or say a word. She was hugged tightly by the scrawny little woman and examined just as Brent had been.

"Mammy's an institution," Brent said once the old slave had ceased her wild chatter. He looked up at that moment, and his eyes met Laurel's. God, but she's beautiful, was his first reaction. He supposed that he'd imagined she would be an old, tired crone after the passage of nine years. And Drew. A man now. Brent broke away from Mammy Bath, his stride firm, his eyes intent.

The two men met on the bottom step of the veranda.

"Brent," Drew said. "As I live and breathe, you do exist. Lord, but you're big."

"And you're all grown up. I remember a skinny little kid who was always covered with blobs of paint."

They embraced. Laughed. Embraced again.

Laurel stood stiffly quiet, her eyes not on the two brothers, but on the woman who remained in the drive beside Mammy Bath. *Brent's wife.* Byrony's face was shadowed by her bonnet. Her clothes were wrinkled and travel-stained, and her hands were clutched in front of her like a nun. She looked like a nonentity. Laurel smiled, and gracefully made her way down the steps. First things first, she thought, and waved.

"Welcome to Wakehurst," she called out. She hugged Brent's wife.

"How tired you look, you poor creature. May I call you Byrony? Thank you. Please call me Laurel. After all, not many years separate us. What a terribly long trip you've had, no doubt. All the way from San Francisco. Did you spend some time in New Orleans? Ah, what a lovely city, so unusual. And your riverboat trip up the Mississippi? A week was all, isn't that right?"

Byrony felt dull-witted. All she was required to do was nod or shake her head.

"Brent," Laurel called. "Come, your wife is ready to sink to the ground with fatigue. You and Drew can reminisce and joke and insult each other to your heart's content, but later. Othello. Lloyd. Come out here and get the master's luggage. Mammy, why don't you see to Brent's little wife. Would you like your own room, dear? No? How odd, well, no matter. Mammy, take her to the master's suite. I vacated it, of course, after my dear husband passed away." She felt a slight frisson even as she said the words. She couldn't wait to be gone from that dreadful, dark room with its smell of sickness. "It's Brent's now. Come along."

"Thank you," Byrony finally managed to say, and trailed after the beautiful woman.

Laurel felt a knot of fury build in her stomach. The girl was so young, damn her. And lovely. Dear God, what was she to do?

No sooner had all of them come into the gigantic entrance hall than they were surrounded by Negroes of all ages, all crying out, yelling actually, Byrony thought, blinking, all crowding around Brent. All she heard was "Massa. Massa."

The outside of the plantation had struck Byrony with its clean, simple lines, the two and a half stories supported by slender white columns, and graceful galleries surrounding three sides of the house. But the interior carried the Spanish influence that Brent had described to her. The walls were painted a soft pink, and a black wrought-iron staircase gently curved to the upper floors. Fresh cut flowers were in delicate vases on every surface. She tried not to feel overwhelmed, but she did, nonetheless. Ira's home in San Francisco had been elegant, rich, but it had none of the Old World grace of this mansion. It looked new and ugly by comparison. She wondered what Brent was thinking. Did it seem to him that their apartment above the saloon was a meager hovel compared to his old home?

"Byrony, come and meet all the house slaves."

Brent introduced her to several of the older slaves, then paused to allow Laurel to give the names of the newer slaves.

Othello, Desdemona, Portia, Lear, and on and on. Good grief, Byrony thought, it was like a Shakespearean festival. She wondered what their real names had been. She smiled until she felt her face cracking. Everyone smiled back at her, calling her the Little Missis. There wasn't a shoe on any foot present.

Suddenly Mammy Bath clapped her hands. "Enough. Off with you, you lazy blackies. Missis, you come with me. We'll get you a nice bath."

Byrony smiled at Brent, and he nodded. "Yes, go on upstairs. I'll join you shortly."

She looked over her shoulder as she preceded Mammy Bath up the stairs. Brent was talking to Laurel. She looked incredibly fragile and delicate and her charming laugh seemed almost intimate. Well, he'd known her intimately. She felt an alarming wave of jealousy. She met Drew's eyes for a moment, and had the feeling he'd read her feelings. He winked at her, an action so unexpected that she very nearly laughed.

The long hall on the second floor was covered with a thick, patterned carpet. Mammy Bath kept up a nonstop monologue until they reached the end of the corridor. She threw open the double oak doors.

Byrony shivered at the sight of the dreadful room. The furnishings were dark and heavy and thick, and musty-smelling gold draperies covered the windows. Byrony walked quickly to the windows and pulled back the awful brocade. Sunlight poured in. Mammy Bath dutifully opened the glass doors and Byrony breathed in the sweet warm air.

"That's better, I think," she said more to herself than to the hovering Mammy Bath. She walked out onto the gallery and leaned over the white wood railing. "So beautiful," she said, breathed in deeply as she stared down into the immaculate garden.

"Old Massa have bad eyes and the sunlight hurt him. All that change now, missis. We get rid of all this stuff, give it to Josh. Make that boy feel more important than he does already. He's the head driver, a smart boy."

Mammy Bath turned at the entrance of two slaves and directed the placement of their luggage. Within twenty minutes Byrony was submerged to her neck in a huge cedar tub filled with jasmine-scented water. I've died and gone to heaven, she thought, in my first full bath since I left New Orleans.

She leaned back and closed her eyes. I'm in Mississippi, she thought vaguely, taking a bath. And there are barefoot slaves about who *belong* to Brent. Her mind skimmed over the long weeks of travel, dwelling more on her husband's behavior than on the strange places they'd visited. Just when she thought she was beginning to really understand him, he would change, withdraw. He'd passed part of his time gambling, and they'd arrived in New Orleans with an extra thousand dollars. He'd spent most of it on her. She pictured the new gowns now hanging in the oak armoire in the corner of the bedroom. Had he been afraid that she would shame him? But of course he'd also had new clothes made for himself. She found herself a bit uncomfortable with the elegant Southern gentleman he'd become during the past week. His accent had broadened and he had developed an inexhaustible charm. She wondered if she would ever understand him. And now there were Laurel and his brother, Drew. Beautiful Laurel, who looked at him so intimately.

Byrony forced herself not to stir when she heard Brent's voice.

"Hello, mermaid. You look as if you're getting as much pleasure from that bath as I give you."

She opened her eyes at that and saw his smile. She gave a soft, replete sigh and his smile widened.

"Shall I join you?"

"I'm sure you need to, but with your size you'd best wait." She began to wash her hair, saying in her most off-hand voice, "Your stepmother seems quite charming, as does your brother."

"Were you expecting recriminations and screams of rage? My dear, this is the South. Ladies are ladies, at least superficially. Laurel will bide her time." He paused a moment. "This was my father's room. He refused to allow Laurel to make changes, according to Drew. Lord, it's depressing. Do what you wish to—anything would be an improvement."

"Will we be here that long?"

She watched him shrug. "We've traveled a long way. I, for one, want to feel firm earth beneath my feet for a while."

"New Orleans was the most unusual city I've ever seen," Byrony said.

"Wait until I give you a tour of Natchez."

"It will have to be an improvement over Panama."

"True enough. Perhaps on our return trip the railroad will be completed."

"None of the slaves wear shoes," she said abruptly.

"At least they're clean, and dressed well enough. That's Laurel's doing, of course. As a boy, I remember nothing but filth. At the dining table, we'd be served by footmen who had the dirtiest fingernails you've ever seen. Made one lose one's appetite."

"Apparently you didn't lose all your appetites."

"Thank the Lord, no," Brent said, grinning at her. Byrony lathered her hair a second time as she watched Brent shrug out of his coat. He said over his shoulder, "It would appear that Laurel has softened a bit."

"She's very lovely," Byrony said, willing to be fair, at least for the moment.

"Oh yes, she is indeed," Brent agreed. He tossed his shirt on the floor and sat down in an ugly wing chair to pull off his boots. He paused a moment. "Drew has become a man. It's disconcerting."

"Makes you feel old, does it?"

Brent grinned at her and rose, his fingers on the buttons of his trousers. "You want to see how old this old man really is?"

"Brent, stop that. You're getting water all over everything."

Opulent, Byrony thought. The dining room could accommodate eighteen people. The walls were painted a soft green, and draperies were drawn back from the long windows with gold cords. The furnishings were obviously French, even to Byrony's untutored eye. The dining table was covered with a pristine white linen cloth and white china edged in gold. "What is that?" she asked Brent in a near-whisper, pointing to a large hand-carved wooden bell-shaped adornment hanging down from the ceiling over the table.

"It's a punkah—"

"A fan is a fan, Brent," Drew said. "You'll be grateful for it within the month, I promise you, Byrony. During the meal, a house slave pulls the fan back and forth with a long cord. It cools the face and the vegetables. In the South we're all very proper. No sweating on the table."

"That will be the day," Brent said. "I can remember

sweating like a pig here during the summer months. Byrony, you'll feel as though you've been wrung out to dry, only you don't—dry, that is."

"How is the weather in San Francisco?" Drew asked.

"Blessedly cool," Brent said. He slanted a look at Byrony and added, "Except at certain times, of course."

Drew laughed. "He's always been outrageous, Byrony— ignore him—even when he was no larger than a mite."

"Tell me about Paris, Drew," Brent said. "Did you keep yourself out of trouble and your gentlemanly dignity intact?"

"Most of the time. It's as different as night is from day, Brent. Everything is so very old and established, despite all the political upheavals, and there is so much to experience, and to paint, naturally."

"You miss it," Byrony said, seeing the faraway look in Drew's eyes.

"Yes, but—"

He paused at the sound of swishing skirts. The men and Byrony turned to see Laurel glide into the dining room, looking as delicious as any dessert, Byrony thought, in a gown of light pink silk that bared her white shoulders and the tops of her breasts. One would have imagined that pink with auburn hair would have been dreadful, but it wasn't. Byrony suddenly felt complete dowdy, her own gown of dark blue silk—the color of Brent's eyes, she'd told him— purchased in New Orleans, seeming like a schoolgirl's next to Laurel's.

And her hair was still damp. She felt like a scraggly dog in comparison to the vision smiling so sweetly at the assembled company.

Laurel never let her smile falter. Indeed, it grew wider as her gaze flitted dismissively over Byrony. However had Brent gotten himself trapped by *that*? As for Brent, she felt herself responding to the man as she had to the boy. He was so handsome, she thought, his black hair thick and shiny, his face so strong and chiseled, even the scar on his cheek romantic and dashing. She met his eyes, still so compelling and fathomless, but they were unreadable as they rested on her face.

"Frank won't be joining us this evening——our overseer, Frank Paxton," Laurel added. "I trust everything is to your satisfaction?"

"Certainly," Brent said. "Byrony, my dear," he continued, a half-smile on his lips, "you will sit at the foot of the table. You are now, after all, the mistress of Wakehurst."

Byrony had the sudden awful memory of the dinner party when Irene had taken her seat at the table. She wondered if Brent remembered too, and thus had ensured that it wouldn't happen here. She smiled up at her husband as he pulled out her chair.

Laurel made no demur, motioning Drew to seat her. She said brightly, "Glasgow, you may serve now."

Glasgow? Byrony stared at the tall black man who was wearing a livery of sorts, black wool trousers and a yellow shirt, and a ragged jest of a white wig on his head.

"Yes, missis," he said, and clapped his hands.

Two other black men—boys, actually, Byrony realized—trooped into the dining room, each bearing a silver tray. They were wearing the same black wool trousers that ended well above their ankles, no shirts, and wool jackets. Byrony could practically feel their flesh itching.

"The usual fare in the South," Brent said to her as he dipped creamed corn from a bowl held by one of the boys. "Chicken, black-eyed peas, corn, and our own special kind of bread, made from corn."

"It all looks delicious," Byrony said. Actually everything looked very heavy. However did Laurel remain so slender? "You were talking about your work," Byrony said to Drew.

"Yes," he said, "and I should very much like to paint you, if my big brother doesn't mind, of course."

"We must find a more appropriate hairstyle, I think," Laurel said, her tone making it clear that she didn't think it possible.

"My fault," Brent said.

His words hung in the air, and Byrony blurted out, "He wouldn't let me out of the tub."

Drew very carefully placed his fork beside his plate, then threw back his head and laughed.

Byrony ducked her head. She heard Brent chuckling with his brother. No, she thought, he most certainly hadn't let her out of the tub. In fact he'd joined her, his large naked body snaking around hers, sending floods of water onto the bedroom floor. She felt herself grow even warmer at the image of lying against her husband's chest, her legs between his, his hands in her wet hair, his mouth caressing her throat.

"Now, if you were a mermaid," he'd said, "I wouldn't have to worry about those two gorgeous legs of yours—just your lovely tail."

Byrony was brought from her pleasurable memories back to the present by Laurel's acid voice. "Please, Drew, Brent." Lord, she wished she could pull out every one of Byrony's damp hairs by the root. "Enough, I don't want the slaves to hear such talk."

"I suppose things do change occasionally," Brent said, drawling out his words so that Byrony stared at him. His lilting accent was thick as honey. "Don't worry, Laurel, when Drew paints Byrony, I'll see to it that she's completely presentable."

Byrony had the awful feeling at that moment that Brent had made love to her only in order to throw it up to Laurel. The black-eyed peas were suddenly hard and cold in her mouth. No, she thought, she was being ridiculous. She could still hear his groans, feel his arms holding her tightly.

Drew said, "Oh, I don't know. Perhaps I could attempt another Venus emerging from the sea."

"I must show you the portrait Drew painted of me," Laurel said. "It's hanging in the drawing room, of course. Visitors believe it to be one of his best efforts. How long have you been married?"

"Three months," Byrony said automatically. "The journey here took a very long time."

"How did you two meet?" Laurel asked. Three months. Hardly any time at all. Brent would be bored with the girl soon enough.

Byrony's eyes flew to her husband's face. Her confusion was not lost on Laurel.

"In San Diego actually," Brent said easily, sipping his wine.

"Where is that? I've never heard of that place."

"It's in the southern part of California. You have heard of California, I trust?"

"You're so instructive, Brent. I thank you. But how interesting. I thought perhaps you were one of the females in Brent's saloon."

My, what sharp fingernails, Byrony thought.

"Oh no," Brent said, grinning. "My wife has none of the skills or attributes of a saloon girl, thank God."

No, Byrony thought, she probably didn't. She felt him looking at her at that moment, and raised her face. His beautiful midnight-blue eyes were filled with wicked amusement.

"But there are so very few ladies in San Francisco, is that not true?" Laurel said.

"More ladies than gentlemen, I'd wager," Drew said.

"That's right, Drew. Men dare to soil their hands in California, But you know you're alive there. There's no stagnation, no carrying on of meaningless traditions as there is, for example, here in the South."

His drawl had disappeared, Byrony noticed, and his voice was clear and crisp. "We create our values and our modes of life as we go along. A man's brains make him important, not accidents of birth that place him willy-nilly in a privileged position."

"I can't imagine what your father would say to such sentiments," Laurel said.

"He'd probably kick my butt out—again," Brent said. His eyes met Laurel's and he grinned. He raised his wineglass in a mocking toast.

Byrony took another bite of fried chicken. It hit her stomach like a rock. She began to envision their life here as a series of skirmishes between Brent and Laurel.

Drew looked from Brent to Laurel, but said nothing. He doesn't know, Byrony thought. She wondered if Brent would ever tell him. She'd hated the trek across Panama, the heat, the butchering insects. She wished at this moment that she and Brent were back there again, this time headed west.

TWENTY-FIVE

"Where the hell have you been?"

Byrony paused a moment, her hand tightening on her riding crop at the cold anger in Brent's voice. "I've been riding, with Drew," she said. "Why?"

"I've been looking everywhere for you."

"You could have asked Laurel. She knew."

"Laurel's taking a bath. It wouldn't be precisely appropriate for me to join her, now, would it? Where is Drew?"

"He's still at the stable. His horse lost a shoe. One of the sla—servants is helping him."

Brent, whose arms were folded across his chest, his legs spread, studied his wife, his eyes narrowed. "Why didn't you tell me you wanted to go riding?"

Byrony flicked the riding crop against her leg. Why was he acting the outraged husband? "I didn't know where you were," she said. "You didn't come to bed last night, nor were you anywhere to be found this morning."

It seemed to Brent that she was a bit furious herself. Jealousy? It pleased him. Perversely, he said in a deep drawl, "No, I wasn't, was I?"

With a measuring look, she said, "Then why are you so concerned where I was? When we were sailing on the *Connecticut* you had no choice but to stay near me." She gave him a marvelously indifferent shrug. "On dry land, you seem to want to rove again. So why shouldn't I do just as I please?"

"Because you are my wife, and you—" He broke off, seeing her insolent expression. "Enough. You will always tell me if you wish to do anything, and you won't go off with other men."

Byrony held her temper. She wanted to thrash him; she wanted to make him howl with pain, the kind of pain she'd felt through the night. Instead she said abruptly, "The slaves' compound I saw is in terrible shape. And I met your overseer, Mr. Paxton. He was very pleasant—to me."

"You've been here scarcely twenty-four hours and you're already finding fault," Brent said as he strode down the veranda steps.

"What I saw was deplorable," Byrony said in a steady voice. "And this was the compound for the house slaves. I understand from Drew that the field slaves live like animals."

"I want you to change into something more presentable," he said, ignoring her words. "We're going into Natchez to have dinner with the Forresters."

Only he had the ability to provoke her so thoroughly. She raised her chin and demanded, "Where were you last night, Brent?"

"That, my dear, is none of your business. Just as Celeste was none of your business, or, may I add, this plantation. Go change your clothes. Mammy Bath has assigned Lizzie to you. And, Byrony, watch what you do with that riding crop."

She said nothing, merely raised her chin higher and walked into the house. Brent stood quietly watching her. How dare she leave with Drew? Of course he'd seen Laurel, but she hadn't said a word, merely observed that Drew seemed much taken with Byrony. And why, you fool, didn't you simply tell her that you spent most of the night talking with Josh, a childhood friend whom you came back specifically to free? Brent shook his head at himself. He'd learned more from Josh about the condition of Wakehurst during the course of one night than he would have from Frank Paxton, a vicious man, according to Josh. But, in reality, no worse than any other overseer. Shit, what was he going to do?

About what, you fool? Byrony or Wakehurst? Brent sighed, running his long fingers through his hair. At least he'd done one good thing. Josh had told him that Frank Paxton was sniffing around Lizzie, and Brent had assigned her to Byrony. She would be safe with Byrony in the big house.

He saw Frank Paxton, dressed in severe black, walking up the drive toward him. He'd been at Wakehurst for nearly twelve years, and had been trusted completely by Brent's father. At least he had been before Brent had left nine years before. Brent remembered Josh telling him that Paxton had bought slaves from Brent's father during his illness, and sold them at a huge profit in New Orleans. A natty dresser was Frank Paxton, Brent thought, watching the overseer wave to him.

"Well, my boy, welcome home. It's been quite a long time."

Brent shook the man's outstretched hand. "Hello, Frank."

I've grown or he's shrunk, Brent thought as he stared down at the overseer.

Tough-looking bastard, Frank Paxton thought, his smile of welcome never wavering. "I've got all the records ready for you, Brent, when you've got the time. I met your little wife this morning. Charming lady, charming. She doesn't understand the way we do things here in Mississippi, but—" His voice trailed off a bit, because he knew the terms of Avery Hammond's will. What was Brent Hammond going to do about Wakehurst?

"We're leaving shortly for Natchez," Brent said. "I'd forgotten that in the South socializing always comes before work."

"True enough," Frank said.

"Tomorrow morning, Frank, if that's convenient for you."

"Certainly, my boy. Oh, incidentally, I'm looking for a little black gal—Lizzie's her name. There are things I want her to do."

Yeah, I'll just bet you have *things* for her, Brent thought, disgusted. "She's been assigned to my wife as her maid," he said. For a moment he thought Paxton would object. His thin lips pursed and his pale gray eyes narrowed. But he held his peace.

"The girl's awfully young to wait on your wife," was all he said.

Young enough to be your daughter, Brent thought. She was even a bit young for Josh, but at least he loved her, wanted to marry her.

"I'll see you tomorrow, then," Brent said, and turned away.

Two hours later, all the Hammonds left Wakehurst for Natchez, a carriage ride of ten miles along the bluffs overlooking the river.

"Did you enjoy your ride with Drew, my dear?" Laurel asked Byrony.

"It was informative," Byrony said.

"Oh?" Her one drawled-out word carrying a wealth of innuendo.

"Indeed," Drew said easily. "I had intended showing Byrony the lovely flora and fauna, but she wanted to see the slaves' compound. She was greeted royally, since she is, of course, the mistress of Wakehurst." Drew saw Laurel's lips purse, and continued to his brother, "I understand you and

Josh spent most of the night together, old man, talking over bygone days."

Brent grinned at his wife. "Yes, that and current events, as it were. Josh is the headman," he added for Byrony's benefit. "We grew up together. Josh was fascinated by my stories of California. I hope he and Lizzie will accompany us when we return to San Francisco."

"When you return to San Francisco," Laurel repeated.

"I thought California was a free state," Drew said on a frown.

"It is."

"Surely you don't mean to free him, Brent," Laurel said. "Why, he's worth at least three thousand dollars."

"True enough," Brent said.

"And Lizzie. She's a strong girl and still a virgin—"

"I should trust so. She's only thirteen years old."

"Come, Brent," Laurel said, anger surfacing now, "even though you've been gone awhile, you must know that the plantation can't exist without slaves. And Frank Paxton wants Lizzie, if Drew doesn't take her first."

All eyes turned abruptly toward Byrony, whose incredulous gasp hung in the silence.

"No," she said. "You can't mean that, Laurel. Frank Paxton is a white man, and he's old. Surely he doesn't—"

She was cut off by Laurel's high, patronizing laugh. She reached out a lavender-gloved hand and patted Byrony's knee. "My dear, you have quite a bit to learn about our ways. Slaves are dealt with as one sees fit."

"Laurel is perfectly right, Byrony," Brent said. "And I've dealt with Lizzie as I deemed appropriate. She will remain your personal maid until we leave or until I decide otherwise. She will not share Paxton's bed."

Brent intercepted Byrony's look filled with warmth and gratitude. Did she think she was the only one who found the prospect repulsive? He could well imagine how the slaves greeted her that morning. Petitions, requests for cloth, food, easier work. He wondered cynically if it had made her feel like the lady bountiful.

Laurel said, "Are you certain you're saving the girl for Josh? Or do you want her for yourself, Brent? Your father told me stories of all the slave girls you took to your bed."

Brent reached over and calmly grasped Byrony's hand in his. "Boys will be boys, right, Laurel? Now, enough. Byrony, did you know that the Spanish owned all this territory until 1795? I believe I mentioned that to you, didn't I? Thus the Spanish influence at Wakehurst."

"Yes," Byrony said quietly, "you did."

Brent continued talking of the different landmarks they passed. She felt again that he'd outflanked her. Why hadn't he simply told her that he'd spent the night with a friend, a male friend? Would she never understand him? She understood well enough that Laurel was the reason for his distrust of women. Maybe too there had been others during the years before she'd met him. But he had to know that she hadn't married him to use him, for heaven's sake. She heard him ask Drew, "Do you intend to remain at Wakehurst or return to Europe?"

"I'll probably return to Paris. I couldn't leave, though, until I'd seen you again."

"I am glad you stayed. So you wish to pursue your art and not become a plantation owner?"

Drew was thoughtfully silent for a few moments. "I believe that I can no longer tolerate slavery. Being gone for years changes one's perceptions. Seeing a man or woman flogged for no greater reason than that it is what the master or the overseer wants turns my stomach. Odd how I didn't react that way when I was a boy."

"I trust neither of you will express those views to the Forresters," Laurel said. "I should like to continue meeting my friends socially. This abolitionist talk won't endear you to anyone, you may be certain."

"I know," Brent said.

"How grand to see you again, Brent," Mrs. Amelia Forrester said again at the dining table. "So many years. I never did learn why you left Wakehurst so precipitately. A young man's wanderlust, I believe your father said."

Brent looked at his hostess, wondering if she had spoken facetiously, but she hadn't. So his father had kept everything to himself. Brent couldn't blame him for that. He'd regretted that day so often during the past nine years, regretted his boy's lust and stupidity. Had he been his father, he probably would have done more than just strike him with a riding crop. He'd also wondered many times what would have happened to him if he hadn't left Wakehurst. Probably he would be an indolent gentleman now, married, the proud father of heirs to carry on Southern traditions. He nearly traced his fingertip over the old scar, but caught himself. He forced a smile. "A difference of opinion between me and my father, ma'am—and wanderlust too, if you will. I understand that sort of thing frequently occurs. I suppose that a young man wants to accomplish things on his own."

"I wish our Stacy had your attitude, although not to such an extreme," said David Forrester. "The boy's probably losing his shirt in New Orleans even as we speak."

Byrony listened to them speak of people she didn't know. She found the Forresters delightful people, thoughtful, kind, and charming. Their daughter, Melinda, however, gave her pause. She flirted with Drew one moment, and looked soulfully at Brent the next. She was quite pretty, with her black hair and her dark brown eyes, but so vapid. She wondered if Southern ladies were all so very pale and languid in their movements. If the weather became warmer, she imagined there was good reason.

"What are you doing now, my boy?" David Forrester asked.

"I own a saloon in San Francisco, sir. The Wild Star."

Mr. Forrester seemed a bit nonplussed, but quickly recovered. He said comfortably, "An unusual enterprise, but now that you're home, you've a plantation to run. An absentee owner is not at all the thing, my boy, as you well know. I myself bought a couple of field slaves from Paxton just before your father's death. My overseer was pleased with the purchase, but I wondered why Paxton and your father would sell two such valuable slaves."

"I'm certain to find out why very soon, sir," Brent said, although he knew very well why. Old Frank was feathering his nest against an uncertain future. Had his father been too ill to realize what was going on? And what about Laurel?

"Wild Star," Amelia Forrester mused aloud. "An unusual name for a saloon, isn't it, Brent?"

Brent smiled. "A bit of whimsy, I guess, ma'am. The star I seemed to follow when I was younger was never of the tame sort." Not quite the truth, but close enough.

"We're giving a ball in two weeks, Mr. Hammond," Melinda Forrester said brightly. "You will come, won't you? And your wife, of course."

"It will be our pleasure," Brent said, and ate a bite of glazed ham.

Lizzie bounded to her feet when Byrony and Brent entered their bedroom a bit after midnight. She rubbed her fists over her eyes, just like a child. Which she was, Byrony thought, shuddering a bit at the thought of this poor girl being forced to bed Frank Paxton.

"Lizzie," Byrony said, "go to bed, for heaven's sake. I had no idea you would still be awake."

"But missis, Mammy Bath say—"

"Lizzie, do as your mistress says. I am quite capable of unfastening all those little buttons." Brent stopped the girl at the bedroom door. "Oh, another thing, Lizzie. You will sleep in the house, on the third floor. You may pick up your things from the compound tomorrow."

Byrony saw the girl's lips tremble, saw the wash of relief in her dark eyes.

"Yes, massa. Thank you, massa."

"That is kind of you, Brent," Byrony said.

"Perhaps," he said. "I don't want her raped by Paxton."

"I can't believe he would really do something so despicable."

"Believe it, Byrony. However, you are another matter entirely. Come here and let me assist you." She moved toward him and presented her back. She felt his deft fingers working down the buttons on her gown. "I wonder," she heard him say, "if Lizzie could be Paxton's daughter. It's possible you know. Her skin is lighter than usual. I can remember him taking Millie, Lizzie's mother, to bed. In fact, I remember hearing that she fought him. It's probably true, because he flogged the flesh off her back. My father was perturbed. He didn't want her away from her tasks for too long a time."

"That's unbelievable. Barbaric."

"Hold still. Yes, it would seem so." Brent slowly slipped the gown off her shoulders. She felt his lips lightly brush the nape of her neck.

"Am I truly the mistress of Wakehurst?" she asked abruptly, turning to face him.

"You're the massa's wife," he said.

"Is the house my responsibility? And the servants?"

"Oh, no," he said, his frown becoming a grin. "Is there going to be domestic trouble shortly?"

"Brent, must you jest about everything? Can't you see that—"

"Just remember, my dear, that I am the master. In the South, the master rules—everything. Do you understand?"

She searched his face, but he was looking over her shoulders and breasts. She clutched the loosened gown over her chemise.

"Do you understand?" he repeated.

She held her ground. "You're a tomcat," she said.

Brent stared at her a moment, then threw back his head and laughed deeply. "And all little female cats are the same in the dark?"

"No, I think you enjoy comparing and contrasting all your women. And I'm just the new cat, one who happened to come into your house through the back door. It's just a matter of time, isn't it, until you want to go roving again?"

"Your metaphor is straining common sense, Byrony. I think, if given the choice, that I'd prefer being the stallion. More noble than a ratty tomcat." His voice hardened, all lightness gone from his eyes. "But since you are my own legal little cat, you are quite in this tomcat's power. Take off your clothes. It's late and I want to go to bed."

Was he giving her outrageous orders because he couldn't do so to Laurel? The complexities of his mind gave her a headache. She sank onto the soft feather bed, pulling only a sheet over her, and watched him strip off his clothes. Naked, he doused the lamps, then strode onto the balcony to smoke a cheroot. The moonlight outlined his body, the hard lines, the sculptured shadows, the smooth muscled planes. Why couldn't he be a gnome? Why did he have to be so beautiful? She called out, "It's a pity I have no comparisons to make. Who knows what I would learn?"

She saw him grind out the cheroot and walk back into the bedroom. "If you ever get the urge," he said, standing over her, "I will tie you up and lock you away."

"Why?" she asked, goading him. "Why shouldn't the cat have the same options as the tomcat?"

"Some cats do, my dear, but not you. You are mine."

"Does it not go both ways? Aren't you then mine?"

He grinned at that and scratched his fingers over his chest. "My, but you're in a feisty mood tonight, aren't you?" He stared down at her, taking in her glorious hair, loose and full, framing her face. He felt lust and knew she was aware of it. Her eyes grew darker, falling to his groin. "I don't think," he said very quietly, "that I shall pull out of you tonight. I think I will fill you with my seed, watch your face while I do so. I think I will stay inside you even as you sleep."

The words poured out of her mouth before she could stop herself. "You love me then? You want our child?"

But he only chuckled. "I am certain my feelings for you rival yours for me."

"You don't know what my feelings are," she said.

Brent grasped the sheet and pulled it off her. He looked down at her. "Why don't you tell me," he said as he reached out his hand and laid it on her belly. He felt her quiver beneath his fingers. He watched her face as his fingers roved lower. "Tell me, Byrony."

He eased down beside her, balancing himself on his elbow. "Tell me," he repeated, his fingers now lightly caressing her. "Nothing to say? I would say, my dear, that your feelings are so soft right now as your woman's flesh." He deepened the pressure, and Byrony couldn't help it. She moaned. "This tomcat knows what he's about, doesn't he? Many men don't, of course. That is, they know perhaps, but they don't care. You're very lucky. I've always enjoyed a woman's pleasure."

She turned on her side to face him and touched him. He was hard and warm, and she stroked the length of him.

"Brent," she whispered, her voice soft and desperate. "Please."

She felt his finger ease inside her and tightened her own fingers around him. To her delight, he groaned, pushing against her. His fingers found her again and she lurched against him, arching her back. "That's it, love. I want you to burst with pleasure just as I will inside you. I want to feel you do it, and admit to yourself that no other man could ever make you feel thus."

She wanted to ask him if he would admit that no other woman could please him as she did, but his words sent her reeling, and she wasn't aware of anything save the intense wash of sensation that made her cry out. But Brent was. He watched her closely, felt her body surge in climax, and knew such pleasure at her release that it frightened him. "Byrony," he said. He quickly drew her beneath him and came into her.

"I can feel you." Her body continued to convulse in small shocks of pleasure. "I can feel you inside me." He arched upward, moaning deeply, and she felt his seed.

She wrapped her arms tightly around his back, buried her face against his shoulder.

Brent was still hard inside her. Her words had made him crazy. Suddenly her soft keening words, other words, crystallized in his mind. It was her pleasure that made her say them, he thought. He eased onto his side, bringing her with him. He remained deep inside her. He stroked her hair away from her face, still telling himself silently that she hadn't meant those words. "Byrony," he asked against her temple, unable to help himself, "did you mean what you said?"

She nestled closer against him, lightly rubbing her cheek against his shoulder.

He pressed his hand against her buttocks, keeping her close. "Did you?"

She was asleep.

He drew a deep breath. I'm a fool, he thought. How could

she possibly love him? He'd been her escape, that was all. He'd taught her woman's pleasure, that was all. Passion made people say things they didn't mean. He, of all people, knew that. No, she couldn't have really meant to say it. She couldn't really love him. Jesus, he'd certainly given her no reason to. He didn't want her to. He felt her thigh move over his belly. No, he didn't want that kind of feeling from her. But he did, of course.

TWENTY-SIX

Brent seated himself at his father's desk, a huge oak affair that he remembered so well from his childhood. His father had looked larger than life seated behind that desk, with its neat piles of important-looking papers, the inkstand of black onyx, the gold antique French clock. He closed his eyes for a moment, leaning back in the well-worn leather chair, remembering.

"I trust you and your brother will treat your new mother with proper respect, my boy."

By turns cocky and sullen, Brent had said, "Hardly a mother, sir. My mother is dead." If his father wanted a girl who was only four years older than his elder son, what could he say? He wanted to demand why his father had married the bit of fluff, but wisely he didn't.

"Yes, your dear mother is dead. For five long years now." Avery Hammond sighed, stroking his fingers over his thick side whiskers. "I've been lonely, Brent, damned lonely. Do you understand?"

No, he didn't, but he nodded. He wanted to go hunting with Russell Longston from a neighboring plantation.

Brent, startled from his memories by a knock on the library door, quickly rose behind the desk. "Come in," he said. He wondered now, pain filling him, how he could have been so crassly insensitive to his father's needs. And now it was too late to make reparations, nine years too late. You spawned a stupid ass for a son, Father, yet you left me my legacy. What am I to do?

Frank Paxton walked into the room. He'd used this room before Brent Hammond had come home. He'd sat behind the master's desk. He smiled and extended the ledgers toward Brent. "Here you are, Brent. The records of our purchases, expenses, and profits for the past five years."

"Sit down, Frank," Brent said pleasantly, "and let's see what we've got here."

Byrony, in the sitting room down the hall, was speaking to Mammy Bath. Laurel was reclining gracefully on a rosewood swivel chair, her look mildly inquiring.

"I want summer material—cotton, I think—to be distributed to all the house slaves, Mammy. I think it's ridiculous that our people have to wear wool all year around."

"So," Laurel said, "the slaves have been crying all over you. They'd do the same if you gave them silk to wear. They—"

"Also," Byrony said, ignoring Laurel, "we need to hire a seamstress. The sla—servants I've met haven't the foggiest idea of how to sew anything but the roughest seams. Nor, with all their responsibilities, do they have the time. I'll speak to Mr. Hammond about additional material for the field hands as well."

"I should trust that you would. They're all lazy, whining—well, it's a waste of money. My husband would never have consented to such a ridiculous use of funds. Brent isn't stupid. I doubt he will either."

"If you don't mind, Mammy, I should also like to meet with Cook. What is her name?"

"Mile, missis."

"Mile? How unusual. Yes, well, if you don't mind, I'll just visit the kitchen and speak with her."

Mammy Bath sent a sideways look at Miz Laurel. She looked fit to kill, at least her eyes did. "Yes, missis," Mammy Bath said to Byrony.

Laurel rose suddenly in a swirl of pale yellow silk. "Mammy, have you made my perfume yet?"

"Yes, missis. It's in your room."

"It's about time. Now, you may leave. I wish to speak to the—to Mrs. Hammond."

Byrony wanted to say something, but she held her peace for the moment. Mammy Bath walked from the room, leaving the door open.

"Yes, Laurel?"

Before Laurel could vent her spleen, they heard raised voices coming from the library.

"I want an answer, Paxton, and I want it now." Brent was speaking very quietly now, but was angry, very angry. Damned lying bastard.

"Look, Brent," Frank Paxton repeated, also lowering his voice, "I'm not used to being questioned like this. I sold those slaves to Forrester because your father asked me to."

The money transacted was neatly printed in the ledger. Brent realized he should have spoken to Mr. Milsom, his father's banker, before confronting Paxton.

"What is your salary, Frank?"

Frank Paxton named the amount. It wasn't at all outrageous.

Another thing to check with Milsom.

Brent closed the ledger. "I'll study these later. This afternoon, I would like to visit the fields."

"As you wish," said Frank Paxton. Damn, he'd done nothing more than any other smart overseer. He drew in his breath. He would show no more anger. Hell, when he wished, he could simply leave Wakehurst; he had enough money now to buy his own plantation.

Laurel turned to Byrony after a few moments. "Well, it

sounds as though Brent wants to squeeze some more money out of the estate. I doubt he'll want to authorize any of your precious material for the slaves."

"We'll see," Byrony said.

"Yes, we will, won't we? Just how poor are you and Brent?" She shuddered. "I can't believe Brent came down so far as to own a saloon. I can't imagine what his father would say."

Byrony rose from her chair to stand beneath the gilded bronze chandelier. "Brent isn't at all poor, Laurel. We are both very proud of the Wild Star. He has financial interests in other ventures as well."

"So that's why you married him? For his money?"

"No, that's not why I married him, but it is why you married Brent's father, isn't it?"

"I think, Byrony, that you—" She paused. *What was I supposed to do? Fade away in oblivion in my parents' rotting mansion?* "You don't know what you're talking about, miss."

Byrony sighed, raising her hand in silent apology. "It's none of my business, Laurel. Nor is it any of your business why I married Brent."

Brent paused at the open doorway. He smiled, a bit unwillingly, at Byrony's words. She hadn't been so calm the night before, he thought, and his smile became broader, until he remembered the words she'd cried to him when she climaxed. He'd left her before she'd awakened this morning, not wanting to, but knowing he must for his own peace of mind. He hadn't wanted to see the lie in her eyes. *If* she even remembered what she'd said to him.

He walked into the sitting room. "Ready for lunch, ladies?"

Byrony couldn't meet his eyes. Like an utter fool, she was—telling him she loved him. She'd given him unwitting power over her. *Am I like my mother? Loving a man who* only takes, who only hurts? *At least he doesn't raise his hand to you in anger or when he's drunk.*

"Yes, of course, Brent," Laurel said, walking gracefully toward him. "How did your meeting go with Frank? Is the plantation bringing in enough money to please you?"

"We'll see," he said.

Laurel continued, "Frank Paxton is an excellent overseer. It's a pity that you two didn't seem to be getting along. Indeed, we could hear your argument in here."

"There are a great many things that are a pity," Brent said. "Byrony, are you coming?"

"Yes," she said.

"You have a worshiper, Brent," Drew said over a lunch of baked catfish, fresh crunchy bread, and stewed sweet potatoes. At Brent's raised eyebrow, Drew added on a smile, "Lizzie. The girl won't shut up, so Mammy Bath tells me."

Brent grunted.

Laurel toyed a moment with the slab of butter on her knife. "If you're bound and determined to keep the girl out of Frank's bed, then why not give her to Josh now?"

"So she can give birth to another slave?" Byrony asked. "To add to the profits?"

"That's quite enough, Byrony," Brent said. "Drew, I'm riding into the fields after lunch with Paxton. Would you like to come?"

"My dear brother, I will come with you if you cannot manage without me. Actually, though, I'd planned to ride into Natchez. I need to buy some paints so I can begin Byrony's portrait."

Brent said, "I'll try to muddle through without you."

"May I come, Brent?"

"A lady doesn't venture into fields," Laurel said, appalled. "It's unhealthy and immodest."

"Immodest?" Byrony said.

"The males slaves wear only short trousers, some even

loincloths. I can't imagine that Brent would want you eyeing his property."

But Brent was thinking about the unhealthy part. He remembered well the conditions in the fields. There was a chance of infection, and he had no intention of allowing Byrony to expose herself.

"No, Byrony," he said. "You will remain here, or visit the local ladies with Laurel."

As they were walking from the dining room after lunch, Byrony laid her hand on Brent's sleeve. "May I speak to you before you leave?"

"Very well. Shall we go into the library?" She was silent a moment, and he added in a deeply drawling voice, "Would you prefer the bedroom? Perhaps you would have another surprise for me?"

"The library."

He closed the door behind him and leaned against it. "What is your pleasure, sweetheart?"

"Did you not say that I have the responsibility for the house?"

"Did I? You seem so certain, that I must have."

He saw the frustration in her eyes. "Yes, Byrony, you are the mistress of Wakehurst. Come, you didn't need to ask me that."

"I need to spend money for material for clothes. The servants have only one allotment of cloth a year, Brent, and it's wool! It must be utterly wretched for them in the summer months. And I need to hire a seamstress. I wasn't certain if I needed your permission. Laurel said that I would."

"Yes," he said, "you do need my permission."

"Do I have it?"

He flicked a bit of lint from his coat sleeve. "Your request sounds reasonable enough." He heard her sigh of relief.

"Thank you, Brent."

"There is one thing, Byrony. Normally, in the South, expenses are handled through the overseer. However, I wish everything to be cleared through me. I do not want you ever to speak to Frank Paxton about any money needs you might have. Do you understand?"

"It would never have occurred to me to ask Frank Paxton for anything. Why may I not accompany you this afternoon?"

"Because I said so." he knew he sounded curt, but he didn't want her to worry, and he knew she would if he told her his reasons. "Now, my dear, if there's nothing else, I will bid you a fond farewell." He opened the door, then paused. "Oh, Byrony, if you take a rest this afternoon, think of me, all right?"

Again he paused, his eyes searching her face. "You might also think about anything you wish to say to me during your pleasure, that is. I truly would like to know what you think."

He left her standing alone in the middle of the library, trying to fathom what was in his mind. He's a man, you silly ninny, and a man doesn't have to make sense.

Byrony didn't nap that afternoon, though she thought about it. Word had gotten about that the new missis was providing the slaves with clothes. Several women slaves, so tired and miserable-looking that Byrony wanted to cry, approached her. She was still taken aback at their flow of outrageous flattery to the little missis, the beautiful, kind little missis. Ophelia, ebony-black and so bent she came to Byrony's shoulder, begged for an allotment of meat for her six children. Shy, furtive Sabilla was pregnant and her back hurt her so badly from the field work that she was afraid she would lose the child. It was her first child and she was only fifteen. Old Die wanted relief from her work because of all the canker sores on her body. The list went on and on. Byrony felt helpless to the point of tears at their plight. To each she repeated that she would speak to the master. She was in her bathtub, thinking longingly of San Francisco and her friends. What would Saint say, she wondered, if he were confronted with all the misery? She would tell him about it when they returned home. Ah yes, home as Maggie, the Saxtons, the Newtons—

Laurel walked lazily into the bedroom.

"Doesn't one knock in the South?" Byrony asked, pushing back wet hair that had escaped the cluster tied atop her head.

"I told you what would happen," Laurel said, disregarding Byrony's words. "I can't imagine Brent appreciating you mucking in his affairs."

"Laurel, these people are wretched. It staggers me that human beings are treated worse than animals."

"What is Brent going to do with Wakehurst?"

"I don't know. Why don't you ask him?"

"Oh, I will, you may be certain of that. Where did you grow up, anyway, to be such a pious little preacher?"

"In Boston."

"Ah." Laurel gave her a long look, then turned to leave. At the door she said over her shoulder, "You do realize, don't you, that several of the slaves who spoke to you today are field slaves. Each field slave has so much to accomplish every day. If they don't complete their work, they're flogged."

Byrony was out of the bathtub in but a moment, her heart pounding. Lizzie stood gaping at her as she quickly toweled herself dry and began to jerk on her riding habit.

"Missis," Lizzie wailed, "you suppose to call me for help."

"I will, Lizzie, next time." Ten minutes later, Byrony was racing out of the house.

Oliver, a bent old stablehand, saddled a mare, muttering under his breath that the massa went to the fields with Mr. Paxton.

He pointed toward the north. Byrony click-clicked her

mare, whose name was Velvet, in that direction. Dear God, what had she done? She rode beneath thick-branched elm and oak trees that allowed only slivers of late-afternoon sun to knife through the green leaves. There were horse paths into the fields. She'd seen them on her ride with Drew. She veered onto the one that was nearest to being toward the north. The cotton fields were flat and seemed to stretch endlessly. There were small trails between the rows. She was beginning to wonder if old Oliver had sent her astray when she saw a group of black men clustered in a small clearing.

The sun was setting when she saw Frank Paxton, the only white man present, coiling up his whip. Ragged slaves stood in a loose circle about an oak tree. She felt her stomach turn as she reined in the mare. Sabilla, the pregnant young woman who had begged her for fewer hours in the fields, was hanging by her bound hands to a low branch, naked to the waist. Her back was crisscrossed with bloody welts. From Paxton's whip. Byrony heard her soft, keening moans.

She slipped off the mare's back and rushed to Paxton. "Cut her down, this minute."

"Mrs. Hammond," Frank Paxton said, closing his fingers over her arm, "the woman deserved the punishment. Don't interfere in things that don't concern you."

"Don't concern me?" She shook her arm free of him. "This woman is pregnant, Mr. Paxton. Cut her down this instant."

"No, ma'am," he said finally. "She will stay as she is until dark. Those are the rules."

"Then animals made the rules." She started toward Sabilla.

Frank Paxton moved swiftly to block her way. He said, his voice deadly soft, "Listen to me, Mrs. Hammond. You will get back on your horse and ride out of here, back to the house. I will not tolerate any interference from you. White people don't argue in front of slaves, do you understand?"

Byrony heard the soft rumbling sounds from the dozen or so male slaves. She didn't know what to do. Oh God, it was worse than a nightmare.

"What is going on here?"

Byrony could have yelled with relief at the sound of Brent's voice. She turned to watch him gracefully dismount from the back of a huge black stallion.

"Nothing at all, Brent," Frank Paxton said easily. "I was just telling your wife that she should return to the house."

"Brent," Byrony said quietly, "he's flogged Sabilla. I must help her, for it's my fault. She's pregnant."

There was a long moment of silence; then Brent said in a calm, emotionless voice, "No, Byrony. She isn't, not any longer."

"No." Byrony's eyes fell to the rivulet of blood that streaked down Sabilla's legs. So much blood, making splotches on what remained of her coarse wool dress.

"Get on your horse and ride back to the house now."

She raised her eyes to her husband's face. "But, Brent—"

"Do as I tell you. I will see that the woman is taken care of. I promise you. Go, now."

Slowly Byrony walked to her mare. She felt Brent's hands close about her waist and lift her into the saddle. She let the mare gallop wildly back toward her waiting stall.

The lamp flickered, then filled the room with light.

"Get up and get dressed now. You will not miss dinner."

Byrony stared at her husband, but didn't move. "Sabilla?"

"We will speak of it later." He turned and walked to the door and called, "Lizzie. Get in here and help your mistress."

As soon as the words were out of his mouth, he felt like a perfect fool. He couldn't very well bathe and change with the girl in the room. When she came skittering to a halt in front of him, her eyes wide on his face, he said, "Never mind. Have water sent up here, now. That's a good girl."

He said over his shoulder. "You can hide in bed for a while longer, I have yet to bathe. Lord knows I need it."

"I'm not hiding."

"Oh? Are you ill then?"

"No, not in the sense you mean. Please, Brent, what about Sabilla?"

"She's all right. She's weak, of course, but she will be fine, I promise."

"It was my fault that she was flogged. She came to me to beg for fewer hours in the field. It was her first child, Brent, and she was in pain. I can't believe that things like that happen."

Brent very carefully folded his coat and laid it on a chair back. He said over his shoulder, "Byrony, stop blaming yourself. It isn't your fault, what happened. You can believe me that I've spoken to Paxton. There won't be any more floggings."

She sighed deeply, and watched him strip off his clothes. The differences between them hadn't really struck her before. They did now. His tall body was powerful, strong, and muscled. But even if he were short and flabby, she thought, veering back to the horrible incident, he would still control everything and everyone in his little kingdom. It was because he was a man that he was powerful, and because she was a woman, she was nothing more than a supplicant. She could do nothing more than beg, perhaps cry to get her way. She wanted to demand that he flog Paxton. She thought of her father. He had no kingdom, yet he was all-powerful to his wife. He could beat her, curse her, throw things at her at will.

"I will not be a party to this," she said.

Brent turned to face her, naked, but oblivious of it. "Would you care to explain yourself?"

Two black boys carrying wooden tubs of hot water came into the bedroom. Byrony slipped deeper under the covers until they left the room.

She silently watched her husband climb into the tub.

"I'm waiting."

"I want to leave."

There, she'd said it.

Brent said nothing until he'd finished bathing. When he stepped from the tub, he slowly began to dry himself. "I was quite smelly," he said. "I don't suggest you use my water."

"I bathed earlier."

"Then get out of that bed and dress yourself."

"I am also tired of taking orders from you. I am not one of your slaves. I will stay in bed if I want to."

He laughed. Damn him, he laughed. She grabbed a small clock from the bedside table and flung it at him. It struck his arm and bounced on the carpet.

His laughter stopped as abruptly as it had begun. He rubbed his arm, a thoughtful expression on his face. "So you want to stay in bed, do you?"

"No, Brent, I don't want any of that. I'm angry and I feel guilty—and—no."

"There's one thing a man's entitled to, and that's obedience from his wife. Haven't I mentioned that fact to you before?"

He joined her in bed and when he took her cries into his mouth he felt her words to his soul. "I love you."

TWENTY-SEVEN

"Brent. I'd heard you were home. Welcome, son."

Brent took James Milsom's offered hand and shook it. For an instant he stared at the man who was one of his father's closest friends, one of his father's contemporaries. He looked old, his face wrinkled, his iron-gray hair thin. Had his father looked this old when he'd died? He swallowed. Nine years was a long time.

"Yes, I returned to Wakehurst just last week. I must speak to you, Mr. Milsom."

"I've been waiting for you, Brent. Sit down."

Brent eased down in a large leather chair opposite James Milsom's mahogany desk, and looked about the dark-paneled office. "I remember your desk and those pictures so well," he said. "Do you still race your horses, sir?"

"Yes, indeed. There's a new picture added to the lot—" Milsom pointed to a painting of a roan quarter horse. "His name is Bullet. Poor old fellow died several years ago. I'm pleased I had him painted before he went down. I suppose it was for the best—a race, you know, and he broke his leg. But, enough of that."

"Natchez has changed a bit also," Brent said. "New buildings, more bustle on the docks, many more boats on the river."

"True." He shook his gray head. "The steamboat you traveled on for a while—*Fortune's Lady*—blew up some five years ago. The idiot captain was racing, of course. Killed some fifteen people. I understand you're newly married. My congratulations."

"Thank you, sir."

James Milsom sat back at his desk and studied the young man across from him. He was a man now, he thought, shaking off the memories of the handsome, arrogant youth he remembered. He said abruptly, with no preamble, "Your father regretted what happened, Brent. Oh, not at first, he was too enraged." He watched Brent raise his fingers to the scar on his cheek.

"I gather he told you. All of it?"

"Yes, but only I know what happened. Forgive me if I'm probing at old wounds, Brent. But you came to talk to me about your father, did you not?"

"That and other things." Brent sighed. "Had I been in my father's shoes, I would have probably killed me. I was an excellent son to him, was I not?"

"It's over and done with, Brent."

"Yes, he's dead, too late for me to make reparations."

"Did you know that he devoured your letters to your brother? He followed your progress, you know. When you bought your saloon in San Francisco, he was pleased. I remember him telling me that at last you'd settled down, finally come to terms with yourself."

Brent remembered that letter, the last one he'd written. He realized now that it had been filled with his excitement, his satisfaction, his hopes. And his father had read it.

"It's a pity he didn't live long enough to learn of your marriage. That would have pleased him greatly."

"Would it? I wonder. Perhaps he saw my son sometime in the future in bed with his father's seductive new young wife. The final irony, the final justice."

"I can't imagine that your young wife has any intention of dying," James Milsom said.

"I can't imagine that my mother did either."

Milsom frowned as he leaned back in his chair. "I believe it's time to cease this spate of guilt, Brent. I certainly don't blame you, and your father ceased to very shortly after you left." He paused a moment, carefully choosing his words. "I do not believe it is wise for a man or a woman to marry outside his generation. Your father realized his mistake very quickly. It's just that he couldn't admit it to himself until after he found you in bed with Laurel. He never approached her as his wife after that."

"Why? Because I'd defiled her?"

"No, because he was sick at his own foolishness, his own blindness. Listen to me, Brent. Your father didn't spend those last years alone. He found someone, and he was happy."

Brent started forward in his chair.

"I won't tell you the lady's name. Suffice it to say that he was discreet, and again, I am the only person who was in your father's confidence."

"I am relieved," Brent said. "Lord knows he deserved it. If only I hadn't been such a selfish little bastard, if only I'd understood."

"I haven't met any young men of eighteen who were saints, Brent. Now, I have something else to tell you. I was with your father just before he died. He wanted to write you a letter to relieve his own conscience and yours, I believe. But there wasn't time. A pity. As to his will, he did disinherit you, but only briefly. It was changed back some eight years ago."

A letter. Yes, Brent thought, clenching his hands, it was a pity. "Had I been my father, I should have made Drew my heir."

"Your brother cares only for his painting—you know

that. As for Laurel, I find it quite interesting that he left her in your hands, so to speak."

"A problem I haven't yet resolved." Brent paused a moment, then said carefully. "There's another reason why I'm here, sir. It's about Frank Paxton."

"Ah, yes, of course."

"I believe Wakehurst's overseer has been lining his pockets over the years, particularly after my father became ill."

"It's probably true, but I have no proof. An ill master or an absentee master allows for that sort of thing, you know. Were I you, Brent, I'd simply fire the fellow."

Then who would run Wakehurst?

"I'd rather wring his neck first. Does Paxton bank with you, sir?"

"No, he's not stupid. Is your new wife a Southern lady?"

Nor am I stupid, Brent thought, realizing well what Mr. Milsom was getting at. "She spent her formative years in Boston, then returned to California last year."

"Then she doesn't understand our ways."

"No, not at all. But as a matter of fact, sir, I don't either, not anymore. To be perfectly frank, I don't know what to do."

"About Wakehurst?"

"Wakehurst and Laurel, as I mentioned."

"I can certainly assist you to find a new overseer."

"No, it's not that. As I said, I think I've become something of an abolitionist. You know, of course, that California entered the union as a free state. I can no longer abide the way things are here."

"You know as well as I, Brent, that there will be no real change until the economics of the situation shift completely. It's really that simple. The South can't exist economically without slavery."

"I will not be a party to it."

"This is a problem indeed. What do you intend to do with your inheritance?"

Brent shook his head, smiling a bit ruefully. "I can just see myself returning to California, leading five hundred freed Negroes."

"It does present a problem. I don't know what to advise you, son. As a banker, my assets aren't directly tied to slavery, thus I won't rant and rave about what you owe to your birthright and your fellow plantation owners. Perhaps if you sold the plantation?"

"The Negroes wouldn't be any better off, would they?"

"Have you spoken to Laurel about this?"

Brent shook his head as he rose. "I have a lot of thinking to do. Thank you, sir, for seeing me."

James Milsom shook the younger man's hand warmly. "If you wish to speak to me again, Brent, I will be here."

Brent rode thoughtfully out of the city, guiding his stallion closer to the high bluffs that overlooked the Mississippi. At a deserted spot he reined in and tied his stallion to the low branch of an oak tree. Slowly he walked to the edge of the bluffs and stared down into the swirling brown water. He sat down, his back against an ancient elm tree, and stretched out his legs.

What was he going to do?

He was so deep in thought that he didn't notice the horse or the rider until they were upon him. He looked up to see the swirl of blue velvet riding habit and charmingly tousled auburn curls beneath a jaunty riding hat.

"Well," he said lazily, not bothering to rise, "my dear Laurel. How ever did you find me?"

TWENTY-EIGHT

Laurel stared down at him from her mare's back, and felt that same almost overpowering pull she'd experienced again the moment she'd seen him arrive at Wakehurst. No, she corrected herself, it wasn't overpowering; she could control it this time. Still, she continued to look at him, saying nothing. His black boots, as glossy as his tousled hair, came nearly to his knees. He drew her like a magnet. Finally she met his eyes, and flinched at the amused sarcasm she read there. Slowly she dismounted, tying her mare beside Brent's stallion.

Couldn't he at least rise? All the gentlemen she knew would by this time have been filling her ears with pretty compliments. She walked gracefully to him, flicking her riding crop against her shirt.

"I don't know if I'd tie the mare right next to him, Laurel," he said lazily. "She's a pretty filly, and he, well—"

"I saw your horse," she said "And stopped. You went to Natchez?"

"Yes."

"Why?"

He cocked a brow at her. "Is this an inquisition?"

"Ah, did you go to see a woman, then? And you're afraid I'll tell your little wife?"

"Do you know someone who would please me, Laurel?"

"Oh, stop it, Brent."

"Actually," he said after a moment, "I went to see Mr. Milsom. He told me many interesting things."

"I'll just bet he did. If I were you, Brent, I wouldn't heed that old man. Your father distrusted him mightily—indeed, they scarcely spoke to each other the last several years."

Brent wondered why she was lying about James Milsom. Hadn't he been one of the fools sniffing about her? "My, but you're vehement, aren't you? You needn't worry, Laurel. Mr. Milsom is a gentleman, and a gentleman never speaks unkindly of a lady."

"Unlike you?"

"Unlike me. Did you want to speak to me about something, Laurel? Or do you wish to continue your ride?"

Laurel paused a moment, aware that his eyes had fallen to her bosom. He still admires me, she thought, he still wants me. She wanted him too, had always wanted him, but this time she must go carefully. She'd always used her beauty and her body to get what she wanted. What else could a woman do? She said, "Actually, we've had no time alone together. To talk."

"I see," Brent said.

"I left Byrony posing for Drew, so I came out riding."

Brent briefly remembered telling Byrony how he would pose her, naked. He felt himself tensing and was annoyed with himself. "What do you want to talk about, Laurel?" he asked. "Are you going to keep standing over me, or will you sit down?"

She sat gracefully beside him, arranging her voluminous skirts about her.

He said, "You know, I thought you'd look old. After all, I was only eighteen when I left, and it has been nine years. You're probably more beautiful now than you were then."

"Thank you."

He wondered silently if Byrony would be more beautiful in nine years than she was now. It didn't seem possible to him.

"What do you want to talk about?" he asked again.

She shrugged, but her eyes were intent upon his face. "I'm worried about the future, of course. My future. Your father left everything in such an odd way. I want to know what you intend to do."

"That's straight speaking," he said. He looked out over the calm waters of the river. "I used to come here when I was a boy, particularly after my mother died. I missed her very much."

Laurel was wise enough to say nothing.

He turned to face her. "I will tell you the truth, Laurel. I haven't decided yet what I shall do."

"You could of course stay here. It is where you were born and raised. It's what your father wanted and expected."

I wonder, Brent thought, remembering James Milsom's words about his father being pleased at his purchase of the saloon, his finally coming to terms with himself. If his father had truly believed that, then why had he left him his heir? He must have known that Brent would have to return.

She reached out her hand and lightly touched his sleeve. "There could be a lot for you here, Brent."

He would have had to be a blind man not to see the offer in her eyes. He thought of Byrony, posing for Drew, laughing with Drew.

"You're doubtless right," he said, and quickly rose. "Shall I accompany you back to Wakehurst?"

She nodded and accepted his hand to help her rise. He released her immediately. She looked up at him and said very quietly, "I was very young nine years ago too, Brent. Young and foolish, just as you were."

Brent said nothing. He lifted her into the saddle.

* * *

Byrony and Drew were seated on the veranda drinking Mammy Bath's special mint julep when Brent and Laurel cantered up the drive. Byrony saw Brent lean closer to Laurel as she spoke, then throw back his head and laugh. If she'd had a rifle, she would have shot him. She turned to speak to Drew. She'd said two words when Laurel interrupted. "Have you two finished working for the day?"

Before Byrony could speak, Drew said easily, "Ah yes. It's too lovely a day to be cooped up inside. You must see the sketch I've made of Byrony, Brent. See what you think."

Brent gave Byrony a look that made her turn red to her hairline. She jumped to her feet and shook out her skirts. "Yes, why don't you? I believe I shall change and go riding." She paused a moment, her chin going up a good inch, as she looked at her husband. "I'm taking food and more clothes to the field slaves."

"No," Brent said quietly, "no, you aren't."

"Why not?"

"Because, dear, it's a ridiculous waste of money, just as I told you," Laurel said.

Brent couldn't help himself; he grinned widely at his stiff-backed wife. She looked ready to tear his ear off. "Tell you what, Byrony, why don't you change, then I'll ride with you and we'll discuss your plans."

He loves to toy with me, she thought as she stomped up the stairs. Lizzie was there waiting to help her change. The girl seemed quiet, something very unusual. Usually Lizzie chattered like a parrot as her small deft fingers fastened buttons, twitching out wrinkles. But Byrony's mind was whirling, and she said nothing.

When she returned to the veranda, Brent was seated close to Laurel, a mint julep in his hand.

"I'm ready, Brent."

"Already?" he said in his affected drawl. "Well, then, it

would be most impolite for me to keep a lady waiting, particularly my wife."

Some fifteen minutes later, they were riding side by side toward the fields. Byrony turned suddenly in the saddle and said, "You asked me last night what I wanted, Brent."

"I did, didn't I? It was probably most foolish of me. Well, what is it? You wish to return to Boston? With jewels and lots of money? Lots of my money, I should say."

Her hands tightened on the reins, and her mare skittered a bit. It took her several minutes to calm the horse.

"No," she said, not looking at him. "I want food and more clothes for the slaves."

"My selfless little wife," he began, his drawl even more pronounced than before.

"Brent," she said, "enough of this foolishness."

"What foolishness?" he asked, but she saw that she'd taken him aback. She wasn't going to let him bait her, not anymore.

"Why," she said, quite calmly, "don't we talk about those demons that are driving you?"

His eyes narrowed on her face.

"Maggie told me once that it took a bit extra to get some men's attention. That's why I bought the whip."

"I think it's time we went back to the house," Brent said.

"Oh no, not yet. Do you truly believe that all women are dishonest and conniving? That all women want something?"

"That's enough, Byrony."

"Is it? Nine years of encouraging yourself to think like that is more than enough, Brent. If Laurel only realized how much influence she's had over you, she'd probably be speechless. She seduced a healthy young boy and turned him into a distrustful, bitter man."

He cursed.

"Brent, listen to me, please. Maggie is a woman and she's your friend, isn't she? Don't you trust her?"

"Shut up, Byrony. You don't know what you're talking about."

"Just maybe I do," she said, her eyes searching his face. "I think you're afraid to be nice to me, afraid that you might come to care for me, afraid that I'll hurt you if you do." She grabbed his sleeve. "Isn't that the truth?"

He shook off her hand, and tightened his hands on his stallion's reins.

"Brent, wait. What about the clothing and food for the slaves?"

"As you said, Byrony, all women want something. Today you appear to be the selfless little lady of the manor. But tomorrow? I wonder."

"Brent, please!"

"Why don't you sell Ira Butler's necklace? It would bring you enough to play lady bountiful."

He wheeled the stallion about and was soon gone from her sight.

Byrony stood very still, staring after him. She'd been right, of course. She just hadn't realized the extent of the boy's guilt, the boy's betrayal, and the woman's part in that betrayal. She never would have realized it, she thought, if they hadn't come back here to Wakehurst. He was so damned closemouthed. And stubborn. And he became absolutely impossible when she got too close. She straightened her shoulders and urged her mare back to the house.

What would her husband do now?

She saw what her husband was going to do over dinner that evening. He was at his most urbane. And closed off from her, Byrony thought as she chewed on a bite of baked ham.

"The fried okra is delicious," she heard Brent say. "I'd forgotten how marvelously different Southern cooking is."

"You're right," Byrony said, smiling brightly at everyone. "In Boston all we consumed was fish. By the time I was fifteen, I was certain that I would begin growing gills at any time."

"Didn't your Aunt Ida tell you the facts of life?" Brent said, turning his attention and that drawl of his on her. "At fifteen I'm certain you were growing far more interesting sorts of things than fish gills."

For a moment she wanted to hurl her lima beans at him. Instead, she said, "Aunt Ida was never married. She didn't speak—" She broke off at the sound of Laurel's laughter.

"You are amusing, Byrony," Laurel said, lightly wiping her lips with her linen napkin. "I suppose every girl has a female relation like that."

"Unmarried and ignorant and prudish?" Brent said.

"You were unmarried until very recently, Brent," Drew said, "but somehow I can't imagine applying the same words to you."

"I can't imagine applying those words to most women," Brent said. "Of course, if a woman doesn't have the face and the form to attract a man, I suppose she must make do with charities and good works. The ladies at this table are fortunate, don't you agree, Drew?"

"And I suppose if a man doesn't have the face or form to attract a woman, he must make do also?"

Brent said easily, "Oh no, my dear, if he has the money, he can simply purchase what he wants."

"If women had any power at all, it wouldn't be that way," Laurel said.

"Thank God, women don't have men's power," Brent said, shaking his head. "All of us poor mortal males would become lapdogs, begging for favors."

Byrony cast a quick glance at Laurel. She was right, of course. If Laurel had had power—and money was power— would she have married Brent's father? *If I had had money, I never would have married Ira.*

And Brent? She'd wanted him, she'd been drawn to him.

But then again, she'd had no choice, not really. She heard him say in that damned bored drawl of his, "I wonder how many ladies would succumb to us poor men if they weren't constrained to by circumstance?"

He's thinking about us, Byrony thought. Or perhaps all the women he's paid. His mistresses.

"Come now," Drew said, "don't be so bloody cynical. There is such a thing as love, you know. A rather far-flung emotional state."

"Love, Drew? I think you mean unrequited lust. Once requited, well, what is there then?" He shrugged.

"Caring? Trust? Children?" The words came out of Byrony's mouth before she could stop them.

Brent laughed. "Well, children certainly keep a man tied in one place. Clip his wings and all that."

Byrony closed her eyes a moment. She lightly touched her hand to her stomach. Why wouldn't the wretched man face himself?

"Then why do you suppose a man gets married?" Laurel asked lightly. "Your precious theory of unrequited lust again?"

Brent was silent a moment. He drank some of his wine, then carefully set the crystal glass down again. "That or he finds himself in a situation where he has no choice."

"You mean like seducing a lady?"

"Ah, Laurel," Brent said, "I still find myself wondering if there is such a thing."

Byrony flung her napkin onto the table. She wanted to scream curses at him, but she gained control of herself. Not in front of Laurel or Drew. She smiled and rose. "If you will excuse me," she said in a voice that was so calm it could have been dead, "I think I shall retire now."

She left the dining room without a backward glance. When she entered the bedroom, she looked at the door, wishing there were a lock.

She was so tied up with her own thoughts, she didn't at first hear the strange sound coming from the corner of the room, near the balcony.

"Lizzie?"

There was another hiccuping sob. Byrony walked quickly to the glass doors and saw Lizzie huddled down in the corner.

"Lizzie," she said, falling to her knees to face the girl, "What's wrong? Why are you crying?"

Lizzie rubbed her fisted hands over her eyes, thinking furiously. She'd heard that the massa had refused to let the missis give food and clothing to the field hands. So had Frank Paxton. He'd caught her near the house, telling her that he'd have her soon, very soon.

But the missis couldn't do anything. Paxton was a white man, the overseer. "Nothing, missis," she said, refusing to look at Byrony.

Byrony sat back on her heels. "Are you certain you don't want to tell me what's bothering you?"

Lizzie's head shook from side to side.

Byrony rose slowly, feeling utterly helpless and useless.

"Very well, Lizzie," she said finally. "Help me undress, then go to bed. If you wish to speak to me tomorrow, I will be here."

Toward midnight, Brent walked quietly into the bedroom. Moonlight streamed through the undraped windows. He saw Byrony lying on her side, her cheek pressed against her hand. Slowly he walked to the bed and stood staring down at her. He felt a powerful tug, and laughed at himself silently. Lust, he thought. I still feel lust for her. He leaned down and lightly clutched a curl that lay over her shoulder. He closed his eyes a moment as he felt the texture of her hair. She stirred but didn't waken. He'd thought of all the things she'd said. She was right, of course. But being right didn't always change things for the better. He knew only that he wanted her now.

He stripped off his clothes and eased into bed beside her. He pulled up her nightgown to her waist, turning her onto her back. He eased her legs apart and slid gently and deeply into her.

Byrony came awake with a jerk at the feel of him.

"No."

"Hold still," he said. "God," he groaned, and lost his control.

She saw the cords standing out taut in his neck as his head went back and he moaned his pleasure.

Brent fell panting on top of her.

Byrony didn't move. She couldn't have moved in any case.

"Are you through with me?"

He pushed himself up on his elbows and looked down at her face, pale and washed-out in the stream of moonlight. Her words sounded like a monotone, like she didn't care.

"Perhaps," he said. "Then again, perhaps not. I like being in your body. You're warm and soft."

"And you won't have to pay me."

Something deep within him stirred. It was hurt, bad hurt.

"Of course you've been drinking. That excuses a man everything, doesn't it, Brent? And of course, now that your lust is slaked, there's nothing more for you."

He stirred the embers of hurt into anger at her. "Next time I'll ensure that your lust is slaked also, wife. You're always so cuddly and affectionate after I've given you pleasure." *And you tell me you love me.*

He pulled out of her, pausing a moment on his knees between her wide-spread thighs.

"It's not worth it, Brent. I wish to go back to sleep now. Please, leave me alone."

He fell onto his side, his back toward her.

She didn't move. He would have heard her had she moved. He pictured her in his mind, lying on her back, her nightgown rumpled at her waist. He had an overwhelming urge to take her into his arms and hold her close to him and tell her— Tell her what, you fool?

TWENTY-NINE

Byrony handed the necklace to the fussy Mr. Dubois. She knew he was thinking it a beautiful piece, but of course he couldn't say that to her, since she wanted to sell it to him.

Aloud Mr. Dubois said, "The workmanship is not quite what one would expect, but of course with stones of mediocre quality, I suppose it is adequate."

She said nothing, merely cocked her head at him and waited. Please, she thought, let him offer me more than the others did.

Mr. Dubois continued to study the pearl and diamond necklace, then sighed. "I'm afraid I can't offer you more than three hundred dollars, Mrs Hammond. The current market for—"

"No, thank you, Mr. Dubois," Byrony said, and held out her hand. "May I have my necklace?"

She saw him clutch it tight in his fist.

"Perhaps, ma'am, I can go a bit higher," he said. "Say, four hundred dollars?"

"No, thank you, Mr. Dubois," Byrony said again, her hand still held open toward him.

"How much do you want?" he asked at last, his voice a whine.

"I can accept nothing lower than five hundred."

He began a diatribe that lasted a good three minutes, but Byrony, having experienced three other jewelers in all their bargaining glory, simply allowed him to demonstrate his art.

"No, ma'am, I simply can't do it—why, I can't sell it for more than—"

She cut him off. "It's your decision, sir. May I please have my necklace?"

He cursed very softly, and she wanted to dance with joy.

Ten minutes later, she joined Lizzie in the landau, a wide smile on her face.

"Where to now, missis?" Oscar asked.

Byrony drew a deep breath, still surprised by her success. "To a clothing warehouse."

"Where have you been hiding?"

Byrony looked up at her husband standing on the bottom step of the veranda, his hands on his hips, an unreadable expression on his face.

"Well? All Mammy Bath could tell me was that you and Lizzie drove into Natchez early this morning. It is now near to sunset. Where have you been, Byrony?"

Suddenly she wasn't certain that she should tell him. Could he stop the warehouse from delivering all the cotton trousers, shirts, and skirts? The barrels of salted meat were already on their way to the field slaves' compounds, so that part was safe. Or was it?

Not only could he stop it, she realized, he, as the master, could confiscate everything. Could he be that cruel?

She ran her tongue over her suddenly dry lips "I'll tell you," she said, knowing she had no choice. He'd find out soon enough.

"Well, I'm waiting."

"I sold the necklace, Ira's necklace, and bought clothing and meat for the field slaves."

Brent felt as though he'd been struck in the belly by

someone the size of Saint Morris. Never, during the long day, had he imagined her doing that. He'd gone from indifference to her whereabouts, thinking she was angry at him for his taking of her so callously the previous night, to gnawing worry, to rage that she would simply leave and not inform him. Hell, he'd felt every damned emotion experienced by man.

"I see," he finally said.

"You did tell me I should provide the funds myself, if you remember."

"Damnation, Byrony—" He broke off, plowing his long fingers through his hair. Suddenly he saw the entire situation as an outsider might see it, a hilarious, cross-purposed argument with no real foundation. He threw back his head and laughed.

"What is going on here? Brent, why are you carrying on like this?" Laurel looked from Brent to a stiff-backed Byrony.

"The little missis make him laugh," Mammy Bath said complacently as she scratched her scraggly bun with a very long fingernail.

Brent got control of himself and said to his wife, "Won't you come with me into the library? I think we should discuss this privately."

He sat on the corner of his father's desk, watching her as she came into the room. She'd taken off her plum-colored bonnet and was dangling it by its ribbons. Her lovely hair was tousled. He wished at this moment that her expression would be as winsome as her appearance. He mentally stripped off her pale blue gown, remembering how he'd bunched her nightgown around her waist, coming inside her. He closed his eyes for a moment, surprised at himself for the shot of desire that went through him.

"What is it you wish to say, Brent?"

Her challenging voice brought him to alertness in an instant. He grinned at her. "I simply wanted to tell you that our people will be the best-garbed slaves in the entire South. I met with a Mr. Cranford here at Wakehurst this afternoon. He will be delivering many different items of clothing the end of the week. Not only for the field slaves, but for our artisans and house slaves as well, and, of course, all the children."

Byrony could only stare at him. "Why didn't you tell me? Why did you make me think that you didn't care?"

He gave her a long measuring look. "As I recall, you were very busy telling me what was wrong with me. And I—well, I do like to keep some things to myself."

"Yes, I was, wasn't I? I wonder if it did any good at all."

He walked to her, and was appalled at her wary look and her quick dodging step back. "Why are you running from me?"

"I'm not running," she said. His long fingers lightly stroked over her jaw. She watched his blue eyes darken to almost black.

"Unrequited lust again, Brent?"

"There's nothing unrequited about you, Byrony. And I'm not touching you, at least not yet."

She slowly turned back to face him, her eyes fastened on the top button of his white shirt. "No," she said, "It doesn't matter. It's just that you make me so angry."

"Or so happy?"

She raised her eyes to his face. "I don't understand."

"My dear Byrony, I was thinking about all those meaningless endearments you spout to me when you're happy."

Her gaze was steady, her voice very calm as she said, "Love can be quashed, Brent. I used to believe—girlish romantic foolishness, of course—that once one fell in love, it was forever. But maybe that isn't always true."

"I should think it had to exist first," he said, his voice

mocking, but he felt trapped and bitterly uncertain. Of her and of himself.

"If you don't mind, I should like to bathe before dinner."

He automatically stepped back, allowing her to leave the library. He listened to her light footsteps on the marble entranceway as she walked toward the stairs.

Lizzie was back to her old self again, Byrony thought as she listened to her chatter happily as she helped her off with her clothes and into the tub.

"Josh look so manly in new clothes," Lizzie said as she laid out Byrony's evening gown and underthings.

"And you will look very pretty in a new dress," Byrony said. Several new dresses, if Brent were to be believed. But what would happen when they left? All the new clothes in the world would make not one whit of difference. All five hundred souls would remain the property of Wakehurst. If they left, would Brent leave Frank Paxton in charge? If only she owned Wakehurst. Yes, and what would you do? Myriad considerations flashed through her mind. Why, she wondered, was life never so simple as it was when one was a child?

Byrony came awake with a start and sat up in bed. It took several moments for her eyes to adjust to the darkness. Brent wasn't beside her. The sheets and pillow were smooth. He'd never come to bed.

Fine, she thought, let him do just as he wishes. "Oh, damn."

The sound of her own voice startled her. She lay back. She heard the night sounds: the tree branches lightly hitting the balcony, the chirping of crickets. Where was Brent? Was he still with Laurel?

It was warm. Byrony slipped out of bed and quickly pulled on her dressing gown. She walked to the French doors and opened them. The air was sweet with the smell of gardenias and magnolias and roses. She padded on bare feet to the edge of the balcony and leaned her elbows on the wooden railing. The gardens below were shadowy and mysterious in the moonlight. She wondered briefly if Drew were still awake painting. She couldn't see his bachelor apartment from here. Bless Drew, she thought. He'd been on her side during dinner when Laurel had exploded with fury when Brent had announced of the Wakehurst slaves' newfound wealth.

Her mind suddenly froze. She'd heard something, someone, moving about in the garden. She strained to see through the shadows. Was that a garbled cry? A man's voice?

Without further thought Byrony gathered up her dressing gown and raced from the bedroom, along the long corridor, and down the stairs. The house was completely quiet.

She quickly unlocked the front door. She made her way to the side of the mansion toward the garden, walking carefully since she'd forgotten her slippers.

A gentle early-summer breeze ruffled her hair as she rounded the side of the house. She paused a moment by a magnolia tree, listening. Nothing. She continued her way through the garden toward the stables. Her toe hit a loose piece of gravel and she winced. She stopped cold at the sound of a woman's cry and a man's low curses. She began running toward the sounds.

She skidded to a stop at the far end of the garden. There was a man dragging a woman onto his horse. She saw the woman struggle, saw the man cuff her as he yanked her onto her stomach over the saddle in front of him.

It was Frank Paxton. She stared unblinking, not understanding, until he whipped up his horse. At the last moment, the woman managed to rear up, and she recognized Lizzie.

"Stop," she said, running toward them. She tripped and went sprawling, breaking her fall with her hands. For a moment she lay stunned.

She forced herself up. Paxton hadn't heard her. And now she could no longer see his horse. She hadn't visited Paxton's house, set by itself on a small rise near to the artisan's compound. Would he take Lizzie there?

What to do? Where was Brent? There was no one else. Just her. Five minutes later, Byrony was running back downstairs toward the library and the gun case. She pulled a rifle from the case. There weren't any bullets. She grabbed the rifle and slid open the casing. There were two bullets.

She ran outside toward the stables. She should stop by Drew's apartment. She wasn't stupid, though her rage at what Paxton had done, was doing, was formidable. She took time only to bridle her mare; then she was urging the horse to a canter toward Drew's apartment. It was dark. She jumped off the mare's back and ran to the door, pounding on it with all her strength. She called his name.

No answer. Nothing.

As she rode toward Paxton's house, she wondered if the man were insane. Hadn't Brent said anything to him? Hadn't Brent had Lizzie move into the big house to protect her? And what was Lizzie doing down in the garden?

Frank Paxton's house was a white man's house. It was well maintained, its white paint fresh. It had an obvious air of prosperity. There was a light in the window.

She pulled up her mare at a short distance from the house and slid off her back. No, she realized as she rushed toward the house, Paxton wasn't insane. He must have seen how Brent had drawn back from interfering with his power. He must not know that Brent had ordered new clothing for the slaves. He must feel that he was free again to do just as he pleased.

She wanted to beat the man's brains. She slowed as she climbed up the front steps. Peering into the window, she saw Paxton ripping at Lizzie's dress. Lizzie was fighting him, and he hit her, throwing her to the floor.

Byrony forgot everything but her rage at what he was doing to the girl. She rushed at the front door and flung it open. The sight that greeted her eyes would have been ludicrous in the extreme had she not been so furious.

Frank Paxton was on his knees between Lizzie's open legs, his breeches open, one hand fumbled to hold Lizzie still, the other pulling out his thick sex. The girl was naked, her dress in rags beside her on the floor.

Paxton whipped about, staring toward Byrony, his mouth falling open.

"Missis," Lizzie cried. "Help me."

"Shut up, you silly little slut," Paxton said, and slapped her face.

"Let her go, Mr. Paxton. Now."

"Get out of here, Mrs. Hammond. You've no right—"

He broke off abruptly as Byrony lifted the rifle and aimed it at him.

"Get off her, you pig."

Frank Paxton felt himself shrivel. He eased his hold on Lizzie and she scooted away from him.

Slowly he fastened his breeches and rose to his feet. The damned bitch. How dare she—He drew in his breath, knowing he had to get control of himself. Women, he knew, feared guns. He had to get it away from her before she hurt herself or did something stupid.

"I suggest, Mrs. Hammond, that you put down that weapon before you hurt yourself. Then, ma'am, I suggest that you leave." There, he thought, satisfied, that should put her in her place.

"You're doing quite a bit of suggesting, Mr. Paxton."

Her cool, mocking voice made him quake with renewed rage at her damned interference. He raised his fisted hand. "See here, you've no right to interfere. She's nothing, do you hear? Nothing, merely a dirty little slave."

"And you, sir, are a dirty pig."

"I can do just as I please with the slaves. The girl was waiting for me in the garden. She wanted it."

"No, missis, no. It was Josh."

Byrony ignored the girl's pitiful cry, her eyes fastened on Paxton. "Now, sir, I have a suggestion for you. You will be gone from Wakehurst by morning."

He drew himself up to his full height. "You giving me orders, Mrs. Hammond? A woman doesn't give orders. And from what I've heard, you and your precious husband are about as friendly as birds and cats. I fancy Mr. Hammond just might give me this little trollop for my trouble. He likely wants to take her himself first. Why else would he move her into the big house?"

"Because, you stupid fool, she's a child, and like most men who have the slightest claim to honor, I tend to protect children."

Byrony whirled around to see Brent standing in the open doorway, his eyes as cold as his voice.

"She's a slave, damn you, Hammond. I've always had my pick of them. You know how they are, hot and ready for a man—"

Byrony heard a roar of fury. She saw Josh hurl himself past Brent.

"Dammit, Josh, stop."

She saw Brent grab the huge black man's arm with such force that it jerked him around. For an agonized moment, she thought Josh would strike Brent to get to Paxton.

She blinked at the very brief struggle. Josh was held firmly, his arm twisted behind his back, panting with pain and rage.

"He's not worth it, my friend," she heard Brent say quietly to Josh. "I'll handle it, I promise you."

Brent turned his attention to Paxton. "I believe," he drawled, "that I heard my wife give you a suggestion." He paused a moment, then continued in a very soft voice, "Consider it an order. You will be gone from Wakehurst by the morning, Paxton, or I'll kill you. Do you understand, you scum?"

"Just where do you think you'll find another overseer? Don't be a fool, man. The little slut is nothing."

"No, Josh," Brent said quietly to his friend, feeling his rage at the overseer. "Actually, Paxton, I'm a bit disappointed that you could be so stupid. You see, I've just begun to dig into your activities. I would have preferred to see you in jail for your cheating. But no matter. Not to see your ugly face again will have to be enough. Byrony, keep your rifle pointed at him until I give Lizzie my jacket."

Byrony stood quietly as she watched Brent walk to the cowering girl and cover her with his jacket. She heard him say very gently, "You've no reason to be scared now, Lizzie. Everything will be all right."

"You're a stupid fool, Hammond. What man lets a woman tell him what to do?"

Brent smiled, actually smiled. "You know, Paxton, you're becoming a complete bore. I have a suggestion for you now: shut your mouth and start packing. I intend to remain here until I see the last of your dirt."

"Brent, I—" Byrony paused as her husband's eyes met hers.

"You will return to the house with Lizzie and Josh. I will see you in a couple of hours. Go now, Byrony."

He sounded abrupt, angry, and she didn't understand him. But she felt too grateful to him to worry about it at the moment.

"Yes, Brent," she said only. Lizzie scurried to stand beside her, but Byrony was looking at Josh. "You will accompany us back, Josh. I need your protection."

The big man looked undecided, his black eyes darting back to Paxton.

"Please, Josh," Byrony said again. "Brent will handle everything."

The bedroom was bathed in early-morning light. Byrony doused the lamp, then returned to her chair to wait. She'd slept a bit during the long night, only to jerk awake after a few minutes, straining to hear Brent.

When she finally heard his steps in the corridor, she jumped to her feet.

Brent walked into the bedroom, drawing to an abrupt halt at the sight of his wife.

"What is this? You waited up to see that I kept to my end of the bargain? Yes, Paxton is off my property. He's gone. It's over, all of it."

She saw he was tired—bone-weary, as her Aunt Ida used to say. Even though his words put her back up, she nonetheless walked to him and lightly laid her hand on his arm. "Thank you, Brent. I appreciate what you did, what you've done. You're a fine man."

He shook off her hand and walked away from her. Without a word, he stripped off his clothes, shrugged into a dressing gown, and sat down in the chair she'd recently vacated. He leaned his head back and closed his eyes. "Perhaps you'd be kind enough to tell me what you were doing in Paxton's house."

"I woke up and you weren't here. I couldn't sleep so I went out onto the balcony. I thought I heard someone and went down to the garden to see. I saw Paxton drag Lizzie onto his horse."

"Yes, I'm listening. Continue."

"I got dressed and got one of your rifles. I went to see if Drew could help me, but no one was there. I had no choice but to go to Paxton's house. He was trying to rape Lizzie when I stopped him."

Brent cocked an eyebrow at her and slowly opened his

eyes. "I see. Such a heroine you are, my dear. I suppose it never occurred to you that Paxton could get that rifle away from you? Perhaps even rape you also? No, I see that such a logical flow of mental thought never went through your little mind. Of course, you are a woman. How could I expect logic from you?"

Byrony could only stare at him. She hadn't known what to expect when he returned, but not this attack, and done so calmly, with such a display of disinterest. "How did you know where I'd be?"

"Ah, an excellent question, one, I'm certain, that just occurred to you. You see, my dear, Josh is a man, and thus reacts with logic. It's true that he was waiting for Lizzie, but evidently she was early and Paxton got her. I was returning from Natchez with Drew and came upon him. It didn't require an excessive amount of thought to determine what had happened, particularly when we discovered that you and a mare were missing."

"I did try to find help, Brent, but of course, you weren't here. You were doing whatever men do. I really didn't need your interference. I simply would have taken Lizzie and left his house."

"Ah, I can just picture what comes next. Had you managed to leave his house with your lovely hide intact, Paxton, filled with righteous indignation, would have confronted me the next day. And I'm really not certain that I would have ordered him to leave. But of course, since I witnessed the man's foolishness, I really had no choice."

"Foolishness? That's what you term his attempted rape of Lizzie?"

Brent suddenly rose and stretched his arms above his head. He looked at her thoughtfully a moment, then said, "Byrony, listen to me. You aren't used to the ways here. It's probably very true that Paxton has taken any and every black female slave he wanted. Or hasn't it occurred to you to wonder why there are so many light-skinned slaves around?"

"It's evil and disgusting. Why, you would never—"

"Don't kid yourself, Byrony. I had my share of slaves when I was young. Didn't I mention that to you once? But, of course, they were all willing."

"Unlike me."

She saw his body clench. "Enough. No more from you. I'm bloody tired. And don't back away from me. What you did, Byrony, was stupid as hell. Now, leave me be. I'm going to bed."

THIRTY

Brent stood quietly in front of the portrait, unable to stop staring at it. It was nearly life-size, the colors so warm and vibrant that he wanted to reach out and touch them. Byrony was seated on a marble bench beneath a rose arbor. He recognized the evening gown immediately. It was a pale violet silk, trimmed with narrow ribbons of lavender. She wasn't wearing the lace-and-ribbon headdress and her hair cascaded over her shoulders in loose curls. But it was her face that drew him, her air of sweetness. He'd seen that small, impish smile about her mouth, but it seemed so long ago. Drew hadn't gotten the color of her eyes precisely right, but they invited him to share a naughty secret. She looked utterly delicious, he thought, a beautiful confection that was his alone. How could that feminine confection be the same woman who had flung herself on a horse at midnight to ride off and rescue Lizzie? And face down Paxton with a rifle? Slowly he forced himself to turn away and say, "It's fine, Drew, very fine indeed. Has Byrony seen it yet?"

"No, I wanted you to be the first, though she's been after me since I set down my brush. It's for your birthday, Brent. Won't you be an ancient twenty-eight soon?"

Brent grinned. "In four months, to be exact, but don't let Laurel hear you use the word *ancient*. She'll go after you."

"Drew? Are you there?"

Both men turned to see Byrony come into Drew's studio. She came to an abrupt halt, staring at the portrait.

"Oh dear," she said. "I don't look like that, do I, Drew?"

"Actually, Byrony," Brent said, "you look better. Drew here is something of a beginner."

Drew cuffed his brother's shoulder, then turned in time to catch Byrony in his arms.

"It's so lovely. Thank you, Drew. I did wonder about that dress—all that lavender. I thought I'd look like a sallow chicken. But it's beautiful."

He gave her a quick hug, and at her kiss on his cheek, he felt a gentle flow of warmth go through his body.

"You've made me look so acceptable."

"I'm glad you like it, Byrony. It's for your husband."

Byrony turned slowly, her eyes meeting Brent's. "Do you like it, Brent? Really?"

"Yes," he said. "As I told Drew, it's fine. Now, what are you doing here?"

"Laurel said there were some business matters you had to attend to," she said.

"You two go along," Drew said. "I'll be up to the house shortly. Doubtless, Brent, you'll need my assistance."

They left Drew's apartment, and Byrony turned to walk toward the house.

Brent caught her arm. "A moment, Byrony."

She turned to face him.

"We're going this way. There's a very pretty spot I want you to see first."

She cocked her head at him, but fell into step beside him. "One of your boyhood haunts?"

"Yes," he said, looking straight ahead. "Are you recovered from the excitement of last night?"

Byrony frowned up at his profile. Why wouldn't he look at her? He was still angry, of course. "Yes, I am quite recovered. Indeed, I really didn't feel the need to recover from anything. My delicate nerves weren't overset, Brent."

He saw her in Drew's portrait in his mind's eye. "The expression in your eyes was almost wicked.".

"What?"

"The portrait. How did Drew manage to get that look?"

She said without hesitation, "I thought about you on one particular night aboard the steamboat. You teased me and fondled me and loved me until I thought I'd die of it. And then I seduced you. I thought perhaps you were beginning to love me." She shrugged, "But of course, coming back here put a stop to that."

He looked surprised but didn't say anything and they walked along silently for a while. "Brent, we're going quite far from the house."

"I know. Be patient."

She thoughtfully kicked a stone from her path and watched it jump in front of her. "What will you do about Lizzie? And Josh?"

"I spoke to Josh this morning. He wouldn't tell me how he'd made that rendezvous with Lizzie, but I suspect Mammy Bath is somehow involved. Josh is her grandson, you know."

"No, I didn't know."

Brent sighed. "What can I do? Josh loves the girl and wants to marry her. Lizzie, I gather, feels the same about Josh."

"But she's only thirteen years old."

"Actually, she's now fourteen as of two days ago. Josh thought it was time."

"And what do you think?"

"He can have her, of course. Actually, if our very closed society would allow it, I'd be tempted to make Josh overseer of Wakehurst."

"Oh no."

The distress in her voice made him stop abruptly and turn to face her. "You have no liking for Josh?"

"The people would still be slaves, possessions, your possessions, Brent. It's not right." She saw him frown, saw his eyes narrow. "What of Paxton?" she asked.

"I would imagine that fool is in Natchez at the moment, drinking and telling everyone who will listen what a bastard I am. Lord only knows what he's saying about you."

Byrony had wondered the same thing. "When will we be at your boyhood haunt?"

"We're almost there."

The boyhood haunt was a very secluded, very private spot, Byrony saw. It was nothing more, actually, than a tiny clearing surrounded by thick maple and elm trees. A curtain of nearly impenetrable summer leaves blocked out the outside world.

"It's lovely, Brent."

"Yes, very lovely."

"I meant this small glade, Brent."

"That also."

"Why did you bring me here?"

"To make love to you, of course."

When, after a very long time, he lifted himself on his elbows and studied her smiling face, he said, "You look pleased with yourself."

"I am," she said. "I've brought you to your knees, so to speak."

"Hussy."

She kissed his chest, hugged him tightly, savoring the moment. She wanted to tell him that she adored him, would do anything for him, but she imagined that he would use such voiced sentiments against her later. And he'd never told her he loved her. She wondered if he were capable of such an emotion, after nine years of denying its existence.

"Do you love me, Brent?"

"You are my wife," he said, his voice fierce.

"But do you love me?"

He withdrew from her and came gracefully to his feet. She stared up at him.

"Leave it be, Byrony," he said as he leaned down to re-trieve his clothing. What did she want from him? But he knew what she wanted—ah yes, he knew.

She looked at him with bitter eyes. He was a fine lover, at least she assumed he was from the incredible pleasure he gave her. He probably gave her all the sexual feeling and pleasure he'd given for years to his mistresses. So what was a wife anyway? Someone to berate when the mood struck him, someone to blame when things didn't go the way it suited him.

From the corner of his eye Brent watched her slowly rise and begin to pull on her clothes. So many clothes, he thought inconsequently, so many petticoats and ribbons and ties. It struck him suddenly that she wasn't wearing a corset. He started to ask her why not, when she walked silently away from him into the cover of the trees.

"Byrony," he called after her.

She turned slowly and took the snowy white handker-chief from his hand.

He finished dressing, then leaned against a maple tree to wait for her.

Byrony heard them arguing, but she couldn't make out their words. Drew had left the house some half-hour earlier, and the servants had gone to bed. She frowned and walked quietly toward the closed library doors.

"Dammit, Brent, I tell you that your father hated the man."

"Come, Laurel, you're saying that because he probably didn't praise your eyebrows."

What man?

"You're a fool, Brent," came Laurel's voice.

"A fool simply because I don't necessarily believe you, my dear?" Brent said in a mocking voice. "Now, Laurel, why don't you tell me the real reason you wanted to talk to me."

There was a deadening silence for several minutes.

"I want to know what you're going to do about Wakehurst. Now that Frank Paxton is gone, we've no overseer, no one to make those lazy slaves do their work."

Byrony wanted to stay, but her past experiences with eavesdropping had been too painful. She'd already committed half a sin by listening to as much as she had. Slowly she walked away from the library and back up the stairs. At least, she thought, they were arguing and that was good.

Lizzie had finally gone off to bed. If Byrony had had to endure any more ecstatic chattering about Josh, she would have screamed. Byrony fiddled with the bows on her dressing gown, then walked out onto the balcony. It was so warm, the night still and dark. Not as warm as her lusty afternoon in the woods.

She saw herself astride Brent, crying out with abandon as his fingers caressed her. Oddly, she wondered if Aunt Ida had ever made love with a man. Silly thought. Byrony couldn't imagine Aunt Ida even taking off her clothes in front of a mirror. But Aunt Ida had to feel, didn't she? Byrony shook her head, suddenly feeling so fatigued she could hardly stand. She stared a moment at the empty bed. How she wished Brent would spend the night with her. She missed his warmth, his occasional snoring that made her poke him in the ribs, his gentle kisses that made her wake up to absolute joy.

She fell asleep alone, and awoke the following morning alone, with Lizzie standing over her, chattering away. She felt so tired, but she couldn't go back to sleep. It was Lizzie's wedding day. Brent had paid the Reverend Fletcher

343

a goodly sum to come to Wakehurst to perform the ceremony.

She smiled, yawned, and quickly drank a cup of tea before she went about her dressing.

During the brief ceremony, with Lizzie now silent as a stone as she stood beside Josh, Byrony felt Drew's eyes on her. She swatted at a fly and tried to pay attention to the service. There were at least fifty slaves crowded into the garden to witness the wedding. One woman with six children had run to her and nearly fallen to her knees to kiss Byrony's feet. "De Lord bless you, missis," she repeated over and over. Byrony felt deep embarrassment. No human being should ever be placed in such a position.

Byrony felt absolute relief when it was over and the slaves had dispersed and gone back to their compounds. Brent was in conversation with Josh, Laurel with Drew. Byrony made good her escape and went upstairs to change into her riding habit.

Thirty minutes later, she was riding down the long drive, enjoying the breeze in her face. It was with some surprise that she heard pounding hoofbeats behind her. She turned to see Brent, and a smile lit her face.

Brent reined in beside her, took in her smile, but refused to allow himself to smile in response. "You're not to ride out alone," he said. "I thought you understood that."

"I wasn't going far," she said. "You were busy with Josh and all the other slaves had left to celebrate."

"Josh clearly had other things on his mind. He and Lizzie will live in Paxton's house for the time being. He wanted nothing more than to deflower his bride."

"She's so young," Byrony said. "I hope he doesn't hurt her."

"He's not an animal," Brent said.

"That isn't what I meant."

"Oh? There isn't too much difference between a virgin of fourteen and a virgin of nineteen, and as I recall, you didn't experience too much pain."

She wanted to laugh. "Any pain I felt was worth it, just to see the look of utter chagrin on your face."

He grinned back at her. "You did take me by surprise, I'll admit it."

"How many virgins have you experienced, Brent?"

"Experienced? That's a novel way of putting it. Not more than a dozen, I expect."

"I don't believe you," she said. He merely cocked a black brow at her. "Can I ask you something, Brent?"

"Go ahead. You will anyway."

"Why is it you believe a woman is a trollop if she isn't a virgin?"

His hands tightened on his stallion's reins. "I don't," he said. "What a ridiculous thing to say."

"You believed I was. Indeed, if I hadn't been a virgin, I imagine you would still believe me to be a loose female."

"Don't be a fool. Come on. Let's gallop awhile."

"You are the most stubborn, inconsistent, arrogant man I've ever known," she shouted after him.

When they reached the long drive back to the house some thirty minutes later, Brent grinned over at her and said, "You want to race? Let's see if your mare has as much conceit as her mistress."

They raced neck-and-neck up the drive. Byrony knew Brent was keeping a firm control on his stallion, to tease her. Sure enough, just as they came in sight of the house, he let the stallion go, leaving her to stare at his back.

Laurel and Drew were seated on the front veranda when Byrony, laughing and shouting at Brent, reined in her mare. The mare skidded and Byrony suddenly felt herself falling sideways.

"Byrony!" Drew shouted, leaping from his chair and running toward her.

But Brent caught her easily and straightened her in the saddle. "Easy, I don't want you eating dirt."

"Dammit, Byrony. What are you doing?"

Both Brent and Byrony turned, startled, to face Drew.

"She's quite all right, Drew," Brent said, his eyebrow inching up in question.

"We were just racing."

"For God's sake," Drew shouted. "Both of you are idiots. You could have hurt the baby, Byrony."

Brent froze. He gazed from his wife's suddenly flushed, guilty face to his brother's worried expression. "Baby?" he said blankly.

"Of course," Drew snapped. "Byrony's pregnant."

Very slowly Brent clasped his wife about the waist and lifted her from her mare's back. "Are you pregnant?"

She nodded.

"Go inside. I will speak to you shortly."

She walked into the house. Brent was furious, just as she'd known he would be. He didn't want the responsibility of a child, the commitment it would mean to her. Perhaps he was a bit worried that she could die. How had Drew known? It was still the very early days yet. She was more tired than usual, but she hadn't had any nausea in the mornings.

"What is the matter with you, Brent?" Drew asked, grabbing his brother's arm and shaking it.

"Just how, may I ask, did you know Byrony was pregnant?" Brent asked in a low voice.

THIRTY-ONE

"I'm an artist, Brent. I see things other people don't. It's part of my talent, I suppose. Are you telling me you didn't know?"

"No, my wife hadn't seen fit to inform me. I suppose too that you can tell me just how far along she is."

"Around two months, I'd say."

Brent unconsciously patted his stallion's nose when the horse whinnied for attention. He felt very peculiar, as if the proverbial carpet had just been jerked from beneath his feet. A father. He would be a father.

He felt Drew's hand on his arm. "I've heard that women many times keep such news to themselves for a while. Miscarriage is very common, you know, and they don't want hopes to be raised—"

"Byrony won't have a miscarriage," Brent said.

"Probably not, but she must take better care of herself."

"Such as not dashing off like she did to save Lizzie?"

"Look, Brent," Drew began, only to pause at his brother's expression. He followed Brent's eyes upward to the second floor and saw his hands clench into fists at his sides.

Byrony stood silently in the middle of the room, wondering where Brent was. She heard the door open and turned around to face her husband. But it wasn't Brent. It was Laurel.

"Well, my dear stepdaughter-in-law, what a surprise. Such a pity that Drew couldn't keep his mouth shut."

"It had to come out in any case," Byrony said. "One does tend to gain flesh, you know, Laurel."

"Thank God I don't know. I do wonder what Brent will do with you. Such a pity, as I said, that the proud papa couldn't control his feelings and not speak out so precipitately."

Byrony simply stared at her.

"Ah yes, and here I was beginning to like you, Byrony. Despite everything. I wonder, were you trying to lose the child, on purpose?"

"What a stupid thing to say, Laurel. What do you want? I'm tired and sweaty and I want a bath."

"But first, my dear, you'll have to face your husband. Another month and perhaps, just perhaps, you could have convinced Brent that it was his child you're carrying."

Byrony laughed; she couldn't help herself. "If ever you'd had a child, Laurel, you'd know how ridiculous you're being! For heaven's sake, we've been here at Wakehurst for only a month!"

"I believe you can leave us now, Laurel."

Both women whirled about to see Brent standing in the door, his arms crossed over his chest.

He looks so pale, Byrony thought. She wanted to laugh at her concern.

"Yes, I'll go," Laurel said. "I believe you have a lot to say, don't you, Brent?"

He straightened abruptly, moving into the room as Laurel walked past him. Very slowly he turned to close the door. He said over his shoulder, "One really shouldn't say private things when anyone passing can overhear."

"What Laurel said wasn't particularly private. It was simply ridiculous."

"True. As you told her quite clearly, it's beyond imagination that you could be pregnant by any other man than your husband."

"Ah well, Laurel was just being Laurel," Byrony said.

"Why didn't you tell me, Byrony?" He walked swiftly toward her and clasped her shoulders in his large hands. She looked up at him with wide, calm eyes.

Her eyes fell and he shook her. "Why? Don't you think I'm entitled to know?"

"I was afraid to tell you. I wasn't sure you'd want it."

"It? What do you mean, it?"

"The child. I know you don't want a child. But you're right, regardless of what you would think, I should have told you as soon as I found out. I'm sorry."

Not want his own child. He closed his eyes a moment, hating the pain her words gave him.

She said, her voice still quiet, utterly calm, "I know that you don't love me, Brent. I know also that you distrust women, that you want to be free. I am not sorry that I'm pregnant, I must be honest with you about that. If you don't want the child, he or she will be mine. I will leave. It is your decision."

"How very selfless you sound," he heard himself say, his voice cold and remote. "But I know women aren't selfless, Byrony. If there's anything I've learned, it's that women take what they want or can from men. However, I am your husband. You belong to me, legally. You will take my child nowhere."

She looked at him with bitter eyes. "And when I am heavy with my child, and graceless and no longer able to accommodate you, I will watch you go to other women? I suppose you are right, Brent. I'm not selfless. I won't let myself be hurt that way. I'm very tired. Would you please leave me alone now?"

He said nothing more, merely nodded at her and walked from the bedroom.

Byrony came to her decision while she was soaking in her cool bathwater.

Not want his own child. But what was she to think? He'd been flailing about like a trout on a fishhook, vicious one moment, withdrawing from her the next. Well, it was enough. He thought of her buying that whip, and grinned. Well, my dear wife, he thought, you've finally got my attention.

He entered their bedroom early that evening before dinner. He drew up short.

Byrony was packing.

"What do you think you're doing?" he asked.

"Packing some of my things," Byrony said calmly, not turning to face him.

"May I ask why?"

Byrony sighed. She really didn't want to look at him, it hurt too much, but she did. "I'm leaving, Brent. I can no longer live with your lack of trust, your cynicism. I thought you were coming to truly care for me on our trip here. But that changed, once you were faced with your boyhood indiscretion, with your own betrayal. If you cannot bring yourself to deal with it, how can you expect me to?" She waited, her back ramrod straight, her shoulders back.

"No, Byrony, you're not leaving. You belong to me. My child belongs with me. Look, we belong together, and you know it."

"No, Brent, you look. A child should be raised with loving parents. I should know. Because my mother's husband is as he is, I was sent to Boston, to be raised by my mother's sister. My child will at least know a mother's love."

He drew a deep breath, knowing she was utterly serious. "You have no money," he said.

"I imagine that I can get some easily enough from dear Laurel. I imagine that she would sell her jewels to be rid of me." She drew a deep breath, not looking at him. "After my child is born, I shall get a job. I'm young and healthy. I shall be just fine."

He cursed. Byrony turned to continue folding a petticoat.

She heard him walk to her, felt his hands close around her shoulders. Slowly he pulled her back against him. "Listen to me, Byrony, please. I want you. I want our child. I want us to be together."

"No, I don't believe you."

"Will you believe me if I tell you that I love you? That I've loved you probably from the first time I saw you, your face covered with flour?"

She said nothing, and he sighed. "There's so much I have to make up to you, love. So much between us that shouldn't have been, had I not been so blind about you. And you're right. of course. Coming back here was a mistake, and I've acted like an ass. Everything you said, it's true. Forgiveness is tough. I do love you, Byrony."

He gently turned her around and looked into her face. "I love you," he repeated. "I've said those words before," he continued, almost as if speaking to himself. "To women I knew expected to hear them, but they were just words. I would ask that you try to forgive me. Will you stay with me? You can even keep your whip, just in case I backslide."

She wondered briefly if her father had said such things upon occasion to her mother, then shut out the thought. Brent was nothing like her father. "Why? You value your freedom highly, Brent. If that is the way you are, the way you want to be, then I don't want you to change. I don't want you to be unhappy."

He laughed at that. "I've been an unhappy bastard for as

long as I can remember. Always something missing. That something was you, of course, and the feelings that fill up every part of me. You're such a joy, Byrony. I want you to share yourself with me, always."

For the first time since she'd met him, she saw uncertainty in his eyes. There was really no question as to her feelings, as to what she would tell him. Love was like that, she supposed.

"All right," she said.

She saw the flash of relief in his eyes and felt his arms close around her so tightly it hurt. She buried her face in his shoulder.

"I love you," he said against her temple. He felt as though a great weight had been lifted from his spirit. He felt warm and, oddly, complete somehow.

She wanted to tell him some minutes later that she could imagine no man who could take a woman's clothes off more quickly than he. But she said nothing. She felt too elated, too urgent.

When he came down onto the bed next to her, she raised her hand and gently stroked her fingertips over his jaw. "You're a most beautiful man, Brent."

"And you don't look like you have a babe in your little belly."

"I will be fat enough soon enough."

His strong fingers were caressing her breast. "Does that hurt you?"

She shook her head, her eyes never leaving his face.

He gazed down her body, taking in the flat belly. He drew a deep breath, gently laying the palm of his hand over her stomach. "Give me a little girl, Byrony, one as giving and sweet and forgiving as you."

"I was thinking of a little boy, a hellion who would give you gray hair."

The look in his eyes changed, and she sucked in her breath, responding as if he had been caressing her.

"Do you know something?" she whispered. "I would slay dragons for you, Brent."

"You would, would you? An easy promise, Byrony. I've never seen a one, at least not west of the Mississippi."

She laughed, punched his shoulder. He kissed her long, thoroughly, then pulled back. He gently parted her legs and sat back on his heels. "No," he said as she tensed a bit, "I want to look at you. Don't be embarrassed or shy. You're mine, after all."

She closed her eyes at his words. Then his mouth covered her and she thought she would explode with the pleasure of it.

He knows my body so well, she thought when he raised his mouth, and lifting her hips, came into her. Her own hands frantic on his back. His flesh was so warm, slick with sweat. She took his cries into her mouth.

We are like two children, Byrony thought sometime later, when she and Brent, holding hands, laughing at nonsense, walked down the stairs.

"Good grief," Brent said, drawing to a halt in the doorway of the dining room. "You shouldn't have waited for us."

"We didn't know how long you would be," Laurel said, searching their faces. "After all, there was so much for Byrony to do."

"Yes," Brent said, "there was, wasn't there?"

Byrony gave him a dazzling smile that made him feel like a randy goat. "Are you hungry, wife?"

"Amazingly so," she said.

Even though she was hungry, she scarcely tasted the delicious oyster-stuffed chicken. She was filled with Brent, attuned to his every movement, every nuance in his voice. He was discussing the future of Wakehurst with Drew, and for once Byrony couldn't bring herself to attend to his words.

Brent looked at her plate, then smiled at her. "Why don't you and Laurel go into the drawing room. Drew and I will join you in just a few minutes."

"Just what was all that about?" Laurel said the moment they were alone.

Byrony didn't answer immediately, but walked slowly to the open window and breathed in the soft evening air.

"Well?"

"I'm not leaving Brent," she said. "You'll have to forget what Mammy Bath told you about me packing."

Laurel shook her head. "God, you're a simpleton. He seduces you and you're ready to forget everything. Oh yes, I well recognize the look. You'll regret this, Byrony."

Brent had seduced her, she thought fairly, but she'd wanted him just as much. "He loves me," she said simply. "Ever since he knocked me down and spilled my flour bag."

"Do you have any idea how many women he's *loved* during the past nine years? I should probably make that fifteen years."

"Probably a battalion. But now he's retired."

"I suppose he wants the child?"

"Of course."

There was a moment of silence. Byrony turned back to the open window, aware of the swishing sound of Laurel's silk skirts as she paced the drawing room.

"Don't you realize there's no reason for him to love you? Listen to me, Byrony, you're a sweet girl. You are even reasonably pretty."

"Thank you."

"But consider all the women he's known, women who are truly beautiful, women who very probably loved him as much as you do. Why you? It makes no sense. He's got a reason. Perhaps it's your child he wants. All men want a son—a question of their mortality and all that, I suppose."

"Brent told me he wanted a little girl."

"I tell you he's lying to you! Or perhaps he's lying to himself."

Laurel paused a moment, unable to find more words, more arguments. She wasn't really certain what she believed. But she knew she didn't want Brent leaving with his wife. If he did, he would probably sell Wakehurst and leave her to face all her neighbors with nothing but her charming smile. She remembered asking him some two weeks before just what she was supposed to do if he left. He'd merely grinned at her and told her to remarry. "So many besotted fools chomping at the bit," he'd told her, and she'd wanted to hit him. She deserved to keep Wakehurst. It should be hers. After all, she'd given years to that damned old man. She felt a moment of dizziness and closed her hand over the back of a chair for support. She'd been so young, so very young when he'd discovered her with Brent. But even then he'd been too old to forgive her, to remember what it was to be young.

She opened her eyes when she heard Brent and Drew come into the drawing room. She watched Brent's eyes meet Byrony's and wanted to scream. She turned to see Drew regarding the two of them with a smile.

She jumped when Drew said, "I will be leaving next week to return to Paris."

"Oh no," Byrony cried. "Drew, I'd hoped you would come back with us to San Francisco."

"I will visit you, my dear, I promise. But there's so much for me to do, you see. Paris is where I belong, at least for a while. I trust you will keep me informed. I swear to send gifts to all my nieces and nephews."

"I see," Laurel said. She walked out of the drawing room.

Byrony walked around in dazed satisfaction for the next couple of days. Lizzie was once again her maid, but she was no longer chatting. *She looks as dreamy as I do*, Byrony thought. Even all the problems of Wakehurst, both present and future, didn't intrude. She knew her first bout with morning sickness, and was taken aback at Brent's pale face when she dashed from their bed to the chamber pot. And pleased. He loved her; he loved the child she was carrying. He left Wakehurst in the mornings, and returned only late in the afternoons. When she asked him what he was doing, he merely told her he was trying to come up with a surprise to rival hers. And no more would he say.

She rode in the open carriage with Laurel to visit neighbors. She supposed Laurel quieter than usual, but neither Laurel nor any of the very charming neighbors intruded into her magical world.

And Brent couldn't seem to get enough of her. "Your endurance is amazing," she said to him one late afternoon.

She felt so protected, so cherished, that when Frank Paxton came upon her one afternoon when she was alone, riding at a very sedate walk on her mare, she couldn't at first grasp that it was he and that he was ugly drunk.

THIRTY-TWO

"What do you want?" Byrony asked as she reined in her mare.

Frank Paxton swept off his hat and bowed. "You could say, my dear Mrs. Hammond that it's unfinished business. I've been waiting here for days for you to ride out."

"And drinking for days too, it appears. You have no business here, finished or unfinished. Now, Mr. Paxton, if you will please leave—"

He grabbed her mare's rains as he laughed, a laugh that scared her to her toes. Like a villain in a silly melodrama. No, her father sometimes sounded like that. Before he became violent. This was real, all too real. Her mind cleared suddenly and she stared at him. Before, he'd always looked the gentleman at least, well-dressed, outwardly polite. But now he looked as though he hadn't slept or bathed in weeks. His face was covered with scraggly whiskers, and his eyes were rimmed in red.

"Byrony." He said her name, savoring it. "Odd name, but it'll do, I suppose. We're going to be too close for last names, my dear."

"Mr. Paxton, you're behaving with no sense at all. I suggest that you take your leave. My husband wouldn't be pleased were he to discover you on his property."

"You're right, of course," he agreed as he swiped his hand across his mouth. "I'm glad that you feel so strongly about me, Byrony. Most women do. Come along, now."

She could only stare at him. "I'm not going anywhere with you," she said slowly, calmly. "Indeed, I'm going to continue my ride alone, then return home. Now, give me the reins."

She stretched out her gloved hand, but he made no move, merely smiled at her. She swallowed, thought of her child.

"I prefer white women," he said. "But I wanted that little Lizzie. So young, and a virgin. But not any longer, is she? You married her off quickly enough to that brute Josh." His eyes narrowed and his voice grew venomous. "I wanted to plow that girl, and oh yes, Byrony, she would have loved it. A white man taking her, not some stupid brute."

"Josh is not a brute. He loves Lizzie. And you're drunk, Mr. Paxton."

"Not that drunk, my dear," he said, and leaned over toward her.

Without conscious decision, Byrony raised her riding crop and brought it down with all her strength against his arm. He yelped in pain and jerked back. At that moment, Byrony kicked her heels into her mare's sides and grabbed for the reins as Paxton dropped them. But she missed them.

She leaned over her mare's neck, stretched for the dangling reins. She knew she must turn the mare back, back toward the house.

She heard Paxton behind her, and swiveled in the saddle to see him gaining on her.

I shouldn't be riding at a gallop, she thought, I might hurt the baby. The mare stumbled. Byrony clung to the pommel, feeling more helpless than she ever had in her life. She felt Paxton's arm close around her waist and lift her. Her first thought was that he'd saved her from falling, saved her child.

He slammed her face down in front of him, and she

smelled horse and sweat and dirty leather. She felt his fingers on her hips, pressing against her through her layers of clothes.

"You damned fool," she shouted, trying to rear up. "Get your hands off me."

"Shut up, you little bitch."

She did. If it weren't for the child, she knew she'd be fighting him wildly. Instead, she lay quietly, hoping the galloping horse wouldn't harm the child.

To her surprise, Paxton suddenly jerked his horse to a stop. She couldn't see what he was doing, but she heard her mare snort, heard Paxton slap the mare's rump.

"There," he said, and she wondered at the satisfaction in his drunk voice.

They rode for what seemed an endless period of time to Byrony. She tasted dirt.

When he finally reined in, they were in front of a small shack, a rickety excuse for a house, which looked as if no one had come near it for a decade.

She didn't fight him as he pulled her down from the horse's back.

"Ain't exactly Wakehurst, but it'll do," Paxton said more to himself than to her. "Come along, Byrony."

She closed her eyes for a moment, fighting the pain as he twisted her arm up behind her.

The door was hanging on its hinges, and Byrony wondered why it didn't fall off when Paxton kicked it open.

He released her, and she stood quietly for a moment, getting her breath, trying to think. It was a single room. Rotted wooden planks heaved upward or sank down into the dirt foundation. There was a single bed, a rough wooden table, and two chairs. There were two windows, one of them without glass, and the door.

Byrony drew a deep, steadying breath and turned to face Frank Paxton.

"Why did you bring me here?"

He didn't pay any attention to her. He walked to the table, picked up a jug, and raised it to his mouth. She watched, her stomach knotting, as the raw-smelling whiskey dribbled down his chin.

He slammed the jug down on the table, then turned to her, a wide grin on his face.

"I brought you here, my fine little lady, to plow you until you beg me to stop. That or you beg me to continue."

For a moment she didn't comprehend what he'd said. When she did, she wasn't afraid, oddly enough. She was furious.

"Don't be a damned fool," she shouted at him, hands on her hips. "Look, Mr. Paxton, my husband will be very worried about me. I don't like you, but I don't want you to be killed. And he will kill you if you attempt to touch me. Now, I'm leaving."

"Like hell you are." He grabbed her arm and pulled her around, pressing her against him. "I used to look at you, you know, and wonder what you had for me underneath your pretty little dresses. Now I'm gonna see for myself. Oh yes, I'm gonna see for myself now."

His words were slurred, and although his grip on her was strong, she knew he was very drunk. She felt his hands all over her.

"You like it already," he said, kissing her cheek, biting her neck. Suddenly his entire body seemed to go slack, and she heard him curse.

He released his hold on her and shoved her over to the sagging bed. "I need me some time," he said, and pushed her down onto her back. Byrony bounced up, ready to fight, but all she saw was his fisted hand. It hit her jaw, and she saw nothing more.

She opened her eyes very slowly, aware of an odd ringing in her head. She wanted to sit up, but couldn't. She jerked on her arms, only to realize that he'd tied her wrists above her head to the rough wooden bedposts. She wanted to yell at the top of her lungs for help. Then she stopped, realizing that she was still clothed. He hadn't raped her.

Very slowly she turned her head, ignoring the pain in her jaw, and saw Paxton slouched at the table, the jug beside him, his head pillowed in his arms. He was snoring loudly.

She lay back and gave an experimental tug to the ropes about her wrists. They tightened painfully, but she heard the bedposts give a creaking, straining sound.

She tugged again, her eyes on Paxton's back. She heard him groan, and froze.

Drew ran up the walk, shouting to Brent, "Wait. Her horse just came back to the stable."

Brent quickly dismounted and turned toward his brother. He saw Byrony thrown in his mind's eye, saw her lying in a pool of blood after she'd lost the child. Her face was waxen and she was dying. Like Joyce Morgan had died all those years ago while he'd held her hand, watching, helpless.

"Look, Brent."

"What the hell is that?"

"A note," Drew said, drawing up beside his brother.

Brent grabbed the single piece of paper. "I already took her, Hammond," he read. "She loved it. She wants to go away with me."

It was signed *Paxton*. "No!" It was a howl of rage.

"What is it? What's happened to Byrony?"

Brent ignored Laurel and said to Drew, "Paxton has taken her, that damned bastard."

What an ambiguous way to say it, Brent thought. He became aware of a roar of voices and looked around to see all the house slaves clustering on the veranda, all of them talking at once. He shook his head. He barked at Jemmy, one of the stableboys, "Go fetch me Josh, at once."

"What will you do, Brent?" Laurel asked.

"I'm going to find the bastard and kill him. Slowly. Drew, come with me to the study."

The two men pored over a map. "I bet he's not left Wakehurst property," Brent said. "Nor can I see Paxton sleeping under a maple tree. He's somewhere here, I know it, probably in an abandoned shack."

Drew, who realized all too well the extent of the Wakehurst lands, closed his eyes a moment. They might as well find a haystack and search it.

Josh appeared some ten minutes later, his face calm, his brown eyes as cold as a winter's night. "Tell me what's happened," he said, his eyes locked on Brent's face.

Frank Paxton felt like all the demons in hell were cavorting in a mad dance through his head. He lurched to his feet, nearly knocking over the table, and rushed outside to be vilely sick.

He groaned and cursed and clutched his belly.

Byrony heard him and knew time was short. She gave a mighty tug, using the strength of her shoulders, and one of the rotted bedposts broke off.

Frank Paxton staggered into the shack, wishing he'd never seen that damned peddler who'd sold him that raw whiskey. Poison, that's what it was. He'd forgotten entirely about Byrony Hammond until he managed to lurch through the door.

He looked through bleary eyes toward the bed. How the hell was he supposed to rape her when all he wanted to do was die? His gaze sharpened. She was gone.

He spewed out curses in surprise, and in the next instant he felt a blow on his head. He crumpled to the floor.

Byrony stared down at him and tried to calm her breathing as she lowered her bedpost club. What a pitiful sight he was. She carefully set the thick bedpost on the table and bent down beside him, feeling for his pulse. Oh no, she whispered to herself. The wretched man was in a bad way. She straightened, a frown on her face. What was she to do? At least he was in no condition to harm a mosquito. It took all her strength, but she managed to pull him to the bed. She shoved and heaved until he was sprawled on his back. She stepped back to think. She must get Brent. But Brent would probably kill him. He was a miserable excuse for a man, but she didn't want to see him dead.

There was a lump on the side of his head the size of an egg now from her blow. "Stupid man," she said.

There was no choice. She had to go for help.

She pulled a blanket over him and left the shack.

Brent gazed about at the three different groups of men in the search party. But it was getting late, soon it would be dark. He felt rage sear through him as he again saw Paxton's words in his mind.

Suddenly one of the blacks let out a shout.

Brent turned from Josh to see Byrony riding like a wild woman toward him. She nearly jumped into his arms before she'd stopped the horse. He caught her, holding her so tightly that she thought her ribs would crack. "I'm all right," she said over and over against his shoulder.

He eased his death grip on her and became aware of her appearance. Her hair was flying about her face and down her back. Her riding habit was dirty and ripped. He felt his blood run cold.

"Byrony," he said.

"I'm all right, Brent," she said, seeing the shock in his eyes. "I'm all right, I swear it."

"Where is Paxton?" Drew asked.

"How did you know about Paxton?" she asked.

"He was obliging enough to send me a note attached to your mare's saddle. He said he'd raped you."

"Poor stupid man," Byrony said.

"What?"

Never had Byrony heard such outrage in one word. "He didn't touch me, Brent," she said.

"How the hell did you get away from him?"

"He took me to an old shack, tied me down to the bed, and fell asleep because he was so drunk. I ripped out the bedpost and hit him when he woke up. He's very sick, Brent, and needs a doctor."

"What he needs, the filthy scum, is a visit to the devil."

There was no mistaking the rage in his voice. Indeed, his entire body was vibrating with it.

"No," she said very clearly. "Don't kill him. He's far too pitiful to kill."

Brent looked down into his wife's composed face. He said very slowly, very softly, "Where is this shack?"

She told him.

"Go inside and rest. I will come to you later."

She watched as Brent, Drew, and Josh mounted and rode away. Each man was carrying a rifle.

"God, you're just like a cat."

Byrony turned to face Laurel. "You would have preferred that he raped me?"

"It looks like he did," Laurel said. "You're a mess."

"Well, he didn't, and a bath will take care of the rest."

Why was she worried about Frank Paxton? Byrony wondered for the dozenth time as she paced the bedroom waiting for Brent to return. She realized that it wasn't Paxton that worried her, but Brent. She didn't want to be responsible for violence. She didn't want him to commit murder. But she would have killed Paxton if she'd had to.

What a damnable coil.

"Byrony."

She whipped about to see Brent in the doorway. She flew at him and flung her arms about his back. "I've been so worried," she said, stroking her hands over his beloved face, over his shoulders, and down his arms.

"Are you all right, truly?"

"Yes," she said, pressing herself close. He pushed her back.

"I didn't kill Paxton," he said.

She gave a sigh of relief.

"You were right. He was the most pitiful sight I've seen in a long time. Drew and Josh took him into Natchez to Doc Harrison. He'll probably live."

"Good," Byrony said.

His eyes narrowed on her face. "Did he fondle you?"

"Just a bit when he had me over the saddle, but it was nothing too dreadful. I was too worried about the baby, you see."

"Ah, yes," he said, quickly recalling his anger at his wife after his worry was under control, "the baby. May I ask what you were doing riding out? And by yourself?"

"I wasn't really riding, just walking Velvet. Paxton said he'd been waiting for days to get me. I think he was demented from all that awful whiskey."

He loosed her arms and walked away from her. He was so bloody tired, the strain of the day making him feel like an old man. And here Byrony was acting like Frank Paxton was a pathetic victim. He turned to her and said coldly, "I find your excess of sympathy a bit nauseating."

She stared at him, mute.

"Would you still have begged me to spare his worthless life if he had raped you? What do you think he would have done if he hadn't been drunk as a loon? Can you even begin to imagine? Damnation, woman, you could have lost the child."

365

She heard his voice shake, but thought it was from anger. "The baby is just fine," she said.

"No thanks to you."

Her eyes narrowed. "For a man who didn't want the child in the first place, you're acting mighty possessive about it now."

But it wasn't the baby, at least the baby wasn't his first consideration. He again could see her lying alone and frightened, losing her life's blood.

"God," he growled, "all women should be locked up until they can prove that they have even a grain of sense."

She opened her mouth, but he slashed his hand through the air. "No, no more out of you. I'm dead tired and I'm going to bed."

"You're being unreasonable," she said to his back.

He stripped off his clothes, flinging each piece to the floor. Without saying another word to her, he doused the lamp and climbed into bed.

Byrony stood in the middle of the room, silhouetted only by the shaft of moonlight coming through the wooden blinds. If her husband did truly love her, she thought, he had a very odd way of showing it. She sighed, slowly removed her dressing gown, and got into bed, as far away from him as possible.

When she awoke near to dawn, her body was alive with sensation at the caressing of her husband's hands on her breasts and belly. She moaned, encouraging the pleasure. Then she tensed all over. How could he dare treat her as he had, then want to make love to her? As if nothing had happened?

"Get away from me."

Brent came fully awake, Byrony's words making him cold all over. "I was ready to forgive you your stupidity," he said.

"My stupidity?"

"Why don't you just lie still? Consider your body payment for my not killing your poor wretch, Paxton."

She flung out of bed, dragging a blanket with her. She marched to the bedroom door, so angry she could think of nothing to say. She flung open the door and yelled over her shoulder, "You want a woman, Brent? Go pay for it."

THIRTY-THREE

"California," Lizzie said, her eyes large with excitement and awe. "Just think, missis, my baby won't belong to nobody."

"Yes, Lizzie. You're not pregnant."

"Josh tell me I probably am," Lizzie said, giggling. "He's a big man, my Josh."

Most of them think they are, Byrony said silently. Damn Brent anyway. For the past two days he'd treated her with sublime indifference. He was polite, absently so, not speaking to her of anything but the most inane of subjects. She didn't know what he was thinking.

It had been Drew who told her that Paxton was quite alive. Brent had merely arched an eyebrow at the news.

Where the devil was he now? She wanted to talk to him, she had to talk to him. This silent battle between them had gone on long enough. Stupid, arrogant man. She wanted to shake him, perhaps even kick him, anything to get his attention.

She frowned a moment as she stood quietly while Lizzie fastened up the tiny buttons of her cotton gown. What if something were wrong and he didn't intend to tell her? What did he think a wife was for anyway? Her frown deepened. As if she didn't know.

"There, missis. You lie down, maybe," Lizzie said, but

Byrony wanted nothing more than to get out of the house and into the cool shaded garden. Her second bath hadn't helped much. She walked through the study out onto the veranda. The thick-leaved oak and elm trees looked heavenly. Child, she said silently as she lightly touched her hand to her belly, are you as warm as I am?

She walked through the garden, pausing every few moments to sniff at the sweet-smelling flowers. She paused, a magnolia blossom to her nose, when she heard Laurel's voice.

"—Brent, it's been so long—it's not as if—"

Her feet moved forward without her mind's permission. She saw Brent standing with his back to her, dressed in buff trousers, white shirt, and black boots. She thought she saw Laurel's face before she put her arms around his back. She thought she heard Laurel whisper something to him, but couldn't make out her words. Then Brent, her husband, leaned down and kissed Laurel.

For a moment she weaved where she stood, until she realized she was holding her breath. A fierce pain stabbed through her, and she closed her eyes. "Damn you, Brent Hammond." She was on the point of turning when she saw Laurel strain to clasp his neck, pressing her body against him.

Rage, pure and clean, washed through her.

"Take your hands off my husband!"

Nothing happened. She realized stupidly that she'd only whispered the words.

"Take your hands off my husband."

Her furious shout drew a gasp from Laurel and she dropped her arms, stepping back. Her eyes met Byrony's, dropped a moment, but not before Byrony saw the gleam of triumph.

"Stay away from my husband, Laurel. As for you, Brent—" She broke off as he turned very slowly to face her.

To her fury, he grinned at her. "Hello, Byrony," he said with mild interest. "You're looking a bit warm. Why don't you have Mammy Bath make you some lemonade."

She yelled, "I'm going to shoot you."

His grin never faltered, and he still appeared but mildly interested. "I believe," he said, "that our last conversation ended with something of that sort."

She felt tears, and swiped the back of her hand furiously across her eyes. "As for you, you—painted hussy, I'll—"

She got no further. Brent burst into laughter. "Painted what? Where the devil did you get that? Have you been reading some lurid novels?"

Laurel giggled.

I should have simply left, not said a word, not humiliated myself, Byrony thought, staring at him. No, that's what my mother would do. She marched up to her husband, drew back her hand, and slapped him as hard as she could. His laughter died abruptly. Slowly he raised his hand to his cheek and rubbed it.

Her hand stung. At least her precious husband wasn't laughing at her anymore. She thrust up her chin as she turned, eyes narrowed, to Laurel. "I wonder, just how lovely you'd look with your hair in a rat's nest around your face."

She rushed at Laurel. "Don't you ever go near my husband again." She grabbed Laurel's hair before she could move out of the way. Suddenly her arms were hauled downward and pinned to her sides.

"Enough, Byrony."

Brent drew her back until she was pressed against him. He shook her.

"You bitch." Laurel hissed at her, but she backed up a step, seeing the fury in Byrony's eyes.

"What the devil is going on here?" Drew walked forward, looking blankly from his brother, to his brother's wife, to Laurel.

"She's trying to give Brent orders," Laurel said. "She struck him and tried to attack me. She's crazy."

Brent felt Byrony quiver and tightened his grip on her upper arms. He shot a look at Laurel before saying to his brother, "Just a slight misunderstanding, that's all. Now, my dear, are you feeling more restrained?"

Byrony nodded.

He released her, and in the next instant he yelped with pain from the kick to his shin.

Byrony ducked away from him, but her leg struck a marble bench and she fell back, her arms flailing.

Brent swore even as he grabbed for her. "You little fool," he said, hauling her up again. "Are you trying to hurt yourself, hurt the baby?"

Byrony drew herself up to her full height. "No," she said clearly, "I was trying to hurt you."

"You did. What do you think you deserve in return?"

"Really, Brent—" Drew said.

"She should be locked up," Laurel said.

Brent grinned down at his wife. "That just might not be such a bad idea. Come along, Byrony."

"Brent, what are you going to do?"

"Mind your own business," Brent said. He dragged her through the garden beside him.

"Let me go."

"Now, that would seem more than careless of me," Brent said. "I suppose I should be thankful that you didn't kick me in the crotch. That would have brought me to my knees, as I'm certain you remember well."

"I will, if you don't let me go."

"That," he said, "makes not one whit of sense. If I hold you, you won't be able to. Hush now and stop digging in your heels."

"I want to talk to you, Brent."

"And I, my dear, want to strip you to your beautiful skin.

371

Will I still be an unacceptable husband when you're whimpering with pleasure?"

She closed her eyes a moment, aware that the house slaves were witnessing the master dragging the mistress up the stairs. "I'll make you sorry for this, Brent. Damn you, if you want to be a rutting pig, go back to your dear Laurel."

"You've made me quite sorry innumerable times during the past months. And now I'm a 'rutting pig.' Why don't you forget your jealousy and think about what I'm going to do to you?"

Byrony jabbed him in the ribs. In the next moment he'd pushed her into the bedroom and locked the door. "Now," he said, and walked toward her.

"No."

She was still yelling at him when she was wearing only her white cotton chemise.

Brent, who hadn't said a word, stepped back and began to stroke his jaw. "Very nice," he said at last. "Why don't you strike a seductive pose on the bed? Given your present attitude, it might help my interest."

"I hope you rot."

"I have no intention of looking to see where your eyes are fastened, Byrony," he said as he stripped off his clothes.

"You're a man, and always interested, no matter who the woman. It doesn't matter one whit to you."

"Oh yes it does. Come now, let's get on with it. The sooner I have you yelling with pleasure, the more quickly you'll forget your grievances."

"I find you making love to another woman—your stepmother—and you have the gall—"

In the next instant she was on her back, her chemise yanked up to her waist, her husband lying his full length on top of her.

Very gently he drew her arms above her head. "I've been quite distracted lately, love," he said, nuzzling her neck. "A husband should keep his wife dreamy-eyed and sated. So many responsibilities."

"Don't you dare force me."

He sat back on his haunches and very calmly tore her chemise apart. "Very nice," he said, staring a moment at her breasts. He eased off her, pulled off the torn chemise, and lowered one hand to stroke her breasts. "Our baby is filling you out quite nicely."

"Don't, Brent."

"Don't what? You know, Byrony, if you but learned to trust your husband a bit more, you'd save yourself a lot of wasted energy."

"Trust you? I *saw* what you were doing. But you don't even care, do you?"

He paused a moment, and she would have sworn that she saw a flash of anger in his eyes, but it was gone quickly.

His long fingers moved down her belly to find her and stroke her. She tried to jerk away from him, but he only laughed. "You said something about forcing you, love? I believe it's your heat that's causing this delightful wetness, not the weather."

"It doesn't mean anything!"

"Oh?"

"Do you do that to Laurel?"

"Not for nine years."

"I don't believe you. If I hadn't come into the garden, you would have—"

He cut off her words with his mouth.

She realized then that she was responding to him.

He continued to stroke her, caress her. "Have it your own way," he said, and came up between her legs. He went deep. "Byrony," he said, stilling a moment over her, "give over."

She turned her face away, unaware that her hips lifted to bring him deeper. She heard him growl deep in his throat, felt his powerful body tense over her. It was the oddest feeling to be separate from him. She hated it. He was lying his full length on top of her. She could hear his ragged breathing beside her ear, feel his pounding heartbeat.

"I won't forgive you this, Brent."

He raised his head to look down at her. "And you're a stubborn witch, Byrony. Would be that women were as simple and straightforward as men, then I'd know just how to treat you. You do realize, don't you, that you didn't hurt anyone but yourself? As I said, you're bloody stubborn. Enjoy it. Now, you must excuse me. I have much to to. Not, of course, that I didn't care for this most charming distraction."

He rolled off her and rose. She closed her eyes.

"At least, you won't be ready to pleasure Laurel for a while."

"No faith in me. So much depends on the woman, you know, and her skill. No, I don't suppose you'd know about that, would you?"

Byrony rolled over onto her stomach.

Brent started to say something conciliating. No, he thought, he wanted to talk to Laurel first. He wanted to know why she'd begged him to kiss her, knowing that Byrony was watching them.

"Don't be silly, Brent. I didn't see your little wife. It's just that I'm lonely, that's all, and I still have very strong feelings for you."

"There's certainly no reason for you to be lonely," he said. "Drew was telling me you have all the men in the county after you."

"It's true. But they're waiting, you know, to see what you do with Wakehurst."

"Which one of them will you accept?"

"If you leave Wakehurst and don't leave me penniless, I suppose it will be Samuel Simpson. He had two children by his first wife. They're both boys, but quite a bit younger than you were."

"Thank God for that," Brent said. "I won't leave you penniless, Laurel. Do what you want to with Simpson. Incidentally, I'm leaving Wakehurst. There wasn't much doubt about that. Your game—no, don't deny it—it made no difference. It just so happens that I love my wife. I think she's mad as hell at me right now, but"—he shrugged—"life with Byrony will never be boring."

Drew was in the midst of painting an azalea, a painstaking task that required just the right mixture of paints and the lighest of touches.

"Drew."

Very carefully he stepped back from the canvas. "You nearly made me do in a flower, Byrony," he said, smiling at her.

"You're all packed," Byrony said.

"Yes,"

"I'll miss you."

"And I you. Perhaps you can talk that brother of mine into traveling to Paris. You'd enjoy it there, Byrony."

Drew watched her walk silently about his studio, running her fingertips over holland-covered furniture.

"What is it, Byrony? You're not sill brooding on that ridiculous fiasco in the garden? Brent is an honorable man, I promise you."

She stopped, drew a deep breath, but said nothing. Drew would stand with Brent. He was a man, after all, and men stood together. "Nothing is wrong, Drew. I merely wanted to talk to you a moment. Your azalea is very pretty."

"Thank you," he said, watching her closely. "Byrony, Laurel is a lovely woman, you know that. She's also somewhat manipulative. Don't regard anything she does."

"Why should I?"

"You shouldn't. Now, I believe it's getting near time for dinner."

Byrony didn't want to see her husband. She got her wish. He didn't appear for dinner.

"Lord only knows where he is," Laurel said pleasantly as she eyed Byrony. "Doubtless he's found something—or someone—to keep him busy. You know how he is, Byrony."

"Yes," Byrony said, "I know how he is."

"Shut up, Laurel," Drew said. "Byrony, would you please pass me a piece of that delicious chess pie?"

At five o'clock the following morning, Byrony slipped out of the house and walked briskly toward the stable. She kept looking behind her. Brent hadn't returned the previous evening, and the slaves weren't about yet. She had no reason to sneak about. She had one valise and six hundred and fifty dollars she'd taken from Brent's strongbox. She saddled the mare, Velvet, took one long last look at Wakehurst, and urged the mare into a gentle canter. She wasn't running away. She was giving Brent a choice. It would be up to him.

Besides the money, she'd taken his gold cufflinks. She'd detailed everything in a letter to him. Oh yes, she thought, she'd given him a choice. Dear God, he had to make the right decision.

Two hours later, the steamboat *New Orleans* belched smoke into the air and pulled away from the Natchez dock. Byrony stood on the deck, her hands on the railing. She found herself searching among the crowd of men and women on the dock. Suddenly she thought she saw him. But no. She turned her thoughts to her plan. She couldn't wait to see what he would do, what he would say. He would eventually return to San Francisco, at least she believed he would, despite what he wanted to do about her. And when he did, he'd find her running his saloon.

My child, she said silently, touching her fingers to her

stomach, I won't cheat you out of what is rightfully yours. She was spinning her plans and developing more and more outrageous alternatives by the time Natchez faded from view.

Brent reined in his horse in front of Wakehurst, exhausted, but inordinately pleased with himself. Everything was finally set in motion.

He was met with pandemonium.

THIRTY-FOUR

The mare Byrony had hired from Luke Harmon's stable in San Diego shied at the sound of a woman's loud shout.

"Byrony, my darling girl, what a surprise. I can't believe it. What are you doing here?"

Byrony scrambled from the mare's back, quickly tethered her to the stable fence, and rushed into her mother's arms. She felt tears sting her eyes at the burst of love she felt. She hugged her mother to her, talking all the while. Suddenly Byrony became aware of her fragility. My God, she thought, loosening her grip abruptly, she could feel her mother's ribs clearly.

"Mother," she said, her voice choking a bit as she drew back a bit to look into her beloved face. "I came to see you for a little while."

"I'm glad, love," Alice DeWitt said, wiping the edge of her apron over her eyes. "Come inside and we'll chat while I make dinner. Oh, Byrony, it's so good to see you!"

Byrony looked around as she walked beside her mother toward the house. The small homestead looked much better than it had before. The house was whitewashed, the sagging front porch railing repaired. There were at least a dozen squawking chickens pecking about near the stable.

"Yes," Alice said, "it does look a bit better, doesn't it?

The money from your hus—from Ira Butler comes on time each month."

"And your husband doesn't spend it all."

"No, he doesn't." Alice hugged her daughter to her side. "Where is Mr. Hammond?"

Byrony said smoothly enough, "He's still in Natchez, Mississippi, working at the plantation. He will join me soon in San Francisco."

"I wanted to meet him. He is good to you? He treats you well?"

"He doesn't beat me, if that's what you mean."

Alice sighed. "Your father has known so many disappointments, Byrony, you really shouldn't—"

"Everyone knows disappointments, Mother. Most people don't resort to hitting others who can't defend themselves."

"Please, Byrony—"

"I'm sorry, Mother." Dear God, would her mother go to her grave defending that man? She said abruptly, "Where is Charlie?"

"In Mexico, I believe. He writes occasionally. I'm not quite certain what he's doing."

He probably writes when he needs money, Byrony thought, but she didn't say it. "And your husband?"

"He's in town. He'll be home soon."

Byrony clasped her mother's careworn hands. "There isn't enough money for you to hire someone to help you?"

"Not yet," Alice said cheerfully. "But your father has plans, you know."

"I know," Byrony said. Things never changed, she thought. Her mother wouldn't allow her to do anything. She sat at the small kitchen table watching her peel potatoes.

"I'm pregnant," she said.

Alice wheeled around, her tired eyes lighting. You must have been so beautiful once, Byrony thought, pain flowing though her. Was life ever fair?

"That's wonderful. Oh, my darling girl, let me get you a cup of tea. When? Do you feel well?"

Byrony laughed. "I feel disgustingly healthy. I felt a royal bout of nausea but once, and that was during a storm near Panama that left all the passengers hanging over the railing. I am just fine, Mother. Indeed, the voyage here was depressingly boring, but for that one storm. The baby is due in about five and a half months," she added, answering another question she saw in her mother's eyes.

"I'm going to be a grandmother," Alice said with relish. "How marvelous. Will you remain here, Byrony, until the baby is born?"

She said very gently, "I'm sorry, but I must return to San Francisco. I have an excellent doctor there, Saint Morris is his name. He'll take very good care of me, I promise you. And I have other good friends as well. One woman, her name is Chauncey, she has a little girl and will help me, I'm certain."

"But what about Ira?"

"He and Irene don't bother me. They keep a goodly distance. Actually, Ira is someone to pity. He found himself in a terrible situation and I suppose he did what he thought he had to do to save himself and his half-sister. He does love her, you know."

"As I said, he still sends money every month."

"He should," Byrony said in a clipped voice. "It was part of the agreement."

"So, you're back."

Both women turned at the sneering voice. Madison DeWitt stood in the kitchen doorway, his hands over his chest. He'd added flesh, Byrony thought, observing him, and doubtless he needed to bathe.

"Did your precious husband kick you out?" her father asked, furious at the distaste he saw on her face.

Byrony saw her mother raise her hands in a pleading gesture, and said coldly, "Which precious husband are you referring to?"

"Don't shoot off your mouth to me, girl."

"Madison, please—"

"Shut up, Alice. What are you doing here, girl?"

"Visiting my mother."

"As long as you're here in my house, you little slut, you'll keep a respectful tongue in your mouth."

"She's pregnant, Madison."

Byrony suffered in silence while her father ran his leering gaze over her body.

"Whose is this one?"

"Why, I'm really not sure. With a slut, there are so many men. We'll have to wait to see the child's features."

Her father growled, and Byrony smiled. "Such a pity that it can't be Gabriel's. You would so much love to have a grandchild who is half Californio, wouldn't you? Perhaps you could even extort more money from his father."

"Byrony."

"Forgive me, Mother," Byrony said. "There's no reason for unpleasantness, is there? If your husband will but be reasonably civil, I will be also."

"Think you're so above us, don't you, girl?"

"Certainly not above my mother."

"Just where is this husband of yours?"

"I'm meeting him in San Francisco."

Madison gazed down at his hands for a brief moment, but not before Byrony saw the glitter of greed in his eyes.

"So, is the man going to send along money to your parents?"

"If I could be guaranteed that it would belong to my mother, I would send it myself. But you'd never let her see a bit of it, would you?"

"You're an ungrateful child," Madison DeWitt said. "Here I am, trying to make a go of things for your mother."

Ah, she thought, so you're trying a new ploy. It fit so ill on his shoulders.

"Shall I help you, Mother?" Byrony asked, ignoring her father.

"Yes, please," Alice DeWitt said, casting a nervous look toward her husband.

"Just what do you expect me to do with that horse of yours? We don't have any help, you know."

"Why, I'll take care of the mare. I wouldn't want you to strain yourself, not after all the hard work I'm sure you've done today. Mother, I'll be back in a moment. Do you mind if I put her in the stable?"

Madison DeWitt shrugged, wheeled about, and left the house.

How, Byrony thought as she stripped the saddle off the mare's back, could her mother bear that officious man? He'd looked even more dissipated and slovenly than he had the year before. And her mother looked so worn, so bone-tired. At least Charlie wasn't here. She'd tried to find at least some theoretical caring for her brother in her heart, but there wasn't any. He was indeed his father's son.

The baby suddenly moved, and Byrony drew a startled breath. She straightened slowly, smiling. She wondered briefly what Maggie would say when she heard that Byrony would be running Brent's saloon. Not Brent's, she added silently. Ours. All three of us.

She was laughing when she returned to the house.

She didn't laugh at night, alone in her narrow bed. Once she awoke in the middle of the night, her breathing heavy, her body alive with sensation. "Damn you, Brent Hammond." She missed him. He was always present in the back of her mind, emerging when she was least prepared, his beautiful eyes on her face, his marvelous hand stroking her, giving her such pleasure that she wanted to yell from it.

What was he thinking? And doing? Was he on his way to San Francisco even now?

Nearly a week later, she rode into San Diego. There would be a ship due, she learned, on the following Friday. She booked passage to San Francisco.

When she returned, her father wasn't there. He was probably off drinking and playing cards with some of his cronies. She cornered her mother, hugged her tightly, and whispered, "I have some money. If I give it to you, will your husband know?"

"Yes," Alice DeWitt said simply. "I'd tell him."

Byrony stepped back, studying her mother's face. "Why?"

Stupid question, she thought a few moments later, her mother's litany of his disappointments playing over and over in her mind.

"Come back to San Francisco with me," she said.

"I'd dearly love to visit you, my dear girl, but—"

"I know. Your husband wouldn't like it."

"He needs me, Byrony."

"What about your needs?"

Her mother looked at her blankly, and Byrony sighed. Was there nothing she could do?

Several evenings later Madison DeWitt didn't appear for dinner. Byrony was delighted, but Alice was distraught. She kept raising her head at each sound, and wringing her hands.

Maybe he got drunk and his horse threw him in a ditch. Byrony tried to dredge up some guilt for the image, but failed.

He had gotten drunk, but he was far from dead. Byrony heard him the next morning in the front of the house. She heard her mother's soft, pleading voice. Quickly she buttoned up the fastenings on her gown and rushed downstairs. She stood a moment, frozen.

"You miserable bitch." Madison DeWitt was yelling at his cowering wife.

"There's some breakfast for you, Madison. Come inside and rest for a while and eat. You'll feel better."

"How the hell is your miserable cooking going to make me feel better? Dammit, woman, I lost all my money in a crooked game."

Byrony closed her eyes a moment. He wasn't suffering from a hangover, he was still drunk.

"Please, Madison, come into the house and lie down for a while." Byrony saw him raise his hand and heave it with all his strength across her mother's shoulder. She staggered from the force of the blow.

"Lie down? With you? Jesus, it's all that little slut's fault. If she weren't here, you wouldn't back-mouth me."

"I'm not, Madison, truly. Please—"

He struck her again, this time with his fist.

"Leave her alone, you godawful bastard."

Too late, Byrony realized she was facing him down without a weapon to protect herself and the baby. She whirled about and ran back into the house.

"That's right, slut," he yelled after her. "Run. I'll catch you and show you."

But Byrony was back before he could come after her. She was holding her riding crop.

"Get away from her," she said in a voice of deadly calm. "If you touch her again, I'll kill you."

His eyes narrowed in drunken fury. "You won't do a damned thing." Very slowly he pulled back his arm to strike her mother again.

Byrony saw red. She rushed toward him, the riding crop raised.

"You touch me, girl, and I'll see that you don't birth more than a clot of blood."

The riding crop came down against his neck and chest.

"You filthy scum." She struck again with all her strength across his belly. He fell back screaming. She struck again, laying open his cheek. He was yelling, rolling in the dirt, clutching his face.

"Byrony, please don't hurt him."

She turned blankly at her mother's words. She was holding her arm, tears flowing down her face, and still she wanted to protect him.

And I want to kill him.

The stark, clear thought brought her up short. If she struck him again, she'd be as bad as he was. If she struck him again, her mother would hate her, blame her forever. It was all too ridiculous, and too sad. She flung the riding crop away from her.

"I hope you die, but I won't kill you," she said.

"I'm going to beat the hell out of you," Madison DeWitt staggered to his feet.

Suddenly there came the sound of loud clapping.

Byrony turned slowly to see her husband standing but a few feet away. For an instant she didn't believe it was really he.

"I'm proud of you, Byrony," he said, smiling at her. He turned toward her gaping father. "As for you, if you raise a hand to my wife or her mother, I will kill you, with great pleasure."

"Who the hell— You aren't supposed to be here."

"Leave my wife unprotected with her loving father? Not a chance, old man. I think it's time you sobered up."

Brent grabbed her father by the collar of his shirt and the seat of his pants. He dragged him, cursing furiously, and dumped him into the horse's watering trough.

"That's your husband?" Alice DeWitt said.

"Yes," Byrony said with great relish. "That's my husband." She burst into laughter.

The two women watched as Brent dunked Madison De-

Witt repeatedly, then hauled him out. "He'll be just fine, ma'am," Brent called to Alice as he dragged Madison De-Witt to the stable. "He just needs to sleep awhile."

"I'm sorry, Alice," Brent said some minutes later to Byrony's mother, "but he truly does need to rest a bit."

"Probably," Alice said, looking toward the stable. "Would you care for a cup of tea, Mr. Hammond?"

"Brent, ma'am. Yes, I think I would."

"Mother," Byrony said, "if it's all right with you, I'd like to speak to Brent for a moment." She said nothing more until her mother disappeared into the house. "I'm surprised she didn't run after you and attack you for hurting her sweet husband."

"It's her life, Byrony. Leave it be. There's nothing you can do."

"What are you doing here?"

He heard the uncertainty in her voice, and forgot his anger at her. Actually, by the time he'd reached Panama, he'd felt so damned proud of her, he couldn't wait to see her. He was certainly right when he'd told Laurel that Byrony would never bore him. He smiled down at her. "Well, I figured it would be the gentlemanly thing to do to escort my wife from San Diego to San Francisco."

"I don't need your escort." She raised her chin. "You know very well what I'd planned to do, Brent. I meant it. After all, the saloon is mine and the baby's too."

"You did, did you? Well, I just might let you, love. Follow through with your plans, that is. I'll have more than enough to do to keep me busy."

"What do you mean by that?" She eyed him suspiciously.

"Later, Byrony. I'll tell you later."

They left San Diego three days later, with Byrony humming to herself. Brent was as slippery as the proverbial eel. But it didn't matter. Let him be as silent as a clam. Let him play with her, joke, and tantalize. She kept asking him to explain things to her, and when he put her off, she lowered her head so he wouldn't see her wicked smile when he kept saying "later" to her.

She waved to her mother from the deck of the *Flying Billy*. She drew back, startled, when her father appeared suddenly beside her mother and waved to them.

"What the devil is he doing here?" she wondered aloud.

"I imagine Madison DeWitt is a happy man," Brent said.

"What do you mean by that?" She smiled impishly back up at him. "I know. You'll tell me later."

"That's right."

Their cabin was small, holding but one narrow bed and a tiny armoire, and a caned chair.

"This is the best I could do for the three of us," Brent said, tossing his coat on the single chair.

Byrony eyed her husband from a distance of three feet, her arms crossed over her bosom. "Well?"

"Aren't you going to tell me how deliriously happy you are to have me with you again? All to yourself, as it were."

"I'll contain my delirium." Her heart was pounding with excitement.

Brent unbuttoned his vest and shirt. "I hope you aren't hungry."

"Why?"

"I don't intend to let you out of that bed for quite a while, that's why."

"Brent, you are the most contrary man. You're acting like a man with nothing more on his mind than—"

She couldn't find the right words for her comparison.

"Hush, woman. I'll tell you everything you want to know after I've loved you silly."

Byrony had no intention of arguing. "Just know for the moment, Byrony," he said against her mouth, "that I love you, and if you ever leave me again, I'll—"

"What?" she said, grinning up at him.

"Later," he said, his hand caressing her throat. "I'll tell you later."

"How ever did you manage that?" Byrony asked, her eyes on the trays of food delivered by a steward some three hours later.

"My charm," Brent said. He placed the trays between them on the bed. "While you regain your strength—here's some chicken—I'll tell you everything you want to know."

Byrony bit into the roast chicken breast. "I would like to know if there is some salt for the chicken."

He looked taken aback. "So," he said, "all I ever have to do in the future when you become recalcitrant is throw you on your back."

"Yes," she said. "That's about it, I suspect. The salt, please."

"Dammit, Byrony, don't you want to know about everything?"

She was eyeing one of the trays. "Can I have a slice of that delicious-looking bread?"

"Here," he said, and tossed it to her.

Some minutes later, Brent interrupted her enthusiastic description of her voyage to San Diego. "Are you nearly through?"

"Why, yes. The chicken was marvelous, the carrots were nice and crisp just as I like them, and—"

"Enough."

Byrony looked at him beneath her lashes, then fell back onto the pillows, laughing.

Brent put the dinner remains to the floor, then stretched himself beside his still-giggling wife. "Is your strength back up, Brent?"

"You're no lady," he said.

"Aren't you glad?"

"I'll be glad only when you let me tout all my greatness to you."

"You sold Wakehurst, freed all the Wakehurst slaves, gave them each money, and brought many of them to California. You're going to buy a ranch south of San Francisco and start your own town, replete with black citizens. You gave Laurel the proceeds from the sale and sent her on her way, her pockets well lined. I imagine that you arranged for my mother to have help, and hired a man to deliver money to their house. Is there anything else?"

"I went to bed with Laurel, for old times' sake."

"No, you didn't. And Josh is in charge of all the former slaves."

"May I ask how you know all this?"

"You talked in your sleep. As for getting money to my mother without my father getting his greedy hands on it, I figured that out for myself."

"Damn," he said. He rested his hand on her rounded belly, his eyes thoughtful. "No one has ever told me I talk in my sleep before, and in such splendid detail."

"You didn't. However, after I've loved you silly, I'll tell you about that letter I found from Mr. Milsom and shamelessly read."

"All my array of good deeds, designed to prove to you that I'm not really such a bad sort of fellow after all."

"I'd decided you weren't a bad sort the moment I saw you applauding at my parent's house. Indeed, even though you've been closemouthed as a cat these past three days, I've decided to forgive you. I've decided also that you simply can't live without me. So my one good deed is to be your loving wife and keep you on the straight and narrow. Just what do you think of that, Brent Hammond?"

"I repeat," he said slowly, "you are no lady."

New York Times Bestselling Author

Catherine Coulter

Evening Star

Giana Van Cleve, the heroine, has fallen in love with a vicious fortune hunter. Her mother, the renowned shipowner and builder Aurora Van Cleve, is desperate to save her daughter. She agrees to support Giana's wedding if Giana agrees first to spend an unusual three months in Rome with her uncle Daniele. But Giana's uncle takes his bargain far beyond what Aurora ever imagined.

Midnight Star

The story of Delaney Saxton, a man who struck it rich in the California gold rush of 1849 and stayed to build a great city, and Chauncey FitzHugh, an heiress from England who travels to San Francisco to avenge her father. She belives Delaney Saxton ruined him and plans to destroy Saxton in the same way he destroyed her father—leaving him betrayed and penniless. But her prey isn't what she expected. He is charming, too handsome for his own good, rich—and elusive as a wisp of smoke.

The Song Series *by*

CATHERINE COULTER

~~~~~

Fire Song

Earth Song

Secret Song

~~~~~

Available wherever books are sold or at
penguin.com